Praise for *Bearing Witness*

"The Rachel Gold series is intelligent and fun."

—Nelson DeMille

"Kahn's likable characters and well-managed plots make this entertaining read a solid addition to its series."

—*Publishers Weekly*

"In this compelling thriller, Kahn makes good use of historical material and offers a revealing look at Orthodox Judaism. Rachel Gold and her eclectic entourage deserve more attention."

—*Booklist*

"Counsel is deadly serious."

—*Kirkus Reviews*

"*Bearing Witness* takes the reader on a tense journey featuring local landmarks. . . . But, it also takes the reader on a far darker journey. . . . This well thought-out book should appeal to mystery fans everywhere."

—*St. Louis Post-Dispatch*

"The plot is well constructed and keeps you plunging ahead to the next revelation."

—*The Mystery Review*

"Kahn draws on his deep St. Louis roots, his strong and positive Jewish identity, his English-major writing ability and his academic and practical knowledge of the law which combine to give his novels the ring of authenticity and credibility. . . . Like the five previous Rachel Gold mystery novels, *Bearing Witness* is another tautly written page-turner which keeps the reader in suspense until the very last paragraph. Kahn's work has been compared to that of John Grisham and Robert Ludlum. . . . Kahn continues to set a higher and higher Gold standard."

—*The St. Louis Jewish Light*

P9-DWM-972

BEARING
WITNESS

Other Books by Michael A. Kahn

Bearing Witness
Trophy Widow

BEARING WITNESS

A RACHEL GOLD NOVEL

Michael A. Kahn

TOR®

A TOM DOHERTY ASSOCIATES BOOK
NEW YORK

This is a work of fiction. All the characters and events portrayed in this book are either products of the author's imagination or are used fictitiously.

BEARING WITNESS

Copyright © 2000 by Michael A. Kahn

A Tor Book
Published by Tom Doherty Associates, LLC
175 Fifth Avenue
New York, NY 10010

www.tor.com

Tor® is a registered trademark of Tom Doherty Associates, LLC.

ISBN: 0-812-57983-6
Library of Congress Catalog Card Number: 00-031697

First edition: September 2000
First mass market edition: April 2003

Printed in the United States of America

0 9 8 7 6 5 4 3 2 1

To my awesome daughter, Kayla

ACKNOWLEDGMENTS

I am especially grateful to my father, who spotted the germ of a chilling tale in a box of dusty archives, and to Steven Miller of St. Louis Station Associates, who gave me a behind-the-scenes tour of the architectural star of this novel. Thanks, Dad. Thanks, Steve.

BEARING WITNESS

CHAPTER 1

There are a quarter of a million civil lawsuits pending within the federal judicial system—everything from fender-benders to complex class actions, from two-bit torts to billion-dollar battles. But of all those cases in all those district courts across the nation, no more than fifteen are genuine Elephant Orgies. And an even smaller number fall into that rarest of categories: the Jurassic Park Blue Plate Special.

Every litigator dreams of landing a role in an Elephant Orgy—one of those massive, complicated cases that lumber along for years, featuring an entourage of gray corporate plaintiffs and defendants shuffling through interminable pretrial proceedings, occasionally mounting one another, and all the while generating astounding quantities of legal fees. In my years as a junior associate in Chicago, I had worked on the mother of them all, *In re Bottles & Cans*, now entering its thirty-second year, and still no trial date in sight. Even the towel boy at an Elephant Orgy can be set for years.

By contrast, no one wants to be the featured item on a Jurassic Park Blue Plate Special. That's the litigation equivalent of being the tethered lamb in the *T. rex* compound. But lately, to my increasing dismay, the simple age discrimination lawsuit that I'd filed on behalf of one of my mother's friends had gone prehistoric. These days my sixty-three-year-old client and I spend a lot of time just trying to keep the bell from tinkling.

But that could all change tonight, I told myself, as the next highway sign came into view and snapped me out of my Mesozoic reverie.

SPRINGFIELD—18 Miles

I checked my watch. 7:03 P.M. On schedule so far.

I was supposed to meet Gloria Muller at seven-thirty at the Applebee's restaurant off Highway 55 in Springfield, Illinois. She was my secret weapon in my lawsuit against Beckman Engineering Co.

Or so I hoped.

I sure needed one.

I'd learned of her during a telephone conversation last week with Charlie Hartman, a private investigator I had working on the case. Charlie had called from Springfield, where he'd gone to interview a man named Dobson. Dobson had worked in Beckman Engineering's government contracts division for seven years before taking a job with one of Beckman's competitors, Muller Construction, headquartered in Springfield. Depending upon your view of reality, Muller Construction was either an innocent competitor of Beckman Engineering or one of its evil co-conspirators. We claimed the latter, and I was hoping that Dobson might be willing to talk. But Charlie had called with bad news.

"Forget about him, Rachel. He's spooked."

"Beckman's lawyers got to him?"

"Last night, and now he's sweating bullets."

Charlie explained that Beckman Engineering's attorneys had sent out a battalion of couriers to hand-deliver threatening letters to a large group of ex-employees, including Dobson. The letters reminded them of their nondisclosure agreements and warned that Beckman Engineering Co. would "vigorously prosecute any breach thereof." Among lawyers, that kind of epistle is known as a hammer letter.

But Charlie also had a bit of good news as well. "I found someone who wants to talk—or rather, she found me."

"She?"

Surprised, I'd reached for my list of key ex-employees, which lately I'd been keeping on my credenza. These were the people most likely to have knowledge about Ruth Alpert's claim. There were thirty-six names on the list. Only two were women, and neither lived within a thousand miles of Springfield.

"What's her name, Charlie?"

"Gloria Muller."

"Muller? Any relation?"

Charlie chuckled. "His ex-wife."

And, as Charlie explained, no ordinary ex-wife. Gloria Muller had been married for thirty-seven years to Edgar Muller, founder of Muller Construction Co. She still had plenty of contacts within the company, and she'd learned from one of them that Charlie was in town trying to set up a meeting with an ex-employee of Beckman Engineering. Although Charlie spoke with her only briefly, it was clear that she detested her ex-husband and savored an opportunity to make his life miserable. More important, she claimed to have damaging firsthand information about Muller, Beckman, and, in her words, "their disgusting scheme." She refused to say anything further to Charlie. She told him she'd only talk to me, and only if she decided that I was okay.

I told Charlie to try to set up a meeting. He called back a day later with her terms: she'd start with a screening interview at a neutral site in Springfield. If I passed that test, we'd go back to her house to discuss things in more detail; if not, we'd part and never talk again. I'd mulled it over. Springfield was a ninety-minute drive from St. Louis—a three-hour round-trip after work. Even worse, Gloria Muller sounded like a vindictive witness, which meant that there'd be major credibility issues with her testimony. But, I'd reminded myself, she was also a living, breathing witness—a rarity in my lawsuit against Beckman Engineering. That alone had made the trip worth the gamble.

I took the second Springfield exit off I-55 and followed her instructions to the restaurant. I pulled into the Applebee's lot, parked my car, and entered the restaurant at exactly 7:30 P.M. I told the hostess who I was meeting. She had me follow her back to the smoking section.

We reached the booth just as Gloria Muller was stubbing her cigarette into an ashtray that was already festooned with filter-tipped butts, each smudged red with lipstick. I shook her hand and slid in on the other side of the booth. Glancing at the stuffed ashtray, I said, "You did say seven-thirty, right?"

Gloria nodded and reached into her purse to pull out a platinum cigarette case engraved with her initials. "You're right on time."

She had a raspy voice. I could smell alcohol on her breath. I glanced at the fancy glass coffee mug. Irish coffee, I assumed.

She opened the cigarette case and held it toward me.

I shook my head. "No, thanks."

There was a gold Dunhill lighter on the table near her coffee cup. She used it to light her cigarette and then tilted her head back and blew the smoke to the side. She watched the smoke dissipate and turned to fix me with a hard stare.

"Well," she said in that raspy voice, "is someone finally going to nail that miserable prick?"

I paused, uncertain. "Which miserable prick?"

She burst into laughter—one of those cigarette cackles that ended in a coughing fit that ran aground on what sounded like a glob of phlegm. The waitress arrived as Gloria was clearing her throat. I ordered a cup of decaf and a slice of cherry pie.

As Gloria Muller studied the dessert menu, I studied her. Two adjectives immediately came to mind: rich and unpleasant. She was thin bordering on bony, with that angular look that comes from a strict diet and a stricter personal trainer. Whatever her original hair color, it was now a lacquered, frosted blond. She was wearing a designer suit in scarlet wool and plenty of expensive jewelry, including big diamonds on her fingers and a heavy gold Y-link bracelet on her wrist. She must have been a striking beauty during her twenties and thirties, but decades of sunbathing and sun lamps had left her in her sixties with a leathery, wrinkled face and a stringy turtle's neck blotched with age spots.

"I'll take a slice of your fat-free, sugar-free coconut cream pie." She handed the waitress her menu. "And another cup of Irish coffee. Make it a double this time."

When the waitress left, Gloria turned back to me with a look of amusement. " 'Which miserable prick?' " she repeated with a smile. "I like that." She stubbed out her cigarette and leaned back in her seat. "So," she said, "I understand you went to Harvard Law School."

I nodded.

She sized me up. "You're a good-looking woman."

I shrugged awkwardly, not certain how to respond.

"I bet some of those professors tried to get in your pants, eh? Men." She snorted in disgust. "Bastards, aren't they?"

"Some are," I conceded.

She chuckled. "Some? You're still young, honey. You wait." She leaned back in her chair and pursed her lips pensively. After a moment, she said, "I asked around. They say Rachel Gold is one tough cookie."

"Oh? Who's they?"

She winked. "Max Feiglebaum."

"Max." I smiled at the memory. "We worked on a divorce case together."

Gloria nodded as she reached for another cigarette. "That's what he told me. He thinks you're terrific."

"He's a good lawyer."

Max Feiglebaum, aka Max the Knife, was one of the most feared divorce lawyers in Chicago. He was a ruthless little ferret who wore dark glasses and Italian suits. His principal victims were the men of the Chicago ruling class who'd had the misfortune (literally) of marrying one of Max's future clients.

Gloria flicked the lighter, got her cigarette lit, and exhaled the smoke through her nose. "He's a barracuda."

"How do you know him?" I asked.

"He was my divorce lawyer."

"Ah." I gave her a knowing smile.

She nodded smugly. "We made that bastard pay through the nose."

"I'm not surprised."

And I wasn't. My investigator had filled me in on some of the details. Gloria's marriage of thirty-seven years had ended in an acrimonious divorce after her stone-drunk husband telephoned from room 203 of the Springfield Holiday Inn one weekday afternoon four years ago to announce that he was in love. The object of Edgar Muller's passion was a twenty-two-year-old redhead from accounts receivable whose high-pitched giggles were audible in the background.

Although Max the Knife had no doubt carved a hefty slab of flesh out of Edgar Muller's hide, Gloria was still bitter. And, I conceded, understandably so. Not only had her husband dumped her for a woman almost young enough to be her granddaughter, but his new bride had already given him something Gloria had failed to do through six miscarriages: Edgar Junior. Add to that her loss of status within Springfield society. Only last month, the same gossip column that had once reported Gloria's victory in a country club tennis tournament or her shopping spree in New York ran a photo of Edgar and his new wife at the Hard Rock Café in Las Vegas during a recent construction industry convention.

As we ate our pies and sipped our coffee, I explained the nature of the claim in general terms, namely, that what had started as a simple age discrimination claim was now something far different. We believed that Beckman Engineering had participated in an illegal bid-rigging conspiracy involving a series of federal government contracts. Although many of the details were still fuzzy, we believed that the co-conspirators included Muller Construction Company and possibly a company in Chicago called Koll Ltd.

At the mention of Koll Ltd., she chuckled. "Oh, yes. Otto was one of them."

I frowned. "Otto?"

"Koll. He owns the company."

"You know him?" I asked, surprised.

She nodded. "You bet, honey. I could probably list the whole rotten gang right now." She paused to light another cigarette. "Now tell me more about your client. Her name's Ruth?"

"Ruth Alpert."

"Tell me about her, and tell me exactly what's going on in your lawsuit."

So I did. I could tell that Gloria responded to my client's plight, perhaps seeing in her another older woman scorned. As I explained the case, it was difficult to contain my growing excitement. For almost six months Beckman Engineering's attorneys had been stonewalling me. They had yet to produce a single document from their files or a witness for a deposition. Moreover, they had intimidated their former employees and others from talking to me. It had been, quite literally, a campaign of silence.

Until tonight.

In Gloria Muller I had finally found a witness who appeared to know something. Better yet, she was beyond the reach of Beckman Engineering and its attorneys. This was no ex-employee they could muzzle with a hammer letter. This was an ex-wife with an attitude who just might know where some of the bodies were buried and who just might be willing to show me where to dig.

"If Ruth is right about what she observed," I explained, "this conspiracy may have lasted for a decade. That's an unusually long time for a bid-rigging conspiracy. If she's right, though, the money at stake is huge."

Gloria chuckled and reached out to pat my hand. "Honey, this conspiracy goes back a helluva lot longer than ten years. It goes all the way back. And the money back at the beginning"—she paused and shook her head in disgust—"believe me, honey, the money back then was a lot filthier than anything since."

She reached for the bill and checked her watch. It was almost nine o'clock. "Well," she said as she stood up, "how about we go back to my house?"

I smiled. "Sounds good."

She gave me a wink. "I think it's time that you and I had ourselves a little heart-to-heart, Rachel."

On the way out of the restaurant she tried to give me directions, but I'm terrible with directions—I lost her somewhere around the fourth left turn.

"I have a better idea," I said, buttoning my coat as we stepped out into the brisk autumn wind. "I'll follow you home. Where's your car?"

"Right there." She gestured toward a huge silver Cadillac parked against the curb along the side of the restaurant. As she stepped toward her car, she stumbled slightly but recovered. There was a lot of Irish coffee zinging through her bloodstream.

"I'm back there," I said, pointing at my red Jeep Wrangler. It was parked in the third aisle, almost directly behind her car, two rows back. "Wait for me, okay?"

She nodded as she unlocked her door and yanked it open a bit too forcefully. A gust of wind snapped the canvas banner overhead. I jogged toward my car. I didn't want to risk her driving off without me.

I could hear her engine rev as I unlocked my car door and got in. I was facing the restaurant and had a clear view of her Cadillac through the row of cars separating us. I started my engine as her red taillights came on.

That's when I spotted him.

He was huge: NFL lineman huge.

He was running toward the Cadillac from the street, where a late-model car was idling at the curb, the passenger door open. My hands gripped the steering wheel. Something was wrong with this scene.

He was wearing a long, bulky trench coat. Big body, big head, crew cut. He stopped directly in front of the Cadillac just as the white reverse lights came on.

I watched in horror as he pulled a shotgun from beneath his trench coat, braced it against his shoulder, and aimed at the windshield.

Ka-Boom!

The first shot exploded the glass.

Ka-Boom!

The second shot splattered the rear window red.

There was an awful hush. I watched as the silver Cadillac drifted backward, arcing slowly to the left. By then, the shooter was running toward the waiting car. He climbed in on the passenger side, and the car squealed off as the door closed. I turned back just as the Cadillac crunched into a parked car.

Stunned, I opened my door and slowly got out, staring all the while at the Cadillac, at those smeared windows. The wind had died. The eerie silence seemed to magnify other sounds. I could hear the low hum of her car engine, and I could hear something else. A faint tinkling noise. It took a moment to identify it. It was the sound of falling pebbles—hundreds of tiny pebbles of glass from the shattered front windshield, tiny pebbles sliding off the car hood and onto the ground.

Unable to move, I stared, horrified, at that rear window splattered red. I squeezed my eyes shut, and suddenly the tinkling was no longer falling glass. Now it was the sound of tiny bells. I shivered. Tiny bells on tethered lambs.

CHAPTER 2

I took a sip of hot coffee as I stood by the window of my office in the Central West End. Out on the sidewalk a teenage boy with long blond hair and headphones zoomed past on a skateboard, his breath vaporing in the chilly air, his flannel shirt ballooning behind him. I took another sip. It was a rotten day for gloomy thoughts—a gray, dreary November morning. Depression weather out there.

In here, too. It was two days after the murder of Gloria Muller. I'd been at the Springfield police headquarters until two that morning giving statements, looking through mug shots and talking to detectives. As of this morning, they hadn't made any arrests.

It was also three days after my creepy encounter with Conrad Beckman. The occasion had been the annual awards banquet of the United Fellowship Council, which I'd originally planned to attend because a client of mine, LaDonna Catrell, was to be one of three award recipients. LaDonna, the Channel 30 meteorologist, was this year's black recipient. Milton Pevnick was the Jewish recipient. He was a local discount furniture peddler who bombarded the airwaves with irritating commercials starring himself and his goofy son Joey, his latest one being the "Bargain Bonanza" spot, a cheesy rip-off of the burning Ponderosa map opening to television's *Bonanza*, with Milt and Joey on horseback riding toward the camera on either side of a Lorne Green look-alike who actually bore such a disconcerting resemblance to Buddy Ebsen that you expected to see Granny kick up her heels and shout, "Yee-hah!"

But LaDonna and Milton were just the warmup acts. The headliner had been Conrad Beckman. It was hardly his first award of the year. As founder and chairman of Beckman Engineering Co., a privately held corporation whose annual revenues exceed $900 million, he spent a not insignificant portion of his year politely declining proffered awards. According to a profile of him that ran in the *St. Louis Business Journal* last spring, Beckman served on the boards of more than a dozen civic, artistic, and charitable organizations in St. Louis, including the Boy Scouts, the Missouri Historical Society, the Council for the Arts, the St. Louis Symphony, the United Way, the Urban League, and the YMCA of Greater St. Louis. By every measure, he was a marquee name on the awards circuit. His company was a major local employer, his philanthropy had left its mark on several local edifices (including the Beckman Sports Complex in the inner city and the Beckman Center for Performing Arts in South County), and his behind-the-scenes intervention was viewed by many as the determining factor in the construction of the new domed stadium and the decision by the Rams organization to move their football franchise to St. Louis.

By the time I got to the grand ballroom of the Hyatt Hotel that night, Conrad Beckman had become my principal reason for being there. From my table off to the side I'd observed him on the dais. I watched the silver-haired Beckman as he sipped his wine, his face ruddy with good health, his eyes a clear blue, and as I did I confronted again the unlikelihood that his fingerprints were anywhere near the illegal conduct at issue in my lawsuit. I'd listened with grudging admiration to his brief but eloquent acceptance speech.

"We are all of us descendants of men and women from other parts of the world," he told the rapt audience. "Like Ms. Catrell, my family came here from a land faraway. Like Mr. Pevnick, I, too, am the son of hardworking immigrants. But tonight, all three of us stand before you as equal partners in the important work of this great city." He'd paused to lift the award, setting off another barrage of camera flashes. "God bless you."

When the event ended, there had been a throng of well-wishers waiting for him at the end of the dais. He'd passed slowly through them, pausing to shake a hand here or acknowledge a friendly congratulation there. I hung back. No sense spoiling his moment of glory.

Eventually, a final handshake, a final thank-you. As Beckman moved past the last of the crowd, I stepped forward.

"Mr. Beckman?"

He'd looked over at me with a tired smile, which faded when I didn't return it. He glanced down at the papers in my hand and then back at my face, his eyes narrowing slightly.

"I'm Rachel Gold, sir," I said, trying to keep my voice firm. "I represent Ruth Alpert."

His face had remained impassive.

I pressed ahead. "This is a subpoena for your deposition, and this check is for the witness fee." I held them toward him. "Here."

My hand was less than twelve inches from his. He looked down at the papers and then into my eyes. We were close enough that I had to tilt my head back to meet his gaze. We stood there, eyeing one another for what seemed a millennium. Although his face remained empty, his steely blue eyes had bored into mine, taking my measure.

I squared my shoulders and took a deep breath. "I'm authorized to serve this on you, sir. Take it."

Watching me with those cold blue eyes, he took the subpoena. He didn't even glance down as he folded the papers and slipped them into the inside pocket of his suit jacket.

And then his lips curled into a smile. Not a sneer, and not a smirk. Not arrogant, or even sardonic. More a smile of regret.

"What a foolish waste of time," he finally said, shaking his head.

His words still bothered me—their force coming not from the opinion expressed but from the fact that someone had finally said it aloud. Over the past few months, as I watched my client's simple age discrimination claim mutate into something far more complex and menacing, I'd found myself wondering more and more whether it was all just a waste of time.

I heard my secretary snort in disgust. "Those jerks."

Turning from the window, I called, "What's wrong, Jacki?"

"Those pencil-necked federal bureaucrats make me sick."

She came into my office carrying a letter. The sight of my secretary buoyed my spirits on this dismal Thursday morning. And what a sight she was. With plenty of ex-steelworker muscles rippling beneath her demure size-22 shirtwaist dress, Jacki Brand was surely the most intimidating legal secretary in town. She was also one of the best.

I noted with quiet approval her makeup and hairstyle. Both were a far cry from the early days, with those awful Dolly Parton wigs and glittery sapphire eyeshadow. We'd been working on Jacki's look for several months now. All things considered, she'd proved a quick study. After all, I'd been female since birth, and it had still taken many years and plenty of false steps to get this woman thing down pat. Jacki had been at it for less than a year. She was attending night law school at St. Louis University and saving money for the surgical procedure that would lop off the last dangling evidence that her name had once been Jack.

"Let me see," I said, gesturing toward the document in her hand.

The letter was on embossed U.S. Department of Justice stationery, addressed to U.S. District Judge Catherine L. Wagner, with copies to me and opposing counsel. It was a terse communiqué, stating that the Department of Justice, having reviewed "the written disclosure of material evidence submitted by Rachel Gold, counsel for relator, hereby notifies the Court and the parties that after due consideration the United States of America declines to take over the matter."

I slumped against the edge of my desk. The gray chill seeped into the room as I reread the letter.

I looked up at Jacki. "This is a flat turndown."

She grunted, shaking her head in disgust. "Wusses."

I sighed, my shoulders sagging. "Oh, Jacki, we're in this alone."

"We always were."

I skimmed the letter again, trying to digest the new reality. Jacki was right, of course. The new reality was just a continuation of the old. Except for one important difference: gone was the hope that the U.S. Cavalry would arrive in time.

I'd placed my call to the Cavalry two months ago when I sent the U.S. Department of Justice a copy of the *qui tam* complaint and the supporting materials, all as required under the Federal False Claims Act. My notice gave the feds sixty days to decide whether to take over the case. I'd been praying they'd say yes. Ruth would still be entitled to 25 percent of whatever the government ultimately recovered; better yet, we'd be able to watch from the sidelines as the government lawyers and their FBI agents shouldered the formidable task of digging up the evidence needed to prove the case.

I stared at the letter. The message couldn't have been clearer. I closed my eyes, recalling the old saying: *It's fun to chase the bear through the woods, but what if you actually catch it?* Well, we'd been chasing a grizzly for months, and now, deep in the forest, just as it turned with a growl, we discovered that we were all alone.

The sound of the telephone yanked me out of the forest. As Jacki started to dash to the outer room for the phone on her desk, I said, "I'll get it." I reached across my desk and lifted the receiver. "This is Rachel Gold."

"Hold for Ms. Howard, please."

Oh, terrific, I grumbled to myself.

A moment later, "Good morning, Rachel." Not an ounce of warmth in that priggish voice.

"Good morning, Kimberly." I tried to keep my tone cordial. "What's up?"

"Actually, a great deal. I have already contacted Judge Wagner's docket clerk. The judge will see us in her chambers this afternoon at two."

"Oh, really? What is it this time?"

"Now, now, Rachel, I think you know perfectly well what the issues are."

With a mixture of irritation and resignation, I said, "Indulge me, Kimberly."

"Number one, your outrageous efforts to induce former employees of Beckman Engineering to breach their contractual obligations."

"Oh, come on."

"It's covered in my letter."

"What letter?"

"The one being faxed to you as we speak. Item number two: your flagrant harassment and humiliation of the chairman of the board of Beckman Engineering the other night in the middle of an awards ceremony."

"That's absurd, Kimberly. You were the one who refused to produce him for a deposition. You and I both know that—"

"You can present your excuses to the judge, Rachel. Item three: as you know, this case is currently under seal. In light of the government's notification, there is an issue regarding the ongoing confidentiality of the case. We intend to ask Judge Wagner to keep the matter under seal, unless, of course, you intend to dismiss the case in light of the government's conclusion that it lacks merit."

I took a deep breath and counted slowly to five, glancing at my desk calendar as I did. I was meeting my mother at noon for lunch but I was free after that. "Two o'clock?"

"Correct. I will see you there, Counselor."

There was a click, and then a dial tone.

Jacki came storming in as I hung up the phone. "This just came by fax," she said angrily, "from that bitch."

I took the two-page document from her. It was a letter from Kimberly Howard covering the subject of our telephone call. As usual, she distorted every key fact, expressed her "astonishment" at my "harassing tactics," and announced her intent to bring my "highly unprofessional conduct to the attention of the Court at the earliest opportunity."

I stood up and walked over to the window. A gust of wind rattled the bare branches on the trees along the sidewalk. I exhaled slowly, shaking my head.

"Mother," I groaned, "this is—"

"—all your fault."

"What, sweetie? Tell me what's wrong." My mother leaned back and looked at me with concern. "Oh, no. Ruth's case again?"

"Again?" I put down my fork and shook my head with frustration. "How about always? Night and day. It's driving me crazy." I checked my watch. "And the next round starts in less than an hour."

"So eat, sweetie. You'll need your strength."

"My strength? What I need is a platoon of Marines."

We were having lunch at the Beaux-Arts Café in the St. Louis Art Museum. Since real women eat quiche, we'd both ordered the quiche of the day: broccoli cheddar. My mother and I tried to meet here once a week, and, when schedules permitted, we strolled through a few of the galleries after the meal. Sometimes my sister, Ann, joined us, although not today; she was at a luncheon event at Plaza Frontenac. Benny Goldberg was supposed to meet us here, but he was running late. We'd ordered without him.

I sighed. "It's overwhelming, Mom, and it keeps getting worse."

She nodded sympathetically. "But there's something there, right? You said so yourself."

I took a sip of iced tea and shrugged. "I think there is. But finding it's the hard part. The company's stonewalling us. The ex-employees are too spooked to talk. Gloria Muller was willing to, but now she's dead. Today, the government wimped out." I sighed. "That means it's just me. Me and Ruth. They have seven lawyers on the other side." I shook my head. "Seven lawyers, a half-dozen paralegals, three consultants, and an unlimited budget. They're playing hardball."

She reached across and placed her hand on top of mine.

"Hardball? You'll show them. You'll kick a touchdown."

I couldn't help but smile. I'd been a cheerleader in high school, and my mother, God bless her, who is bored to death by sporting events, came to every one of the football games to watch me cheer—even that miserable Friday night game at Webster Groves when it was six degrees and snowing. Every game. You'd think something would have rubbed off.

"That's football, Mom, and you don't *kick* a touchdown. You kick a field goal."

"You'll do that, too, doll baby."

I smiled. "Thanks, Ms. Buns of Steel."

She leaned back in her chair and flexed her biceps. "Look at that." She winked proudly. "You should see me with those free weights."

I rolled my eyes. "Oy, mother."

My crazy mother, who never fails to surprise me, had enrolled in a weight-training class at the Jewish Community Center almost two years ago. In fact, that's where she met Ruth Alpert. Ruth was there on doctor's orders to slow her osteoporosis; my mother was there because she'd all of a sudden decided it was time to "tighten up." The two widows became fast friends while pumping iron on Monday and Thursday nights. When Ruth lost her secretarial job at Beckman Engineering Co. last November, it was my mother who insisted that she consult with her daughter Rachel-the-Harvard-lawyer about a possible discrimination charge.

"Don't worry," my mother said as she cut a piece of quiche with her fork. "You won't be alone."

I gave her a puzzled look. "What does that mean?"

"I'll help."

I smiled with weary amusement. "Thanks, Mom, but I'm going to need more than that. It's not quite like my sixth-grade science fair project."

She shrugged, unruffled. "So we'll get Benny."

"Benny already has a job."

She dismissed that with a wave of her hand. "He's a law school professor. What kind of job is that? He'll have time. I'll talk to him." She paused and snapped her finger. "I've got it."

"Oh?"

I was smiling. Sarah Gold to the rescue. My mother is the most determined, resourceful, and exasperating woman I know. Life trained her well. She came to America from Lithuania at the age of three, having escaped with her mother and baby sister after the Nazis killed her father. Fate remained cruel. My mother—a woman who reveres books and learning—was forced to drop out of high school and go to work when her mother (after whom I am named) was diagnosed with terminal cancer. Rachel Linowitz died six months later, leaving her two daughters, Sarah and Becky, orphans at the ages of seventeen and fifteen. Two years later, at the age of nineteen, my mother married a gentle, shy bookkeeper ten years her senior named Seymour Gold. My father was totally smitten by his beautiful, spirited wife and remained so until his death from a heart attack almost two years ago on the morning after Thanksgiving.

"The law school," my mother said. She leaned back in her chair, crossing her arms over her chest triumphantly.

I gave her a curious look. "What about it?"

She waved her hand impatiently. "Don't you see? You need help, the law school has students. We'll get volunteers. Benny can help get them." She paused, looking up. "Ah, here he comes now."

I turned and saw Benny approaching. He had a dark expression.

"What's wrong?" I asked as he pulled up a chair.

He stared down at the table and took a deep breath. He exhaled slowly, shaking his head.

"What?" my mother said. "Talk already."

He looked up at me, glowering. "You're not going to believe this. The dean stopped me after class. He told me that Ray Hellman just announced that he's taking five weeks of sick leave."

"Who's Ray Hellman?" my mother asked.

I explained that he was a professor of law at Washington University.

"The dean wants me to cover one of Hellman's classes," Benny said.

"Which one?" I asked, and then it clicked. "Oh, no. Insurance law?"

He nodded grimly. Benny and I hate insurance law.

"What did you tell him?" I asked.

"I told him I'd rather spend a weekend in a dog collar as Rush Limbaugh's boy toy."

"What kind of toy?" my mother asked.

"Never mind, Mom." I patted Benny on the hand. "It could be worse."

I noted that the female patrons at several nearby tables were eyeing Benny warily. His outfit certainly didn't allay their concerns. Although he had donned a blue blazer in technical compliance with the law school faculty dress code, he was wearing it over a black T-shirt, baggy khaki slacks, and green Converse All-Star high-tops. The black T-shirt, one of his favorites, bore the legend *I Am That Man From Nantucket*. For that final dash of sartorial elegance, he hadn't shaved. As a result, Benny looked ready to answer Central Casting's call for an overweight Bolivian drug courier. Surely none of the apprehensive women at the nearby tables would have guessed that this fat, swarthy, curly-haired phenomenon was actually a hotshot professor with a growing reputation in the field of antitrust law. (Justice Stephen Breyer had recently cited one of Benny's articles in a concurring opinion in *United States* v. *Beal Fuel Co.*—a form of recognition that is the law school professor's equivalent of an Oscar.)

Nevertheless, Professor Benjamin Goldberg was, by any standard, crude and vulgar and obnoxious. But he was also ferociously loyal, wonderfully funny, and—most important—my best friend. I loved him like the brother I never had, although he bore the same resemblance to my dream brother as Divine did to Tinkerbell.

Fortunately, the waitress arrived with a menu. Benny's mood improved noticeably as he scanned the selections. After he placed his order, my mother launched into her plan for student volunteers. By the time I left for court ten minutes later, he was scoffing down a roll while my mother was, quite literally, on a roll.

"What do you mean 'maybe'?" she said to him. "If those kids have any ideals, they should jump at the chance to work on a case against such *goniffs*."

I arrived at Judge Wagner's chambers at five minutes to two. Kimberly Howard was already there, seated primly in the waiting area, back erect, legs pressed together, Little Miss Posture Perfect. She was studying a set of papers.

"Hello, Kimberly," I said coolly as I took a seat across from her.

She looked up from her papers and nodded precisely. "Good afternoon, Rachel."

On either side of Kimberly sat the mandatory smug associate, each in a dark suit and starched white shirt, each wearing tortoiseshell glasses. Kimberly didn't bother introducing Frick and Frack, and I didn't bother acknowledging their presence. I was familiar with the routine. Kimberly would be the sole mouthpiece for Beckman Engineering. Frick and Frack would take voluminous notes during the proceeding, say nothing in the judge's presence, smirk when any ruling went against me, and probably not be seen again in the case for weeks. They were here today primarily because Roth & Bowles was a large law firm. Lawyers in large firms are like wolves: they prefer to travel in packs.

On this case, Kimberly was the leader of the pack. She was a litigation partner at Roth & Bowles, a powerful St. Louis firm, and her specialty was defending employment claims, especially claims of racial discrimination. She was also the firm's only black partner. Today, as always, she was elegantly dressed and perfectly coiffed. She exuded the cool poise of a former beauty queen, and with good reason. Nearly twenty years ago, Kimberly had been the first black contestant crowned Miss Teenage Missouri.

The composure and tenacity that made her a pageant queen had served her well in her legal career, which began as a law clerk to a then obscure U.S. Circuit Court judge by the name of Clarence Thomas. Unlike Judge Thomas, however, Kimberly could not claim humble origins. Her father was a prominent radiologist at Barnes Hospital. Her mother was a genteel product of the Chicago black middle class who was active in several St. Louis charities and had served an unprecedented two terms as president of the Junior League. Kimberly was their only child. She grew up in the wealthy suburb of Frontenac, prepped at Villa Duchesne (a snooty Catholic girls' high school), and earned her B.A. in economics at Smith College. She met her first husband at St. Louis University Law School, divorced him during her clerkship with Judge Thomas, married her second husband during her years in the general counsel's office of the Department of Commerce, and shed him before returning to St. Louis. She was now thirty-eight and unmarried, although one of the gossip columnists had linked her to Barry Silvermintz, a local urologist who, if memory serves, either did Geraldo Rivera's vasectomy or reversed it.

Kimberly's strategy in this case had been obvious from the start: wage a war of attrition. I was outgunned and outmanned. We both knew that I couldn't risk a full-scale battle out in the open, and she exploited that knowledge by objecting to all of my requests for information, swamping me with her own discovery requests, contesting virtually every action I took in the case, and generally doing whatever could be done to make my pretrial preparations unpleasant, arduous, and demoralizing.

We sat in silence across from each other until Judge Wagner's secretary announced that Her Honor was ready for us. With Kimberly in the lead, we filed into the chambers of the Honorable Catherine L. Wagner.

Like their courtrooms, the chambers of U.S. District Court judges are built on a scale for pharaohs. This one had high ceilings and dark paneling. Her Honor was seated in a high-back leather chair behind an imposing desk. She stood as we approached.

"Greetings, Counsel."

Catherine Wagner was in her mid-forties, a tall, willowy blonde, with long hair, piercing blue eyes, and a ski-slope nose. She had been a renowned beauty in her early twenties, and she still cut quite a figure when striding into the courtroom with that long blond hair cascading down her black judicial robe. In her chambers, the black robe hung on the brass rack in the corner. She was wearing a cream-colored silk blouse and a maroon wool skirt. Up close you could see the bags under her eyes and the worry lines on her forehead—the wear and tear of a hectic career squeezed on top of life as a divorced mother of two adolescent boys, whose framed portraits hung on the wall above her credenza.

"Good afternoon, Your Honor," Kimberly answered cheerfully.

"Hello, Kimberly. Good to see you." Judge Wagner nodded at me with somewhat less enthusiasm. "Ms. Gold."

I returned the nod at the same level of zeal. "Hello, Judge."

Although Catherine Wagner was known as a tough but fair judge, the playing field never felt quite level with Kimberly Howard present. The two were active members of the St. Louis University Law School alumni association. They also shared another important bond: the Republican Party. Catherine Wagner's GOP bona fides had been impeccable when she was appointed to the bench eight years ago, and Kimberly Howard was an increasingly visible member of the Missouri Republican Party. Indeed, her name had started popping up when political pundits talked of the next round of elections; some picked her to challenge the incumbent Missouri Attorney General.

"Well, well," Judge Wagner said in a voice laced with sarcasm after we'd taken our seats, "my favorite case." She looked at Kimberly and then at me. "To what do I owe the pleasure today, ladies?"

"Judge," Kimberly began solemnly, "we have grave concerns about Miss Gold's conduct."

Judge Wagner nodded as she lifted a copy of the letter Kimberly had faxed to me earlier in the day. "You're referring to the ex-employees and their nondisclosure agreements."

"That's certainly one important item on the agenda," Kimberly said. "However, there are others. For starters, we have Miss Gold's outrageous attempt to serve Mr. Beckman with a subpoena in the middle of an awards ceremony on Sunday night."

We were off and running. Although I hate squabbling with opposing counsel in front of a judge, Kimberly and I were at each other before long. As for my efforts to contact former employees of Beckman Engineering, she wanted an order requiring my investigators to issue a Miranda-like warning to each prospective witness informing him of the nondisclosure agreement and providing the ex-employee with the name and telephone number of a Beckman Engineering attorney with whom he could consult without charge before answering any questions. In addition, Kimberly wanted twenty-four-hour advance written notice of each witness contacted.

"Your Honor," I said, trying to maintain my composure, "this is nothing less than an attempt to use the power of this Court to intimidate potential witnesses and, in the process, to invade the confidentiality of my trial preparations."

Judge Wagner agreed and disagreed. She granted Kimberly's request for the Miranda-style warning, but ruled that I did not have to let Kimberly know who I contacted. I told myself that I could probably live with that—as if I had any choice in the matter.

I fared worse with the Conrad Beckman subpoena. "Ms. Gold," Judge Wagner announced sternly, "the Court is not unmindful of the fact that Mr. Beckman is an extremely busy executive. Reluctantly, I will allow you to depose him. However, I will limit that deposition to exactly two hours."

"Two hours?" I said, incredulous. "I don't think I could complete it in two days."

Judge Wagner responded with an imperial shrug. "Deal with it. The mere filing of a lawsuit does not give a plaintiff the unfettered right to depose a busy chief executive officer." She paused to jot a note on her docket sheet. "You'll have two hours." She turned to Kimberly. "Anything else?"

"Unfortunately, yes, Your Honor. Given that the trial date is now just two months away, I must remind Ms. Gold that we are still awaiting new dates for her client's deposition."

Judge Wagner looked at me. "Is there a problem?"

"There most certainly is," I said, my temper flaring. "Kimberly has already subjected my client to twelve days of deposition. Twelve days." I shook my head in disbelief. "While Ms. Howard squeals in panic at the thought of having Conrad Beckman deposed for two hours, she thinks nothing of subjecting my client to day after day after day of completely irrelevant lines of questions. At some point—"

"That is preposterous," Kimberly said, acting shocked.

I spun toward her. "Let me finish," I snapped. I looked back at Judge Wagner. "Judge, enough is enough. The defendant is using discovery as a weapon to make this case as painful as it can for the plaintiff. It's a scorched-earth tactic, Your Honor—an attempt to turn the discovery process into a trial by ordeal." I shook my head angrily. "And meanwhile, more than six months have elapsed since defendant was supposed to produce its documents to me. Six months, and I have yet to see a single piece of paper. Ms. Howard is trying to sneak to trial without having to reveal a thing."

Kimberly put on a show. She was "incredulous" and "insulted" and "offended" by my accusations. We argued back and forth until Judge Wagner raised her hand for silence.

"Here's what's going to happen," she announced, turning to me. "You're going to make your client available for one more day of deposition before month end." She looked at Kimberly. "The Court appreciates the efforts you are making to review your client's documents. However, Ms. Gold has a point: six months is a long time. Perhaps we can prioritize the tasks. It seems that the documents plaintiff needs most urgently are those having to do with the bids. Get those to her by the end of the week." She looked at me. "That ought to keep you busy for a while." She turned back to Kimberly. "Get the rest of the documents to her in, let's say, three weeks. By December eighth." She looked at both of us. "Okay?"

"Your Honor," I said, "we're talking about hundreds of thousands of documents. It'll take me weeks to review them, and I'll still have an awful lot to squeeze in before trial, especially with the Christmas holidays." I paused. "Judge, if the current trial schedule stands, Beckman Engineering will have gained an unfair advantage through its tactics. I request that the Court continue the trial to the spring."

"Oh, no," said Judge Wagner with a chuckle. "No way." She shook her head firmly. "I'm getting this case off my docket. Come hell or high water, we're picking that jury on January twenty-third."

She leaned back in her chair and checked her watch. "That's all for today, ladies. I have a sentencing in ten minutes."

As I waited for the elevator, my blood pressure gradually returning to normal, I tried to remind myself that there was nothing personal or spiteful in Kimberly's strategy. It was standard operating procedure. Her goal was to use her client's substantial economic resources to grind me into the ground. My goal was to avoid needless skirmishes and somehow survive until trial. As for today's brawl, my plan had been even simpler: survive without heavy casualties. I had.

Barely.

In the courthouse lobby downstairs, one of Kimberly Howard's smarmy underlings came over. "Here," he said, holding out a slip of paper with dates written on it. "These are the days that we're available to take your client's deposition."

I studied his smug face. He was a typical product of the

big firm litigation department—that macho subculture most closely akin to a street gang, except that this gang carries notebook computers and dictaphones instead of knives and guns. I knew the type. After all, I'd come of age within a big firm litigation department. We were the guerrillas, the SWAT teams of the law. Although there are few battlefields more stylized and bloodless than a courtroom, you'd never know that from the jargon of the big firm litigator. You don't simply "win" a motion to compel, you "blow the other side out of the water." You don't ask a witness difficult questions at a deposition, you "drill him a new asshole." You don't reject a low settlement offer, you "piss all over it." It's a weird warrior cult where men with soft hands and tasseled shoes swagger into court as if they were wearing battle fatigues and ammo belts.

I stared at this Brooks Brothers tough guy with his slip of paper and for a moment I was mightily tempted to suggest a different place for him to stick it. But why play that game again? It was one of the reasons I left Abbott & Windsor in the first place.

I gave him a tolerant smile. "What's your name?"

He seemed taken aback. "Uh, Arthur Brenton."

I took the slip of paper and dropped it into my briefcase without looking at it. "Thank you, Arthur. I'll call your boss after I check my client's schedule."

CHAPTER 3

Jonathan Wolf leaned back in the booth and scratched his beard pensively. "Gloria Muller doesn't match any profile," he finally said.

"How so?" I asked.

"White, heterosexual, Presbyterian." He shook his head, frowning. "That is not a typical skinhead target."

"Are the Hammerskins typical skinheads?"

Jonathan nodded. "Absolutely."

We were having dinner at Cardwell's in Clayton. That afternoon, after returning to the office from Judge Wagner's chambers, I received a call from one of the Springfield homicide detectives to let me know that they'd arrested two men and charged them with first-degree murder in Gloria Muller's homicide. One was an auto mechanic, the other worked on the loading dock of a Springfield factory. Both had rap sheets more typical of hooligans than gunmen: arrests for peace disturbances, barroom brawls, vandalism, and common assaults. But they shared something else: both were members of a local neo-Nazi group known as the Springfield Aryan Hammerskins. Although the police didn't understand the skinhead connection with the murder, they were positive that they had the right men. In one of the car trunks they'd found a shotgun that matched the one used in the parking lot and a trench coat with powder burns. They also had a witness who'd overheard the two bragging about the shooting at a local bar.

Our dinners arrived—a spicy Thai pasta concoction for me, grilled salmon for Jonathan. Like many who kept kosher in their homes, Jonathan ordered only fish or vegetarian dishes when dining out.

The waitress was all titters and fluttering eyelashes as she asked if she could bring him another Anchor Steam beer. He shook his head distractedly, oblivious to her flirting. With a playful giggle she told him she'd check back in a few minutes to see if he was thirsty. I watched her sashay away, shaking my head. Jonathan tended to have that effect on woman, and on juries. It was part of what made him such an effective trial lawyer. Although one might think that a Brooklyn accent and an embroidered yarmulke would be a drawback in front of a St. Louis jury, he was one of the preeminent criminal defense attorneys in town.

Jonathan Wolf was New York City born and bred. He'd been raised an Orthodox Jew, and as a child attended a Jewish day school steeped in bookish traditions. Nevertheless, he somehow fell in love with boxing, and by the time he was eleven years old he'd demonstrated enough skill and mettle to induce one of the black coaches at the neighborhood gym to work with him. From his bar mitzvah on, he fought in every Golden Gloves competition in the area. At the age of seventeen, he won the Brooklyn title and traveled to Madison Square Garden to compete against the title holders from the other four boroughs. He beat them all, and Jimmy Breslin tagged him "the Talmudic Tornado."

He started his legal career in the U.S. Attorney's office in St. Louis, his wife's hometown. During his prosecutor days, he'd been a classic intimidator—a righteous crusader whose bond with the victims seemed almost obsessional and who earned the nickname "Lone Wolf" for the long, solitary hours he spent preparing his cases. For nearly ten years, he'd stalked criminal defendants in the courtroom as if they were prey in his lair, boring in on them with rapid-fire questions, his green eyes radiating chilled heat.

Six years ago his wife died of ovarian cancer, leaving behind two little daughters. According to courtroom pundits, the young widower decided it was time to provide for their future. He resigned from the U.S. Attorney's office and hung out a shingle as a criminal defense attorney. It was an astounding career change, and astoundingly successful. The Lone Wolf became the Wolf Man—defender of the accused, tormentor of the accusers. His significant cases since the switch included the acquittal of Frankie "The Stud" Studzani on first-degree murder charges and two hung juries in the tax fraud prosecution of former Missouri congressman Jim Bob Pegram.

Jonathan and I met as litigation adversaries, and I had detested him from the get-go. My mother, of course, decided from the start that he was the perfect man for me. I told her no way—he was far too arrogant. She told me it was pride, not arrogance. I told her if that was pride, he had too much of it. "Sounds like someone else I know," she answered with a wink, "and on top of that, sweetie, he's such a nice Jewish boy. What could be so bad?"

Well, I wasn't quite ready to concede to my mother, but I was starting to weaken. Jonathan was in his early forties. His close-trimmed black beard was flecked with gray. Standing a trim six feet tall, he still resembled a light heavyweight fighter, right down to the nose that had been broken and never properly reset. Although it scratched him from the pretty boy category, I had to admit that Jonathan Wolf was, as my niece would say, "fine." I could well imagine the younger women on his juries wondering, during a dull moment of trial, whether that yarmulke stayed on when everything else came off.

I did, too.

Dating an Orthodox Jew was a new experience. In addition to the strict observance of the Sabbath from sundown on Friday to sundown on Saturday—no cars, no telephones, no electrical appliances, no work—there were exacting rules about sex. Although few organized religions celebrate the joys of marital sex more than Orthodox Judaism, the counterweight is a stern prohibition against premarital sex. I suppose it added a touch of nostalgic charm to our relationship, as if we were a pair of high school kids from the 1950s going steady. But it sure added plenty of frustration, too—and for both of us.

"What do the suspects say?" he asked.

I shook my head. "Nothing yet. They're being held without bail. The police are going to let them stew in the county jail over the weekend and try another interrogation on Monday."

"That might work."

"Even if Gloria doesn't fit the profile," I said, "they still may have a possible hate crime motive."

Jonathan looked up from his meal. "Oh?" he asked skeptically.

I told him what I'd learned from the homicide detective. Gloria Muller had been having an affair with a Jewish gynecologist whose clinic had been the target of a pro-life demonstration three months earlier; moreover, the doctor had received several anonymous death threats over the past years. Skinheads tend to be fiercely anti-abortion, the detective had explained.

Jonathan shook his head in disdain. "Those cops should know better than that. Hate crime motives are never subtle. Hammerskins have been tied to two other Springfield murders. One was a thirty-one-year-old black man. He was stomped to death in an alley behind a bar by two skinheads who claimed he had danced with a white woman. The other was a gay man. Stabbed to death. Forty-two stab wounds."

"My God," I murmured.

Jonathan nodded solemnly. "That's not unusual. The killer does it to demonstrate his commitment to the cause. In that one, he sliced off one of the victim's ears, presumably as a souvenir. That's how the police nailed him. They found it in his glove compartment."

I silently absorbed those appalling details. Jonathan's knowledge didn't surprise me. Six weeks ago, the Missouri Attorney General had appointed him a special assistant attorney general to supervise the investigation and potential criminal prosecution of Bishop Kurt Robb and the other leaders of "Spider," a white supremacist organization headquartered in St. Louis. Although Jonathan's criminal defense practice was at least a full-time job, he'd been spending long hours poring over state and federal investigative files and talking to various law enforcement officers charged with monitoring hate groups.

I twirled some pasta onto my fork as I thought it over. "Does that Springfield group have ties to Spider?"

"I'm not sure." He took a sip of wine. "Skinheads tend not to have deep affiliations with any of the established neo-Nazi organizations, but they usually know one another. Spider operates in Illinois, so I'm sure there are connections. I'm thinking of going up there myself. See what those two suspects have to say."

"Mind if I tag along?" I asked. "I have a few questions for them, too."

He smiled. "Sure."

I sighed with disappointment. "She was my only witness, Jonathan."

"You'll find others."

"Not after what Judge Wagner did to me today."

"Maybe you're searching for the wrong ex-employees."

I gave him a puzzled look. "What do you mean?"

"You've alleged a conspiracy, right? Beckman Engineering may be the only defendant in your case, but it's just one of the conspirators. Beckman has its guard way up, but the same won't be true of all the others."

"Oh? Look what happened to Gloria Muller."

He shook his head. "You can't assume that her death is connected to your case."

"Come on," I said, frustrated. "I talked to her, Jonathan. She definitely knew something about the conspiracy."

"Rachel," he said patiently, "that wasn't a mob hit, and she was hardly a mob witness. Moreover, look at the incongruity. Even assuming that she had damaging information about an alleged civil conspiracy—and that's a big assumption—is that reason enough to kill her?"

I watched glumly as he finished his salmon. Although I was convinced to my bones that Gloria's death was connected in some way to my case, the objective facts didn't offer much support.

He wiped his mouth with his napkin and gave me a smile of encouragement. "Start with the bid documents," he said. "You're getting them tomorrow, right? They'll include all of the relevant federal government projects. That'll define the bid-rigging universe. Use them to figure out which company won which bid, and see what kind of pattern emerges."

"Wait," I said, giving him a time-out signal. "All I'm getting are Beckman's bids. How do I figure out who won each one?"

Jonathan leaned back in the booth, his green eyes twinkling. "Don't tell me you haven't heard of *Commerce Business Daily*?"

I frowned. "Ruth mentioned it. Something about using it to keep track of the bids. What is it?"

Jonathan winked. "The key to the kingdom."

"Ruth is meeting with me tomorrow. I'll—"

I paused. Coming down the aisle on her way out was none other than Judge Catherine Wagner, accompanied by two other women her age. My surprised look must have caught her eye because she slowed and smiled in recognition. "Why, look who it is. Hello, Rachel."

I returned the smile. "Hi, Judge."

She approached the booth and nodded approvingly toward my nearly empty plate. "I'm pleased to see that my rulings haven't ruined your appetite."

I laughed politely.

She glanced from me toward my dinner companion. Her expression froze for an instant before she regained her composure. "Ah, Mr. Wolf," she said in a much cooler voice.

"Good evening, Your Honor," he answered with a courteous nod.

Her gaze shifted from Jonathan to me as she appraised our situation, her brow furrowing ever so slightly. We didn't have that business dinner look about us—no notepads or pens on the table, no briefcases on the floor. Her two companions stood behind her, waiting quietly.

"Well, Counselors," she said with a perfunctory nod, "good evening."

I turned to watch her leave and then looked back at Jonathan. "You two have a history."

Jonathan inhaled deeply. "Unfortunately."

"Criminal or civil case?"

He gazed at me for a moment. "Neither."

"Neither?" And then it sank in. "Oh, my God." I leaned forward and whispered, "Did you and she ... ?"

He frowned. After a moment, he said, "Not exactly."

"Not exactly?" I repeated, amused. "What in the world does 'not exactly' mean?"

He looked into my eyes for a moment and then shook his head self-consciously. "We had a misunderstanding."

I pried the story out of him as we left the restaurant. It happened seven years ago at the annual Christmas party thrown by the U.S. Attorney's office and attended by several of the judges. When Jonathan went down the hall to his office to get his briefcase and coat, Judge Wagner snuck in behind him. He was at the coatrack in the corner when she closed the office door behind her. She sat against the edge of his desk, facing him with a boozy, carnal smile. He stood there, immobilized.

"It's party time, Counselor," she told him, her voice somewhere between a purr and a growl. "How 'bout a party favor?" She lifted her right leg and planted her high-heeled foot on the armrest of the chair in front of the desk. As she did so, her skirt slid all the way up her parted thighs. "How 'bout you come over here and fuck me till it hurts."

I giggled in amazement. It was a scene out of a trashy novel. I couldn't imagine Judge Wagner doing that. I couldn't imagine any woman doing that. "What happened?"

We were standing under a streetlight outside Cardwell's. He shrugged. "I tried to act responsibly. I told her I was married, that she'd had too much to drink, that she was too fine a person to have a one-night stand. I told her I'd be happy to get her a cab or find someone to drive her home."

I winced. "Oh, Jonathan, she must have been mortified." I slipped my arm under his as we walked up Maryland toward the parking lot behind the church. "She must have been furious."

"She was a little upset." He shook his head ruefully. "Our relationship has been somewhat strained ever since."

I laughed. "I bet it has. Oy, as if I didn't already have enough problems in that lawsuit."

"I don't think she'll hold that against you."

"Oh, come on, Jonathan, she's a woman, too." I shook my head and groaned. "She's already got an antiplaintiff reputation, especially where the defendant is a corporation. Now she'll have an added reason— Oh, my God."

I stopped, dismayed by what I saw. I turned to him. "Is that your car?"

Without answering, he left my side and headed toward the car, moving with grim resolve.

Someone had bashed in the windshield and side windows. As I approached the car, I could see broken glass scattered on the asphalt. In the dim light from a distant streetlamp I could make out what appeared to be white streaks of paint on the car hood. As I got closer, the pattern became clear.

"Oh, no," I said.

Spray-painted on the hood of Jonathan's car was a swastika. He stared down at it, his face implacable. I said nothing, waiting. I could see his jaw muscle flexing. His eyes shifted from the hood to the interior of the car, which was strewn with broken glass. He surveyed the seats and carpet, moving slowly along the side of the car toward the rear and then back to the front.

At last he turned to me, his eyes cold. "Do you have a phone in your car?"

I glanced toward my car, which was a parked a few spaces over, and then I looked back at him. "I do."

He reached into his suit jacket, removed his wallet, and took out a card. "Do me a favor," he said, his voice calm. He handed me the card. "Call this number."

I squinted at the card. It was for a Lieutenant Hendricks of the state police. I looked at Jonathan.

"Tell them where I am," he said. "Explain what happened, and ask them to find Hendricks. Tell them to send someone from Forensics over here."

I nodded. "Okay."

He turned to his car.

"Jonathan."

He looked back at me. His utter composure was almost eerie.

"This is"—I gestured toward his car, struggling for words—"this is terrible."

He nodded.

I gestured helplessly. "I'm sorry."

He mumbled a "Thanks" and turned back to his car.

CHAPTER 4

I was never supposed to represent Ruth Alpert.

When I reluctantly agreed to meet with her a year ago last November, I warned my mother in advance that I wasn't going to take her case, regardless of its merits. Age discrimination cases against large companies are hard enough to prove without the complicating factor of a corporate downsizing that permanently eliminates your client's position. Moreover, Beckman Engineering Co. was a particularly unappealing target, especially in front of a St. Louis jury. It was not merely that Beckman was headquartered here, employed more than two thousand local citizens, and spent millions of dollars a year burnishing its public image, as personified by its revered chairman, Conrad Beckman. No, what made Beckman Engineering especially unappealing was its reputation as a tenacious litigant. It tended to respond to a lawsuit with wrath, indignation, and an abundance of litigators. All of which meant that this was not a company to sue unless you had a deep-pocket client and a large support staff. I had neither back when I met with Ruth, and things sure hadn't changed in the year since then.

So why had I taken her case?

It was a good question.

As I sat at my desk rapping a pencil against a legal pad, I could hear Ruth Alpert's voice in the outer office. She had arrived a few minutes early for our one-thirty meeting and was out there now boring poor Jacki with one of her interminable Lauren stories. Lauren was Ruth's niece, and she played a minor character on *Gold Fillings*, a moronic sitcom about a Beverly Hills dental practice that seemed the nightmare offspring of an unholy coupling between *ER* and *Married With Children*. One of the first rules of survival with Ruth was learning how to interrupt her latest Lauren story before she got rolling. Jacki had yet to master that skill.

So why had I taken Ruth's case?

Partly because of my mother. Ruth was her friend and Ruth had been wronged. What else could I possibly need to know? My mother's powers of persuasion and guilt are wondrous to behold and virtually impossible to resist. Trust me.

Another reason, of course, had been the injustice of it all. Here was a woman—a widow, no less—cut adrift at age sixty-three after more than two decades of loyal service. BECKMAN ENGINEERING ANNOUNCES ADDITIONAL LAYOFFS, read the headline. INDUSTRY ANALYSTS APPLAUD LEANER PROFILE. In an era of perpetual corporate "rightsizing," the familiar headlines could dull you to the individual victims and their pain. Ruth's had been one of 150 JOBS TO BE TRIMMED IN THIRD ROUND OF CUTS and her anguish was palpable. Here was a woman who took great pride in her secretarial skills, who bragged during our first meeting that she had graduated as the top secretarial student in her class at Soldan High, who could type seventy-five words per minute ("eighty-five on a computer, Rachel, but that's easier"), who knew several computer programs, including WordPerfect, Lotus, and DisplayWrite ("that's capital D, capital W, no space"), who had taken only seven sick days in two decades and just two personal days (one to bury her husband, one to sit *shiva*). On the Friday before I saw her, she had applied for unemployment compensation—"As God is my witness, Rachel, the most humiliating experience of my life."

But injustice and a mother's guilt trip will get you only so far. The deciding factor had been Uncle Harry. On that chilly morning a year ago when Ruth and I first met, we'd both started our day reciting kaddish. For me, it had been two weeks before the first anniversary of my father's death. He had no son to say kaddish for him, so that first year I'd gone to the synagogue every Saturday morning to recite the prayer for the dead. For Ruth, it was the fifty-fourth anniversary of the harrowing night her beloved uncle Harry had been seized outside his little jewelry store while locking up. Later that night, his bullet-ridden corpse was dumped from a moving car onto the pavement in front of a police station. His wife died in a nursing home in 1964. His only sibling—Ruth's mother—died in 1973. His two sons died within six months of each other in 1979—one from heart disease, one from cancer.

From then on, there was no one but Ruth to say kaddish for her uncle, and she'd done it every year thereafter, less from a sense of familial duty than of profound devotion. Although she was only nine when he'd been killed, she cherished her vivid memories of him—of the card tricks he used to perform, the penny candies he used to sneak her, the silly bedtime songs he sang whenever she spent the night.

Ruth told me the story of Uncle Harry on that cold November morning last year, and when she finished, we both had tears in our eyes. "It's a *mitzvah*," she explained in her gentle voice, "an honor to be able to say kaddish for that wonderful man." So moved was I by the image of her bearing lone witness each November for her beloved uncle that I agreed to take her case.

Back then, of course, neither of us suspected what was to come. Our first hint: Beckman Engineering's response to Ruth's complaint. It included a vicious, petty counterclaim that accused her of everything from making personal telephone calls on company time to taking excessive lunch breaks. I remember reading through it when it first arrived. I was worried about Ruth's reaction. I'd seen many a client recoil at the first answering volley. Frankly, the best plaintiff in an employment discrimination case is one of those gritty, hard-scrabble types willing to go the distance. Ruth certainly didn't look the part. In fact, she looked more like a storybook Jewish grandmother, right down to the gray hair pulled back in a bun, the soft face, and the dowdy floral-print, calf-length dress. She actually wore granny glasses.

I can still remember the February afternoon she came in

to read the counterclaim. She'd arrived around five o'clock, pausing outside the doorway to stomp the snow off her boots. It had been gently snowing all day—big, fluffy snowflakes floating out of a milky white sky. We talked about the weather and the traffic as I got her a cup of hot tea. I handed her the document and took my seat behind the desk. I watched as she slowly read through it, bracing myself for the tears. Beckman Engineering's counterclaim was startling in its spitefulness—as if the company had decided to stake Ruth Alpert out there on the hillside as an example to all would-be plaintiffs.

As she reached the last page of the counterclaim, I glanced toward the box of Kleenex tissues on my desk. A minute passed. She was still staring at that page, the only sounds the faint hum of my computer and the syncopated clicking of the radiator. I waited and watched, looking for a telltale sign—a sniffle, perhaps, or the trembling shoulders. Finally, she closed the document and looked up. Her eyes were clear, her expression firm.

"So," she said in a calm voice, "they raised the ante."

I gave her a smile of commiseration. "I'm afraid so."

She rubbed the back of her neck thoughtfully. "Then we should, too."

"We?" I asked, puzzled.

She nodded. "I worked there a long time, Rachel." She paused, arching her eyebrows. "A girl hears things."

"Things?"

She nodded again, this time with the hint of a smile.

Jacki brought me back to the present by poking her head in my office to announce, "Ruth's here." She paused, widening her eyes in a show of relief at finally escaping from the latest Lauren saga.

I smiled. "Send her in."

A moment later, Ruth Alpert came in. She was carrying a tin of what I knew were homemade ginger snaps. I loved her ginger snaps.

"Hello, Rachel dear."

"Ruth, I love your hair."

"Really?" she asked, self-consciously touching it. Since we'd last met two weeks ago, she'd had her long gray hair chopped off. "Your mother told me to do it," she said with an embarrassed giggle. Her hair was cut in a close shag. "She told me I looked like an old *bubba*."

"A new outfit, too?"

She nodded. "Your mother again."

Ruth was wearing khaki slacks, a pink cotton Oxford shirt, and a navy blazer. I suppose she was aiming for that country club matron image—or perhaps the zoo docent look—but she actually reminded me of Miss Hodges, my high school field hockey coach who spent her summers in the Wisconsin Dells running a crafts store with her horsy companion, Miss Gulden. Still, it was a definite improvement over her usual outfit.

Despite the new 'do and clothing, she remained the same old Ruth—a woman who seemed a full generation older than my mother, not merely pre-Beatles but pre-Elvis, stuck in a Lawrence Welk world of accordions and tiny bubbles. During a pause in our conversation, she wrinkled her nose and made *tsk, tsk* sounds.

"What?" I asked.

"I keep thinking of that poor woman." She shook her head in consternation. "Killed in front of your eyes. Barbarians." She pressed an index finger against her plump, rouged cheek. "Do you think there might be a connection?"

"The police don't really know what to make of it yet." I shrugged. "Neither do I. That's why I'm going up there on Sunday to talk to them."

"The police?"

"No, the two men in jail."

Ruth's eyes widened in concern. "My heavens, is that safe?"

I nodded reassuringly. "Perfectly. I've done it before, and this time I'll be with a friend who used to be a prosecutor."

"Oh, I could never." She shuddered. "I would be so horrified."

"Well," I said with a weary sigh, "if you're looking to be horrified, you don't need to go to Springfield. There's plenty to horrify you in this case right here—including yet another day of your deposition before the end of the month. Let me tell you what happened in court yesterday afternoon."

I brought her up to date, including the decision by the Department of Justice to pass on our case. "Looks like we're on our own, kiddo," I said with a fatalistic smile.

"What can we do, Rachel?" she said, a tremor in her voice. "Everyone at Beckman pretends they don't know anything. Former employees won't talk to us. That woman in Springfield—good heavens." She was wringing her hands.

I gave her a plucky smile. "Don't bury us yet, Ruth. There's still a heartbeat."

"Barely," she said, her eyes welling up in frustration.

"Hang in there, Ruth." I leaned forward and took one of her hands in mine. "We've had some setbacks, but it's not over. If there was a conspiracy, we'll find it. Trust me, you can't hide something that big and that complicated without leaving behind some stray pieces of evidence. They're out there. We'll just have to keep looking."

"But where?"

"For starters," I said, "the bid documents on the water and sewer projects. Beckman Engineering is delivering them today."

Ruth frowned. "What will that do for us?"

"Define the universe."

"What universe?"

I patiently explained it to her again, for what seemed like the tenth time. Our lawsuit alleged a bid-rigging conspiracy on certain federal water and sewer projects in the Midwest. That meant that the bad guys got together to divide up the bids and decide who would win each one. The documents Beckman Engineering was delivering today would presumably identify the universe of projects involved in the alleged conspiracy. Once we defined that universe—no easy task—we'd have to figure out who had the winning bid on each of the projects, since Beckman Engineering's alleged co-conspirators would presumably be among the winners.

Ruth looked confused. "But that won't be in the bid documents. They announce winners after the bids are in."

I nodded. "But apparently we can get that information from that publication you once mentioned to me. The *Commerce Business Daily.* Do you have any copies?"

"I'm sure I do. I'll drop some off later today."

There was a knock on my door. Jacki opened it and peered in. "They've arrived," she said.

"The bid documents?" I asked.

She nodded ominously.

"A lot?"

She gestured toward my office window. "See that?"

There was a yellow Ryder truck parked out front. Its rear doors were open. A worker was pushing a handcart loaded with three boxes down the ramp from the back of the truck to the street.

"How many boxes?" I asked.

"Thirty-three," Jacki said.

I sat back in my chair and stared at her. "Thirty-three?"

She nodded. "Containing seventy-three thousand pages. I signed the receipt."

I groaned. "Wonderful."

At 5:35 P.M. I leaned over, put the lid on the box, and slumped back in my chair.

"Two down," I announced to the empty office. Glumly, I surveyed the solid wall of boxes. They were stacked four feet high and ran the entire length of the side wall of my office. Two down, thirty-one to go.

Once all the boxes had been unloaded and stacked along the wall, I'd closed the door, taken a deep breath, psyched myself up, and reached for the first box. Three hours later, I'd gotten through a grand total of two. At that rate it would take at least forty more hours to finish them all—and the task would have to be divided into small segments spread out over many days. Examining just two boxes of documents— thousands of pages of technical financial and engineering materials—had turned my mind to mush. I didn't know whether I had enough mental stamina to look at any more documents tonight.

I bent down, grasped box number two through the handhold openings on either side, lugged it over to the side wall, and dropped it on top of box number one. I turned toward the far end of the mountain range of boxes and stared at box number three as I carried on a silent debate. It was 5:45 P.M. If I started another box now, I could finish it and be home by eight with the satisfaction that I'd gotten through one-eleventh of the documents on the first day. On the other hand, if I left now, I could be home by six o'clock. It was Friday night, the beginning of the Jewish Sabbath. I needed to get home to light the *Shabbat* candles—a ceremony I'd performed every Friday night since my father's death. You're supposed to light the candles at sundown to welcome the Sabbath. I glanced toward the window. Too late for that. I turned again toward box number three. Well, if I could knock off one more tonight, that would be three in one session. Three more tomorrow morning, maybe another three in the afternoon, three on Sunday, keep up the pace, and I'd be done by the end of the week.

But that meant box number three tonight. My shoulders sagged.

As I stood facing the rows of boxes, trying to get motivated, there was a knock at the outer door to my office. I turned toward the sound, concerned. I wasn't expecting anyone. Ruth had already been by to drop off several old issues of *Commerce Business Daily*.

Cautiously, I opened my office door and walked through the reception area toward the outer door. There was a spyhole at eye level. I peered through it and saw a most unusual sight:

a grinning Benny Goldberg holding aloft several carryout pizza containers. He was wearing a black T-shirt with the legend, *Please Help Me—I Am An Endomorph*. Behind him stood five young men and women casually dressed in jeans or khakis. One of the guys was holding two six-packs of beer.

"Benny?" I said in amazement, still peering at him through the spyhole.

"Come on, Rachel," he hollered, "open the door already. These goddamn pizzas are hot."

I unlocked the door and pulled it open. Benny moved quickly toward Jacki's desk to set down the carryout containers. As he did, the room filled with the yummy scents of spicy tomato sauce, crusty dough, oregano, and pepperoni.

"Professor?" the young guy with the two six-packs asked. "Where should I put these?"

Benny surveyed the office. "Over there, Jake," he said, pointing to a side table. Benny turned to me with a broad smile. "Well?"

I gave him a baffled look. "Well what?"

The other five had gathered around us. Benny gazed at them with a smile. "Folks, this is the great Rachel Gold— lawyer extraordinaire and total babe, with the brains of a Brandeis and the stems of a showgirl. Rachel," he said, making a sweeping gesture toward the others, "these are your shock troops."

I smiled at them uncertainly, not sure what to make of Benny's description.

Benny turned to me. "Your law student volunteers, re- member? These are Wash U's finest. That's Jake over by the beer, and Zack next to him."

Jake and Zack were a pair of big burly kids with lovely blue eyes and shy smiles. Jake was wearing an Amherst Col- lege sweatshirt and Zack had on a St. Louis Blues jersey.

"They both have engineering degrees," Benny explained, "which means they ought to be good with the technical stuff. And this is Josh." He gave him a playful punch in the arm "This dude is my man."

Josh looked like a dude: a slender athletic build, long brown hair, and one gold earring. He was wearing baggy army pants, a green Miles Davis T-shirt, and a battered St. Louis Browns baseball cap turned backwards. "Hey," he said to me, flashing a marvelously roguish grin that revealed perfect white teeth.

"And this is Kayla," Benny said.

She had short, dark brown hair and stunning brown eyes.

"You're a CPA, right?" Benny asked her.

She nodded and turned to me with a lovely smile. "I used to work at Price Waterhouse."

"That means she can make sense out of all the cost-accounting documents in the bid materials," Benny said. "Believe me, she's smarter than shit. And finally, say hi to Hanna." He pronounced the name to rhyme with Donna.

Hanna stepped forward with a cheerful smile and held out her hand to shake mine. "Benny told us all about the case, Miss Gold." Hanna was striking in a Cindy Crawford sort of way: tall, long brown hair, exotic green eyes. "We're really excited to be able to help you and Mrs. Alpert."

"That's—that's wonderful," I stammered, overwhelmed.

"So," Benny said, rubbing his hands together, "have the documents arrived?"

I nodded. "Thirty-three boxes. They're stacked in my office. I've been through the first two."

"Thirty-three?" Benny said. "No problem. We ought to be able to knock off a third tonight, a third tomorrow, and finish by our deadline."

"What deadline?" I asked.

"Seven o'clock Sunday." Benny winked. "Your mom has invited us all for dinner." He solemnly placed his hand over his heart and looked heavenward. "She's making her brisket, praise the Lord."

He paused as he felt something in the breast pocket of his T-shirt. "Oh, yeah," he said. He removed two blue birthday candles from his shirt pocket and handed them to me. "Almost forgot."

I took the candles from him. "What are these?"

He shook his head, amused. "Now that you're Miss Super Jew, I figured you'd be getting *spilkes* about lighting the *Shabbat* candles." He nodded toward the birthday candles. "It's the best I could do on short notice. God won't mind." He turned to the others. "What do you say, gang? Let's put on the old feed bag."

As the students moved toward the pizzas and beer, I grabbed Benny by the arm and pulled him back.

"Thanks," I said, kissing him on the cheek, my eyes watering.

"Aw," he said, shrugging it off, "no big deal."

CHAPTER 5

It was four o'clock on Saturday afternoon. Two hours ago we'd finished the last of the thirty-three boxes. In celebration and gratitude, I'd taken everyone to lunch at Balibans in the Central West End. After lunch, the students headed back to Wash U and Benny, Jacki, and I walked back to my office.

It had been amazing—no, wonderful—to see how quickly those fresh, intelligent eyes could review and categorize seventy thousand documents. They'd ended last night's session at eleven o'clock, started again this morning at eight-thirty, and finished by two. Even Benny—the man who had earned the nickname "Iron Butt" during our years together at Abbott & Windsor for his marathon document review sessions in *In re Bottles & Cans*—was impressed.

As a result of their efforts, we'd at last defined the universe: one hundred forty-eight federal construction projects in the field of wastewater, groundwater, and other water control on which Beckman Engineering had submitted bids over the past ten years. It was a much larger universe than Ruth or I had imagined. Almost twice as large. Then again, until that snowy day last February, I'd no idea that any such universe existed, large or small.

"A girl hears things," Ruth had told me that day.

"Things?"

"Bad things."

Specifically, she'd heard over the years that something fishy was going on with the bids on certain federal government water-control projects in the Midwest.

"It was odd," Ruth said with a puzzled look, her index

finger pressed against her cheek. "It was as if we knew in advance which contracts we would win and which we would lose." She raised her eyebrows knowingly. "You might want to keep that in mind, Rachel. It could embarrass them."

I can still remember that moment. I can remember turning toward the window to watch those big snowflakes waft down out of a pale sky. I can remember the bottom of the window scalloped with miniature snowdrifts like a Hallmark Cards Christmas scene. I can remember a vision of huge stacks of money, mountains of dollar bills thrusting upward into that pale sky. But most of all I can remember another vision, a far more troubling one—a vision of our tidy little lawsuit morphing into that rarest of litigation weapons, a lethal juggernaut known to few within the law and even fewer outside. Even its name is tinged with portent: *qui tam*.

I had probed gingerly at first, asking in an almost offhand manner whether she had any specifics, any examples of what she had labeled the "inside track." She'd overheard talk among her superiors about certain bids: "This one's ours" and "We don't get that one" and "We're supposed to bid this one at nine point five mill." She'd observed odd conduct surrounding certain bids. Some took weeks to prepare and included several site visits; others were literally slapped together overnight— an impossible time frame for a real bid. Even more unusual, she remembered a major project for the construction of a new wastewater treatment plant on an air force base in Oklahoma; the project team worked around the clock for two weeks to come up with a bid of $9,232,350, and then, unbeknownst to them, one of the higher-ups "rounded" the number up to $10.6 million—and Beckman Engineering was *still* low bidder.

But most of all, I can remember Ruth's complete obliviousness to the implications of what she had observed. She saw it as gossip that might make her former employers squirm— that might embarrass them in the eyes of the federal government the way their counterclaim had embarrassed her in the eyes of her former colleagues. I saw something far different.

If the bits and pieces of what she had observed were more than mere coincidence, then Beckman Engineering was a participant in an illegal bid-rigging conspiracy in violation of the Federal False Claims Act. That meant that Ruth had an opportunity to become a *qui tam* relator—in plain English, a bounty hunter.

Qui tam is derived from the Latin *qui tam pro domino rege quam proseippso*, which means "he who as much for the king as for himself," or, for short, "in the king's name." It's legal shorthand for a special type of lawsuit in which an ordinary citizen is allowed to wrap himself in official garb and take action in the name of the government. It dates back to thirteenth-century England, where clever litigants used the *qui tam* maneuver to avoid corrupt local tribunals, gain access to the royal court, and, by purporting to align themselves with the king's interest, claim as their reward a percentage of the penalties levied against the wrongdoers. The *qui tam* action entered this country in a statute enacted at the height of the Civil War in response to allegations of fraud and price gouging by unscrupulous contractors. The goal was to encourage whistle-blowers by giving ordinary citizens the chance to share in the bounty. In more recent years, Congress turbo-charged the statute by adding treble damages and a bigger slice of the pie (up to 30 percent) for the successful *qui tam* relator.

To move from an employment discrimination plaintiff to a *qui tam* relator was the equivalent of moving from church-basement bingo to Monte Carlo. Beckman Engineering had submitted bids on a hundred forty-eight relevant federal water-control projects over the past ten years. If—and it was still a huge if—we could prove an illegal bid-rigging scheme, than each of those bids constituted a separately punishable act of "false negotiation" under the Federal False Claims Act. Given the size of the contracts involved, the potential recovery was staggering. As an age discrimination plaintiff, Ruth's best-case scenario was an award of roughly $100,000—the difference between her "early retirement severance package" and the regular salary she could have earned through age seventy. As a *qui tam* relator, Ruth's share of the bounty could exceed $10 million.

All of which explained why Ruth and I were now the featured items on a Jurassic Park Blue Plate Special.

This was the first *qui tam* claim I'd ever handled.

It was also the last.

I'd long since taken that vow.

Unfortunately, identifying the universe of one hundred forty-eight bids was just the starting point, and we were still a long way from the finish line. Indeed, there was no way to determine from the bid documents we'd reviewed which of Beckman Engineering's one hundred forty-eight bids had been successful; nor was there any way to determine who else submitted a bid on that project, who won, and what the winning bid had been. Those were crucial facts, since the other winners could be Beckman's co-conspirators.

But the task of identifying the winning bids for those projects seemed even bigger and more tedious than the document review we'd just completed. The crucial information was buried within ten years of back issues of the *Commerce Business Daily*. I'd taken several issues with me to the restaurant and passed them out to Benny, Jacki, and the law students during lunch. I explained my next project: finding out who won each of the one hundred forty-eight bids. I waited as they leafed through the publication, watching as the enormity of the project began to dawn on them.

The *CBD*, as it's known to its readers, is a daily bulletin listing every U.S. government procurement invitation and contract award over $25,000. Printed on flimsy yellow paper by the U.S. Government Printing Office, each edition is 40 to 70 pages long and contains anywhere from 500 to 1,000 notices. The first two-thirds of every issue lists projects open for bids, that is, "U.S. Government procurement invitations." Each invitation is set out in a dense, eye-glazing block of small type, ten to twenty invitations per page, thirty or more pages worth per issue—everything from an invitation for a bid to construct a new pier at the U.S. Coast Guard Station in Surfside, Texas, to an invitation for a bid to conduct a study of krill demographics in Antarctica for the National Marine Fisheries Service. At the back end of each issue are ten or so pages of winners, or "Contract Awards." These were set out in even smaller clumps of type, thirty to forty announcements per page.

To make matters worse for us, there was no connection between the procurement invitations at the front of the issue and the contracts awarded at the back. Indeed, the bids submitted in response to one of those invitations would not be awarded (and reported) until months later. And as a final maddening twist, there was no cumulative index, and thus no way to correlate the contract announced as open for bid in, say, the August 12 issue with the contract award announced two or four or six months later.

Frankly, I felt guilty even mentioning the project. After all, my volunteers had already saved me hours and hours of monotonous work. The next task—essentially searching for one hundred forty-eight needles in a humongous haystack of back issues—would involve far more hours of mind-numbing tedium. It was the equivalent of handing them ten years' worth of Manhattan telephone directories and a list of one hundred forty-eight telephone numbers (just numbers, no names), each of which appeared only twice over the ten years, and asking them to find the match for each number.

"Damn," Benny said, shaking his head, "this could take weeks."

"Not necessarily," Josh said, studying the small print on the cover page of one issue.

If the information reported in the *Commerce Business Daily*, he explained, was also available in a computer database on the Internet, they might be able to do the search far quicker than it would take to do manually. By way of analogy, the full text of the plays of William Shakespeare is available in an Internet database. To find the exact location of Hamlet's famous soliloquy in the "hard copy," you'd need to leaf through the play, page by page, skimming the dialogue in each scene. To find that same text in a computer database, you'd type "To be or not to be," press Search, and in seconds your screen would light up with the entire soliloquy from Act III, Scene 1.

Perhaps, Josh explained, they could conduct the same type of search through the *Commerce Business Daily* database. By entering the contract number, they might be able to pull up the original procurement invitation and the subsequent contract award for each of the one hundred forty-eight bids without having to look through any documents.

The phone rang.

It was Zack calling from the library to fill me in on their progress. When I hung up, I turned toward Benny and said, "These kids are terrific."

He looked up from an issue of *Commerce Business Daily* and beamed. "Of course they are. I picked them. What's the word?"

"They're on a computer over at Wash U, and they found a Web site covering almost forty years of issues. He says they'll have the result no later than tomorrow."

"Whoa." Benny raised his eyebrows, impressed.

I gave him a thumbs-up. "If that works, Kayla has an idea for another search. They'll bring all the results to my mom's house tomorrow night."

Jacki came in with the typed list of one hundred forty-eight bids fresh off the printer. "That's it," she said as she handed it to me. She checked her watch. "I'm outta here."

"Thanks, Jacki," I said, standing up. "Have a good time."

She inhaled deeply and nodded. "Thanks."

"Hey, Jacki," Benny said, "where you off to?"

She blushed. "Oh, just . . . out. Probably dinner."

Benny grinned. "Who's the lucky guy?"

Jacki shrugged awkwardly. "Just someone from my civil procedure class."

Benny winked. "Sic him, tiger."

She turned to me, trying to regain her poise. "You need me to come in tomorrow?"

"Sunday?" I shook my head. "No, I won't be in, either. I'm going with Jonathan tomorrow morning to hear that Nazi creep give a sermon, and then we're driving up to Springfield to talk to the skinheads they arrested for Gloria's murder."

She shook her head in disgust. "Those animals."

I followed her to the outer door. "Wait," I whispered, glancing back to see if Benny was listening. He wasn't. I turned to her. "Let me see."

Uncertainly, she moved toward me. "Do I look okay?"

I smiled. "Extraordinary." Then again, at six foot three and two hundred thirty-five pounds, it'd be hard for her to look anything else.

"Really?" she asked.

"Definitely." We both kept our voices low. "I love the hair. Is it new?"

She nodded. "I bought it last weekend." She touched the side curls doubtfully. "You're sure the permed look isn't too much?"

"Oh, no," I told her. It was a big improvement over her last night-on-the-town wig, a platinum beehive that looked stiff enough to drive railroad spikes.

I turned back again. Benny was engrossed in an issue of *Commerce Business Daily*, oblivious to us. "Let's see," I whispered as I reached over and unbuttoned the top button of her blouse. I stood back, studied her a moment, and nodded in approval. "Perfect."

She took a deep breath. "Thanks."

"See you on Monday. Have fun."

When I came back into my office, Benny looked up from the *CBD* and asked, "How tall is her date?"

I shrugged. "She said he works days at an insurance company."

"Does he—you know?"

I looked at him wearily. "Does he what?"

"Does he know about the magic surprise she's hiding under that skirt? Does he know that Jacki is everything you always wanted in a girl—and more?"

I tried to keep a straight face as I took a seat behind my desk. "That's none of our business." I picked up the list of bids that Jacki had prepared and tried to focus. After a moment, I glanced over at Benny, who was grinning at me. I raised my eyebrows. "Oy, I sure hope he does."

Benny chuckled. "Oh, man," he said, shaking his head in amusement. "What an image, eh?"

I settled back in my chair with the list of bids. Reaching behind me to the credenza, I flipped on the radio. I was just in time to hear the opening chords of the Eagles' "Hotel California."

"Mmmm," I sighed, transported back to the summer before my sophomore year of high school and a cute junior on the varsity football team named Chuck Nathan—back to a time when "cute" and "varsity letter" equaled Mr. Right. Chuck was the love of my life for six whole weeks, and I wore his letter sweater with pride on even the hottest nights that August.

"So what's next?" Benny asked.

I reached for the list of bids. "Depends on what the students find on the Internet." I frowned at the entries. "In fact, the rest of this case depends on that."

"How so?"

I leaned across the desk and turned the list toward him. "If there really is a conspiracy, we ought to be able to see a pattern from the winners. First of all, there ought to be a fairly small group, but large enough to divide up all those jobs—I'd guess somewhere between five and ten. More than ten, I don't see how they could run a conspiracy—too many players, too many variables. So, the first hurdle is the number of winners."

"And then what?" Benny asked.

"A comparison of the winning bids to the cost estimates."

"What cost estimates?" Benny asked.

I showed how each bid invitation in the *CBD* included an estimated cost range for the project—$3 to $6 million for one,

$5 to $8 million for another. Since the central goal of a bid-rigging conspiracy is to allow each conspirator to "win" one contract with a higher-than-competitive bid, the bad guys have to decide in advance what the winning bid will be so that the rest of them can be sure to submit higher bids. How did they decide how high to go with the winning bid? On government projects, Uncle Sam is kind enough to provide that answer with its cost estimates.

"You see?" I said. "If the government's cost estimate for a particular project is four to seven million, and if there really is a bid-rigging conspiracy, which end of the cost estimate would you expect the so-called low bid to be closer to?"

He looked at me and nodded. "Good thinking."

"We'll see if that happened here." I leaned back in my chair. "If so, we still have a case."

"Keep your fingers crossed," Benny said.

"I guess so." I stared up at the ceiling and sighed. "If we still have a case, that means I've got at least two miserable months of trial preparation ahead of me." I shook my head glumly. "Sometimes I wish someone would drive a stake through the heart of this lawsuit."

CHAPTER 6

For more than thirty years, the good burghers of South St. Louis have made the Reavis Banquet Center the place of choice to celebrate their weddings, confirmations, high school graduations, and other special occasions. As such, it's normally a place for merrymaking—drinks flow, buffet tables groan, and big bands play top tunes from decades ago.

But not this Sunday morning.

Today, the main hall of the Reavis Banquet Center felt more like a chapel. Gone were the steam trays and portable bars and banquet tables. In their place were about fifteen rows of folding chairs, sixteen chairs per row, all facing the elevated stage at the head of the room where the big bands normally set up. The stage was empty except for a podium in the center, a flagpole in the right corner, and a large white cross on a stand in the other corner. Taped organ music played softly over the speakers. Every chair was taken.

Jonathan and I were in the back row. I gazed around the room, trying to gauge the audience. It was a white, working-class crowd—mostly blue collar, with a few shopkeepers and bank tellers scattered in the mix. The men looked uncomfortable in their sports jackets. I saw a few adjust their ties or run a finger around the inside of their buttoned collars. The older women looked dowdy; the younger ones favored bleached hair and chewing gum. At first glance there was a Norman Rockwell feel to it, but after a few minutes you sensed the slightly harder edge to this crowd. Any doubts, of course, were dispelled by the presence of all those uniformed cops. I counted a dozen St. Louis police officers positioned along the walls around the room. There was a similar number of state troopers outside, spread around the perimeter of the building, their walkie-talkies crackling. Several had nodded at Jonathan as we walked in.

On our drive down, I had jokingly told Jonathan that we'd probably be the first Jews in the building since it opened in 1957. The irony seemed amusing then. It sure didn't now. Although the crowd was obviously gathered for a Sunday morning sermon, this would be no ordinary religious event. For today we were going to hear from Bishop Kurt Robb, former Green Beret and high school driver's ed instructor, currently the spiritual leader of the Church of the Aryan Jesus and the Grand Commandant of Spider.

Bishop Robb was also the main target of Jonathan's criminal investigation. That was why we were here. Although several of his sermons were available in printed form and on cassettes—through his own mail-order operation for the true believers, in the evidence files of the Attorney General's office for the investigators—Jonathan had yet to observe a live performance. Since he'd soon be observing another type of live performance, namely, Bishop Robb's command appearance before the grand jury to answer Jonathan's questions, he decided to check him out here first.

When Jonathan had mentioned where he was going Sunday morning before our drive to Springfield, I asked to join him. After witnessing Gloria's murder, I was more than a little curious to see one of the skinheads' spiritual leaders in action.

Bishop Robb's followers had rented Reavis Banquet Center for the morning so that he'd have an opportunity to bring his message to the city folk. It was part of his grand plan—to establish a viable neo-Nazi organization near where he believed his true constituents were located: in the larger cities and suburbs. As he was fond of saying, "You can't run a national revolution from a kooky commune in Montana."

Stepping onto the stage was a stout, middle-aged man with thinning, slicked-back hair, wire-rim glasses, and a pencil mustache. The taped organ music ended abruptly as he approached the podium and cleared his throat.

"Ladies and gentlemen," he said in a surprisingly high-pitched voice, "welcome to our special morning with our very special guest. In keeping with the spirit of the occasion, our guest has asked that we not applaud." He paused and looked toward the side, where the door had opened. "Ladies and gentlemen, we are pleased to present Bishop Kurt Robb."

Through the side door filed eight men in their twenties and thirties, moving at a stride somewhere between a march and a swagger. All wore jeans, dark boots, and what looked like black-and-gold high school letter jackets without the letters. All had buzz cuts and all wore aviator sunglasses. They took up positions along the floor in front of the stage and turned in unison to face the audience, their hands clasped behind their backs, their legs at shoulder width.

There was a moment of tense silence, and then a tall man in a white robe entered from the side. It was Bishop Kurt Robb. You could almost feel a shiver run through the crowd as he stepped onto the stage. He was wearing tinted horn-rims and his trademark green beret. He paused to shake the hand of the man who had introduced him. It was a solemn handshake. The man nodded deferentially and quickly stepped down from the stage.

Robb was now the sole figure on the stage. He stared at the audience. Below him, his security guards stood motionless. Robb's straight brown hair was brushed at an angle across his forehead in a creepy echo of his hero. All that was missing was black hair dye and the brush mustache.

After a moment, he nodded somberly. "Good morning, my friends."

"Good morning," they murmured back at him.

"I have come here this morning, good people, to bring you news, to tell you that what happened in Germany many years ago is happening today in this country." He had a deep, modulated voice with a hint of hickory in the accent and honey in the timbre. It was the smooth voice of a folksy radio personality.

"The Jews are grabbing control of everything they can lay their greasy hands on. My friends, this is a replay of Germany in the early decades of this century. But there, as we all remember, the Aryan people had the courage and the character to rise up in indignation to reclaim their birthright, to reclaim their legacy." He paused, his eyes sweeping slowly around the room. "That, too, will happen here, my friends. The Lord Jesus teaches us that it is God's will, and God's will is inexorable."

He leaned forward on the podium, his voice more fervent now. "When that blessed day comes, praise Jesus, in a time not too distant from today, then we must each of us be prepared to fight for that just and holy cause, for that righteous and God-fearing government dedicated to the preservation and propagation of a nation of Christian men and women of Aryan descent." Another pause, and then a pensive shake of his head. "Jesus teaches us that there will be bloodshed and that there will be fighting and that there will sacrifice. But Jesus implores each of us to do our part in this holy cause, in this, His holy war, blessed be He." Another pause, and then, in a louder voice, "It is our destiny."

As the sermon continued, Bishop Robb eased his foot off the rhetorical pedal in order to explain for the newcomers in the crowd the basic tenets of the "Identity Church" movement, within which his peculiar church clearly fit. Anglo-Saxons were the "chosen people"—the lost tribe of the House of Israel, the true descendants of Adam and Eve, the actual chosen people for whom Jesus was sent. Jews were the children of Satan—"Satan's spawn," in Bishop Robb's words, born not of Adam and Eve but of Eve and Satan, set on the earth to destroy the "chosen people" through Talmudic teaching, forced interracial mixings, and sexual perversions. Jews had mated with beasts of the jungle to produce the subhuman "mud peoples"—blacks, Asians, Hispanics. And now, in fulfillment of their mission as Satan's spawn, the Jews were financing guerrilla training of the "mud peoples" to enable them to seize control of the major cities and enslave the Aryan youth of the nation through the dissemination of cocaine, heroin, and other drugs.

It was a theology so warped that at first it sounded like a bad *Saturday Night Live* routine—and then you realized with a shudder that Bishop Robb was real, and these congregants were true believers.

Jonathan had given me a brief bio on the drive down. Robb had returned to his hometown, Baton Rouge, after his final tour of duty as a Green Beret in Vietnam. He took a job as a driver's ed instructor at his old high school, but the place felt even more alien than Southeast Asia. His rage grew as he watched antiwar protesters mock his America. Women's liberation, civil rights marches, gay rights movements—it was an abominable travesty. When he finally attended his first meeting of the Baton Rouge chapter of the American Nazi Party, it was as if he'd discovered that special place he called home.

It was not a smooth homecoming. Over the next two decades he would drift from one white supremacist organization to another, often severing his ties after bitter fallings out over seemingly trivial ideological differences. In the early 1980s, Robb rose to an influential position within the Louisiana-based National Emancipation of Our White Seed, but he disappeared in 1983, only to resurface three years later as the editor of the *Battle Axe News*, the house organ of the Christian Defense League. Before that organization collapsed in the late 1980s amid a blizzard of federal indictments, it had been tied to the firebombing of an Orthodox synagogue in Belleville, Illinois, and the attempted bombing of an oil pipeline from Tulsa to Chicago that ran along southern Missouri curving up through St. Louis.

Then came another gap in Robb's biography until he surfaced in 1994 as the spiritual leader of the Church of the Aryan Jesus, located in a rural area of Jefferson County south of St. Louis. Last year, Robb expanded his responsibilities by announcing the formation of "Spider," an organization whose mission was to bring the neo-Nazi movement into the urban centers of America. "Adolf Hitler created the Third Reich in downtown Berlin," he announced at the opening ceremonies, "not in some remote patch of the Black Forest." He proudly billed Spider's St. Louis offices as the "Midwest Headquarters of the White Race." Although he was savvy enough to keep the swastika off the literature and logos, Spider's official emblem was still spooky: a black widow spider with a grinning skull in place of the spider's thorax.

Robb was reaching the end of his sermon. "Let us rise," he announced as he turned toward the flagpole. He placed his hand over his heart. The congregants got to their feet amid the rumbling and scraping of the folding chairs. They all placed their hands over their hearts.

One of Robb's assistants had stepped onto the stage by the flagpole. He reached down to grasp the end of the limp flag, and then stepped back to unfurl it for all to see. It was a replica of the American flag, except that in place of the stars there was a white cross against a black background.

"We pledge our allegiance," Robb solemnly recited, accompanied in unison by the crowd, "to our fighting Aryans and to a pure, white United States. We offer praise unto Jesus Christ, our Aryan Messiah, and we beseech Him to lead our sacred army to victory and to join us in our holy battle cry: Free America!"

After a long pause, Bishop Kurt Robb turned back to the crowd. "God bless you," he said quietly, dropping his head, "and amen."

"Amen," they answered.

Disheartened, I watched as members of the audience crowded forward to shake his hand or touch his sleeve. With his slight twang and folksy mannerisms, Kurt Robb could have been a commercial airline pilot coming over the P.A. system to tell us that "we're gonna keep that lil' ol' seat belt sign on jes' a bit longer 'cause we may be catching a patch of turbulence up ahead a ways."

There was nothing Hitleresque about this Hitler wanna-be, and that made him even scarier.

*   *   *

H ey, Jew Boy!"
        Jonathan spun toward the voice. There were two of them coming down the sidewalk toward us. White guys with buzz cuts—one tall and one short, dressed like Robb's bodyguards in faded jeans and letter jackets. The short guy had a goatee and crooked, tobacco-stained teeth. He walked with a bowlegged strut. The tall guy had a beer gut and moved more like a bear. In one of his huge hands he was holding a wooden dowel the length of a baseball bat and the diameter of a broom handle. With a snap of his wrist, he sliced it back and forth through the air.

Whoosh. Whoosh. Whoosh.

I glanced behind me. Our car was less than twenty feet away. We'd parked in a residential area two blocks over from the Reavis Banquet Center. The center's lot had been full when we arrived.

Jonathan pulled me close as he moved backward down the sidewalk toward the car. For some reason, I thought of all the new windows and windshield in his car.

"Don't be stupid," Jonathan told them, his voice unyielding.

The big guy looked over at his comrade and chuckled. "Hear that, Bobby? Guy here says, don't be stupid. You feeling stupid?"

Bobby snorted. "Fuck no, partner."

"Me, neither." He turned to Jonathan. "I'll tell you who's stupid, Rabbi. Guy like you who shows up at a Bishop Robb event, sticking that big Jew nose where it don't belong. That's what I call stupid. Ain't that right, Bobby?"

"Fucking aye, partner."

Whoosh. Whoosh.

We were even with Jonathan's car. He reached into his jacket and handed me the keys.

"Get in the car," he said, and then he turned to face them. "Listen carefully," he said, pointing his finger at the big guy. "There are two dozen cops back at the building."

The big guy laughed. "That's back there, Rabbi, but we ain't back there, are we? Two dozen? Shit, man, two *thousand* cops back *there* ain't going do you any fucking good right *here*. Ain't that right, Bobby?"

"Fucking aye, partner."

I'd taken a step toward the car, but stopped. I couldn't just leave Jonathan to face these thugs alone. My heart was racing. I didn't know what I could do, but I refused to abandon him.

He was standing his ground, his fists clenched, seemingly unfazed by the danger. Although I'd taken a self-defense class for six months, it was as if everything I'd learned had vanished in the face of these animals. I glanced around, looking for something to use as a weapon.

"You should leave here now," Jonathan told them in a firm voice.

"Hey," the shorter guy snarled as he jammed his middle finger in the air. "Fuck you, kike." His head was bobbing defiantly, his middle finger still up. "And fuck your Jew bitch, too."

Jonathan stared at him. "Turn around," he finally said in a totally calm voice, "and walk away and no one gets hurt."

"Wrong, dickhead," the big guy said, his face suddenly contorting in rage as he started forward. "You get hurt."

Jonathan burst into action. He punched the big guy in the gut just as the guy was raising the dowel. He hit him again, even harder this time, squarely in the solar plexus. The first blow staggered him, the second one toppled him. As he keeled over, wheezing in pain, Jonathan ripped the dowel from his hand and spun toward the smaller guy, who'd hesitated a moment too long before attacking. Jonathan whipped the dowel against the guy's throat. He lurched backward with an awful gargling noise, both hands grabbing for his neck. Jonathan moved in fast and whacked him again, splintering the dowel against the side of his face. The guy collapsed, curling into a ball as he covered his head with his hands. There was a set of brass knuckles on his right hand. Jonathan stood over him, the shattered dowel raised high, waiting. The guy was moaning, blood streaming from his mouth and nose. He wasn't going anywhere. Neither was his comrade, who was on his back near me, gasping for air, his eyes squeezed shut, his hands pressed against his ribs. The front of his jeans was soaked. The odor of warm urine was unmistakable in the chilly air.

Stunned, I looked at Jonathan, who was standing over the smaller guy with the shattered dowel held high. Jonathan was panting, his breath vaporing in the cold, as he looked from one assailant to the other. With his yarmulke still in place and his close-trimmed dark beard, he looked every inch the Maccabee warrior. He lowered the dowel and seemed to contemplate it a moment before tossing it aside.

He turned toward me and our eyes met.

"Wow," I said.

"Are you okay, Rachel?"

I nodded. "Sure."

He frowned as he reached into his coat pocket. I watched him remove his cellular phone and punch in a number.

"Third-rate goons," he mumbled, shaking his head as he waited for the call to go through. "Hi, this is Jonathan Wolf. You have a dozen officers stationed at Reavis Banquet Hall. Lieutenant Bradley is in charge of them. He knows who I am. Tell him I'm two blocks north on Carter Avenue. Have him send over a squad car with two officers."

This was definitely not shaping up to be a typical lazy Sunday. Having started our day with a Nazi diatribe and a one-round boxing match with two thugs, we were now seated in the reception area of the Sangamon County Jail in downtown Springfield waiting to interview the two skinheads arrested for Gloria Muller's murder.

"Boy," I said to Jonathan, trying to force a smile, "you sure know how to show a girl a good time."

"Hey," he said with a wink, "don't forget lunch."

"My apologies," I said, my spirits picking up a bit. "That was excellent."

Road trips require a little extra planning if you're an Orthodox Jew. Jonathan was as likely to find a kosher meal at a food-and-gas exit along I-55 as he was to find the artist formerly known as Prince—theoretically possible, but the odds were steep. So Jonathan came prepared, having swung by the Tel Aviv Deli on his way to pick me up that morning. He deserved an A+ in deli shopping. During the drive to Springfield we had a feast of corn beef on rye with spicy mustard, potato knishes, tangy cole slaw, kosher dills, plenty of Dr. Brown's to wash it all down, and a slice of luscious apple strudel for dessert.

The food and the drive had helped put some distance between me and the morning's events, but the memories had been catching up during our wait in the prison lobby. Bishop Robb's words had been so hateful and depressing, made even more chilling by his smooth, syrupy delivery—as if we were listening to the headwaiter of Armageddon. I'd felt blue on our way to the car afterward, and then those two thugs attacked. That scene ended so quickly I found myself watching in a daze as the police hauled them away in handcuffs.

Jonathan didn't think Robb was behind the attack. First, he explained, Robb was too smart to order his people to beat up a prosecutor, especially with all those cops nearby. Second, the attackers were amateurs. Although they'd looked plenty menacing to me—so much so that Jonathan's response had seemed right out of an action-hero flick—he shrugged it off, explaining that they were a pair of stumblebums.

We'd arrived at the prison right on time. That was thirty-five minutes ago. Jonathan walked over to the clerk's window to try to speed things up. The delay wouldn't have surprised me if I was alone. I'd had prison officials keep me waiting for more than an hour, and those were times when I was there to see a client. But today I was with Jonathan. These prison officials knew him. He'd been here several times during his years as an assistant U.S. attorney, and he was here today in his official capacity as a special assistant attorney general on an investigation that had the official cooperation of several Illinois law enforcement agencies.

He came back over, shaking his head.

"What?" I asked.

He frowned. "Something's not right."

Ten minutes later, the inner door opened and a woman in her sixties stepped into the reception area. She smiled when she spotted Jonathan.

"Hello, Wolf Man," she said as she came over. She was a vibrant woman with sparkling blue eyes and salt-and-pepper hair cut short.

They shook hands and Jonathan turned to introduce us. "Rachel, this is Ila Frisbie. Ila's with the State's Attorney's office in Springfield, and she one tough prosecutor."

Ila laughed and told me she was a pussycat compared to Jonathan. Pussycat or not, she was obviously a character. She was wearing a white knit T-shirt, a long pleated blue skirt, white socks, and brown leather Birkenstocks. She had dangly earrings and a clunky necklace that she must have found at an arts-and-crafts festival. I liked her immediately.

"So what's going on?" Jonathan asked.

Ila's smiled disappeared. "Well," she said, hesitating and glancing at me.

"Rachel's okay," Jonathan said. "She witnessed the murder."

Ila nodded, all business now. "Let's go inside."

We followed her through a security door and down a narrow hallway to a small conference room. She ushered us in and closed the door.

"We don't know how it happened," she said, shaking her head.

"Both?" Jonathan asked quietly.

"Yep."

"No one else?"

"Just those two."

"Knives?"

She nodded. "All the inmates are on lockdown now."

"Where are the bodies?"

She gestured toward the hall. "The infirmary. The medical examiner's already looked at them. They're moving them to the hospital tonight for the autopsies."

"I'd like to see them," Jonathan said quietly.

Ila raised her eyebrows and shrugged. "Sure." She glanced over at me. "What about you, Rachel?"

I looked at Jonathan and then back at Ila. I hadn't seen either suspect since the arrests. If one of them was the killer, I might recognize him. "Well, okay," I said.

Jonathan looked at me with concern. "Are you sure, Rachel? You can wait right here. I just want to see whether they were killed execution-style. It won't take long."

"I'm sure," I said unsurely.

We followed Ila down the hall, around the corner, past two security checkpoints, and into the jail infirmary. She led us to a closed door near the back.

"In here," she said, opening the door.

I paused in the hall, staring at the floor as I psyched myself up. They didn't teach Dead Bodies 101 at Harvard. *Come on*, I told myself, *you're a big girl*. I took a deep breath and stepped into the room.

The bodies were on steel gurneys. Mercifully, a white sheet covered each man from head to ankle, exposing only the feet. The big toe on the left foot of each corpse had been tagged. From the size of the feet and the outlines of the bodies beneath the sheets, these were large men.

Jonathan was standing between the gurneys up by the head area. I was down by the feet. He leaned over the body on the left and pulled the sheet back, exposing the head, neck, and chest. I had feared that there'd be blood and dreadful wounds, but instead the body looked almost peacefully intact. Except for blue and purple tattoos on the chest and arms, the skin was as pale as wax, as if they'd just pulled him out of a meat locker. I moved slowly around the far side of the body to get a look at the face. The eyes were open, gazing at the ceiling. I peered closer. The face wasn't familiar.

Jonathan was bending over the corpse, studying the neck area. I shifted my focus to where he was looking, and reared back, almost gagging. The neck had been sliced from ear to ear. The flesh along the knife slash had puffed and curved outward, making the wound resemble a pair of slobby lips pressed into an enormous smile. I stepped back, a little woozy, and tried to focus on the wall clock on the far side.

"Where did it happen?" Jonathan asked Ila in a clinical tone.

"In the showers."

Jonathan turned from the corpse to Ila. "Both at the same time?"

She nodded. "According to the guards, they went down together after breakfast around ten. The showers were on the whole time. The place was all steamed up when the guards went in to fetch them a few minutes before eleven. They found them on the tiles, their throats slashed."

Jonathan moved to the other body after covering the first one. As he pulled back the sheet, I forced my eyes to focus only on the face. The skin was chalk white, the mouth sagging open. I stared at the broad forehead and the big chin as I tried to remember back to the night in the Applebee's parking lot. I nodded. It was the face of the shooter.

B ut you don't agree?" I asked.

We were on the drive back to St. Louis.

Jonathan scratched his beard pensively. "I'll concede that there's logic to their assumption. Skinheads hate blacks, blacks hate skinheads. Two skinheads get killed, round up the leaders of the black prison gangs."

"But?"

"If they'd been arrested for murdering someone black, then maybe. But this?" He glanced at me "Where's the motive?"

"They're still skinheads."

He shook his head. "Not enough. Blacks and skinheads co-exist in prison. They have elaborate social codes, and the gangs have enforcers to keep their members in line."

"Even the skinheads?" I asked.

"Oh, definitely. There's a loose affiliation of skinhead prison gangs around the country known as the Aryan Brotherhood. In fact, prison outreach has become an important part of the neo-Nazi movement."

"What do you mean?"

"Take Spider, for example. It has outreach programs in several states. They correspond with gang members, send them a prison-oriented newsletter called *The White Path*, and make prison visits." Jonathan paused. "So the mere fact that these two guys were skinheads doesn't mean that a black man killed them."

"Then who?"

He looked over at me and shook his head. "Unfortunately, it's not that hard to get yourself killed in prison."

CHAPTER 7

Benny leaned back in his chair with a satisfied smile and patted his belly with contentment. "Sarah," he said to my mother, "you deserve a special place of honor in my Hall of Fame."

My mother was beaming.

He turned to me. "Am I right?"

"It *was* delicious, Mom," I told her, "but as your attorney I have to advise you to be careful about allowing your name in the Benny Goldberg Hall of Fame."

"Now, Rachel," Benny said, placing his hand over his heart and feigning offense.

I winked at him. "Let's just say you have some peculiar items in there."

"Such as what?" my mother asked.

I shook my head. "Such as you don't want to know, Mom."

Benny uttered a long, lugubrious sigh. "Oh, to be forced to endure such calumny."

I had to smile. It felt wonderful to smile. To smile and to eat my mother's wonderful cooking. A dinner in the warm cocoon of my mother's house was just the antidote for this miserable Sunday.

Ruth Alpert came out from the kitchen carrying a fresh pot of coffee. The doorbell rang as she started pouring refills.

"I'll get it," I said, checking my watch as I stood up. "It's probably Jonathan."

It was. He looked handsome in his navy pullover sweater, red turtleneck, and tan wide-wale corduroys.

"Hi," I said, giving him a quick kiss on the lips. He had

that clean, musky scent that I loved. "Mmmm, you smell good enough to eat."

He chuckled. "You look lovely, Rachel."

"Well, thanks." I did a playful curtsy. I was wearing a black cotton turtleneck, a denim mini-skirt, black tights, thick white socks, and black Doc Martens. It was one of my favorite cold-weather ensembles: fun and comfortable. "Did the girls have fun?"

"They loved it."

My mother had invited Jonathan and his daughters to come for the dinner, but he was already planning to take them to a Sunday father-daughter dinner event at the JCCA. Nevertheless, he told my mother he'd drop by after he put the girls to bed. He was curious to hear the results of the Internet search.

My mother called from the dining room, "Is that Jonathan?"

"Hello, Sarah," he said as we rounded the corner. All eyes were on the two of us.

"You know Benny," I said to Jonathan.

"Sure. How are you, Benny?"

"Hangin in there, Wolf Man."

"This is Ruth Alpert," I said. "Ruth, this is Jonathan Wolf."

"Hello, Ruth," he said, warmly shaking her hand.

"It's a pleasure," she answered, captivated. "I've heard so many splendid things about you from Rachel and her mother."

"And these are my heroes," I said, turning toward the five law students, who were all seated along the far side of the dining-room table. "This is Hanna, Zack, Josh, Kayla, and this is Jake. Guys, this is Jonathan Wolf."

From the awed expressions of Josh and Kayla, it was clear that they recognized the name. Both were interested in criminal law. To be interested in criminal law in St. Louis and to meet Jonathan Wolf was the equivalent of being interested in baseball in St. Louis and meeting Ozzie Smith. And like Ozzie

Smith, Jonathan's reputation reached beyond the city. He'd made two appearances on Ted Koppel's *Nightline* during the second O. J. Simpson trial. More recently, his defense of Oklahoma lieutenant governor Billy Rimmel in the Indian casino vote fraud prosecution had generated coverage in newspapers around the country.

After politely declining a slice of cherry pie and accepting a cup of coffee, he turned to the students. "Rachel told me you were able to match the bids to the contract award announcements."

They nodded.

"Let's hear what you found," I said.

Josh stood up. "I'll get the charts." He came back from the living room with a sheaf of documents. "We made several copies," he said as he passed them out.

The chart was nineteen pages long, and each page contained summary information on eight or nine contract awards. I paged slowly through the document, studying the entries. By the time I reached page five, the pattern had emerged. Page five was typical:

Contract No.	Estimated Cost Range (in millions)	Winning Bid	Beckman Bid	Winning Company
N44255	$9 to $12.5	$12.2	$12.4	Eagle
AA23165	$8 to $12	$11.8	$11.8	Beckman
56NR-78	$7.5 to $11	$10.8	$10.9	Eicken
MMR3421	$6 to $10	$9.8	$9.9	Koll
R6-5-B3	$10 to $14	$13.6	$13.9	Eagle
TC-62-331	$5 to $10	$9.5	$10	Beek
K4321-T2	$9 to $14	$13.6	$13.8	Muller
S3-3419	$12 to $15	$14.5	$14.5	Beckman

I skimmed the remaining pages to confirm it. The pattern held. The entire universe of winners of the one hundred forty-eight bids over the last ten years was limited to six companies, including Beckman Engineering. I recognized two other names: Muller was presumably Muller Construction of Springfield, Illinois, and Koll had to be Koll Ltd. of Chicago. Owned by Otto Koll, as I recalled from Gloria Muller's comments. Her words still echoed in my memory: *Oh, yes*, she had said with a chuckle, *Otto was one of them*. I flipped back through several pages of the chart. Koll's name appeared at least once on every page. *Oh, yes, Gloria*, I thought, *Otto definitely was one of them*.

I leafed slowly through the document. Each of the six companies had won roughly the same number of contracts over the ten-year period. Most striking, though, were the winning bids: all were crowded up near the high end of the estimated cost range. No matter how wide the spread between the lower and upper end of the government's estimated cost range—$10 to $14 million, say, or $5 to $10 million—the winning bid was always within a few hundred thousand dollars of the high end.

I could feel my optimism grow as I skimmed down each new page. When I finished, I looked around the table. My five volunteers were beaming at me. Benny was studying his copy and nodding his head thoughtfully. My mother and Ruth were sharing one set and staring at it with equally mystified expressions.

I looked over at Jonathan. He'd put the chart down and was sipping his coffee. He winked and said, "You're in business."

"What do you mean?" Ruth asked.

I turned toward her. "These charts back up the rumors you heard. Now we need to get out and dig for the evidence."

"But where?" she asked.

"Right here," I said, pointing at the nineteen-page list of winning bids. "These other five companies." I turned to the students with a sheepish look. "One more favor, guys? Does anyone have time to run these companies through the computer? We need to find who owns them, who runs them, that sort of thing."

"Sure," Kayla said. "I used to do that all the time at Price Waterhouse. It won't take me long. I have two free hours tomorrow morning." She turned to Benny. "I could drop off the results at your office before noon, Professor."

It still cracked me up to hear them call him Professor.

"That'd be super," I told Kayla.

I did a quick mental review of my schedule for tomorrow: a discovery motion in the city circuit court in the morning, a meeting at a client's office at two in the afternoon, my self-defense class after that, and then dinner at my sister's house. I glanced over at Benny. "You eating lunch tomorrow, Professor?"

"Am I eating lunch tomorrow?" He held his palms up, as if I'd just posed the most moronic question of the year. "Does the wild pope shit in the woods?"

"I'm buying," I told him.

"And I'm eating."

Nu?" Benny said, chewing on his sandwich as he studied one of the printouts that Kayla and Jake had dropped off at his office that morning.

We were having a light lunch at Stacks cafe in The Library Ltd. bookstore. Or rather, I was having a light lunch—a bowl of mushroom barley soup, a banana muffin, and a cup of coffee. Benny was devouring what charitably could be called a heavy lunch, and more accurately a pair of heavy lunches.

He stuffed the rest of his second sandwich in his mouth, swallowed it nearly whole, and gestured toward the printouts that were spread between us on the table as he reached for his bottle of Pete's Wicked Ale. "What's your reaction?"

"Surprise," I said, pausing to take a sip of coffee, "and hope."

The most surprising find of the day was contained on several pages of new materials gleaned from the *Commerce Busi-*

ness Daily data bank. Last night at my mother's house, Jake had shown us another chart he'd put together: a random review of construction contracts in an unrelated field, which demonstrated that winning bids in an untainted market tended to be evenly distributed throughout the government's estimated cost range. This morning, acting on a hunch, Jake had sampled contract awards from earlier decades in the same field of water-control projects at issue in our lawsuit. I had alleged a ten-year bid-rigging conspiracy in the Midwest. Jake was curious to see how that market functioned before then. It was another way to test my antitrust hypothesis.

The *Commerce Business Daily* data bank went back to 1956, so he picked four years at random—1957, 1964, 1975, and 1982. The results were completely unexpected. Regardless of the year, the winning bidder was always one of the alleged co-conspirators in our case: Beckman, Beek, Eagle, Eicken, Muller, or Koll. Moreover, the winning bid was always at the high end of the estimated cost range. The implication was plain.

"I thought ten years was pushing it," I said, shaking my head in wonder, "but this is incredible. A forty-year conspiracy?"

Bid-rigging schemes tend to be unruly and inherently unstable beasts that rarely survive their first year. The greed that brings the confederates together is the same force that drives them apart. But here, according to the data, we had a conspiracy that had thrived not merely for years but for decades. It was, quite simply, extraordinary. Moreover, it raised a fascinating question. What was it about these companies that had enabled them to maintain that level of group discipline over so many years?

"Where's that summary page on the six companies?" I asked Benny.

He shuffled through the papers and found it. As Kayla promised, she'd spent the morning searching through various business and commercial data banks for information on the six companies. She'd taken the hodgepodge of information and summarized the basic facts on the one-page chart that Benny and I were studying.

Several points stood out. All six companies were based in the Midwest in a relatively small geographic area: one in eastern Missouri (Beckman Engineering); two in Indiana (Beek Contracting Co. in Gary, and Eicken Industrial in Indianapolis); two in Illinois (Koll Ltd. in Chicago, and Muller Construction in Springfield); and one in western Tennessee (Eagle Engineering in Memphis). All were middle-aged companies, that is, somewhere between forty-five and sixty-five years old—the oldest formed in 1934, the youngest in 1953. Although three of the original founders were still nominally at the helm of their companies, only one—Conrad Beckman—was still in charge. The day-to-day management of the other five had passed to the next generation. Beckman Engineering appeared to be the largest of the six, at least in terms of revenues, but all were significant commercial operations.

"What are you thinking?" Benny asked.

I took a sip of tea as I stared at the one-page summary. "I'm thinking Eagle."

"Huh?"

"These guys." I pointed at the summary information on Eagle Engineering in Memphis. "They're my best bet."

"Why?"

"Look what happened to them in 1994."

Benny leaned forward and studied the entry. "New owners," he said, a little tentatively. "You're thinking maybe they'll be easier to deal with than the old-boy network."

"Benny," I said impatiently, "they're not simply new owners. Look how they did it."

Benny squinted at the entry. "Ah," he said, leaning back with a smile. "An asset-purchase deal."

I nodded. "Exactly."

There are several ways for one corporation to acquire another. It can merge with it, purchase all of its stock, or buy all of its assets (but not the stock). The latter transaction is known as an asset-purchase deal, and one of its most attractive features is that the purchaser buys the assets, but *not* the liabilities, of the seller. A simple example of such a deal is buying a used car: the buyer acquires the asset (the car itself) but not any of the seller's liabilities for, say, a prior speeding ticket or an overdue insurance bill.

If our bid-rigging allegations were correct, Beckman Engineering and its co-conspirators had a staggering joint liability under the Federal False Claims Act. That meant that each of the other companies had good reason to fear my lawsuit, and thus good reason to vigorously resist my efforts to obtain any information from them.

Except for Eagle Engineering.

The new owners of Eagle Engineering had no liability for the prior owner's misconduct. That meant that the new owners had little to fear from my lawsuit, and thus little to fear from a subpoena for all relevant documents generated during the period *before* they purchased the assets of Eagle Engineering.

"Oh, woman," Benny said, giving me the thumbs-up. "You're a goddamn genius."

I mulled it over. "Timing is key. I've got to get that subpoena out no later than tomorrow afternoon." I sat back with a frown. "This is going to take some finesse." Then I remembered. "Oh, rats."

"Now what?"

I shook my head in frustration. "I can't do it tomorrow."

"Why not?"

"I have to defend Ruth's deposition."

"Allow me," Benny said with a grin. "I don't have a class until five-thirty. It would be my pleasure."

"Really?"

"Sure."

"Great. I can go over what you need to put in the subpoena and then—"

"Not the subpoena, for chrissake," Benny said with a dismissive wave. "I'm not messing with that technical crap. I'm talking about Ruth's deposition. Who's taking it? The lovely Kimberly Howard?"

I rolled my eyes. "Who else?"

"Excellent." He rubbed his hands together with delight. "I would be pleased to provide your client with vigorous representation."

I gave him a dubious look. "No funny business."

"Funny business?" He pressed his hand against his chest and pouted innocently. "*Moi?*"

Among Benny's many deposition misadventures during our Chicago years at Abbott & Windsor had been the Reynolds deposition in the *Allied Chemical* case, which terminated abruptly on page 127 of the transcript—a page that was eventually reprinted verbatim in a *Chicago Bar Journal* article on the decline of professional courtesy. The infamous exchange occurred after Benny's adversary had made his fifty-third objection of the day:

MR. KLEMPER: That's too bad, Mr. Goldberg. As you know, I have a perfect right under the Federal Rules of—

MR. GOLDBERG: Forget the Federal Rules, Norman. From here on out we're following the Goldberg Rules, and here's Rule Number One. You open that little trap of yours one more time and I'm going to rip off your head and shit down your lungs. You read me?

MR. KLEMPER: I—you—I cannot believe—do you—this deposition is over.

MR. GOLDBERG: Excellent. Get out of my office before I throw your sorry ass through that window.

I sighed and shook my head. "I must be crazy."

He was grinning. "Hey, I'll take care of your client. You just worry about getting that subpoena served, 'cause I'm going down there, too."

"You are?"

"Memphis? You better believe it, woman. We're going to look at some documents and feast on some barbecue and then"—he paused and solemnly placed his hand over his heart—"we're going to go pay our respects."

"What are you talking about?"

Benny gave me a wink and started humming the Paul Simon song, "Graceland." "We're going to Graceland. . . ."

CHAPTER 8

I am not a Harvard booster. I never learned the fight song, don't wear crimson, and couldn't tell you who won the Harvard-Yale game this year, or any year. Nevertheless, I'll admit that spending three years at Harvard Law School has its advantages, the chief one being my alumni directory. My classmates are scattered throughout the country, and a remarkable number occupy important positions within their legal communities. As a result, my alumni directory was a definite advantage on this Tuesday morning, since my Eagle Engineering strategy required contacts with lawyers in influential positions. Thank you, John Harvard.

Eagle Engineering had its offices in Memphis, Tennessee. According to the data compiled by my student volunteers, it was formed in 1938 by Max Kruppa and remained in the family until Rhodes & Monroe Industries acquired its assets in 1994. Rhodes & Monroe was an international construction and engineering firm with headquarters in Cleveland, Ohio. That meant that Eagle Engineering's brains were now in Cleveland but its body was still in Memphis. My strategy involved its brains and its body.

The alumni directory showed two classmates in Cleveland, both junior partners at major law firms. I started with the one I knew the best—a woman who lived on the same dorm floor as me our first year in Cambridge. I got lucky: her law firm did work for Rhodes & Monroe. Although they hadn't been the transaction lawyers on the Eagle Engineering deal, they had done a fair amount of work on matters relating to Eagle Engineering since then. I explained what I needed and what I was willing to offer her client in exchange. Although she was in her firm's tax department, she was on good terms with Rhodes & Monroe's principal attorney at the firm, a senior corporate partner named Wendell Bingham. She agreed to handle the shuttle diplomacy between Wendell and me.

Ordinarily, the negotiations would have dragged on for days or weeks. While corporate lawyers no doubt have strengths, speed is not one of them. Fortunately, Wendell Bingham was the exception: he was smart, had control of his client, and was quick to grasp that we could offer his client full value for its cooperation. As a result, we were able to work out the details in less than two hours—a pace approaching warp speed for a corporate lawyer. One of his associates faxed me the three-page proposal by one that afternoon.

I read through the proposal. It was a good deal for both sides. Eagle agreed to respond to the subpoena without objection and let me inspect all documents contained in its warehouse in Memphis. Just as important, the lawyers agreed to my timetable: I would serve the subpoena on their Memphis office tomorrow, and then, even though the subpoena would state that the inspection was to occur "on or before" a specified date three weeks off, they would let me inspect the documents the following day (which was, technically, "on or before" the other date).

The timing was a crucial part of the strategy. I would prepare five subpoenas in all: one for Eagle Engineering and one for each of the other four companies. All five subpoenas would have the same "on or before" language, which I hoped would lull Beckman Engineering's attorneys into thinking that they had plenty of time to organize a massive stonewall operation. If my strategy worked, by the time Beckman Engineering's lawyers got around to calling Eagle Engineering—probably early next week—I'd have already reviewed the Eagle documents and obtained copies of the important ones.

In exchange for all this, Ruth would sign an ironclad covenant not to sue Eagle Engineering or Rhodes & Monroe for "any act or omission, whether known or unknown, occurring or alleged to have occurred at any place or at any time from the beginning of the universe until today." Such was the belt-and-suspenders approach of a corporate lawyer.

That took care of the brains of Eagle Engineering. The body was down in Memphis, and that's where the subpoena would be served. Once Beckman Engineering's lawyers got wind of what I was up to, they would run into federal court down there to quash the subpoena. That meant I had to have a well-connected co-counsel in Memphis on emergency standby. I didn't need my alumni directory for that name. Kenny Randall had been a year ahead of me at law school, and we'd worked together on the *Harvard Civil Rights–Civil Liberties Law Review*. He was the epitome of an influential Memphis lawyer: his grandfather was on the Tennessee Supreme Court and his uncle was a federal district judge. Even better, Kenny was a good guy. The summer before law school, he'd married a funny, drop-dead-gorgeous southern belle named Darlene who used to bring us Chinese takeout and a big thermos of mint juleps on those long nights down at the printer as we tried to put the next issue of the law review out.

I caught up with him after lunch. He chuckled as I sketched out my strategy. "Rachel, dahlin'," he said in that familiar Mississippi Delta drawl, "ah'd be delighted to help y'all out. Maybe we'll git a chance to give those Yankee lawyers a taste of some southern-style justice."

B y four that afternoon, Jacki and I had finished all the subpoena details, including making the necessary arrangements with a process server in each of the other cities. Still no word from Benny or Ruth. The thought of Benny defending that deposition, and no doubt tangling with Kimberly Howard, gave me the jitters.

At four-twenty, Jacki buzzed to tell me that Laurence Browning was on line two. Browning was Kimberly Howard's lieutenant on the lawsuit, an unctuous senior associate who oozed the warmth of a moray eel. Reluctantly, I lifted the receiver, half expecting him to notify me to meet Kimberly

Howard in Judge Wagner's chambers to discuss Mr. Goldberg's shocking misconduct.

"Hello?"

"Rachel, this is Laurence."

Never Larry. Always Laurence.

"What's up, Larry?"

"A bit of good news. Mr. Beckman's schedule has developed an unexpected opening on Friday afternoon from three
until five." He paused for one of his world-weary sighs. "If
you still insist on taking that man's deposition, he will be
available then."

I glanced at my calendar. I had a deposition in another
case scheduled for Friday afternoon but I could get it moved.
This was far more important.

"Fine," I said. "Your offices?"

"Of course. Precisely at three, and remember, Rachel, exactly two hours. That's the limit."

"You just make sure he's on time."

He chuckled. "We'll take care of Mr. Beckman. You
worry about you."

Well?"

"Probably," I conceded.

Benny widened his eyes in disbelief as he reached for another tortilla chip. "Probably?" He laughed and pointed at the
transcript with the chip. "Come on, woman. You know I'm
right." He scooped up some fresh salsa with the chip and
popped the whole thing into his mouth. Crunching away, he
said, "There's nothing there. She's got absolutely *bupkis*." He
reached for his Dos Equis beer and took a gulp. "You're home
free."

We were having dinner at Chueys, a noisy Mexican restaurant in the Dogtown area. The evening was on me as thanks
to Benny for defending Ruth's deposition. Jonathan was supposed to meet us here later; he was flying back from Chicago,
where he'd spent a long day at the arraignment and related

matters for a bank president indicted for various federal bank crimes.

Ruth's deposition had lasted all day and ended at five o'clock with an infuriated Kimberly Howard storming out of the conference room. Benny had called me from his car phone on the way back to Washington University, where he was teaching a two-hour seminar on advanced civil procedure that started at five-thirty.

"How'd it go?" I'd asked nervously.

"Okay. We had some fireworks this afternoon."

"Fireworks?" I said, closing my eyes. "How bad?"

"You can see for yourself before dinner," he said with a chuckle. "Kimberly ordered daily copy. The court reporter said she'd drop off your copy by seven."

I groaned, envisioning the scene in court, presumably tomorrow morning: an outraged Kimberly Howard demanding sanctions against my client for the egregious misconduct of her attorney.

"Don't worry, Rachel. There's nothing there. Trust me. The court reporter takes down words, not tone. You'll see. I'm the perfect gentlemen in the transcript."

And, incredibly enough, he was right.

A messenger delivered the 220-page transcript to my house at seven o'clock, and I was able to skim through it before Benny arrived to drive us to the restaurant. The fireworks didn't erupt until the afternoon portion of the deposition. Kimberly spent most of the morning of this, the thirteenth day of Ruth Alpert's deposition, asking questions that she had already asked her in prior sessions of the deposition, which merely confirmed what I already knew was their strategy, namely, to harass and demoralize my client. During the morning session, Benny behaved better than I would have. But midway through the afternoon session, his patience ran out. Fortunately, though, his savvy did not. As a result, he was able to get Kimberly completely flustered while sounding, at least in the black and white of the transcript, like Miss Manners, his sarcasm quite literally invisible. In passage after passage, Benny came off so polite that Kimberly began to sound clinically unbalanced. Typical was this one at page 184:

> MS. HOWARD: At the time that you first saw this bid announcement, which has previously been marked Defendant's Deposition Exhibit 429, had your duties and responsibilities changed in any respect?
>
> MR. GOLDBERG: Bravo, Kimberly. That is what I call an excellent question. Getting right to the heart of the matter, eh? Allow me to commend you.
>
> MS. HOWARD: That's it. That was totally unjustified.
>
> MR. GOLDBERG: My goodness, Kimberly, I merely meant to express my admiration for your estimable talents as an interrogator. You are a veritable heat-seeking missile at a deposition.
>
> MS. HOWARD: Stop it. You hear me? Stop it. Stop it. Just stop it.

Benny shook his head as he reached for his beer, his smile fading. "What a sanctimonious bitch. I hope you kick her ass."

Jonathan arrived around nine-thirty and the three of us moved to a booth near the bar. When Benny got up to go to the restroom thirty minutes later, I leaned across the table and gave Jonathan a kiss.

"I have a wonderful idea," I whispered, nibbling on his lower lip.

"Oh?"

I sat back and eyed him with a naughty expression as I slipped off my right shoe under the table. "Tonight you could pretend that you're a reform Jew," I said, "and you could take me home and ravish me until dawn." I slid my stockinged foot up his leg and along his thigh.

He smiled as he reached under the table to give my foot a gentle squeeze. "Reform Judaism has never seemed more enticing."

Benny returned at that very moment, of course. I banged

my knee under the table pulling back my foot. Benny gave me a curious look and then, as it clicked, he tried to conceal a leer.

In the awkward moment of silence I glanced over at the television above the bar. The ten o'clock news. Footage of the Missouri governor signing a piece of legislation. I watched idly, sipping my white wine. From the governor it was back to a pair of grinning anchors who couldn't contain their mirth as they introduced the next story: a snowboarding standard poodle.

"What dreck," Benny said as we watched the poor pooch, strapped to a snowboard, skid down the slope with a look of pure dread.

Back to the male anchor, chortling with amusement. Then he paused, wrinkling his brows gravely. Time for a serious story. He said something to his co-anchor, a fortyish woman with brown shoulder-length hair. She shook her head somberly and then looked toward the camera, which pulled back to reveal a display terminal in the background above her shoulder. The terminal had a color shot of a man wearing a green beret standing on the courthouse steps.

"Hey," Benny said, "isn't that whatshisname?"

"It is," I said, getting to my feet and moving toward the bar to hear. Benny and Jonathan joined me.

". . . on the steps of the Old Courthouse in downtown St. Louis," the anchorwoman was saying.

The screen shifted to a videotape of Bishop Kurt Robb. He was dressed in his white clergy robe, tinted horn-rims, and green beret. He was holding up a cardboard poster that appeared to be a blowup of a court document. The word "indictment" was clearly legible at the top of the poster.

The anchorwoman continued in voice-over. "Claiming to speak on behalf of all Americans of Aryan descent, Bishop Robb announced a people's indictment of Missouri's governor, lieutenant governor, and attorney general."

"Gentlemen," Robb was saying, "you have exactly thirty

days to resign. Otherwise, we will commence our grand jury inquest as the true representatives of the Aryan citizens of this great state."

Back to the reporter, a still photo of the governor over her shoulder. "A spokesperson for the governor denounced the charges as, quote, 'a cheap publicity stunt by a fascist thug.' "

The screen shifted to stock footage of Missouri attorney general Bob Simmons walking down a hallway. The anchorwoman continued in voice-over. "Sources within the Attorney General's office confirmed that Robb and other leaders of Spider, a white supremacist group headquartered in St. Louis, are the subject of an ongoing criminal investigation." Back to the anchorwoman. "That investigation is headed by St. Louis attorney Jonathan Wolf, a former federal prosecutor who has been appointed a special assistant attorney general on the matter."

I glanced over at Jonathan, who was watching the screen intently.

"Although Attorney Wolf was unavailable for comment," the anchorwoman continued, "Bishop Robb had plenty to say."

Back to a full-screen video of Robb, who was shaking his head sadly. "It's a pitiful state of affairs when the chief law enforcement official in this state has to send his dirty work out to a lawyer wearing a beanie. It kind of makes you wonder who's really calling the shots down there in Jeff City? Our elected officials or these so-called special assistants lurking in the shadows? That's the real mystery here."

Back to the anchorwoman, who frowned seriously and turned to her cohort, who joined her in an instant of solemnity. "Thank you, Sharon," he said. Turning to face the camera, he paused a beat and then immediately perked up. "Well, you won't have to call tomorrow's weather a mystery. In a moment, we'll be back with Big Bob Buckles and his Döppler RadarWatch Weather Update."

*   *   *

I don't care," I said, still furious. "That's outrageous."

Jonathan reached across the seat and squeezed my shoulder. "It's okay."

We were in his car in front of my house. He'd driven me home from the restaurant.

" 'A lawyer wearing a beanie'?" I repeated. "I'm so angry I can't see straight."

"Rachel, that's just phony bravado. Robb is worried. We're tightening the vise, and he's starting to feel the pressure. Now tell me about Memphis."

I explained my Eagle Engineering subpoena gambit.

"You might get lucky," he said.

"I sure hope so. I've got Conrad Beckman's deposition Friday afternoon. If I find something juicy in Memphis, I might spring it on him at the deposition."

Jonathan grinned. "How do you think Kimberly will react?"

I shrugged. "I'm not ruling out the possibility of spontaneous combustion."

Jonathan laughed. "When do you and Benny leave?"

"Tomorrow afternoon. It's about a five-hour drive." I smiled. "Benny's totally pumped."

Jonathan gave me a puzzled look. "About reviewing documents?"

"Benny?" I said with a laugh. "No way. Memphis means two cherished things to him: Elvis and barbecue."

"Barbecue?"

"I forgot," I said, "you poor yeshiva boys don't know from barbecue. Benny's a zealot. He's even compiled a computer data bank on barbecue restaurants around the country." I sighed and shook my head. "And he's driving me crazy. Memphis is unexplored territory for him, which means he's been spending hours sifting through his materials and talking to others on the Internet to find the best spots. I told him we're only having barbecue twice down there." I groaned. "He's already called me three times to go over his choices."

Jonathan chuckled and took my hands in his. "Good luck down there, Rachel. Call me tomorrow night."

We kissed—a gentle, lingering kiss.

Lovely, I said to myself as I floated up the walk to my front door.

CHAPTER 9

"We'll see how much time we have, Benny," I said, raising a hand to calm him down. "No promises."

The light turned red up ahead and I slowed to a stop. It was Thursday morning. We were driving through a run-down warehouse district south of downtown Memphis somewhere near the Mississippi River. According to the directions, we were just a few blocks from the Eagle Engineering warehouse. I peered out the window, trying to find a street sign.

"Come on, Rachel," Benny whined. "We got to make the time. We're not talking mere mortal here. We're talking 'Heartbreak Hotel.' We're talking 'Jailhouse Rock.' We're talking about a guy whose idea of heaven was watching a pillow fight between teenage girls in white panties, whose idea of a gourmet treat was a fried peanut butter and banana sandwich. We're talking about a guy who died on the crapper twenty years ago but still gets spotted two or three times a year scoffing Ding Dongs and Big Slurps at 7-Elevens in rural Michigan. You realize what kind of a guy we're talking about?"

I looked over at him and nodded. "A total loser."

"A loser?! My God, Rachel! We're talking about the King."

The light turned green. "Yeah, right," I said, pulling into the intersection.

"Okay, big shot, name me one other rock 'n' roll singer from that era—just one—who could hold a candle to Elvis."

"One?" I slowed the car and gave him a look. "How about, let's see, five?"

"Five?" He burst into laughter. "No way."

"Chuck Berry, James Brown, Sam Cook, Ray Charles, Stevie Wonder."

That shut him up for the rest of the ride.

"Here we are," I said, pulling the car into a spot across the street.

The faded Roman lettering etched in the grimy slab of granite high above the door read EAGLE ENGINEERING CO.— CENTRAL WAREHOUSE. The sign looked like it dated back to the company's founding in 1938. So did the building. It was your basic two-story, redbrick, tar-paper-roof Depression-era structure. No windows on the first floor, and those translucent pebble-glass windows on the second floor—the kind that open not by sliding up but by tilting out on a chain. There was a buzzer and an intercom box next to the heavy metal door.

I pressed the buzzer. After a moment, it crackled and a voice said, "Who is it?"

I leaned toward the voice box. "Rachel Gold and Professor Goldberg."

I looked over at Benny and winked. Might as well milk that title for all it was worth, although today he looked less like a professor of law than an aging roadie for Neil Young. He was wearing his Portland Beavers baseball cap turned backward, green mirrored wraparound shades, a black sweatshirt with a ZZ Top logo, baggy olive army pants, and red Converse Chuck Taylor high-tops. In fairness, though, he wasn't the only one dressed for comfort: I had on my faded Levi's, a Chicago Blackhawks jersey, and my old pair of Nike Windrunners. No sense putting on office clothes to sort through dusty boxes of old documents.

The buzzer sounded and I pulled open the door. Ahead of us was a steep wooden stairway carpeted in a shabby brown runner. The stairs creaked as we climbed them toward the exposed fluorescent ceiling lights at the top of the landing. We'd been told that we'd be met by Willie, and as we reached the landing a man stepped into view with a security badge that read WILLIE TURNER.

I suppose that because this was the South, I assumed Willie would be Eagle Engineering's version of Boxcar Willie. But this was no Hee-Haw rent-a-cop in overalls and clodhoppers chewing on a stem of hay. No, this Willie was a dignified, middle-aged black man with chiseled features and hard eyes, dressed in sharply pressed security guard blues. Then again, we probably didn't fit his images of a Yankee attorney and law school professor, although you'd never know it from his deadpan expression.

"Mr. Turner, my name is Rachel Gold, and this is Professor Goldberg."

We shook hands and he instructed us to follow him. He led us down a narrow corridor toward the back of what was clearly a functioning warehouse operation—we passed several small offices where men or women were typing at computer terminals or talking on the telephone. We took a stairway down and into a large open area two stories tall that was crowded with rows of materials stacked on pallets on the concrete floor. Off to the right were several loading docks. I saw a forklift with a bale of barrels heading toward an open sliding door on one of the docks.

We followed Willie to a door marked EXIT against the back wall and stepped into a narrow alley behind the warehouse. Across the way was the redbrick exterior of the back side of another warehouse. There were three gray metal doors, each about thirty yards apart. Willie walked to the one on the far right and unlocked the door. Stepping into the darkness, he slid his hand along the wall until he found the light switch and flipped it on.

"We put a table in here for you," he said, "and some folding chairs. If you need to use the facilities or have any questions, just come across the alley and ring the back doorbell. Someone will open it." He paused and nodded stiffly. "Good luck, folks." He crossed the alley, unlocked the back door to the main warehouse, and disappeared inside.

"Argh," Benny groaned.

We were standing in a dimly lit space about the size of a

basketball half-court—roughly forty feet by forty feet. The room was illuminated by a half dozen naked lightbulbs hanging by cords from the ceiling. Two folding chairs and a rickety wooden table were in the center of the room, positioned directly beneath one of the bulbs. A network of pipes crisscrossed the plaster ceiling, which was water-stained in some places and crumbling in others. The concrete floor was littered with cigarette butts and rat droppings. The walls were hidden behind boxes. Stacks of boxes. Boxes of different sizes and shapes. Easily more than one hundred of them. Piled in uneven heaps all along the walls.

Benny stood in the middle of the room with his hands on his hips surveying the piles of boxes. After a moment, he walked over to the mound of boxes stacked along the back wall. He studied the label on the top box and then lifted the lid to peer inside. He let the lid drop down and turned to scan the room again. Looking toward me, he shook his head as his shoulders sagged.

"Shit," he groaned.

S hit," he groaned.
      I patted him on the back. "Come on, champ," I said. "We've been to the shrine, we've seen the King's tomb, we've eaten more barbecue, and best of all, we're at least halfway through. What could be bad?"

Benny gave me a dubious look and trudged over to the next pile of unopened boxes.

It was ten minutes after three in the afternoon. We'd reviewed documents for four and a half hours that morning. At twelve-thirty, bleary-eyed and hungry, we'd staggered out of the warehouse, climbed into the car, and drove to a place called Neely's, where we had two more plates of excellent barbecue. (Last night it had been a joint called Interstate.) After lunch it was south on Elvis Presley Boulevard to Graceland for the grand tour. I watched Benny go gaga in the Jungle Room, which looked like what you'd get if you gave LSD to a hillbilly decorator and set him loose in a Pier 1 Imports warehouse. In the Meditation Garden out back, Benny stood at the foot of Elvis's grave for a long time staring silently at the words engraved on the slab of marble covering the grave. The Christmas season had arrived at Graceland, and the grave was surrounded with floral arrangements and long-stemmed red roses and wreaths and Teddy bears and little Santas and kneeling porcelain angels. The only thing missing was the Velvet Elvis.

By the time we got back to the Eagle Engineering warehouse, we'd both forgotten how miserable our morning had been. It came rushing back, though, the moment Willie unlocked the door to our document dungeon. Although we were now more than halfway through—specifically, sixty-five boxes reviewed, including all of the ones along the left wall and two-thirds of the ones along the back wall—our progress was deceptive. We'd found nothing of value and very little that was even colorably relevant. Just thousands and thousands of seemingly irrelevant documents—boxes of reports by structural engineers, of drawings by architects, of inventory lists and reconciliations going all the way back to the 1950s, of change orders on unrelated construction jobs. Mainly old junk. Boxes and boxes and boxes of it. The only startling thing we'd found that morning was a dead rat in a box of invoices and subcontractor bills on a wastewater treatment plant built during the 1970s near the town of Newport, Tennessee.

We'd brought along dozens of packs of those yellow Post-its with the idea of sticking a note on each document we wanted copied. In all sixty-five boxes reviewed during the morning, we'd stickered exactly seventeen documents, and none was significant—a few organizational charts, a couple of corporate franchise tax filings, a handful of financial statements.

Benny lifted the top box off the pile and lugged it over to the table in the middle of the room. He looked down at the box and then looked up at me with a scowl. "This sucks."

I nodded sympathetically. "Big time."

"Bigger than big." He looked down at the box and shook his head. "This is a colossal suck." He pulled off the lid and stared at the jumble of documents. "A black hole suck."

Ninety minutes later, Benny broke the silence. "Aw, no."

I looked up from my box, which was on the table. Benny was standing along the side wall, where he had just lifted a box lid and peered in.

"What?"

He turned to me with a look of disgust. "Expense reports. I hate expense reports."

"Whose?" I asked.

He leafed through a few pages. "Some guy named Kruppa. Oh, Jeez, these things date back to the sixties, for chrissake."

"We need to review them."

He turned to me with an dubious expression. "What do you mean 'we,' Keemosabe?"

I sighed. "Okay, Tonto, bring me the box."

He carried it over and dropped it on the table behind the one I was looking through.

Forty minutes later, he broke the silence, this time with a question. "San Carlos de Bariloche?"

I looked up from the expense reports. "Who?"

Benny was holding up a thick file he'd pulled out of one of the boxes. "Some town."

"Where?"

He paged through a few documents. "Beats me."

"What about it?"

"These guys did some sort of a groundwater treatment plant for the town of San Carlos de Bariloche."

I shrugged. "They did a lot of big groundwater treatment jobs."

"Yeah, but this one's outside the country." He was studying the document. "Somewhere down in South America."

I mulled it over. "Well, outside the country is probably outside the lawsuit."

"Maybe, but this was a joint venture." He looked up from the documents with puzzled expression. "With Beckman Engineering."

"No kidding?" I stood up. "What's the name of that place?"

"San Carlos de Bariloche."

I brought over a legal pad. "How recent was this job?"

"Not too: 1958."

I looked at one of the documents with the town's name on it and copied the name onto the legal pad. " 'Fifty-eight," I mused. "That's a long time ago."

"But it's evidence of dealings between these two companies."

I mulled it over as I returned to the table. "Evidence of a joint venture in another country? Not exactly killer evidence."

"You never know." He pointed toward the packs of Post-its on the table. "Toss me one of those doohickeys. Might as well copy the file."

Twenty minutes later, I looked up. "Benny."

"You rang?" He was over by the wall, sorting through the contents of one of the boxes.

I held up a stapled packet of documents, my eyes wide. "Bingo."

He came over. "Bingo?"

I handed him the set of documents. The cover page was an Eagle Engineering travel expense form. Stapled to it were about a dozen receipts, including hotel, rental car, and restaurants.

Benny studied the cover page. "A two-day trip to Chicago, eh? Back in late March of 1983." He glanced down at me. "Who'd you say this Max Kruppa was?"

"The founder of Eagle."

Benny glanced down the entries on the cover page. " 'Business purpose,' " he read, " 'meet with suppliers and others.' "

"Look at the American Express receipt," I said. "The one for dinner in a private room at Morton's."

Benny found it. "More than five hundred bucks, eh? That was a lot of dough back then." He looked at me. "So what's the punch line?"

"Turn it over."

Because the receipts were stapled together, he had to turn the documents around and fold them back to read the reverse side of the American Express receipt, which is where the cardholder writes down a description of the expense.

Benny squinted as he read Max Kruppa's barely legible handwriting. When he finished, he looked down at me with his eyes wide. "Holy shit."

I nodded.

Scrawled on the back of the receipt was the following "business purpose":

> *Meet w/Koll, Muller, Beckman, Beek & Eicken to divide up pending federal IFBs.*

An IFB is contractor shorthand for an "invitation for bid," which is what Eagle Engineering's people would have called the notices of federal government procurement invitations that appeared each day in *Commerce Business Daily*. Koll, Muller, Beckman, Beek, and Eicken were, of course, the heads of the other five companies back then. Thus, according to the American Express receipt, on March 26, 1983, the presidents of the six companies involved in the alleged bid-rigging conspiracy met in a private room at Morton's steakhouse in Chicago for the purpose of dividing up the pending federal contracts, which is a slightly oblique way of saying that these six men met in secret one night to decide who would submit the winning bid on each of the pending federal contracts.

Benny turned the receipt over. "March of 'eighty-three." He looked at me. "Beyond the statute of limitations."

"That's okay. It's still evidence."

He chuckled as he waved the packet of receipts. "You better believe it, woman."

Although that meeting occurred outside the time period covered by my lawsuit, I would argue for its admissibility at trial under the theory that bid-rigging meetings are like cockroaches: when you stumble across one, you can be fairly certain there's more where that one came from.

I pulled the next stapled expense report out of the box. "Keep your fingers crossed," I said. "Maybe there's another needle in this haystack."

There wasn't, but we did find some other things worth copying. For example, the Eagle Engineering federal contract bid documents we located fit the pattern we'd seen with the Beckman bid documents: thick files on the bids they'd won, thin ones—or just empty file folders—on the others, all of which tended to suggest that Eagle Engineering knew in advance which jobs it was going to win, and thus which jobs were worth the time and effort necessary to make an accurate assessment of the likely costs of the project.

In addition, the documents revealed that the groundwater treatment plant in San Carlos de Bariloche was not Eagle's only joint venture down there. In 1968, Eagle and one of the other alleged co-conspirators, Beek Contracting, built a floodwater-control system on Lake Nahuel Huapí, which appeared to be on the outskirts of San Carlos de Bariloche.

Although I found no additional incriminating American Express receipts, there were two boxes filled with Max Kruppa's appointment calendars and personal papers. The calendars covered the period 1956 through 1993. (Kruppa died in 1994.) Although I didn't have time to go through each one, I spotted a few cryptic entries that suggested illegal meetings among the co-conspirators.

Even more tantalizing was a collection of yellowed carbon copies of typed correspondence dating back to the company's founding in 1938. The letters covered the period 1938 through 1945. Although they were addressed to people in the United

States, five of them were written in what appeared to be German. One of the letters was addressed to Otto Koll in Chicago, and another was addressed to Conrad Beckman in St. Louis. Although the letters were far outside the statute of limitations, if the topic was bid-rigging, they could be even more valuable than the American Express receipt or the calendar entries. Much the way adults will spell certain words or use a secret code when discussing certain topics around their children, perhaps Max Kruppa was less circumspect when communicating with his co-conspirators in a language he may have assumed most law enforcement officers would not understand.

I'd already made arrangements with a Memphis copy service that, according to Kenny Randall, specialized in big copy jobs. Two of the copy guys met us at the Eagle warehouse at five-thirty that evening. I showed them the various documents I wanted copied. They promised to have them delivered to St. Louis at least an hour before the start of my deposition of Conrad Beckman tomorrow afternoon.

The delivery deadline was important. My two-hour deposition would be my only shot at him before trial. I might just decide to spice up those two hours with a few surprises from Memphis.

CHAPTER 19

Precisely at three.

Just another example of the petty oneupmanship that the Roth & Bowles litigators had cultivated to a high art—or a low farce. So long as I was there by three o'clock, the one thing that definitely would not begin on time was the deposition of Conrad Beckman. Instead, I'd be kept waiting whatever length of time they deemed necessary to score another point in the silly power game that only they were keeping score in. Nonetheless, I had to play along, for if I showed up at, say, 3:10 P.M., they would all be waiting for me in the conference room and Kimberly Howard would imperiously announce that I'd already used up ten minutes of my allotted two hours.

Accordingly, at 2:52 P.M. on Friday afternoon I got off the elevator on the fifty-first floor. The words "Roth & Bowles" were engraved in the slab of gray marble over the portal. I stepped into the pretentious wood-paneled reception area. The prim receptionist with the British accent announced me to Kimberly Howard's secretary and directed me toward the waiting area behind her, where my court reporter, Jan, was already seated. They let us cool our heels until 3:15 P.M., and then Kimberly's secretary arrived to lead us down the hall, around the corner, and down another hall. She opened the door to a huge conference room. It had a mahogany conference table as long as a bowling lane and a state-of-the-art panel of video screens and teleconferencing equipment along the far wall. The side wall along the length of the conference table was solid floor-to-ceiling windows with a dramatic view of the St. Louis riverfront.

We were alone in the huge room. God forbid Kimberly and her entourage should have to wait for us. Jan set up her shorthand equipment at the far end of the table, and I arranged my stuff next to her along the side of the table. No doubt, Kimberly and Beckman would set up camp across from me. After a few minutes of idly clicking my nails on the tabletop, I stood and turned to look out the window. From fifty-one stories up, the Arch was a silver croquet wicket below. I checked my watch—3:21 P.M. I took a seat with my back to the windows and waited.

And waited.

At 3:43 P.M., the conference-room door swung open and in marched the forces of darkness in single file. Kimberly Howard was in the lead. Behind her came Laurence Browning, the obsequious senior associate, and behind Laurence came one of the two younger male associates who had flanked her at the status conference in Judge Wagner's chambers. And finally, striding into the room behind the others but towering over them all at six foot three, was Conrad Beckman. He wore a dark blue suit, crisp white shirt, and a gray-and-navy-striped tie. With his silver hair combed straight back, thin lips, strong jaw, and steely blue eyes, he looked every inch the intimidating chairman of the board. Although he was now in his early seventies, he radiated a strength that was athletic and surprisingly rugged. This was no elegant, white-haired fencer with épée and black tights. No, this was an aging bare-knuckles boxer who'd knock you on your butt if your attention wavered for just an instant.

Kimberly took the seat directly across the table from me and put Beckman to her immediate left. Laurence Browning sat next to Beckman, and the junior associate sat next to Browning.

Deposition preliminaries are often casual, friendly events, with the lawyers shaking hands and catching up on recent events while they wait for the court reporter to take down the names of the parties and the attorneys and to confirm the caption, court, and cause number of the lawsuit. This one, however, felt like a psych-out contest before the start of a heavyweight boxing match. Kimberly said nothing, and her underlings followed suit, of course. Beckman sat placidly with his hands on the table in front of him, his fingers interlaced. I arranged my papers for the tenth time and waited for the court reporter to get ready. Finally, she finished jotting down information, put down her pen, poised her fingers over her shorthand machine, and looked at me with a nod.

"Let the record show," I said as I turned from her toward Kimberly Howard, "that this is the deposition of Conrad Beckman. By Court order, the deposition is limited to two hours."

There was a stirring across the table. I paused to watch Laurence Browning remove a stopwatch from the pocket of his suit jacket. He ostentatiously positioned the stopwatch in his hand with his thumb on the start button. He turned to me with a smirk. With his pudgy cheeks, thick pursed lips, and round pop eyes, he could have been a cartoon blowfish in an underwater production number in Disney's *The Little Mermaid*.

Checking my watch, I announced: "The time is now 3:54 P.M. That means this deposition will last until 5:54, unless objections are made to any of the questions I ask Mr. Beckman." I glanced over at Laurence. "To avoid any disputes about timing, I have asked the court reporter to bring a stopwatch with her. Do you have it, Jan?"

Jan nodded and lifted it to show everyone.

"Whenever there is an objection," I explained, "Jan will stop the time, take down your objection, and then restart the stopwatch." I looked over at Laurence and winked. He made an indignant *harumph* and turned toward Kimberly, who was writing something on her legal pad.

"Are we ready to begin?" I asked.

"We are," Kimberly said without looking up.

There are several approaches to taking a deposition. The one I normally favor is to make the witness comfortable at the outset. I try to make my questions and his answers seem closer to a conversation than an interrogation, and usually start with a leisurely exploration of the one topic the witness is most familiar with and most comfortable talking about: himself. His background, his education, his prior job experiences—the goal being to get the witness relaxed. The more relaxed he becomes, the more talkative and less on guard he'll be, and thus the more I'll learn from him.

This was not one of those depositions. To begin with, I had only a limited time. Two hours for a deposition of this magnitude was but a blink of the eye. In a typical case, Conrad Beckman's deposition would last several days. Moreover, the usual approach would never work with Beckman, especially within the time constraints. He was far too savvy and there was far too much at stake for him to allow himself to get relaxed and talkative. So, instead, I decided that I might as well get him uptight and keep him uptight for his two hours. Turning to the court reporter, I said, "Swear the witness."

Jan turned to Conrad Beckman. "Raise your right hand, sir. Do you swear that the testimony you are about to give will be the truth, the whole truth, and nothing but the truth?"

Beckman nodded. "I do," he said in his deep raspy voice.

"Mr. Beckman," I said to him, "you understand you are under oath?"

"Yes."

"You understand that if you answer a question here untruthfully, you could be guilty of perjury?"

"Objection," Kimberly said indignantly.

I ignored her and kept my focus on him.

He contemplated me with those icy blue eyes. "Yes."

"Good," I said, checking my notes. "Sir, do you maintain a personal appointment calendar?"

He smiled at my naïveté. "My secretary does."

"When a new year begins, sir, what does she do with your calendar for the prior year?"

"I presume she places it in the file."

"Which file would that be?"

He chuckled without a trace of warmth. "The one for old appointment calendars."

"How far back does that file go?"

He shrugged. "Several years, I suppose."

"Ten years?"

"Perhaps."

"Longer?"

"Perhaps."

I nodded. "In order to recall your activities on a particular day, say, fifteen years ago, would you need to refer to your appointment calendar?"

"On a particular day fifteen years ago?" he asked with mild amusement. "I should think so, Miss Gold."

"And the same would be true for a particular day, say, five years ago?"

"Certainly."

"Or twenty years ago?"

He nodded. "Yes."

I turned to Kimberly. "Plaintiff renews its previous request for copies of Mr. Beckman's appointment calendars going back as far as they are maintained."

Kimberly gave me a frosty smile. "And defendant renews its previous objection to that request."

I turned back to Beckman. Might as well cut to the chase. "What is an IFB?" I asked.

Kimberly looked up from her notes.

Beckman frowned slightly. "In what context?"

"In the context of government contracts."

He rubbed his chin. "An IFB is shorthand for an invitation for bid."

"Is that the shorthand term used within your industry for the notices of proposed U.S. government procurement actions that appear in the *Commerce Business Daily*?"

"Excuse me," Kimberly said. "Would you repeat the question?"

I turned to Jan, who had paused to click the stopwatch.

"Jan," I said, "please read back the question for Ms. Howard."

When Jan finished reading the question, I turned to Beckman. I heard her start the stopwatch again.

"Yes," Beckman said.

"You understand the nature of the claim against your company, correct?"

His nostrils flared slightly. After a pause he said, "I have read the allegations."

"Then you understand that my client claims that your company conspired with five of its purported competitors to divide up the pending federal IFBs on certain wastewater treatment plants, correct?"

In a voice that remained impassive but with a hint of cold steel, he said, "I have read the allegations, Miss Gold."

"And you understand that those five competitors are Eagle Engineering, Koll Limited, Muller Construction, Beek Contracting, and Eicken Industrial, correct?"

"I have read the allegations, Miss Gold." This time more steel.

"And you deny those allegations?"

He crossed his arms over his chest. "Absolutely."

I shuffled through my papers and found the photocopy of Max Kruppa's American Express receipt. I studied it for a moment and looked up at Beckman. As I did, I lowered the sheet of paper until it was flat on the table facing me. Making sure that everyone on the other side of the table could see that I was referring to it, I asked, "On March 26, 1983, Mr. Beckman, did you meet for lunch in a private room at Morton's restaurant in Chicago with representatives of Eagle Engineering, Koll Limited, Muller Construction, Beek Contracting, and Eicken Industrial for the purpose of dividing up the pending federal IFBs?"

There was a long silence. Kimberly and Laurence subtly leaned forward, trying for a better look at the photocopied receipt without being obvious about it. I kept my focus on Beckman as I watched him consider the question and his answer. You could almost see those unruffled features getting winched a few turns tighter. He shifted his gaze toward me. "I have no present recollection of where I was or who I saw on March 26, 1983."

"No present recollection," I repeated. "In order to refresh your recollection, sir, would you need to refer to the March twenty-sixth entry in your appointment calendar for that year?"

A pause. "Perhaps."

I looked at him curiously. "Perhaps?"

I knew what he was up to, but I might as well hear it now. We were both shooting in the dark, since neither of us knew what his appointment calendar showed for March 26, 1983.

He gazed at me coolly. "An entry in an old calendar may not refresh my recollection." A pause. "Additionally, the entry may not be accurate."

"Why would that be?"

He gave me an imperial shrug. "Occasionally an appointment is changed without the change being noted in my calendar."

I nodded, suppressing the urge to smile. He'd been careful to carve himself an escape hatch just in case his personal calendar contained corroborating evidence of a Chicago meeting.

I turned the photocopy facedown on the table and reached for a set of photocopies from Max Kruppa's appointment calendar.

Again, I placed the first page—the one that included May 25, 1975—faceup on the table. Even when viewed from across the table and upside down, it was obvious that I had before me a page from someone's appointment calendar.

"What about May 25, 1975?" I asked, looking up from the page. "Did you attend a meeting in Chicago at the O'Hare Hilton with representatives of Eagle Engineering, Koll Limited, Muller Construction, Beek Contracting, and Eicken Industrial for the purpose of dividing up the pending federal IFBs?"

"What is that?" Kimberly asked, pointing at the photocopied calendar page.

I ignored her. "Well?" I asked Beckman.

"I asked you a question, Rachel," Kimberly said, her voice rising. "What is that document you're reading from?"

I glanced toward the court reporter, who lifted the stopwatch and clicked it to stop the time. I waited until her fingers were poised again over the shorthand keys. I turned toward Kimberly. "This is my deposition," I said calmly. "That means I'm the one who asks the questions. I don't answer them. That's your client's job today."

Kimberly stood up, her eyes wide. "Are you refusing to answer my question?"

I ignored her and turned to the court reporter. "Could you please read my question back to Mr. Beckman?"

"Did you hear me?" Kimberly demanded.

I kept my eyes on the court reporter. "Go ahead," I told her.

Kimberly remained standing as the court reporter leafed through her shorthand tape. "Here it is," Jan said. " 'What about May 25, 1975?' " she read. " 'Did you attend a meeting in Chicago at the O'Hare Hilton with representatives of Eagle Engineering, Koll Limited, Muller Construction, Beek Contracting, and Eicken Industrial for the purpose of dividing up the pending federal IFBs?' "

Beckman crossed his arms over his chest. "I have no present recollection of where I was or who I saw on March 25, 1975."

I turned over the next calendar page and asked the same question for September 12, 1975, and received the same answer. All the while Kimberly remained standing, unsure of her next move but unwilling to concede a thing by sitting down.

Ignoring her, I turned over the next calendar page. "What about October 8, 1987, Mr. Beckman? That was a meeting in St. Louis with those gentlemen. Over at the Missouri Athletic Club. Do you remember that meeting, sir?"

"No," he said forcefully.

I nodded. "Tell you what," I said. "Let's leave aside the particular dates, sir, and even the particular years, okay? Instead, let me ask it this way: at any time during the last thirty years, have you met with representatives of Eagle Engineering, Koll Limited, Muller Construction, Beek Contracting, and Eicken Industrial for the purpose of discussing pending federal IFBs?"

Again the stare. "I should think not, Miss Gold."

I smiled. "Is that a no, Mr. Beckman?"

He leaned forward, his face dark. "That's a 'Hell no,' Miss Gold."

He had his story, and he was sticking with it. It was up to me to prove it false—a task better left for trial. As for now, I'd been able to fire an important warning shot across the bow. Although Conrad Beckman had far too much self-control to reveal any reaction, Kimberly was clearly rattled. So much so that she took a seat without another word.

I put the photocopies back in my briefcase, trying to look more confident than I felt. Although I'd had enough ammo for the warning shot, I had nothing else—no kill shots. At least not yet. Barely twenty-four hours had elapsed since we'd found the American Express receipt in the Eagle Engineering warehouse. Now there'd be witnesses to interview and documents to examine and plenty of opposition to battle, especially once Kimberly discovered that I'd outfoxed her in Memphis. She'd never let that happen again.

I shifted tactics and nibbled for a bit around the periphery of his daily obligations and responsibilities. I didn't get much. When I checked my watch, I still had fifty minutes left. That was too much time and not enough, since I still didn't have the types of documentary evidence I needed to put together one of those thorough examinations designed to back the witness into a testimonial corner—assuming a witness as savvy as Beckman could be backed anywhere he didn't want to go.

Which still left me with fifty minutes.

Might as well go fishing.

"Mr. Beckman," I said, watching him carefully, "tell me about San Carlos de Bariloche."

He sat back in surprise. "Pardon?"

"Your company has done work there, correct?"

He paused, frowning. "I believe we may have. It was a long time ago."

"Where is San Carlos de Bariloche?"

"South America."

"Where in South America?"

He was glaring at me. "Somewhere in the Andes Mountains, I believe."

"Your company built a groundwater treatment plant there, correct?"

"Objection," Kimberly said, more out of bewilderment than anything else. "What does a groundwater treatment plant in South America have to do with this lawsuit?"

I ignored her. "Correct, Mr. Beckman?"

He shrugged nonchalantly. "Perhaps. It was many years ago, Miss Gold."

"I believe you did that project as a joint venture with Eagle Engineering; correct?"

Beckman's eyes narrowed slightly.

"Objection," Kimberly said. "Irrelevant."

I kept my eyes on the witness. "You may answer the question, sir."

"Perhaps it was a joint venture," he said. "I don't recall the details."

"Mr. Beckman," I continued, "how did a St. Louis company end up building a wastewater treatment plant in South America?"

"We have occasionally performed work outside of the United States," he said.

I turned to the court reporter. "Jan, please read the question to the witness."

She nodded and reached for the roll of shorthand tape. " 'Mr. Beckman,' " she read, " 'how did a St. Louis company end up building a wastewater treatment plant in South America?' "

Beckman stared at me, his jaw clenched. This was obviously a new experience for Mr. Chairman: having to actually answer someone else's question. Finally, he said, "I don't recall."

"How did your company end up in a joint venture with Eagle Engineering on a project in South America?"

This time the answer came quicker and more forceful. "I don't recall."

I spent the next thirty minutes moving around the periphery of the case, asking him about bidding procedures, industry meetings, chains of command within each of the divisions.

When there were less than ten minutes left, I reached for the last of the photocopies. This was the carbon copy of one of the letters in Max Kruppa's file. I hadn't yet received the English translation. Jacki had sent a copy to a professor of German when the documents arrived earlier today, but he wouldn't get to it until the weekend. I was hoping that Beckman might be able to do the translation at the deposition. After all, the letter was addressed to him.

"Mr. Beckman, who was Max Kruppa?"

"He was the president of Eagle Engineering."

"Was?"

"He is no longer alive."

"Did you know him?"

"Yes."

"When did you first meet him?"

Beckman paused as he tried to recall, or pretended to. "Many years ago," he said.

"Did you know him as far back as 1939?"

"Objection," Kimberly said. "Irrelevant."

I waited.

Beckman shrugged. "I don't recall."

"Back in 1939, did you live at 1923 Pond Avenue in St. Louis?"

He rubbed his chin. "I don't recall."

"Did you ever live at 1923 Pond Avenue?"

A pause. "Yes."

"You're just not sure whether you lived there in 1939?"

"Correct."

"You may have, right?"

"Yes," he said impatiently. "I may have."

"If independent documentary evidence showed that you lived at that address in 1939, would you dispute it?"

He eyed me warily. "I suppose not."

"What's the point of this?" Kimberly snapped.

"I'm going to hand you a document, Mr. Beckman," I said, ignoring her. "A letter. As you will see, it's written in what appears to be German. Please read it and tell me whether it refreshes your recollection as to where you lived in 1939 and whether you knew Mr. Kruppa back then."

I handed him the photocopy of Kruppa's letter. Kimberly got to her feet to stand behind him to read over his shoulder. Beckman stared at the letter, his brows furrowed.

Although the text of the letter was indecipherable to me, the addressee at the top of the page was quite legible: Conrad Beckman, 1923 Pond Avenue, St. Louis, Missouri. At the bottom it was signed "Max Kruppa." The letter was dated October 4, 1939.

"Where did you get this document?" Kimberly demanded.

I heard the click of the court reporter's stopwatch. With a sigh, I looked up. "This is a deposition, Kimberly. If you have questions about particular documents, put them in writing and I'll respond in due time."

"I've never seen this document before," she said.

"Put it in writing." I glanced toward to the court reporter and nodded. She started the stopwatch again.

I turned toward Beckman, who was still staring at the document. "Have you had an opportunity to review the document?"

He looked up, his face a blank mask. "Yes," he said, his voice flat.

"Does it refresh your recollection?"

"No."

"Do you recognize the language it's written in?"

"It appears to be German."

"Can you read it?"

"No."

"Why not?"

"I don't understand the language."

"Were you ever able to read German?"

"When I was much younger."

"But not anymore?"

"Not anymore."

I leaned over and took the document back from him. "Did you receive this letter from Mr. Kruppa?"

"I don't recall."

"Do you have any reason to doubt whether you received it back in 1939?"

He stared at me. The vein in his right temple was pulsing. "I have no reason to believe anything about this document."

Kimberly interjected, "Where did you get this document?"

I ignored her. "Did Max Kruppa send you other letters in German?"

"I don't recall."

"Rachel," Kimberly snapped, "I asked you a question."

I kept my eyes on him. "Was Max Kruppa born in America?"

"I don't recall."

"Did he speak with an accent?"

"I don't recall."

The court reporter cleared her throat. We all looked at her. "Two hours," she said.

Kimberly stood up. "This deposition is adjourned." She pointed at the photocopied letter. "I want a copy of that document."

Conrad Beckman was studying me.

I glanced up at Kimberly. "Put it in writing."

"We can make a copy right now," she said.

I shook my head. "No, we can't, Kimberly. Send me a written request and I'll consider it."

"That's ridiculous. I'm clearly entitled to the document. It's far more efficient to make a copy now."

"Kimberly," I said evenly, "your client has at least seven

attorneys and four paralegals on this case. You outnumber me by more than ten to one, yet not once have you made an effort to accommodate me. Not once in this case have you responded to any of my requests in a way that could remotely be described as 'more efficient.' You've made me jump through every procedural hoop you can dream up. You want this document?" I put it into my briefcase. "Start jumping."

She stared at me, incredulous. "I cannot believe this." She spun on her heels and stormed out of the room.

"Harumph," Laurence Browning added as he got to his feet.

Beckman placed his hands flat on the table and stood up, his eyes on me the whole time. They'd gone from frosty to subzero.

"Well," Browning tsk-tsked to no one in particular, "this is certainly a lamentable day for professional courtesy, eh?"

Beckman brushed past him without a word and stalked out of the room. Browning and the junior associate exchanged uncertain glances and then filed silently out of the room.

I glanced over at the court reporter. She raised her eyebrows and exhaled slowly.

"Wow," she said.

CHAPTER 11

I expected repercussions, of course. Conrad Beckman had been one unhappy camper at the end of his deposition, and I could assume he'd demand retribution.

After dinner that night, I'd curled up on the couch in the den with my golden retriever Ozzie snuggled next to me and listened to my favorite Chicago bluesman, Junior Wells, as I imagined the range of possible repercussions. As Junior wailed out a harmonica solo on "Why Are People Like That?" I tried to brace myself for the incoming barrage of motions and discovery requests that would start Monday.

But the one repercussion I hadn't expected was the phone call at noon on Saturday. I'd just returned from a seven-mile jog through Forest Park with Ozzie. The call caught me off guard. It also caught me in the shower. Wrapped in a towel and dripping wet, I grabbed the phone in my bedroom.

"Hello?"

"Rachel?" asked a hearty male voice.

"Yes?" I could feel the water pooling around my bare feet.

"This is Stanley Roth, Rachel. How are you?"

"Uh, fine."

Rachel? Stanley? I'd never met the man before in my life.

"Rachel, I am terribly sorry to disturb you at home over the weekend, but I'm off to Washington, D.C., on Monday and won't be back until Thursday. I certainly don't want to let this matter linger that long. I was wondering if you were free tomorrow night for dinner? I could reserve a private room at Briarcliff. That way we could discuss the matter in confidence."

"Discuss what matter?" I asked, baffled.

He chuckled. "Why, your lawsuit against Beckman Engineering, of course. How does Sunday for dinner sound? Just the two of us."

I was having trouble processing the conversation. Stanley Roth, the Roth of Roth & Bowles, wanted to meet with me alone at his country club to discuss the Beckman Engineering lawsuit? Roth was Beckman Engineering's principal attorney and had handled their legal matters for more than twenty years. Rumor had it that Beckman Engineering's annual legal fees exceeded $4 million, which made it by far the largest client of Roth & Bowles.

Well, I said to myself, *what's the harm?*

"Sunday night won't work," I told him, remembering my plans with Jonathan and his girls.

"Then how about Sunday brunch?" he asked cheerfully. "Say, eleven o'clock?"

"Well," I said uncertainly, "okay."

"Excellent," he said. "I shall look forward to it."

I pulled my car into the parking lot at Briarcliff Country Club on a brisk Sunday morning. The bright sun made me squint as I walked toward the imposing portico and entrance to the clubhouse. This was hardly my first visit to Briarcliff. But no matter how often I came here, my feelings remained the same. I detested the place.

Briarcliff is the most exclusive Jewish country club in St. Louis. It is thus a place where my people—victims of prejudice and exclusion since the time of Abraham—can inflict those despicable practices upon their own kind. Indeed, for years, one of the basic prerequisites for membership was the purity of one's Germanic ancestry—a macabre standard for a people nearly exterminated by those of pure Germanic ancestry. Briarcliff is a world of affectation so somber as to be silly—a place where you can stroll through the Great Hall, a kitsch homage to King Arthur, and as you pass beneath the rows of heavy flags emblazoned with English heraldry, you can almost forget (almost) that your family coat of arms is, at best, a gefilte fish rampant on a field of chopped liver.

This was Stanley Roth's world. Indeed, his grandfather, Julius Roth, had been one of the club's founding fathers. But Stanley Roth was far more than just a member of Briarcliff. And he was far more than a typical "leader" of the Jewish community—one of those perpetual student council presidents who spend their lives campaigning like rats in heat for high office in various local and national Jewish organizations while making sure that their smiling faces appear constantly on the front pages of the Jewish weeklies.

No, Stanley had actually crossed the great divide. Now in his early sixties, he was a name partner in a preeminent law firm, had served as trusted counselor to members of the St. Louis business elite for more than four decades, was on the boards of directors of several prominent St. Louis companies, and was one of three non-CEO members of Civic Progress, that shadowy group of St. Louis power brokers who help run the city. Indeed, it was Stanley Roth, an influential member of the Missouri Republican Party, who had lured the politically ambitious Kimberly Howard back to St. Louis, and it was Stanley Roth who would no doubt help launch her career in Missouri politics.

And now this same Stanley Roth was waiting for me.

The white-coated maître d' nodded deferentially as I stepped into the main dining hall. He was a plump, pink-cheeked man in his fifties, with thinning gray hair combed straight back. "Yes, madam."

I scanned the room, trying to spot a man that I might be able to recognize on reputation alone. I couldn't.

"I'm supposed to meet Stanley Roth," I told the maître d'.

He smiled respectfully. "Ah, yes. Mr. Roth has arranged for a private dining room." He turned and gestured for me to follow. "This way, if you please."

We moved through the dining room and past a groaning buffet table filled with Sunday brunch goodies. Because this was Briarcliff, the table was heaped with bacon, ham, pork sausage, shrimp, and other *traif*. I did notice a platter of lox, although here they called it smoked Norwegian salmon.

Down a short hall off the main dining room we came to a heavy wood door. The maître d' rapped twice and then opened it. Poking his head in, he said, "Mr. Roth, sir, your guest has arrived."

"Excellent," I heard from within. "Send her in, Ronald."

The maître d' turned to me and opened the door with a bow. "Mademoiselle."

The room overlooked the golf course, which was visible through the lead-glass windows. The walls were paneled with carved wood. The table was large enough to serve eight, although today it was set for just two, facing one another across the center of the table. Stanley Roth was seated on the far side of the table as I walked in. I noticed that his coffee cup was half full. He stood with a friendly smile and came around the table to greet me.

"Hello, Rachel," he said, taking my right hand in his and covering it with his left. "I'm delighted you could join me." He gestured toward the table. "Please have a seat. I've asked them to bring you juice and coffee along with a menu."

By the time I'd taken my seat across from him, a pair of waiters had appeared, one carrying carafes of tomato juice and fresh-squeezed orange juice, the other carrying pots of regular and decaf coffee. I chose orange juice and regular; Stanley opted for tomato and more decaf.

As they poured the beverages and handed out menus, I studied Stanley Roth. He was taller than I had expected—perhaps six foot one—with a slender build and an athletic posture. Bald on top, he had gray, close-cropped hair on the sides. He had the tanned, healthy look of a middle-aged tennis buff, which in fact he was. As I recalled, he had played on Princeton's varsity squad during college. He had bright hazel eyes, good teeth, and a strong nose echoed by a strong Adam's apple. Today, he was wearing a brown Harris tweed jacket over a blue-and-white-striped Oxford cloth button-down shirt and pleated, crisply pressed chinos.

After we placed our orders—an Egg Beaters mushroom

omelette and wheat toast for him, a fresh fruit salad with yogurt for me—we exchanged pleasantries. Roth had obviously done his homework on me, or had instructed someone to do it. I didn't delude myself: as a solo practitioner with middle-class roots and Eastern European ancestors, the only function I normally had in Roth's world was, in Hamlet's words, to swell a progress. But like most powerhouse attorneys, Roth viewed information as leverage, and he'd acquired plenty of it on the subject of Rachel Gold. I was hardly flattered. By the time our opening pleasantries were concluded, my internal defense systems were flashing red alert.

"Rachel," Roth said, setting down his fork, his demeanor downshifting from affable to serious, "I think a little background may help you understand the purpose of this meeting." He paused to take a sip of coffee. He neatly set the cup back in the saucer and brushed his lips with the napkin. "Twenty-one years ago, Conrad Beckman came to me. He was disgusted with the law firm that was handling his company's litigation. Apparently, they would talk tough up until the time of trial, but then panic on the courthouse steps and force him to settle." He shook his head in long-suffering amusement at the memory. "Conrad Beckman may have been born and raised in South St. Louis, but he had some Old World notions about the way a lawsuit ought to be handled. 'A lawsuit is war,' he once told me. He viewed a settlement as a capitulation, and a dishonorable one at that."

He paused for another sip of coffee and then carefully placed the cup on the saucer. "Conrad Beckman came to me twenty-one years ago because he wanted a firm that wouldn't buckle under pressure, that wouldn't force him to settle a lawsuit. Rachel, I looked him straight in the eye that day and promised that my firm would never try to talk him into settling a lawsuit." He leaned back with a steadfast expression. "I've kept that promise for twenty-one years."

I nodded politely. After a moment of silence, I tried to fill the void. "Well, that's really something." It sounded even lamer than I feared.

"Twenty-one years, Rachel. Until today. I've decided to break that promise."

"Oh?"

He nodded gravely. "My client has no idea I'm here. In fact, I am quite sure he will be unhappy to learn of this meeting or what I am about to suggest."

I sipped my coffee and waited, keeping my expression neutral. I'd believe in Santa Claus before I'd believe that his client didn't know about this meeting.

He rubbed his knuckles along his jawline in a contemplative manner. "I would like to try to convince my client to settle your lawsuit. I caution that I have reached that conclusion not based on the merits of our clients' respective positions. Kimberly assures me that Beckman Engineering's defenses are rock solid, and I have no reason to doubt her. Even so, I am well aware of the extent of the pretrial preparations still to come for both sides. I truly believe that this is a case where an early resolution would confer a substantial benefit on both parties by eliminating the additional time, expense, and distraction of litigation. Moreover, we are at a stage where the matter can be resolved quietly. The case is still under seal. I'm sure your client would have no problem agreeing to keep the settlement terms confidential, would she?"

I smiled. "For the right price."

He chuckled. "But of course."

"There are some complicating factors," I cautioned. "This is a *qui tam* case. It can't be settled without the government's approval. Also, keep in mind that my client will only be entitled to twenty-five to thirty percent of that settlement amount."

But Stanley Roth had already devised a solution to those problems. Beckman Engineering's settlement payment would be deemed attributable only to Ruth's original employment discrimination claim, which meant that she could keep 100 percent of the payment. The *qui tam* claim would be dismissed without any additional settlement payment.

"But we'd still need the government's consent," I said.

He smiled. "I am confident that we can obtain the government's consent."

I leaned back in my chair and crossed my arms over my chest. "Okay, Stanley, what's your client want to pay?"

He chuckled. "Nothing, of course." He rubbed his chin pensively. "What I'd like to do is for us to come up with a number that I could recommend to my client. Obviously, it would have to be a number your client would accept, and thus you'd need to talk it over with her first. But if it is a number your client would accept *and* that I can recommend, I will give you my word, Rachel, that I will do my level best to deliver it."

It was an old negotiating technique: try to get the other side to commit to a number while pretending that you have no authority to negotiate. I'd used the technique myself in other lawsuits. I was willing to bet that Conrad Beckman had already given Stanley Roth the precise dollar amount of his settlement authority. Regardless, if Beckman Engineering was willing to settle the case on reasonable terms, I didn't care what kind of face-saving charade they needed to go through in order to get there.

"Let's cut to the chase, Stanley. Tell me your number."

He crossed his arms over his chest and nodded. "Your client received a generous early retirement package when she left the company."

"Except she didn't retire. She was fired."

"Regardless. I've had someone calculate the difference between the present value of that severance package and the present value of the salary she could have earned through age seventy. I have the actual calculations in my briefcase if you'd care to see them."

I shook my head. "Not now."

"Your client's maximum recovery, assuming she could even prove age discrimination, is ninety-eight thousand five hundred dollars." He leaned forward. "Rachel, I'd be willing to recommend to my client that they round the number up to one hundred thousand and add another fifty thousand dollars to cover attorney's fees and costs."

"Your offer is one hundred fifty thousand dollars?" I asked, keeping my tone neutral.

"Actually, it isn't an offer yet. If your client is willing to accept that amount in settlement of all claims, I'm prepared to sit down with Conrad Beckman and urge him to do the deal."

I leaned back in my chair and studied him. "One hundred fifty thousand."

He nodded. "It's a generous offer, Rachel. It's at least as much as she could hope to recover in an age discrimination case."

I shook my head. "But this is no longer an age discrimination case, Stanley."

He shrugged indifferently. "Call it whatever you want, Rachel. One hundred fifty thousand dollars is a lot of money."

"Your client will spend four times that amount just getting ready for the trial."

He nodded slowly, his lips pursed. "Perhaps."

"Don't you see, Stanley? Your client will spend a million dollars to defend a claim where its exposure could exceed one hundred million dollars, but it'll only offer a hundred fifty thousand to settle it."

"Correction, Rachel," he said, wagging his finger in good-natured chiding. "My client is willing—or at least I hope it is willing—to offer one hundred fifty thousand dollars to settle a claim that it believes is frivolous." He leaned forward, his eyes suddenly cold. "If that offer is declined, I can assure you that my client is prepared to spend whatever it takes to defend this case." He leaned back and shook his head. "One million, two million—it won't matter. War is war."

I gazed at him a moment. "I'll convey your offer, Stanley."

"Talk to your client, Rachel." There was a trace of sympathy in his voice. "Pass on what we've discussed. This is her last best chance. Help her understand that."

*   *   *

I talked to Ruth that afternoon. We met in her breakfast room, seated across from each other at the table. I told her what Stanley Roth had said. I told her that $150,000 was a lot of money. I told her that Stanley Roth claimed that it was her last best chance. I told her I didn't know whether that was true.

I also told her that I assumed Conrad Beckman was fully apprised of the meeting in advance and had approved the $150,000 "offer." I told her that I thought there was some give in the number and that we might be able to goose it to $200,000. I told her that it was my best guess that there was a direct causal link between Conrad Beckman's deposition on Friday afternoon and my meeting with Stanley Roth on Sunday morning. I wasn't sure what the actual link was—at least not yet—but I'd place my bet on Max Kruppa's American Express receipt.

I also warned her.

I warned her that we still didn't have any hard evidence of a bid-rigging conspiracy. Circumstantial evidence, yes—but nothing direct. The American Express receipt and the calendar entries, while harmful to Beckman Engineering, fell outside the statute of limitations. Same with the letter in German from Max Kruppa, whatever it said. All of which meant that we still had a difficult path ahead of us, and it was possible that $150,000 would be more than the jury verdict we might end up with.

Ruth listened carefully and nodded as I explained the situation. When I was finished, she asked me one question:

"Are you still willing to represent me if I say no?"

I smiled and placed my hand on top of hers. "Absolutely."

"The money isn't important, Rachel. I don't have fancy tastes, and my Sidney, God bless him, left me more than enough to live on." She paused and shook her head. "This is just not right. What they're doing is stealing money from the government. We caught them, and all they want to do is sweep that dirt under the carpet. They want to buy me off cheap and then go back to business as usual like they're a bunch of choirboys. It's not right." She looked at me earnestly. "Don't you agree?"

A wave of fatigue washed over me. Yes, I agreed with her. But the lawsuit had worn me down. I was outnumbered and outgunned by Roth & Bowles. There were lots of them to one of me, and they'd been pummeling me for months.

Nevertheless, Ruth was right. The offer was too low. She shouldn't settle cheap—at least not until we'd run down all of the leads. Of course, I wasn't thrilled about being the one to run down those leads. At that very moment, I was sick to death of the case. I would have gladly passed this baton to another lawyer. Let someone else lug this load to the finish line.

But there was no one else. It was just Ruth and me. We'd started this obstacle course on our own, and we were going to have to try to finish it that way, too, or fall down trying.

I gave her a weary smile. "Yes, Ruth. I agree."

"Good." She nodded firmly. "We're doing the right thing, Rachel. I just know we are."

I sighed. "I hope so."

There was a moment of silence. I waited, holding the telephone receiver against my ear.

"Is there a counteroffer?" Stanley Roth said, his voice spiked with irritation.

"No, Stanley. My client has strong feelings. I don't think further settlement discussions will be worthwhile unless your client is willing to place a seven-figure number on the table."

Another long silence.

"You are making an enormous mistake, Rachel."

"I hope not."

An exasperated sigh at the other end. "I have done what I can, Rachel. You and your client will have to live with the consequences of your unfortunate decision."

"All of us will, Stanley, including your client. That's the chance we're willing to take."

"Chance has nothing to do with it. Good-bye, Rachel." A
pause. "I am sorry for you."

"Don't be. I'm a big girl."

"Not big enough for this."

Click.

CHAPTER 12

The girls and I had a wonderful time. Jonathan dropped them off at two-thirty that Sunday afternoon. I sat them down at the kitchen table and poured each a tall glass of fresh-squeezed lemonade. Leah, in fourth grade, had long auburn hair and her father's dazzling green eyes. Her younger sister Sarah, age eight, could almost pass for my daughter with her dark curly hair and almond-shaped hazel eyes. They sipped their lemonade and listened carefully as I went over the menu. I'd planned what seemed a safe meal to serve a family that kept kosher at home: pasta with pesto sauce, steamed asparagus, grilled salmon, Italian bread, and chocolate ice cream. Their eyes got big when they realized that we were going to knead our own bread and roll our own pasta and churn our own ice cream. They were adorable, and their excitement over our dinner plans swept away any lingering sour notes from my meeting with Stanley Roth.

During the rest of the afternoon they turned my kitchen into a cookfest filled with precious images. There was little Sarah kneeling on a kitchen chair, her sleeves rolled up, splotches of white flour on her nose and cheeks, as she kneaded the bread dough. And Leah cranking the handle of my old-fashioned pasta machine and watching wide-eyed as the long ribbons of fettuccini emerged. And the two of them hanging loops of fresh pasta onto the arms of the wooden drying rack while Ozzie watched curiously from below, his tail occasionally wagging. There was Leah, pursing her lips thoughtfully as she sampled a spoonful of chocolate ice cream that I had scooped out of the ice cream maker. And Sarah, a dish towel tied around her neck for a bib, standing on a chair in front of the kitchen sink and licking the dasher paddles clean, her face smudged with chocolate ice cream. And, finally, the three of us scrambling to get the table set before Jonathan arrived. We used a blue tablecloth and good china and a pretty glass vase for the irises I'd picked up at the grocery store on the way back from Ruth Alpert's house.

The girls barely had time to wash up and comb their hair before their daddy arrived. He bestowed a long-stemmed rose on each of us—white for the girls, red for me. He also brought a fancy chilled bottle of white grape juice for the girls and a chilled bottle of sauvignon blanc for us. With proud, solemn expressions, the girls showed their father to his seat and then joined me at the counter to help serve our feast.

Dinner was delicious and, with one exception, proceeded without a hitch. In all of the commotion I'd forgotten about the salmon. I remembered halfway through the salad course. It was too late to start the grill, so we improvised. We served the pasta as a separate course and changed our entrée from mesquite-grilled salmon to oven-broiled salmon. It worked out fine. By the time we finished our bowls of chocolate ice cream, we were stuffed and content.

For one last time, Jonathan filled his wineglass and mine with the sauvignon blanc and his daughters' with grape juice. Holding aloft his glass for a toast, he looked around the table and said, "Ladies, that was unquestionably the most scrumptious meal I have ever eaten in my life."

The girls basked in the praise, their eyes shining with pride. Leah looked over at me. I gave her a wink.

Jonathan helped clear the table and clean up as the girls went into the den with Ozzie to play with my old Barbie doll stuff. As we washed the dishes, I told him about Conrad Beckman's deposition and Stanley Roth's settlement offer.

"You've got them rattled," he said.

"A hundred fifty thousand dollars doesn't sound too rattled."

"It is for that company."

"Maybe." I was suddenly sick of talking about my lawsuit. "Tell me about the Spider investigation."

He rinsed the soapsuds off the plate and handed it to me. "I've divided the group into two teams."

"What do you mean?"

As he scrubbed the inside of the ice cream churn, he explained that one task force was now focused on the more traditional law enforcement role of solving hate crimes and preventing future ones through surveillance, informers, and undercover operations. He was heading up the other group, which was handling the financial probe.

"Which is what?" I asked.

"You can't run an organization like Spider without a lot of money. Cutting off the flow of money is like cutting off the flow of oxygen: you'll kill it. That's my goal."

"What's their source of funds?"

"It's a mystery."

"Really?"

He nodded. "We can trace the little stuff—the contributions they get through direct-mail solicitations, the plugs during Robb's radio broadcasts. But his operation requires a big additional source of revenues. That's the missing piece."

To find it, Jonathan explained, he'd been serving subpoenas on area banks. It was a two-pronged strategy. First, bank records might reveal one or more sources of funding. Second, and just as important, the threat of disclosure might put pressure on the sources of funds, who might be anxious to keep their connection to Spider confidential. If so, one or more might be willing to cooperate with the investigators in exchange for anonymity.

"What have you found so far?" I asked, fascinated. We'd finished the dishes and were now having tea at the kitchen table. We were within earshot of the girls, who were still playing Barbie dolls in the den.

Jonathan paused to stir honey into his tea. "We located Spider's main account," he explained, taking a sip. "It's at Sunset Bank in South County. Over the past year there've been six big deposits into that account totaling nearly half a million dollars."

"Wow. From whom?"

"From a trust account at Patriot Bank & Trust on South Grand."

"A trust account?" I said.

He nodded.

"Who owns the account?"

Jonathan shook his head. "Don't know."

"Is the bank the trustee?"

"No," he said. "Paulie Metzger."

"Who's that?"

"A criminal defense lawyer."

I shook my head. "I've never heard of him."

"Paulie's a fringe player," Jonathan explained. "Strictly a ham 'n' egger, a little storefront office on the far south side. He's in his late sixties now—maybe even seventy. Has a reputation as a real sleazeball, which he definitely deserves. Back in my prosecutor days, I convicted one of his clients on a firearms possession charge. The trial took seven hours, including jury deliberations, and after a full day with Paulie, I felt like I needed to get fumigated."

"Sounds like Prince Valiant."

Jonathan nodded, pursing his lips. "Paulie is going to make a special command performance before my charm school."

I raised my eyebrows. "The grand jury?"

"Yep."

"Here?"

"Down in Jeff City. Probably in two or three weeks. That'll give us enough time to see whether our subpoenas turn up more sources of funds."

I stood on the porch with Jonathan. The girls were already in the car.

"That was a wonderful meal, Rachel," he said, taking my

hands in his. His green eyes sparkled in the porch light. "Thank you."

I smiled. "We had fun making it."

I couldn't read his thoughts, but I assumed they were in the same realm as mine, and just as muddled. We had started off as litigation adversaries and gradually became wary allies. But when our relationship shifted unexpectedly from professional to romantic a few months back, it quickly pushed us to this confusing edge. Because of Jonathan's religious beliefs, we could be friends but not lovers. We couldn't take that next step without first becoming husband and wife, and that was a huge next step—for both of us. As much as I might fantasize about making love to Jonathan Wolf or just snuggling with him in front of the fireplace on a winter night, the prospect of becoming Mrs. Jonathan Wolf—with all the traditional Orthodox observances that might entail, from keeping kosher to the monthly visit to the *mikva*—gave me pause. More than anything, the two of us needed time to discuss it, to sort these issues out.

Unfortunately, time was the one thing neither one of us had these days. Meanwhile, our bodies remained oblivious to the bigger religious questions. I had trouble keeping my hands off him, and I knew he had the same problem with me. Even washing dishes together felt like foreplay, which only made our situation all the more frustrating. I was still guilty about my lapse at the restaurant the other night. Although playing footsies under the table had been fun, it wasn't fair to him. I've always despised women who do that to men.

"Good night, Rachel." He leaned over and gave me a gentle kiss on the lips.

I ended it just as gently, resisting the sudden urge to turn it into a from-here-to-eternity kiss. "Good night," I whispered.

As he walked toward his car, I waved to the girls and they waved back.

Oh, well, I told myself as I watched them drive off, *we'll manage somehow—at least for now*. If the couples in my beloved Jane Austen novels could manage, so could we.

CHAPTER 13

As expected, the bombing runs began Monday morning. There was an irate letter from Kimberly Howard emerging from my fax machine as I walked into the office. Twenty minutes later, while I was sipping my first cup of coffee and skimming through Kimberly's angry demands—*and immediate production of all previously undisclosed documents shown to Mr. Beckman at his deposition, including but not limited to*—a Roth & Bowles messenger arrived with a stack of five motions to quash, one filed in each jurisdiction where I'd served a subpoena. By noon, two more packages arrived by messenger delivery; they included a set of interrogatories, a set of requests for production of documents, a set of requests for admission, and a motion to shorten the time to respond to each.

I didn't study any of them carefully. When you're outnumbered the way I was outnumbered, there's no sense trying to match the other side's firepower. Roth & Bowles, like most large firms, had a massive but lumbering war machine. They fought litigation battles the way the redcoats fought the colonists, and the only way to resist was the way the colonists had. The Memphis maneuver had been a classic example: get in and out quietly before the B-52s start darkening the skies overhead.

Moreover, I had the sense that Kimberly was starting to overplay her hand. While Catherine Wagner was surely no friend of mine, she was nevertheless a U.S. district judge, and U.S. district judges are never eager to resolve discovery squabbles among lawyers. Jacki had checked with Judge Wagner's docket clerk last Friday, as she does every Friday, and learned that Her Honor was starting a two-week criminal docket this morning that included a carjacking case with two defendants and a kidnapping case where the U.S. Attorney was asking for the death penalty under the new federal statute. According to the docket clerk, neither criminal case was likely to end in a plea. That meant that Judge Wagner was going to have plenty of other things on her mind for the next two weeks. As a result, there was a good chance that Kimberly's latest motions and demands would sink without a trace into the court files.

Benny called at 2:10 P.M. from the law school, where he'd just finished teaching his civil procedure class. "I did some poking around in the library this morning," he told me. "Dug up some interesting shit on San Carlos de Bariloche. When's your self-defense class?"

"Six, and then I'm having dinner at my mom's house."

"How 'bout I drop by around five? It won't take long."

"Perfect."

I t's a resort town."

"A resort town?" I sat back in my chair, surprised. "Where?"

"In the Andes Mountains," Benny said. "On the western border of Argentina, near Chile, about eight hundred fifty miles southwest of Buenos Aires. It's supposed to be a real a picturesque postcard spot: gingerbread houses, fondue shops, chalet-style hotels, pine forests. Surrounded by jagged, snow-capped mountain peaks. The town overlooks a huge clear lake."

"Lago Nahuel Huapí?" I said, recalling the documents we'd looked at in Memphis.

"Yep."

"San Carlos de Bariloche," I mused. "I've never heard of it."

"Apparently it's an Argentine version of Aspen—a ski resort for international jet-setters during the winter, a fishing and hiking mecca during the summer. Chalet-type buildings, surrounded by mountains." He paused and reached into his briefcase. "Here," he said, handing me a sheet of paper. "I copied this from the *Encyclopaedia Britannica*."

I took the sheet from him and read the two-paragraph entry. About the only item of real interest was: "The picturesque scenery of the area, designated as a national park (1934), inspired the setting for Walt Disney's film *Bambi*."

I looked up at him curiously. "Strange."

"What?"

"I showed the stuff on the Eagle/Beckman joint venture in Bariloche to Ronald Milton along with the stuff on the other Eagle joint venture down there."

Ronald Milton—formerly the chief financial officer of a large construction company, now a professor at one of the local business schools—was one of the expert witnesses I'd retained for the lawsuit. If, as I'd alleged, the bid-rigging conspiracy had inflated the price of the government contracts, I needed an authority to analyze the bids and offer expert opinions on various pricing issues.

"What did he say?" Benny asked.

I frowned. "He can't figure it out. He says it looks like they did the work down there at below cost—both Beckman's joint venture and the other one." I shook my head. "It doesn't make sense."

Benny thought it over. "It's a resort town, right? Maybe they got to spend some extra time down there for free."

I gave him a skeptical look. "Since when do contractors do work in resort areas below cost? If anything, they'd tack on a premium."

Benny rubbed his chin thoughtfully. "Kickbacks?"

"Possibly." I sighed and shook my head. "There are still too many loose ends."

"So you'll tie them up."

"When?" I said, discouraged. "I'm running out of time, Benny. The trial is barely a month away. You should see the pile of motions they filed today." I rolled my eyes and groaned. "I know exactly what they're up to. They're going to turn this thing into a seven-ring circus to make sure I don't have enough time to prepare the case."

"So," he said, leaning forward and lowering his voice, "fuck 'em."

"Yeah, right," I said in frustration.

"I mean it, Rachel. Fuck 'em and fuck the horses they rode in on and all seven rings of their asinine circus." He leaned back and crossed his arms over his chest. "January is a slow month at the law school. I can help get this case ready. We can handle these Roth & Bowles turkeys. Don't forget, Rachel, we were weaned at Abbott & Windsor. We went through basic training in the seventh level of hell. And now we're supposed to be intimidated by a bunch of pencil-neck geeks from a St. Louis law firm? A *St. Louis* firm? Excuse me? You know what I say, woman?"

I couldn't help but smile. "No, Benny. What do you say?"

"I say we put on the old war paint, cry havoc and let slip the dogs of war, eh?" He gave me the thumbs-up sign. "How's that sound, partner?"

I nodded wearily. "Okay, partner."

"Goddamn," he said, he eyes blazing, his fists clenched. "I feel like Henry at Agincourt. Bring on St. Crispin's Day, eh? I'm pumped, woman! We're gonna kick some butt."

Fifteen minutes later, I left the office for my self-defense class. It was snowing lightly. As I headed toward the front walk for the car, a local courier service car pulled up to the curb.

"Miss Gold," the young messenger called as he got out of the car. He held up a sealed manila envelope. "This is from Dr. Geissler. He wanted you to have it right away."

I thanked him and took the envelope. Hubert Geissler was a professor of German languages at St. Louis University. I'd retained him to translate Max Kruppa's 1939 letter to Conrad Beckman. This must be the translation. I slipped it into my briefcase as I headed toward my car. I was running late to my self-defense class. I could read it later.

* * *

I looked up at her in wonder. "This is awesome, Mom."

She put another forkful in her mouth and chewed seriously. "Halfway decent," she finally said with a shrug.

"What do you call it?"

"Red bean stew with ancho chili salsa."

I smiled in admiration as I scooped another forkful. "You're incredible, Mom, but you better be careful."

"What?"

"When the word gets out you're cooking up meals like red bean stew with ancho chili salsa and that unbelievable risotto last month—what did you call it?"

"Risotto with purple and white rices and julienne mushrooms."

"Right. When word leaks out, they're going to drum you right out of the Hadassah."

"Hey," she said in mock outrage, pointing her finger toward heaven for emphasis. "For which of my two daughters did I cook that cholent two weeks ago?" She paused and gave me a wink. "Now tell me about Ruth's lawsuit."

"That reminds me," I said, standing up. "I have something."

I went out to the front hall, got my briefcase, and brought it back in. "Remember that German letter I told you about? I just got the English translation."

I pulled out the sealed envelope and tore it open. I skimmed at the cover letter from Dr. Geissler as I handed the translation to her. I came around to read it over her shoulder:

4 October 1939

Conrad Beckman
1923 Pond Avenue
St. Louis, Missouri

My Dear Conrad:

I know that these have been gloomy days in St. Louis, especially with the departures of Kessler and

Metting over the summer. As you know, we have suffered here as well.

But my hopes are climbing again! Yes, after those dismal days of summer, when dark forces were choking our dreams, a new era is dawning at last!

I speak of my unforgettable evening with Wilhelm Kunze. I first met the gentleman two summers ago in Philadelphia, when he was chief of their group. But last night I was so aroused by his speech that I walked the city streets until three in the morning with his words ringing in my head:

"Jewish Reds and their Gentile stooges even have their own organization: the American Civil Liberties Union, whose Jewish lawyers get Communists out of jail whenever patriots try to convict them. And never ignore the Negroes. I tell you that the Jewish Reds plan to use these loathsome beasts as the shock troops of the revolution.

"But the day of reckoning will soon be here. The Jews are grabbing control of everything they can lay their sticky hands on. When that happened in Germany, the people finally rose up in resentment, and that great day will come here as well. It is inevitable. And when it arrives we must be prepared to fight for the right kind of government. We must win the masses, the good people to our side. When we get through with the Jews in America, they will think the treatment they received in Germany was nothing. Judaistic gore will soon flow in the streets of Memphis."

When Kunze finished, we jumped to our feet, cheered and applauded for twenty minutes. Kunze later told me that he will be in St. Louis on 12 October to speak at your Liederkranz Club. You must go hear him, Conrad. While no one can ever replace Kuhn in my heart, I assure you that Mr. Kunze is a man of noble vision. I implore you, Conrad: Go hear the man. Your soul will be invigorated.

Yours faithfully,
Max Kruppa

"My God," my mother whispered.

I walked back to my chair and took a seat facing her across the table, my thoughts roiling.

She was studying the text. "How old was Beckman in 1939?"

"Twenty," I said. "He was a plumber's apprentice and worked for his uncle Max. Beckman's Plumbing. When his uncle died in 1944, he took over the business and changed the name to Beckman Engineering."

She gave me a determined look. "I have time tomorrow. I'm going to the library." She gestured toward the translation. "I want to look some things up." She frowned at the text. "Kuhn," she mumbled.

"Do you know who that could be?"

She stared at me. "I know one Kuhn. Fritz Kuhn."

"Who was he?"

Her eyes narrowed. "He used to work at the Ford Motor Company. Before World War II he was the head of an organization known as Friends of the New Germany."

"I never heard of them."

She nodded. "They changed their name in 1936."

"To what?"

"To the German-American Bund."

"Oh," I said quietly.

My mother knew about these things. Although she was too young to have any memories of American Nazi activities back then, she had good reason to learn about them: most of her family had perished in the Holocaust. She'd read widely on the subject and on anti-Semitism. For the past two years she'd served as a docent at the St. Louis Holocaust Museum and Learning Center, where she gave tours to visiting school groups.

I reached for the translation of Kruppa's letter and examined it again. "You think that's the Kuhn he's referring to?"

"Maybe." My mother tugged at her ear solemnly. "That's why I want to go to the library."

"There were four more letters in German," I said, pensively.

"To Beckman?"

I shook my head. "To others. One is to Otto Koll. He's the founder of one of the other companies."

"You need to get them translated."

I nodded. "I know."

It had stopped snowing by the time I reached home. I took Ozzie for a long walk in the fresh snow as I mulled over the Kruppa letter. While a youthful flirtation with Nazism was not necessarily ruinous—after all, history was filled with great figures who'd overcome ugly episodes in their youth—it was still an enormously embarrassing document for Conrad Beckman. Its disclosure could inflict far more damage to his standing in the community than an allegation that his company had been involved in an illegal bid-rigging scheme. Kruppa's letter, after all, was personal, and Conrad Beckman had reached a stage in his life where his personal reputation was his most treasured asset. He had also reached a stage in his life where he knew that the years remaining might not be sufficient to erase such a blemish. All of which suggested an alternative explanation for Stanley Roth's sudden settlement offer.

Then again, I cautioned myself, the document in question was a 1939 letter written by someone else. It was not Conrad Beckman who had been so aroused by denunciations of Jews and promises of "Judaistic gore" that he walked the city streets "until three in the morning" with those inspirational words ringing in his head—an important distinction, since it meant that Beckman could have an innocent explanation, namely, that Kruppa's letter was merely an unsuccessful attempt to recruit Beckman. It was certainly an explanation that Max Kruppa—now dead—could not refute. Moreover, I conceded, it was an explanation that just might have the additional virtue of being true.

CHAPTER 14

I shmael called me."

"Not a bad opening," Benny said. "Needs work, but not bad."

I gave him a curious look. "What?"

"Never mind," he said with a grin. "Ishmael, eh? So what's on the old boy's mind?"

I waggled my eyebrows mischievously. "Otto Koll."

Benny smiled. "Ah, yes. And what, pray tell, is on Otto Koll's mind? Perhaps his upcoming deposition?"

I nodded and reached for my iced tea. It was close to one in the afternoon, and we were having a quick lunch at the Station Grille in St. Louis Union Station, which just happens to be my favorite building in the city. When it opened a century ago, Union Station was the nation's grand railway terminal, and it soon became the busiest train station in the world. During the glory days of rail travel you could stroll along the midway and watch porters tote luggage onto trains whose names have passed into railroad legend: the Katy Flyer, the Wabash Cannonball, the Twentieth Century Limited, the Lone Star. Indeed, it was from the back of one such train on Track 32 on election night, 1948, that a beaming Harry Truman held up the front page of the *Chicago Tribune* with that infamous headline, DEWEY DEFEATS TRUMAN.

But that was decades ago. By the time the very last train departed on a stormy Halloween night in 1978, the splendor of Union Station had long since faded. Rainwater cascaded through holes in the rusted roof of the train shed, once a marvel of Victorian engineering with huge sweeping arches and butterfly trusses. But, to quote native son Yogi Berra, never say never. Union Station had been reborn—a jewel of urban restoration, its sweeping arches refurbished, its train shed reglassed and reroofed, its midway bustling again with specialty shops and eateries and bars and colorful handcarts, its travelers of yesteryear replaced by tourists and shoppers.

The rich heritage of the place seems almost palpable, even in the restaurant we were in. Sixty years ago, it was the home of the renowned Fred Harvey eatery, whose waitresses became household names with the 1946 release of MGM's *The Harvey Girls* starring Judy Garland. Reopened in the 1980s as the Station Grille, it's been restored to its earlier charm, with oak ceiling beams and plaster panels frescoed in tapestry effects. Add to that the stiff white tablecloths, heavy silverware, sparkling glasses, fresh flowers, and good light, and the effect is enchanting, as if you'd stumbled through a time warp into a graceful never-never-land where you might find a young Audrey Hepburn at the next table sipping champagne and laughing gaily with Cary Grant.

It was, in short, the last place you'd expect to find Benny Goldberg chomping down on a thick cheeseburger with extra grilled onions and pickles. Nevertheless, it was the perfect location for us to today. I'd just finished meeting a client at her office around the corner, and Benny had a presentation downtown after lunch.

Almost two weeks had elapsed since I'd received the English translation of Max Kruppa's 1939 letter to Conrad Beckman. I'd been spending a good portion of that time fighting the motions to quash that Roth & Bowles had filed in Chicago, Springfield, Gary, Indianapolis, and Memphis, while trying to interview prospective witnesses. My mother had been busy, too. She'd confirmed her initial suspicion that the Kuhn referred to in Kruppa's letter—"While no one can ever replace Kuhn in my heart"—was Fritz Kuhn of the German-American Bund. Her research showed that Kuhn had served as head of the Bund from 1935 until he resigned in the summer of 1939 under accusations of stealing Bund funds—accusations that quickly blossomed into an embezzlement conviction and a four-year prison term. In the late summer or early fall of 1939, the Bund named a new national führer, G. Wilhelm Kunze, who had started as head of the Philadelphia local. Kruppa's letter to Beckman, dated October 4, 1939, describes his "unforgettable evening with Wilhelm Kunze," whom Kruppa first met "two summers ago in Philadelphia, when he was chief of their group."

Kruppa's letter to Beckman opened with words of consolation for the gloom in St. Louis, "especially with the departures of Kessler and Metting over the summer." Working backward in old microfilm from the date of Kruppa's letter, my mother found an article in the July 23, 1939, issue of the *St. Louis Post-Dispatch* headlined:

10 ST. LOUIS BUND LEADERS
HAVE GONE TO GERMANY

The news report opened:

> At least 10 members, including most of the onetime officers of the St. Louis division of the Amerika-Deutscher Volksbund, the American Nazi group, have gone back to Germany within the past year, and more Bund followers are preparing to go. . . .

Kessler and Metting appeared in the fourth paragraph:

> Recent departures include Albert Mueller and Anton Kessler, former leaders of the St. Louis division, and Ernst Metting, first leader of the group when it was still known as the Friends of the New Germany. . . .

According to an unidentified source quoted in the article, "The departures have left the St. Louis Bund without any leader. They have no officers and few meetings."

There were still open items in Kruppa's letter. For example, he mentioned Kunze's upcoming speech in St. Louis at the Liederkranz Club. My mother found no report of any such speech in the issues of the *Post-Dispatch* and the *Globe-Democrat* for that period.

Nevertheless, her research efforts had certainly pushed Conrad Beckman a few important steps closer to the American Nazi movement in the late 1930s. Kruppa's letter, read in light of what my mother had turned up, sounded like a communication between Bund members. And that, oddly enough, might be relevant to my case. My mother's research had planted the kernel of a theory: the possibility of a German-American Bund connection between these two young contractors, one in St. Louis and one in Memphis—a connection that perhaps led to other important connections in business ventures. Perhaps the trust and camaraderie they developed back then enabled them to join forces years later to implement a bid-rigging scheme. After all, an antitrust conspiracy was another sort of relationship that requires a high level of trust and camaraderie among the participants. And maybe, just maybe, Otto Koll had also shared a youthful flirtation with the American Nazi movement.

I had now received translations of the other four letters written in German by Max Kruppa. Three were directed to officials of the German-American Bund, and revealed Kruppa as an active and enthusiastic American Nazi. But the fourth was to Otto Koll. Although it was far more circumspect than the one he sent to Conrad Beckman two years earlier—no proper names, no quotations from speeches, no references to the Bund—Kruppa signed off with a "Heil Hitler." Presumably, one did not close a letter that way in the United States in 1941 unless the author believed that the addressee was a kindred soul.

"So tell me about Ishmael," Benny said. "Is Abbott and Windsor going to represent Koll at his deposition?"

I nodded. "Yep."

Ishmael was Ishmael Richardson, chairman of Abbott & Windsor, where Benny and I had started as young associates.

Although I eventually left to open my own practice, the firm had retained me on a few occasions to handle sensitive matters that they were unable to handle for one reason or another. My contact on each of those matters had been Ishmael Richardson, and over the years we had developed about as nice a rapport as possible between a silver-haired charter member of the Chicago power elite and a Jewish female solo practitioner young enough to have gone to college with his granddaughter.

"And?" Benny asked.

"Ishmael didn't come right out and say, but I got the sense that they're reluctant to let Koll testify."

"Oh?" Benny snorted. "Like they have a choice? Did you remind Ishmael that you already defeated their motion to quash?"

"Benny," I said patiently, "you're missing the point. Just because he shows up for his deposition doesn't mean he has to testify."

After a moment, Benny's frown changed to a smile. "Ah, are we talkin' Amendment Number Five?"

I nodded.

"Goddamn," Benny said with a cackle. "They're thinking about having Otto take the fifth? I love it." Benny rubbed his hands together. "Oh, baby, I call dibs on Otto's deposition. This could break the case wide open."

I smiled. "It could."

That was because Ruth's case was a civil action. In a criminal case, the defendant's assertion of his Fifth Amendment privilege cannot be used against him, and the jury is not permitted to draw a negative inference from his refusal to answer a question. But that rule doesn't apply in civil actions. Here, if Otto Koll refused on Fifth Amendment grounds to say whether he was involved in an illegal bid-rigging conspiracy with Beckman Engineering, his refusal to answer the question *could* be used against him *and* against his alleged co-conspirators, and the jury would be permitted to draw any negative inference it saw fit.

"Oh, baby," Benny said, grinning savagely, "I can't wait to go to Chicago. I'm going to make that Nazi bastard shit bricks."

That afternoon I took a four-hour journey back to the 1930s and the netherworld of the St. Louis Nazi movement. It was a journey made possible by the late Abram Levine, the charismatic head rabbi of Temple Shalom from 1929 until his retirement in 1954. Rabbi Levine had also served as executive director of the St. Louis Jewish Defense Alliance (JDA) from its founding in 1931 until its merger into the St. Louis chapter of the Anti-Defamation League in 1949. The JDA's principal activity had been the gathering of intelligence on various organizations viewed as a potential threat to the Jews of St. Louis, and thus its principal focus during the years before World War II was the American Nazi movement.

Rabbi Levine had planned to spend his retirement years writing both his memoirs and a major history of American Jewish life in the heartland during the years between World War I and the Korean War. Over his professional career he had amassed a substantial collection of personal papers and documentary records that were to serve as his source materials. Sadly, a heart attack killed Levine less than a year after he left the pulpit. All that remained of his ambitious literary plans were eleven uncatalogued boxes of papers. The papers had resided in the corner of a musty storage room in the basement of Temple Shalom's dignified old quarters in the University City Loop until 1979, when the synagogue moved west to its fancy new digs off Clayton Road, the one with the wrought-iron bema that looks like a stage set from *Mad Max Beyond Thunderdome*.

After the move, the synagogue's new librarian placed the eleven boxes in an archive room in the back of the library and issued an open invitation to scholars and Judaica librarians to come review the treasure trove. Alas, the personal papers of one reform rabbi from the Midwest, to paraphrase Bogart in *Casablanca*, didn't amount to a hill of beans in the modern historian's world. But they did merit an entry in the St. Louis Holocaust Museum's directory of resource materials on the German-American Bund, and that's how my mother discovered their existence.

Unfortunately, the contents of those eleven boxes were in complete disarray. For example, sandwiched between a sheaf of Rabbi Levine's sermons from 1947–48 and the minutes of a March 8, 1951, meeting of the St. Louis Rabbinical Council was an undercover report on the celebration of Hitler's birthday on April 20, 1937, at the St. Louis Deutsche Haus (German House) attended by German consul Reinhold Freytag.

On the wall behind us in the archive room was a framed photographic portrait of Rabbi Levine, and he seemed no more pleased by the disarray than we were. He was glaring into the camera from behind his enormous desk, a pipe clenched between his teeth, his scowl amplified by the dark, bushy eyebrows that joined over a tomahawk nose. Under his baleful eye, my mother and I spent hours sorting and reorganizing and reading the materials.

Gradually, the outlines of the story began to emerge, starting with the founding of the Hitler Club in March 1933 by a Dr. R. L. Groellefeld. Although the Hitler Club was soon to merge into the Friends of the New Germany (Freunde des Neuen Deutschland), it was around long enough to host a visit from ex-prince Louis Ferdinand of Hehenzollern, son of the former crown prince of Prussia, who delivered a speech to the members exhorting them "to atone for their sins in forgetting the fatherland in World War I by rendering every aid possible to our exalted führer and the New Germany."

This all according to the undercover report filed by someone identified by the initials H.A.R. H.A.R appeared repeatedly throughout the materials, along with three others: M.M.N., L.A.B., and B.P.P.

As we sorted through the papers, we could see the American Nazi movement grow and expand like some insidious fungus in an old horror flick. The Hitler Club metamorphosed

into the Friends of the New Germany, which in turn metamorphosed into the German-American Bund. At the 1938
observance of Hitler's birthday, Anton Kessler, *Sturmtruppen-
führer* of the local group, addressed a crowd of celebrants at
the German House. The men, dressed alike in black pants,
black boots, brown shirts, black ties, and Sam Browne belts,
cheered Kessler's words (recorded, once again, by H.A.R.):

> Why shouldn't the Gentile majority of St. Louis take
> arms against Jewish Anti-American subversions? This
> country is on the eve of a Communist revolution. The
> Stars and Stripes will be safe only so long as they hang
> between the Black-White-Red and the Swastika flag.

The Bund was hardly the only manifestation of Nazi
fervor in the St. Louis area during the late 1930s. There was
the German-American Commercial League (Deutsch-
Amerikanische Berufsgemeinschaft), a branch of the Foreign
Division of the Hitler Labor Front, which organized boycotts
of Jewish businesses throughout metropolitan St. Louis. There
was the Hitler Youth Camp, which opened on July 4, 1938,
on Funk's Farm near Stanton, Missouri, and drilled the children in Nazi marching formations while instructing them in
fascist propaganda. There was a group known as the Hitler
Youth Group and an agency called the Nazi Employment Service. And on and on.

My mother found an account of Kunze's speech at the
Liederkranz Club on October 12, 1939—the one Kruppa had
urged Conrad Beckman to attend. H.A.R.'s report read, in
pertinent part:

> Wilhelm Kunze, newly appointed national leader of the
> German-American Bund, spoke at the Liederkranz Club
> before a group of about 150 persons at a secret meeting
> at which the doors and windows were sealed. Men in SS
> uniforms moved through the crowd passing out pieces of
> anti-Semitic literature bearing the official stamp of the

German government. Kunze said that the Democratic
Party was a puppet of American Jewry, that Jews con-
trolled the newspapers and radio stations, had a strangle-
hold on industry and the CIO, that Roosevelt was under
Jewish domination, and that the recent sit-down strikes
were a Jewish idea. Kunze announced that it was time to
purify the American race. As the crowd cheered, he
promised that "Judaistic gore will soon flow in the streets
of St. Louis."

We found page after page of thumbnail profiles of St.
Louis Nazi activists during the late 1930s—a paperhanger, a
perfume salesman, a watchmaker, an electrical contractor, a
dentist, a sports editor, a mechanical engineer, a "naturopath,"
a waiter. Bit players of the Apocalypse, foot soldiers at Armageddon.

It was fascinating and it was creepy, but it wasn't quite
what I was hoping to find.

And then my mother found it.

"Oh, my God, Rachel," she said, looking up from the fifth
box. "Come here."

It was a typed undercover report by M.M.N. prepared in
July 1939 in which he described a sunny afternoon at a Bund-
sponsored family camp called the Deutsche-Horst (German
Nest), located near the Meramec River south of St. Louis. The
day's events opened at noon as fifty members of the Bund, all
dressed in storm-trooper uniforms, gathered at the two flag-
poles on the parade ground in front of the clubhouse. An
unidentified commander supervised the raising of an American
flag and a Nazi flag. The ceremony ended with the storm-
troopers lifting their right arms in a stiff-armed salute, shouting three "Heil Hitlers," and goose-stepping in double file off
the parade grounds to the cheers and applause of approxi-
mately one hundred spectators, mostly mothers and fathers
and children. As the storm troopers left to change out of their
uniforms and rejoin the group, the spectators drifted off in
groups for the afternoon's recreation. For much of the re-

mainder of the day, according to M.M.N., the camp "had the appearance of many other Meramec River clubhouses."

The words that caught my mother's eye were on the last page of the report:

The operations of the Deutsche-Horst family camp are under the auspices of Otto Groshong, a former druggist who now works during the week at the German House. He curses Roosevelt and calls him a Jew. Working as counselors under Groshong's direction are three young men: Rudolphe Schober, Herman Warnholtz, and Conrad Beckman. All three were in uniform at the flag-raising ceremony at the beginning of the day and at the pledge later that afternoon. Schober, age 19, loads trucks at the Lemp Brewery. Warnholtz, 20, is a custodian at a St. Louis public elementary school and an active member of the storm troopers. He has a short temper and has been arrested three times on assault charges. Beckman, age 18, is a plumber's apprentice in his uncle's business. For one week every June since he was 15, Beckman has worked as a boxing instructor at the Hitler Youth Camp.

We continued sorting through the boxes, and as we searched, we drew whatever conclusions one could draw from Rabbi Levine's disjointed and incomplete records of the era. It appeared that the Bund's power in St. Louis began to fade after 1939; by the end of 1941, it was all but irrelevant. But part of the decline was deceptive. As law enforcement shone their spotlights on the Bund, its members scurried into darker corners. Some of the splinter groups appeared to be close to mainstream organizations, while others were far more malignant. Perhaps the most sinister of the post-Bund organizations, according to a January 9, 1942, letter to Rabbi Levine from the Chicago offices of the Anti-Defamation League, was a secret outfit called the American SS-Death's Head Formation (Amerikanische SS-Totenkopfverbände). This band of thugs got its name from the German storm-trooper division of the same name that was in charge of the Nazi concentration camps. Like their counterparts in Germany, members of the American Death's Head Formation wore a skull-and-bones insignia on their black storm-trooper tunics. According to the letter from the Anti-Defamation League, the Death's Head Formation was based in the Midwest with chapters in several cities, and "a somewhat reliable source in Springfield claims that the leaders of the local unit are Edgar Muller and Fritz Voerster."

I stared at those names, thinking again of Gloria Muller and her vague allusion to her ex-husband's dark past. I handed it to my mother.

"Here," I said to my mother. "Look at this."

She looked up from the document she was reading and took the letter from me. She read it with a frown and nodded. On the table in front of her was a folder of materials she had removed from the last box. She lifted the top sheet from her folder. "Read this."

It was a carbon copy of a half-page typed report from H.A.R. dated February 27, 1942:

Efforts to obtain substantive information about the operations of the SS-Death's Head Formation unit in St. Louis have been unsuccessful to date. Given the small size of the unit, the prospect of finding a reliable informer is low and the likelihood of infiltration is nil. The current fuhrer (leader) of the unit is rumored to be Herman Warnholtz. According to a source who was at Sauters Roadhouse on Telegraph Road late one night after Warnholtz and a man named Haupman had consumed several pitchers of beer, Warnholtz bragged that his storm troopers are prepared, if necessary, to engage in acts of violence to further the cause of Nazism in America.

The remainder of that last box contained more than a dozen drafts of Levine's proposal for an updated Passover Haggadah (and letters of rejection from various publishing concerns) and copies of his correspondence with various national Jewish organizations during the late 1940s and early 1950s on a variety of topics wholly unrelated to the American Nazi movement. There was no further mention of Conrad Beckman, the Death's Head Formation, or anything having to with the American Nazi movement in the 1930s and 1940s.

As I walked to my car in Temple Shalom's parking lot, I thought of the creepy bonds between my investigation and Jonathan's. I was trying to unravel an American Nazi connection dating back fifty years while Jonathan was trying to unravel a different Nazi connection right here in the present. I let the car engine idle in the cold weather as I recalled the hateful words of G. Wilhelm Kunze's speech that Kruppa quoted in his letter to Beckman and the hateful words of Bishop Robb's sermon from that Sunday morning several weeks ago.

My mother's family had died in the Holocaust. "Never Again" was the motto of those who insisted that we never forget the lessons of that terrible moment in history. Yet here we were, more than a half century later, and the grand march of progress had delivered up a modern version of the same old monsters. What a dismal parallel. Were we just Time's captives, running nowhere forever on ancient treadmills?

CHAPTER 15

My secretary was able to match initials with names through records at the Anti-Defamation League, which had merged with the Jewish Defense Alliance in 1949. All four men had been volunteers, doing their investigative work at night and on weekends. Two of them—Myron M. Newman (M.M.N.) and Lester A. Bronkowski (L. A. B.)—had been dead for close to twenty years. A third, Bernard P. Proskower (B.P.P.), was alive but far beyond reach; according to a nurse at the Jewish Center for the Aged, he was in the final stage of Alzheimer's disease and spent his days curled in a ball.

But H.A.R. was alive and well. Harold A. Roth was now eighty-nine years old, a widower who lived alone in a one-bedroom apartment on the third floor of an older building on Waterman Avenue in the Central West End. Back in the 1930s, according to the materials Jacki obtained on him, Harold Roth had been a plant manager in a metal-casting factory in South St. Louis. He first learned of the American Nazi movement from leaflets brought into the plant by some of his workers. Although not a religious Jew, he was a proud and defiant one. On the schoolyards of his youth, he had fought the neighborhood bullies who taunted the smaller Jewish kids. Accordingly, he was outraged by the Bund literature. Eager to join the fight against Nazism, he went down to the offices of the Jewish Defense Alliance after work that day to enlist as a volunteer.

I pulled my car into a space in front of his apartment building on Monday morning. The trial against Beckman Engineering started in one week. My five student volunteers were hard at work at my office this morning, and Benny was up in

Chicago taking the deposition of Otto Koll. Although my to-do list of trial preparation tasks seemed to keep growing, I had to see Harold Roth. It was one loop I felt compelled to close.

I found his name on the lobby mailbox for apartment 3C and rang his bell to let him know I'd arrived. The inner lobby door, once a security door through which guests were buzzed, no longer served that function. The entire doorknob was missing—there was a clean round hole where it had been—and the door pushed open at the touch. The steam was hissing and clanging in the stairwell radiators as I walked upstairs. The gray carpet tread was old and frayed, and the smells from last night's dinners—the roasted meats, the fried onions, the cooked garlic—still hung in the air. It had snowed again yesterday, and there were snow boots, some still wet, in front of the four doors on each landing.

The door to apartment 3C opened as I reached the landing. Holding it open was an elderly man with fierce dark eyes magnified behind heavy black horn-rims. His upper torso curved forward, which made him seem to peer up at me even though we stood at eye level to one another. He was wearing off-brand tennis shoes, black trousers belted high on his waist, and a freshly pressed red-and-gray-plaid flannel shirt buttoned to the collar, which seemed about three sizes larger than his neck. His bald head was covered with age spots.

"Miss Gold?" he said in a thin, reedy voice. He was leaning on a wooden cane. There was a hearing aid in each pendulous ear, and his head shook with a slight palsy.

I introduced myself. He nodded, unsmiling, and gestured me in, turning to lead the way down the short hallway. Although he took small steps and leaned on his cane, his physical frailties were offset by an aura of sheer resolve.

The living room was small and sparsely furnished with odds and ends that looked as if they once stood in the showroom window of a 1950s discount house. He moved toward an easy chair covered with a brown corduroy fabric. At the side of the chair was a TV tray. Resting on the tray were an empty mug with an old tea bag that stained the bottom brown and a well-used set of red bicycle playing cards dealt in an unfinished game of solitaire. He settled into the easy chair and pointed me toward a sagging grayish couch against the side wall.

I took my seat, placed my purse and briefcase on the floor beneath the coffee table, and gave him my friendliest smile. "Thank you for meeting with me, Mr. Roth."

He had the cane resting between his knees, with his hands crossed on top of the cane handle. He was watching me with a distinctly guarded expression. Yesterday, I'd had to practically beg him on the phone before he reluctantly agreed to see me. He frowned. "Where'd you find my reports?"

I explained.

He listened carefully. "Levine, eh? Good man. Even if he was a rabbi. Don't like rabbis." His voice grew louder. "Never did. Don't trust 'em." He snorted. "Steal your eyes right out of your head if you gave 'em a chance." He glared at me. "Haven't been in a damn synagogue since the day I married Mrs. Roth. Fifty-seven years ago. Never gone back." He thrust his chin forward. "Never will."

I nodded silently.

"Don't get it," he said with a frown.

"Pardon?"

He grunted. "You. Your interest in this." He shook his head. "Ancient history. What do you care?"

I gave him a short description of the lawsuit and how I thought Conrad Beckman's dark past might have some relevance to at least the origins of the bid-rigging conspiracy, especially his relationship with Max Kruppa in Memphis.

"Kruppa," he mused, squinting as he tried to remember. "Rings a bell." He paused, eyeing me dubiously. "What else?"

I gave him a puzzled look. "I'm sorry, Mr. Roth, I'm not following you."

He made a dismissive gesture. "That Bund stuff—ancient history. Has to be more than that."

I thought it over. "Well, my friend—a boyfriend, actually—has been investigating one of the modern Nazi groups. Their headquarters are here in St. Louis. They're called Spider." I paused for a moment, and then shrugged. "I guess that's not a logical reason for me to be here, but it makes me want to know more about what happened then."

"Spider?" he repeated.

I nodded.

"Jesus Christ," he said, angry. "Those bastards again."

"Again?"

He shook his head in disgust. "Nazi bastards." He pronounced "Nazi" to rhyme with "snazzy."

"In addition," I said slowly, hesitantly, "there's another reason. Probably the most important reason." I reached for my purse and opened my wallet to the photograph of my mother. I walked over to him. "Here," I said. "This is my mother."

He held the photograph close to his face and squinted at it. He looked up at me.

"When the Nazis came to power," I said quietly, "she was a little girl in Lithuania. She was lucky. She lived. So did her sister and so did her mother—my grandmother Rachel. They escaped. But her father—my grandfather—didn't. Her uncles and aunts didn't. Her grandparents didn't. They all died in the concentration camps. The Nazis murdered them."

He handed me the wallet. I walked over to the couch, surprised by the rush of emotions, trying to keep them in check. I took a deep breath, searching for the words. He was leaning forward on his cane, waiting.

I shook my head helplessly. "I'm not sure what the connection is, Mr. Roth, but I know that I have to do this, to see it through. When I started this lawsuit, I had no idea that there was this other stuff, but now I do. I'm not sure what's hidden back there, but I have to find out. I have to try to close the loop." I gave him a sad smile. "I'm not kidding myself, Mr. Roth. Believe me, this is no crusade. I know that what I discover isn't going to bring my mother's family back. But still . . ." I paused, wiping a tear from my cheek. "I feel that I owe it to them."

He studied me. I met his gaze, blinking.

Finally, he grunted. "Okay."

"Thank you, Mr. Roth."

"Call me Harold, young lady."

I smiled and sniffled. "Okay, Harold." I paused to open my briefcase. "I've read all of your reports. Or at least I think I did. I read the ones on the Bund and the ones on the other groups."

"Been a long time. Don't know how much I can recall."

"I can help," I said, pulling out a folder.

I went over his various reports. His mind was sharp and his memory excellent. Before I could finish a description of a report he had written more than fifty years ago, he would have already recalled most of the key facts in that report and a subsequent one on the same topic. When I reached the last one—his half-page report on the Death's Head Formation— I paused to pull a photocopy of it out of my briefcase.

"This is the last one in Rabbi Levine's archives," I told him as I stood up and came over to his chair, "and the only one on this organization."

He took the report from me and read it slowly, holding it close to his face. I returned to the couch and waited. When he finished, he looked up, his lips pursed solemnly.

"Did you write any others on that group?" I asked.

He shook his head gravely.

"Any other reports at all?"

He scowled as he considered the question. "Not a report," he finally said.

I waited.

"Kept a journal," he said. "On those people. Others, too. All those Nazi bastards."

"What kind of journal?" I asked carefully.

He gave me a proud look. "What I saw. What I learned."

"Did that include the Death's Head Formation?"

"You bet," he said fiercely.

"Do you still have it?"

He leaned back and eyed me warily. "Might."

I caught myself, realizing that I was moving far too fast for him. According to what Jacki had been able to glean from the Anti-Defamation League records, his wife had died of lung cancer twenty-one years ago. Their only son had died in Vietnam in 1967. Harold Roth had been living alone for many, many years. And now, out of the blue, a young woman arrives eager to pry into a chapter of his life that had been closed for more than half a century.

I gave him a sheepish smile. "I'm sorry, Mr. Roth. I guess it's because I have this trial coming up and I'm so excited to have found a person who might be able to shed a little light on Conrad Beckman's past. Every time I think I might be on to something important, it seems like five lawyers from his firm pop up to block me." I sighed and shook my head. "Some people put themselves to sleep at night counting sheep. Well, I do it by counting lawyers from Roth and Bowles."

"Roth and Bowles?" he said sharply. "That's his lawyers?"

"Technically, they represent his company. Why, do you know of them?"

He nodded darkly. "Stanley Roth."

"Really?" I was intrigued. "How?"

"Bastard's my nephew. My brother's son. Beckman's lawyer? Jesus Christ." He shook his head. "Poor brother. Spinning in his grave."

I was as surprised as he, but the unexpected link seemed to lessen his distrust of me. I tried to work him gradually back around to the journal. We talked some about his brother and the rest of his family and some about how he used to do his surveillance of the Bund in the early days. I told him about Max Kruppa's letter in German to Conrad Beckman.

"Memphis, eh?" He leaned forward and rested his chin on the top of his cane. "Rings a bell. What business was Kruppa in?"

"Back then? Construction, I think. Maybe plumbing. The

company grew into a pretty big contractor over the years."

"Successful?"

I nodded. "Definitely."

"Your lawsuit." He paused, frowning in thought. "You think there's a connection between that Memphis company and Beckman's company?"

"Definitely."

"Run that by me again."

I gave him a brief outline of the bid-rigging allegations.

He nodded as he listened. When I finished, he nodded his head slowly. "Any other connections?"

"Not really. Well, actually, they did do a joint venture outside of the United States back in the 1950s. A water treatment plant. It doesn't seem relevant to my case, but my expert witness tells me that the two companies had to have lost a lot of money on the project."

"Where was it?"

"Down in South America."

"Where?"

"A little resort town in the mountains. San something—I can't remember the name."

"San Carlos de Bariloche?"

I looked at him, stunned. "How did you know?"

"Memphis, eh?" he said, ignoring my question. "Had a unit down there."

"You mean the Bund?"

He snorted. "Later. Death's Head, and all the rest."

"All the rest of what?"

He scratched his neck as he stared at me.

I waited.

"Die Spinne."

I wasn't sure of what he said. "Spin?" I repeated.

"Spinne," he said. "S-P-I-N-N-E."

"Spinne? Die Spinne?"

He nodded.

"What is it?"

He studied me for a moment. "It's in my journal."

I paused, not wanting to force the issue. I gestured toward the photocopy of his last undercover report. "According to your source at that tavern," I said, "the leader of the Death's Head Formation was bragging that his storm troopers were willing to commit violence to further the cause." I paused and looked at him. "Did they?"

He crossed his arms over his chest stubbornly. "Don't need my journal for that."

"But where else would I look?"

"In the damn newspaper."

"But when? Which days?"

"When?" he said irritably. "Big celebration days."

I frowned. "Like July Fourth?"

He laughed. "Nazi days."

"But isn't that information already in your journal?"

He paused, sizing me up again. "Might be."

"Is your journal here? In the apartment?"

He chuckled. "Oh, no. Don't keep it on the premises." He paused, his eyes narrowing. "When I die, it's going to that Holocaust Museum in Washington. Got the whole thing laid out in my will." He sat back, pleased and defiant. "People are going to sit up and take notice." He nodded firmly. "You bet."

I paused. "Could I see it, Mr. Roth?"

He pursed his lips. "Maybe."

"Today?"

"No."

"Tomorrow?"

"Tomorrow?" he repeated.

"It's important to me, sir," I said. "I'll be happy to go with you to the safe-deposit box or wherever you keep it."

"I'm not saying where I keep it," he said testily. He studied me for a moment. "Eleven o'clock tomorrow. Give you an hour. No more. One hour and then out."

I smiled. "Fair enough, Harold. It's a deal."

He wagged a finger at me. "Eleven o'clock. Don't be late."

I saluted him. "Yes, sir."

He studied me for a moment, and then he showed me something I hadn't seen before. He showed me a smile. It was a lovely smile.

CHAPTER 16

I spent most of that afternoon in the chambers of Judge Catherine Wagner. The occasion was our final pretrial conference—a standard meeting of the attorneys and judge scheduled one week before trial. Typically, the final pretrial conference is an opportunity for the parties to resolve any remaining evidentiary disputes and for the judge to once again explore settlement possibilities. Kimberly Howard was there for the evidentiary disputes, and Stanley Roth was there for settlement discussions. I was there alone, with my client waiting in the courtroom alone.

The judge focused on the areas of contention first, but after two hours of wrangling, the key issues remained in dispute. Kimberly Howard objected to my plan to introduce evidence of the relationships among the various co-conspirators during the decades prior to the period covered by my lawsuit, and I objected to her motion to exclude all evidence of what she characterized as Conrad Beckman's "entirely irrelevant childhood curiosity in certain aspects of German nationalism." Although Judge Wagner was leaning toward granting Kimberly's motion, she agreed to defer her ruling until the trial began in order to give me an opportunity, outside the jury's presence, to try to demonstrate that Conrad Beckman's involvement in the American Nazi movement of the 1930s enabled him to forge an important link with at least some of his co-conspirators in what became the bid-rigging scheme.

"Time's running out, Counselor," she told me sternly, "but I'll give you until the first day of trial."

When Judge Wagner turned to settlement, Stanley Roth took over for the defendant. He gave a lengthy spiel on Beckman Engineering's innocence and then magnanimously announced that in the interest of saving the parties and the court the time and expense of a lengthy, acrimonious trial, his client was prepared to raise its settlement offer from $150,000 to $250,000, the payment to be characterized as an "enhancement" of Ruth's retirement package and paid in full following her dismissal of the *qui tam* claims with prejudice.

I conferred briefly out in the courtroom with Ruth Alpert and returned to chambers to decline the offer.

To say that Judge Wagner was unhappy with our response was an understatement. She sent the other side out of the room, gave me a blistering lecture on the risks of litigation, and demanded that my client and I come up with a counteroffer. I again conferred in the courtroom with Ruth and this time returned with a counteroffer: $10 million, to be treated as a settlement of the *qui tam* claim (under which 30 percent of the settlement would be paid to Ruth and the rest to the government). In the language of diplomacy, our proposal triggered a full and frank exchange of viewpoints followed by a consensus among those present that conditions were not yet sufficiently propitious to justify a continuation of negotiations.

But on the way down the hall toward the elevators, Stanley Roth asked me to join him for a moment in an empty jury room. Once inside, he turned to me and said, "Your settlement position is preposterous."

I shrugged. "I don't agree."

"Ten million dollars?" He snorted. "Come on, Rachel. What's your real number?"

"Two hundred and fifty thousand dollars?" I said with a smile. "Come on, Stanley. What's *your* real number?"

"That *is* a real number, Rachel. My God, that's an extraordinary amount of money for your client. And for you. What's your contingent fee deal?"

"None of your business."

"A third? Do the math. It's more than eighty grand in your pocket. Better yet, both of you get your money today.

Look at the alternative: the two of you can spend four grueling weeks in this courtroom and walk out of here with absolutely nothing."

I shrugged. "Stanley, you're a corporate lawyer. I'm a trial lawyer. Corporate lawyers earn their living resolving matters. Some things can't be resolved." I looked around the room. "That's why we have courthouses."

He shook his head, exasperated. "You're being completely irrational." He paused lowering his voice. "And this American Nazi nonsense is preposterous. Worse than preposterous—it's a totally unjustified diversionary tactic. Conrad Beckman is a great American citizen. Your allegations are nothing short of defamation. Do you truly believe he's the only man of stature to have made a mistake in his youth? His story is no different from dozens of great men. Look at Supreme Court Justice Harlan Black, a man who rose above his racist youth to become one of our country's greatest defenders of civil liberties. Look at St. Augustine. Look at Moses, for God's sake." He shook his head angrily. "Same with Conrad Beckman. So what if he had an adolescent flirtation with Nazism? Look at him now."

"It was more than a flirtation, Stanley."

He snorted. "Says who?"

I gazed at him calmly. "For starters, your uncle Harold."

That answer seemed to stagger him. "Harold Roth? What in God's name would Harold know?"

"Enough," I said.

He gave me a puzzled look, and then he shook his head in disbelief. "Oh, for God's sake. Not that old Jewish Defense Alliance nonsense? Harold's unreliable. He's a bitter old paranoid."

I shook my head. "I don't agree."

"Come on, Rachel," he said impatiently. "This is a federal trial. You're going to need more than the ramblings of an old man. You're going to need real evidence."

He paced around the room, shaking his head as he did. He stopped in front of me. "Look at me, Rachel." He patted his chest. "I'm a Jew. Just like you. I understand what it means to be a Jew. I understand that the Nazis tried to exterminate us, to wipe us off the face of the earth. Do you honestly believe that I would represent a man that I thought was once *seriously* involved in the American Nazi movement? It's ludicrous. It's unthinkable."

I shrugged. "Then you may be in for a surprise, Stanley. That's all I can say."

He nostrils flared in anger. He straightened up and pointed a finger at me. "And you may be in for a surprise yourself, young lady, if you start throwing around baseless allegations in court."

I stared at him. "Is that supposed to be a threat?"

He stared right back. "I don't make threats."

I tried to keep my voice calm. "And I don't throw around baseless allegations."

After a moment he stepped back and took a deep breath, trying to compose himself. "I apologize, Rachel. I didn't ask you in here to pick a fight. Look, talk to your client. Please. Beckman Engineering is offering a lot of money. A quarter of a million dollars, Rachel. That's far more than she could ever have hoped to win on that age discrimination case." He paused. "I might even be able to squeeze another fifty grand out of the company if that's what it'll take to get the deal done. Talk to her, Rachel. Please."

I walked out without responding. I found Ruth seated in the courtroom with her knitting on her lap. "Well?" she asked.

I gave her a wink. "They're starting to worry."

"How are you feeling?" Jonathan asked, studying me with concern.

"Okay, I guess." I sighed. "I need someone to clone me. Trial starts next Monday and I have too much to do."

It was eight-thirty that night and I was sitting in Jonathan's breakfast room. I took of sip of my second cup of tea with honey and lemon. I'd come by for dinner. Leah and Sarah were upstairs getting ready for sleep; the housekeeper had just finished the dishes. I glanced at my watch. I had to leave for the airport in about thirty minutes to pick up Benny, who was coming back from Chicago after taking the deposition of Otto Koll.

It had started snowing again. Out the window I could see the wispy flakes floating by. I thought for a moment of Ozzie. I'd put him in the backyard after dinner. He'd be okay. It wasn't supposed to snow hard, and if it did he could find shelter on the back porch. I reached for another piece of homemade *rugalach*, a yummy Jewish cookie that Jonathan baked on Sundays with his daughters.

I leaned back in my chair. The breakfast room was a circular nook that protruded from the edge of the house with windows on all sides. Jonathan had left the light off so that the room was only dimly lit from the kitchen. The shades were open. With the snow gently falling all around us, it seemed that we were all alone in a snug igloo in the middle of a fairyland.

"I love this room," I said.

We sat in silence. It was a cozy silence. After a while, I noticed that he was staring at me. I gave him a wink.

He smiled. "What?"

"Distract me, handsome. Tell me about Spider. How goes it with those bank subpoenas?"

"Slow."

"What now?"

"We've traced the Spider funds through a series of bank accounts all the way back to 1955, but that's where the trail ends."

"Why?"

"From 1955 until 1964, the funds were at Mercantile Bank. That account was opened on May 23, 1955, with a deposit of nine hundred fifty thousand dollars. I've seen the microfilm of the check. It was drawn from an account at the Gravois State Bank and Trust."

"Where's that?"

"It used to be on the south side, down by Bevo Mill."

"Used to be?"

He nodded. "It went under in 1962. We've traced the bank's records to a microfilm storage facility in a Utah salt mine."

"You're kidding."

"No. Actually, lots of old Utah salt mines have been converted into storage facilities. Anyway, the only records on microfilm for that bank were its loan accounts and certain types of trust accounts." He shook his head in frustration. "There are no records on this account. We don't know who opened it or where the money came from."

"Maybe that sleazy lawyer can tell you. What's his name?"

"Paulie Metzger. We'll find out on Wednesday."

"Is that when he goes before the grand jury?"

Jonathan nodded. "Grand jury in the morning, and if that doesn't pan out, me alone after lunch."

I giggled. "Someone better tell Paulie to eat a light lunch. Oh, wait," I said, suddenly remembering. "That's going to be in Jefferson City, right?"

He nodded. "Why?"

"When are you going?"

"Tomorrow afternoon."

I mulled it over. "I've got to go down there, too."

"What for?"

I explained. Two months ago I'd served written requests for disclosure on various state and federal agencies seeking to find out whether any of them had ever investigated Beckman Engineering for business misconduct. It was a total fishing expedition, a shot in the dark, but two weeks ago I'd received a response from the Missouri Trade Commission: in 1978 they'd conducted an investigation of Beckman Engineering regarding "certain averments of antitrust infractions." I called the commission's general counsel the day I received their response. Although he was reluctant to disclose the results of an investigation that had been closed for almost two decades, he finally agreed to let me, and only me, review the file, but only if I did so in his office in Jefferson City. He refused to tell me anything in advance about the contents of the file. I realized that the materials would most likely prove irrelevant to my lawsuit, but I couldn't be sure without examining them, and that fact kept pestering me as the trial date approached. With so much at stake in the case, I'd never forgive myself if it turned out that there was something valuable in a file that I'd neglected to examine.

"Would you like to drive down with me?"

I shook my head. "I can't take that much time. But maybe I'll take the train down Wednesday morning. I could bring along some pretrial stuff to do on the ride, review the commission's file when I get there, and hitch a ride home with you."

He smiled. "Sounds great."

As Jonathan was saying good-bye to me in the foyer, Leah came down the stairs in her pajamas. She was carrying a gift-wrapped package.

"Daddy," she said, holding out the package, "I forgot about this. It was in my backpack."

He kneeled down. "What is it, honey?"

She shrugged. "I don't know. It's for you."

Jonathan's smile faded. "From you?"

She shook her head. "A man gave it to me."

I tensed.

"Who was the man?" Jonathan asked in a calm, fatherly voice. He took the package from her.

She shrugged again. "I don't know. He came up to me on the playground at recess."

"At school, honey?"

She nodded. "He asked me if I would give you this present."

Jonathan held the package to his ear in an almost casual way. "Did he know who you were?"

She nodded. "He called me by my name."

I could feel my heart pounding.

"He called you Leah?" he asked, not a trace of alarm in his manner.

She nodded.

"Did he tell you his name?"

She shook her head. "He said you'd be able to figure it out when you opened your gift."

He gave her a reassuring smile. "What did he look like?"

She shrugged. "Big."

"Do you remember his hair?"

"No, he was wearing a ski cap."

"Do you remember anything else?"

She frowned for a second and then shook her head.

Jonathan kissed her on the forehead. "Thanks, honey. You can go up to bed now."

"Aren't you going to open your present, Daddy?"

"Later. Good night, Leah."

"Good night." She turned to me. "Good night, Rachel."

I forced a smile. "Good night, Leah." My voice was hoarse.

Jonathan waited until he heard her enter her bedroom upstairs.

"Oh, God," I said.

He felt around the edges of the package. "I think it's a book."

The state troopers responded quickly. Within twenty minutes there were two investigators in the kitchen, both wearing rubber gloves. I stood next to Jonathan and watched as they carefully opened the wrapping paper. They'd already dusted it for prints and had lifted several. No doubt all belonged to Leah.

I looked up at Jonathan. My heart went out to him. Although he appeared as implacable as ever, he had to be churning inside. I wanted to comfort him somehow, but I knew that reassuring words were just words now. His car had been vandalized, two thugs had tried to beat him up, and now this. I put my arm around his waist and gave him a squeeze, knowing even as I did it that his ordeal had moved beyond the hugs and kind words. There'd be bodyguards for his daughters, increased surveillance, and heightened security as his investigation pressed on.

I glanced over at the wall clock. I had to leave in a few minutes to pick Benny up from the airport. Although I wanted to remain here by Jonathan's side, I knew it was probably better that I go. The men in this house were in their criminal investigative mode, and there were more investigators on the way, including two FBI special agents. There was nothing helpful I could add, and soon I'd just be in their way.

"It's a book," one of the investigators said as he pulled back the wrapping paper.

The other said, "Dust it."

"Check inside first," Jonathan told them.

With the wrapping paper open but still shrouding the book, one of the investigators lifted the cover and flipped quickly through the pages.

The investigator turned to Jonathan and shook his head. "Nothing inside."

He closed the cover and removed the wrapping paper. I was staring at a hardbound copy of *Mein Kampf*.

N ot even once?" I asked when Benny finished his description.

We were parked in front of his house. On the drive from the airport I was still so freaked out that I had to tell him about Jonathan's "gift" and get my chance to vent before I'd listen to his account of Otto Koll's deposition.

Benny shook his head. "Nope."

"Rats," I said.

Benny shrugged. "Hey, it could have been worse."

I gave him a look. "It could have been better."

"It's really not bad, Rachel. As soon as I realized his dodge, I just started firing questions at him. He may not have taken the Fifth, but he did the next best thing. We're talking two solid hours of 'I don't remember.' To every goddamn question I asked him. 'Were you active in the German-

American Bund?' Answer: 'I don't remember.' 'Did you ever attend a meeting of the German-American Bund?' 'I don't remember.' 'Did you ever meet with representatives of Beckman Engineering to discuss an upcoming bid on a wastewater treatment plant for the federal government?' 'I don't remember.' Over and over and over." He paused to give me a wink. "I think the transcript is going to read better than you think," he said. "Trust me, kiddo. You read that bilge to the jury and it won't take them long to figure out that ol' Otto has suddenly contracted the most suspect case of amnesia in medical history."

"Maybe," I said, "but I'm going to need more than Otto Koll's amnesia to meet my burden of proof."

"Keep your fingers crossed," he said. "Sounds like Harold Roth's journal might blow them right out of the water."

I held up my fingers. They were crossed.

Benny grinned. "Hey, what's the worst that could happen? Even if his journal turns out to be the mad ravings of a lunatic, you can still use it to squeeze another hundred grand of settlement money out of them."

"Harold Roth is no lunatic, Benny," I said.

"Then all the better, eh?"

I gave him a weary smile. "What a day." I leaned over and planted a kiss on his cheek. "Thanks, Benny. You're the best."

"Ain't that the truth." He opened the car door. "Take care, gorgeous."

CHAPTER 17

The skies were blue, the sidewalks were shoveled clean, and the temperature was a sunny forty-two degrees. I'd been hunkered down in my office since seven-thirty that morning grinding through myriad trial preparation tasks. After three hours of that drudgery I needed some physical activity, so I decided to walk to Harold Roth's apartment. It was just twenty minutes by foot.

He'd told me not to be late, and that was fine with me. I was eager to see his journal and hear any other nuggets of information he was willing to share. If he was willing to talk, I was ready to listen. My briefcase contained a fresh legal pad, a portable dictation machine, and three blank cassette tapes. Depending on what he had heard and what he had observed back then, Harold Roth might be an important witness for me. I smiled at the irony of calling Stanley Roth's uncle to the witness stand.

On the way over to Harold's apartment I ran through my schedule for the rest of the day. Since I'd be in Jefferson City for most of tomorrow, my pretrial preparation schedule had become even more compressed. I'd allowed myself two hours for Harold—perhaps an overly optimistic estimation of how much time he'd be willing to give me. Then came Otto Koll. The court reporter in Chicago had promised to modem down a copy of his deposition transcript by one o'clock. I'd budgeted ninety minutes to read the transcript. Which reminded me: I made a mental note to ask Harold about Otto Koll; in fact, I'd ask him about the founders of each of the five companies. He seemed to have recognized Kruppa's name.

The rest of the afternoon was booked solid. Professor

Kenneth Chalmers, my economist, was arriving at three this afternoon so that we could go over his testimony. It would be our third session. Chalmers had performed a computer analysis of the relevant bids and awards over the past twenty years and compared them to a control group of federal contracts in another area. His conclusion: the most likely explanation for the pattern of bids and awards was an agreement among the six bidders. It was a complex mathematical analysis, and it was also a critical building block in my proof of the conspiracy. Thus the real challenge for us was to come up with a way to present it to a jury of laypeople.

Benny was also coming by this afternoon, and he was bringing along my law student volunteers to start getting the trial exhibits and related computer records in order. That would be at least a two-day project.

The walkway to Harold's apartment building was unevenly shoveled. I got increasingly irritated as I skirted icy patches on my way to the entrance. Surely Harold was not the only elderly tenant, and even if he was, the landlord owed him better treatment than that. I rang the bell to apartment 3C to let him know I was here, and then I pushed through the broken security door and headed up the stairs.

Unlike last time, he wasn't waiting for me when I reached his landing, but his door was slightly ajar. I knocked gently, holding the doorknob as I did so that the door wouldn't swing open. I listened for the sounds of his footsteps. When I didn't hear any, I knocked harder. No sound.

Remembering his hearing aids, I opened the door a little wider and called, "Mr. Roth?"

Again no sound. I leaned my head in and called louder, "Harold? It's me, Rachel . . ."

My voice trailed off because suddenly I knew. I knew without even stepping into his apartment.

Oh, God, I said to myself as I stumbled back a step. *Oh, God.*

I flashed back to my father, who had died of a massive

heart attack on the morning after Thanksgiving two years ago. My mother had found him on the kitchen floor when she came down to make breakfast. The sports section of the *Post-Dispatch* was clutched in his left hand, his reading glasses were hanging from one ear. The mug of coffee on the kitchen table was cold.

I took a deep breath, steeling myself, and stepped into his apartment. I turned left and moved slowly toward the tiny kitchen, wincing as I peered around the doorway. On the little kitchen table there was a half-empty mug of black coffee—cold—but the room was empty. I moved farther down the hall, conscious of the silence in the apartment and the loud thumping of my heart. The bathroom was empty. So was the bedroom.

Standing at the bedroom door, I slowly turned. The living room was at the other end of the narrow hallway. I stared down that hallway, almost woozy with anxiety.

He might not be there, I thought, trying to persuade myself to start down the hall. *He might still be out. It could have taken him longer to retrieve his journal than he anticipated. Maybe the sidewalks near the bank weren't shoveled.*

I took a few tentative steps toward the living room, cringing each time the floorboards creaked. I paused when I reached the front door, remembering with a wave of dizziness that it had been open when I arrived.

But he's old. Maybe he forgot to close the door when he left. You've done that yourself.

I moved on toward the living room. One step, another, and then I saw him.

I backed against the wall. For one eerie moment, I thought he was alive. I thought he was smiling at me. I thought he was about to say something.

"Oh, God," I moaned, covering my mouth.

I squeezed my eyes closed.

When I opened them, nothing had changed. He was still seated in his easy chair, his feet flat on the floor, his arms on the armrests. He was wearing the same white tennis shoes and black trousers as yesterday, but his shirt today was brown flannel, buttoned to the collar as before. His head was tilted slightly back and to the side, and his eyes were open. His face was set in a grimace that I'd first mistaken for a smile. There was a neat black hole above his right eyebrow and a corresponding stain on the nubby brown fabric behind his head.

The indignity of it bothered me, even though Harold Roth was long past caring about such things. Like all murder victims, he was now stuck in that grisly way station between person and dearly departed. He was "the body." Never mind that this body still had a head, was still dressed, was still seated in his favorite chair with his eyes open, his mouth frozen in that awful smile, half his brain bunched against the back of his neck. He was no longer a person. He was a corpse.

They milled around him, the uniformed cops, the evidence techs, the two homicide detectives, the police photographer, the ambulance jockeys. Some talked homicide talk, the two uniformed cops talked bowling, the ambulance driver played Game Boy. And throughout it all, there in the middle of the crowd, untouched by the commotion, sat Harold Roth, gazing across the room at the darkened screen of his battered portable television.

It took another forty minutes, but finally one of the homicide detectives, a forty-something black man named Ray, was able to leave the scene to come with me to the branch office of Mercantile Bank that was two blocks from Harold's apartment. The reason? The receipt. We'd found a battered leather briefcase in the corner of Harold's living room. There was nothing inside it but a Mercantile Bank receipt for the withdrawal of $100. According to the receipt, Harold had withdrawn the cash from the branch office at 9:28 A.M. that morning.

The bank had its procedures. Even when faced with an irascible homicide detective and an impatient attorney, it took more than an hour for the bureaucracy to disgorge someone with sufficient authority to drill open Harold Roth's safe-deposit box. By then it was a mere formality. Whatever we might find in there, I knew what we wouldn't find. According to the security guard I talked to while we waited, Harold Roth had been standing at the entrance when the bank opened at nine o'clock. He hurried straight to the safe-deposit vault where, according to the log, he'd signed in at 9:05 A.M. and signed out thirteen minutes later. The vault clerk remembered that Harold showed up with an old leather briefcase, took his safe-deposit box to one of the privacy cubicles, and stayed in there for about two minutes. He came back out acting furtive and clutching the briefcase against his chest.

"Here we go, Detective." It was one of the bank vice presidents. He was holding a safe-deposit box. "If you don't mind," he said, gesturing toward a dour, gray-haired woman standing behind him, "Vera here will take an inventory of what you find inside."

The contents proved easy enough to verify: thirty shares of May Company stock, five Israel bonds (total face value: $3,400), $2,050 in fifties, an expired passport, and a photocopy of the Last Will and Testament of Harold A. Roth.

"Anything else?" Vera asked.

I held up the empty box so that she could see inside.

I stormed past the flustered receptionist, not even bothering to identify myself.

"Oh, ma'am," she called after me.

I headed down the corridor, ignoring her. I'd been on this floor often enough to know the exact location of his corner office with its panoramic view of the Arch and the riverfront. In fact, he was standing by that window when I came storming in.

He turned, surprised, just as a male voice came booming over his speakerphone. "They just might go for that approach, Stanley. I like it."

He leaned over and quickly lifted the receiver. His courtly smile faded, no doubt in reaction to the wild expression on my face. "Run it by the mayor first," he said, his voice smooth. "See whether he thinks it'll fly. You'll be at the dinner tonight, right? We'll talk then. Got to run, Donny. Be sure to give your lovely bride a big hello from me. Certainly. Take care, Donny."

He hung up and gestured toward the upholstered chair in front of his antique table desk. "Well, hello, Rachel. I wasn't expecting you."

I remained standing. "Who did you tell?" I demanded.

He looked perplexed. "Tell? About what?"

"About what I told you yesterday. About your uncle Harold."

He settled into his high-back chair and steepled his hands beneath his chin. "I don't believe I am following you." He spoke cautiously.

"Did you tell your client? Did you tell Conrad Beckman?"

He took his time, seeming to contemplate the question. "Rachel, I certainly do not want to seem evasive, but I believe that question crosses the boundary. I should think that any discussion I may have had on the subject of Harold Roth is protected by the work product privilege and the attorney-client privilege."

"I want an answer," I said, practically shouting.

"What makes you think you are entitled to one?" he responded, trying to sound self-righteous, to reclaim the high ground.

"Because of what happened, that's why."

"Ah," he said with the hint of smile, "has someone served my uncle with a subpoena?"

I stared down at him. "No, Stanley. Someone has killed your uncle with a gun."

He lurched back his chair. "My God. When?"

"This morning. Sometime before eleven. Who did you tell?"

"Maybe it was a burglar." His voice was unsteady.

"Come on."

He looked at me, perplexed, defensive. "Why do you doubt that?"

"Because the police found his wallet on top of the bedroom dresser. In plain view. With one hundred seventeen dollars still in it. Whoever killed him wasn't looking for money. Answer my question, Stanley. Did you tell Conrad Beckman?"

He stood up and walked over to the window. After staring out at the Mississippi River for a moment, he turned back to me. "Rachel," he said, his mask partly back in place, "the death of my sole surviving uncle comes as a complete shock to me." He came back to his desk and took a seat behind it. "I can assure you that I have absolutely no reason to believe that our conversation yesterday afternoon or any subsequent conversation I may have had played any role whatsoever in his death." He stared at me calmly. "Accordingly, I am afraid we have nothing further to discuss today."

I placed my hands on his desk and leaned toward him. "Your own uncle." I shook my head in revulsion. "My God, Stanley, what runs through your veins? Antifreeze?"

I straightened up and stared down at him.

He said nothing, his face expressionless. He tried to meet my stare, but after a moment he looked down at his desk and picked up his Mont Blanc fountain pen.

I turned and left.

CHAPTER 18

"**W**hy Hitler's birthday?" Benny asked.

I shrugged. "Seems as good a place as any to start."

This was the last thing I had time for. It was Tuesday night—T-minus six days to trial—but I was totally consumed by the vision from that morning of Harold Roth in his easy chair. I had an eight-page list of pretrial tasks to complete by Monday morning, I was going to be in Jefferson City most of tomorrow, and I'd already given up an hour I didn't have tonight to drop by Jonathan's house to read his daughters a bedtime story and, in the process, to check on the level of police security in place during his absence. (He'd left for Jefferson City that afternoon.) My schedule was so hectic that my dinner tonight had been an apple and a Snickers bar on the drive to the library. But none of that mattered now. I was obsessed with Harold Roth's missing journal. I had to see whether I could reconstruct it, or at least certain parts of it, and Benny, God bless him, had agreed to help. We were in the main library at Wash U.

I gestured toward Harold Roth's last undercover report, the half page of typed material concerning his unsuccessful efforts to obtain information about the SS-Death's Head Formation unit in St. Louis. That was the report in which he repeated Herman Warnholtz's boast that his storm troopers were prepared to do violence in furtherance of the cause of Nazism.

"Why Hitler's birthday?" Benny asked again.

"Harold was kind of cagey, but he seemed to confirm that there was some act of violence—maybe more than one. When I asked when, he told me to focus on Nazi celebration days. What could be bigger than Hitler's birthday?"

Benny nodded thoughtfully. "It's worth a try."

We were seated at one of the microfilm readers. Benny got up and went over to the file drawers filled with microfilm of issues of the *St. Louis Post-Dispatch* dating back to the 1920s. He turned to me and with a frown, "When was that scumbag born?"

"April 20, 1889."

"April twenty," he repeated as he kneeled down to study the dates on the file drawer labels. "Which year should we start with?"

I glanced at the date at the top of Harold Roth's final report: *February 27, 1942.*

"Nineteen forty-two," I said.

Benny returned with a roll of microfilm and threaded it into the machine. "So if something happened on April twentieth," he mused aloud as he used the fast-forward button to advance the film in starts and spurts, "it'd be reported in the April twenty-first edition."

When one of his fast-forward spurts landed us in the middle of the features section for April 20, 1942, he slowly advanced the film until we were staring at the front page of the April 21 edition of the *Post-Dispatch*. The headline immediately yanked us back to World War II:

U.S. AND FILIPINO FORCES
FALL BACK IN PANAY BATTLE

SOVIET GAINS IN LENINGRAD
AND CENTRAL PARTS CLAIMED

We carefully scanned each page, looking for an act of violence that could somehow be linked to the American Nazis. As we moved through the newspaper, page by page, the black-and-white images pulled me back into an era before I was born, to a time that seemed in some ways more exotic than ancient Rome. All the men wore hats, the women gloves. Lawrence Welk and his Champagne Music were held over at the Casa-Loma Ballroom on Cherokee, admission 50 cents. Wool sweaters were on sale at Stix, Baer & Fuller for $3.59, and "luxurious furs" were available at Scruggs•Vandervoort• Barney for $69.95. A fifth of Hiram Walker cost $1.79. The Esquire was showing Spencer Tracy and Katharine Hepburn in *Woman of the Year*. The Uptown had Robert Taylor and Lana Turner in *Johnny Eager*. According to the box scores, the Browns had beaten the Indians the day before, and the Cards had knocked off the Reds.

"Oh, Jesus," Benny said quietly, pointing at the small headline on the screen.

The headline read:

MAN DIES IN PAWNSHOP FIRE
OFFICIALS SUSPECT ARSON

The story was just three paragraphs, cobbled together in time for the deadline. Myron Bernstein, owner of the Southside Pawnshop, had died when flames consumed his place of business late on the night of Monday, April 20. He was fifty-seven years old, married, and the father of five children, all grown. His wife said he usually stayed down after hours on Monday nights to count his inventory, do his books for the prior week, and go over his records. The article reported that the fire marshal and the police believed the fire was deliberately set, that the arson squad had opened a file, and that the police captain had assigned two homicide detectives to the matter. Nevertheless, the article was silent as to what had triggered that level of investigative activity so promptly.

The reasons began to emerge over the next several days of coverage as Benny and I followed the story on microfilm. The presence of several empty gasoline cans strewn around the store was strong evidence of arson. The homicide part was just as obvious: the dead man's feet and arms had been bound by baling wire. Then came the Nazi connection. On the day of the fire, a city desk reporter at the *Globe-Democrat* received an anonymous telephone call announcing that in honor of Adolf Hitler's birthday, "we're going to barbecue a fat Jewish pig tonight." The reporter had dismissed it as a kook call—one of many he received each day—until he learned of the fire that night. The connection seemed clinched by the pair of dripping red swastikas painted on the outer side walls of the building.

The horrible crime possessed the city, or at least the newspaper, for several weeks. The mayor, the governor, and both U.S. senators denounced the crime and condemned the perpetrators. There were daily front-page updates on the investigation for nearly three weeks. But then, like most such crimes that aren't solved quickly, it dropped from view. The last investigation update appeared on May 27, 1942. We skimmed through another month's worth of newspapers but found no further mention of it.

With a sense of unease, we moved ahead one year to April 21, 1943. Had those Hitler celebrants struck again? But there was nothing in that day's edition of the *Post-Dispatch* or, for that matter, the rest of the week. Nor was there any mention of the arson murder that had occurred the prior year. The institutional memory of a newspaper didn't seem to extend that far.

We checked the 1944 and 1945 editions as well, but Hitler's birthday seemed to have passed both years without incident.

"I wonder if they ever solved it," I said to Benny as he rewound the roll of microfilm that included the edition for April 21, 1945.

"It could take us forever to find out," Benny said. "There's no index for this microfilm."

"I'll ask Jonathan. He has plenty of contacts with the police and prosecutors. Maybe one of the older guys will remember."

Benny walked over to the file drawers and put the roll of microfilm back in its slot. "Any other Nazi holidays?" he asked

"Let's try May first," I said. "I read in one of those reports that Hitler declared May Day a Nazi holiday."

Benny shrugged. "Worth a shot."

But we came up empty. We searched through the first week in May for the years 1942 through 1945, but found no acts of violence that appeared to be in any way related to the American Nazis.

Benny turned to me as he held the rewind button for the May 1–15, 1945, roll. *"Nu?"*

I leaned back in my chair and crossed my arms over my chest. I frowned in thought. "You know what that arson job reminded me of?"

"What?"

I gazed at Benny. "Kristallnacht."

He raised his eyebrows and nodded solemnly. "When was it?"

"Sometime in the late thirties, right? Toward the end of the year, I think."

We confirmed it with an encyclopedia. Kristallnacht, or the "Night of Broken Glass," began on the evening of November 9/10, 1938. Joseph Goebbels's SS troops, urged on by his denunciations of the Jews, poured into the streets to wreak vengeance. Other Germans joined the SS troops, and soon an angry mob was raging through the streets in a frenzy of anti-Semitism. By the following morning, 91 Jews were dead and hundreds seriously injured, 177 synagogues were burned or demolished, and nearly 7,500 Jewish businesses destroyed.

We started with 1942. Benny threaded the microfilm and advanced it until we were staring at the front page of the November 10, 1942, edition of the *Post-Dispatch*:

YANKS TAKE ORAN; DARLAN CAPTURED

**Another American Column Drives
Toward Rommel Army in Libya**

**Gen. Eisenhower's Mother Hopes
"Dwight Will Be Good," Return Soon**

We paged slowly through the issue, but there were no reports of any violent crime in St. Louis for the prior day. Or for any of the remaining days that week.

"Try one more year," I told Benny.

He came back with the microfilm roll covering November 1 through 15, 1943. As I watched him thread it into the reader, I said, "Did I tell you that Harold Roth knew about San Carlos de Bariloche?"

Benny glanced over at me. "How?"

I shook my head. "He wouldn't say, but he guessed the town's name as soon as I told him about the joint venture in a South American resort town."

"That's weird."

I nodded. "It tells me that there's another piece of the puzzle we're missing. And remember, Beckman Engineering wasn't the only one involved in a joint venture down there. Beek Contracting did that floodwater system on the lake down there in 1968."

"Oh, yeah."

"That one was a money loser, too, according to my expert witnesses."

Benny squinted at the screen, which was displaying the second page of the sports section for November 8, 1943. "Maybe I'll do some poking around tomorrow," he said as he pressed the fast-forward button. "See if I can find out anything else about that town."

"There," I said as the film stopped at the front page for November 10, 1943. I pointed at a smaller headline near the bottom of the page:

**Action In Boston Urged
On Tracts Against Jews**

The one-paragraph blurb reported that the Massachusetts Public Safety Commissioner had urged Boston officials to confiscate anti-Semitic pamphlets in the wake of nearly forty assaults on Jews throughout the city over the past several weeks.

A small article on page three described a memorial service held for the German Jews who had perished on that night five years ago on Kristallnacht. The service had been lead by Rabbi Abram Levine of Temple Shalom. With a twinge of poignancy, I saw his portrait again—that face glaring into the camera, pipe clenched between his teeth, those dark bushy eyebrows over fierce eyes. It made me sad.

"I wonder whether Harold Roth was at that service," I said.

Benny silently advanced the microfilm page by page. We found it on the first page of the city section:

JEWELER MURDERED ON SOUTH SIDE
POLICE SUSPECT NAZI SYMPATHIZERS

In a crime that had veteran police officers shaking their heads in shock, the unclothed corpse of a south side jeweler was dumped from a moving car outside the third district police headquarters at midnight last night. The corpse was riddled with bullet holes and painted with swastikas, the symbol of the German Nazis.

The victim was identified as Harry Rosenthal, age 51, of the 5900 block of Enright. Rosenthal was the proprietor of Mound City Jewelry on the 3200 block of South Meramec.

According to the police, a missing persons alert on Rosenthal had been issued by 9 p.m. after the police received a report from a passerby who claimed to have seen Rosenthal grabbed outside his jewelry store by a masked man around 6 p.m. The witness said that Rosenthal was dragged into the alley and shoved into a car, which promptly drove off.

Police Captain Clarence O'Bannion said that the list of suspects included every known Nazi sympathizer in the area. He said his investigators would begin bringing in suspects for questioning beginning today.

Rosenthal is survived by his mother, a sister, his wife and two sons.

I leaned back in my chair, numb. "That's Uncle Harry."

Benny turned to me, aghast. "That poor guy was your uncle?"

I shook my head. "Not mine. Ruth's. The day I met her she had just said kaddish for him at the synagogue. Two Novembers ago." I pointed toward the screen, where the date at the top of the newspaper page was visible. November 10, 1943. "We first met on Uncle Harry's *yahrzeit*."

CHAPTER 19

It was soon apparent that the main value of my trip to Jefferson City was the solitude on the train. No phones, no interruptions, no distractions. I'd stuffed my briefcase with trial preparation materials and got more done on that two-and-a-half-hour train ride than I would have accomplished in a whole day at the office.

As for the sole purpose of the trip, it took less than thirty minutes with the Missouri Trade Commission's file on Beckman Engineering to conclude that its 1978 investigation had nothing to do with the claims in my case. Apparently, some eager staff attorney named Robert Hennepin—no doubt an ambitious recent grad with a fuzzy grasp of antitrust law—decided that Beckman Engineering's acquisition of a small engineering firm in Cape Girardeau posed a threat to free enterprise in southeast Missouri. Regardless of the merits of his concerns, it didn't take long for a platoon of lawyers from Roth & Bowles to hit the beach armed with reports, charts, and affidavits from a Princeton economist and a University of Chicago professor of law. They drove their Sherman tanks right over poor Mr. Hennepin, leaving treadmarks across his back.

At least I was able to make good use of the extra time. I spent about an hour in the law library in the Missouri Supreme Court building running down a few legal issues in Ruth's case, and then I located an open phone in the attorney room and spent another hour collecting and returning my phone calls. I caught up with Jonathan around three-thirty. He was still meeting with Paulie Metzger, so I took a seat in the waiting room outside the small conference room and pulled out another sheaf of pretrial materials.

At four-fifteen the door opened. I didn't need a name tag to identify the fat, balding man in his late sixties who stepped out of the room shaking his head in exasperation. Paulie Metzger was wearing a plaid sports jacket, wrinkled brown slacks, and scuffed black shoes. He had a pencil mustache, a Mr. McGoo nose, and an unlit cigar clenched in his teeth.

A moment later, Jonathan appeared in the doorway, his tie loosened, his shirtsleeves rolled up to the elbow. He crossed his arms over his chest as he leaned against the doorjamb and stared at Metzger's back.

"Your choice, Paulie," he said.

"Come on, Wolf," Metzger said in a raspy voice as he turned to Jonathan. "How many times I gotta tell you? I'm just the lawyer for the trust here."

"Save your speech for the parole board, Paulie. You're as much a suspect as any of them. Today's Wednesday. The offer stays open until sundown Friday."

"Sundown? What are you—Wyatt Earp?" And then he chuckled. "Oh, yeah, the Jew Sabbath, right?" He turned with a dismissive wave. "Don't hold your breath, Wolf."

I watched him board the elevator. When the doors slid closed, I turned to Jonathan. "What a creep."

Jonathan pursed his lips together and nodded.

"Any luck?"

He shrugged. "We'll see. I gave him some heavy stuff to mull over."

On the drive home from Jefferson City I brought Jonathan up to date on the Harold Roth situation. He already knew Harold was dead—I'd told him yesterday before he left for Jefferson City—but the two homicides from the 1940s were news to him. I read him the articles I'd photocopied from the microfilm. He was intrigued. As we headed east on Highway 70, he called one of his contacts with the St. Louis police and asked him to see what he could find out about the results of the two homicide investigations.

*   *   *

What is it?" I asked.

We were about fifty miles outside St. Louis. Jonathan had been checking his rearview mirror with concern. I turned around to look. In the falling darkness I could make out a brown GMC van about a hundred feet behind us.

"Probably nothing," he said. "It's been back there since we left Jefferson City. Can you read the license plate?"

I squinted. "Looks like an Illinois plate, but it's too dirty to read."

Twenty minutes later, it was night. We'd just passed St. Charles and were now on the outskirts of St. Louis. The highway traffic was moving smoothly in the dark.

The first hint of peril came just beyond the Lindbergh exits off I-70. We were in the right lane and I was flipping through the radio stations in search of a good song.

"What's this?" Jonathan mumbled.

I turned to watch as a van pulled into the middle lane, passed us, and pulled back into our lane right in front of us.

"Is that the same one?" I asked.

He nodded. "Look at the plates."

Illegible Illinois plates, covered with mud.

As we approached the airport exit, a large pickup truck pulled into the middle lane directly alongside our car. A quarter mile, a half mile—it was keeping exact pace with us. I glanced over at the speedometer: 64 miles per hour.

"What's going on?" I said, peering through Jonathan's window at the pickup. It was a dark-colored vehicle with a raised cab. The passenger window was opaque.

We had just entered the intricate network of overpasses at the I-70/I-170 interchange when our car was bathed in light, as if someone had set off a phosphorescent flare in the backseat. I turned and squinted into huge headlights. They were less than ten feet from the rear fender. I looked at Jonathan just as the headlights behind us jumped from high beam to spotlight. Momentarily blinded, Jonathan lowered his head to avoid the glare.

"Look out!" I yelled, pointing ahead.

The brake lights on the van in front had just come on. As Jonathan moved his foot off the gas toward the brakes, the pickup truck whipped to the right and rammed into us hard, knocking our car onto the shoulder. Jonathan's window exploded into a thousand pieces. The wind howled as broken glass whistled through the car.

Jonathan had both hands on the steering wheel, fighting for control.

The pickup rammed us again. Our car careened to the right, wheels squealing.

"No!" I shouted, grasping for the dashboard as the car smashed through the guardrail.

We were airborne—

plunging—

the night sky above us—

below us—

above us—

then a crashing jolt . . .

I opened my eyes to the wailing.

There was a blurry image in front of me.

A tombstone?

I blinked.

A tombstone.

An upside-down tombstone, half sunk at an angle in the upside-down snow. A brightly illuminated tombstone. It cast a long, stark shadow.

I blinked again. The tombstone was still there. So was the loud wailing.

My brain seemed to be operating in slow motion. Gradually I realized the wailing sound was actually a car horn. I wasn't dead. The tombstone wasn't upside down. I was.

Something was pushed hard against me. I looked down— or was it up?—and felt with my hands. My sluggish brain processed the information: an inflated air bag was pressed against my body, holding it in place. I was strapped inside a car upside down, suspended by the seat belt.

I stared out at the tombstone. The faded engraving was all but unreadable, especially upside down. I could only make out the first name—*Jeremiah*—and the date of birth: *March 8, 1897.*

My head was throbbing. My neck was stiff. My hands were cold. Numb.

The wind was blowing. An icy winter breeze. I could feel it against my face, on my hands, ruffling my hair. The windshield was gone. Crystallized pieces of glass clung from the corners nearest me.

"Rachel?"

It was a whisper, barely audible over the howling. At first I thought I was hearing voices—words from inside my head.

"Rachel?"

The voice was familiar. I frowned.

The wailing. The car horn. Jonathan's car horn. Jonathan's car.

Jonathan!

I turned my head, grimacing from the pain.

"Oh, no," I moaned. "Oh, Jonathan."

He was suspended at an odd angle by his seat belt, his upper torso crammed against the steering wheel. The roof had partially caved in on his side. His air bag hadn't inflated. He turned his head toward me. There was blood on his forehead, blood in his hair, blood dripping slowly down—up?—onto the roof of the car.

"Rachel?" he asked softly.

"It's me, Jonathan. Oh, my God."

"Tell me what hurts."

"What hurts?" I paused, and did an inventory. "My head. My neck."

"Is anything broken?"

"What?"

"Try your arms and legs. Can you move them?"

I tried. I could. "They're okay. But what about you?"

He winced. "My left wrist is broken. Maybe my ankle, too. The right one."

"Oh, Jonathan."

"My phone has to be somewhere."

"I'll find it for us." I slid my hand down along the shoulder harness, looking for the buckle. "Oh, Jonathan, I'll get us help. Don't worry. You'll be okay. I promise."

It took me a full five minutes to unlatch the seat belt, brace myself against the roof, wrench the door open, and drag myself through it onto the frozen ground. I kneeled in the snow, drenched in perspiration as I tried to catch my breath. By the time I'd stopped panting, I was shivering. It took no time for the frigid air to seep through my silk blouse, gabardine skirt, stockings, and loafers. My coat was still in the car. I'd slipped it off on the drive back. My teeth were chattering as I crawled halfway into the car to retrieve it. Standing in the snow, I fumbled with the coat buttons, my fingers nearly crippled from the cold.

I climbed back in the car and checked on Jonathan. Fortunately, he'd kept his winter coat on during the drive. He told me he wasn't cold, but I didn't know whether to believe him.

I gave him a gentle kiss on his ear. "Hang on, Jonathan. I'll find the phone and call for help."

I searched inside the car but couldn't find it. I clambered out and stood up to survey the area. Although the car's engine had died upon impact, the headlights remained on, and they were illuminating a scene right out of a low-budget horror flick. The car had come to rest in the middle of Washington Park Cemetery, the run-down graveyard near the airport where several generations of poor black families are interred. The headlights were creepy stage lighting for the dilapidated burial grounds.

Massaging the back of my sore neck, I tried to get my bearings. The path of the car would likely dictate the location of any items flung from it. High above the cemetery grounds, the highways crisscrossed on their overpasses, the exit and entrance ramps looping in big sweeping arcs. I located the smashed guardrail. The rest of the path was easy to trace from the trail of broken glass, debris, and slide marks below. The car had tumbled down the embankment, hit a concrete drainage ditch, and flipped over, landing on its roof in the snow. It slid through the cemetery, barely missing several grave markers before coming to rest right in front of Jeremiah's half-buried tombstone.

After twenty minutes of searching—during which I came across my purse and Jonathan's sunglasses—I found his phone half buried in the snow on the near side of the drainage ditch. Stumbling through the snow, I carried it back to the car and kneeled in front of one of the headlights to see what I was doing. Holding my breath, I flipped the phone open and pressed the Power button. Nothing at first, and then the little number screen lit up, blinked several times, and flashed *Ready*.

I exhaled slowly. "Thank you," I whispered as I pressed *55, the emergency number for the Highway Patrol.

The emergency-room physician told me Jonathan never lost consciousness. Although he had suffered a severe concussion and a gash in his scalp when the car flipped over, along with a broken wrist, a broken ankle, and internal bruising, he'd remained conscious the whole time. Apparently, that was a good sign. The best sign, though, was that he was about to be transferred from intensive care to a regular hospital bed where I'd finally get to see him. By comparison, I'd come through the accident practically unscathed. Just a contusion on my forehead and a stiff neck that probably wasn't whiplash.

Jonathan had certainly been conscious when the Highway Patrol and ambulance arrived. Indeed, by the time the ambulance reached the hospital, the paramedics had already called ahead, at Jonathan's insistence, for two homicide detectives. Although the emergency-room physician refused to let the police near the patient until he'd been stitched and X-rayed, his broken bones set, and his condition stabilized, as soon as the doctor gave the okay, the detectives filed in with their notebooks and recorders.

I'd slept for about two hours on a waiting-room couch after the emergency-room physician came out to give me a status report at four A.M. The detectives woke me at 6:45 A.M. after they interviewed Jonathan. One of them was Poncho Israel, a huge black man with the build of an aging offensive tackle and a perpetually melancholy expression. We knew each other from a prior case.

Poncho tugged at his Fu Manchu mustache as he spoke. "An incident like that," he said, shaking his head slowly, "car smashing through a railing, the Highway Patrol should get half a dozen calls from passersby on car phones. But not here. No one noticed a thing. That's how they planned it, Rachel. Those trucks did more than pin you in. They screened you from view."

"Skinheads?" I asked.

"Maybe, but Mr. Wolf put a lotta punks behind bars during his prosecutor years. Some of them don't believe in letting bygones be bygones, especially now that he's no longer in the U.S. Attorney's office."

"Come on, Poncho," I said, shaking my head stubbornly, "it has to be the skinheads. They know he's tracing their source of funds. That's why he was down in Jeff City. They know he's coming after them, and they're getting nervous." I crossed my arms over my chest and stared at both detectives. "That pickup truck has paint from Jonathan's car scraped along the passenger side. And don't forget about the brown van with the Illinois plates. Find one of those trucks and I'll bet you'll trace it right back to Spider."

At the pay phone down the hall from his hospital room, I called Jonathan's housekeeper again to give her a status report. Then I called my secretary to explain why I'd be in late.

"What can I do?"

"I'll be okay," I said, studying my pocket calendar. "You and Benny keep pressing ahead on the pretrial stuff. See if we can move the prep session with Steiner to after lunch, okay?"

"Oh, my God, Rachel."

"Hang in there, Jacki. We'll pull through this."

Jonathan was still asleep when I tiptoed back into the hospital room. He was on his back with his arms at his side and his right leg suspended in a canvas sling about a foot above the mattress. The ankle cast ran from his foot to his knee. His left arm was in a cast up to the elbow. There were bruises on his face, his left eye was blackened, and his head was wrapped in gauze. He had an IV drip in his right arm and several monitor wires running from different parts of his body to a bank of machines on a cart beside the bed. Nevertheless, he seemed to be sleeping peacefully. Thank goodness.

As quietly as I could, I lowered myself into the chair next to his bed and closed my eyes. Not to sleep, even though I was totally exhausted. No, I closed my eyes to shut off the turmoil for just a moment. It didn't work. I seemed to be running on autopilot somewhere out there along the edge of chaos. I'd just survived an assassination attempt on Jonathan and an automobile crash right out of a stuntman's bad dream. It was the kind of night that merited at least a week of recovery time, preferably on a warm beach somewhere in the Caribbean. Instead, I had the biggest trial of my life starting in four days. Faced with far too many pretrial tasks for the hours remaining, I didn't have time to do what any normal person ought to do: enjoy a tidy little mental breakdown. I didn't even have time to do what I really wanted to do: collapse into someone's arms sobbing hysterically. Worse yet, the only person whose arms I wanted to collapse into had a cast on one and bandages on the other. So I did the next best thing: I sat there with my eyes closed and wallowed in self-pity.

"Good morning, Rachel."

I opened my eyes. His were open, too. They looked drained. I stood and leaned over him, banishing my selfish thoughts.

"Hi," I whispered. I kissed him softly on his nose.

"How's your head?" he asked.

"Just a bump." I shook my head nonchalantly, trying to conceal my neck pain. "It's nothing."

I gently laid my hand on his chest. He looked battered and worn, but he also looked resolute. I thought of his Golden Gloves days. He looked like he'd been pummeled hard for the first eleven rounds but was determined to answer the final bell.

"How bad does it hurt?" I asked.

"I can't tell. They have me on painkillers."

"Oh, Jonathan."

"Don't worry. It'll be worth it."

I gave him a puzzled look. "What will?"

"This." With an effort, he turned his head to look down at his casts. He looked back at me, his green eyes fatigued but unyielding.

"What do you mean?"

"They're not clever enough to cover all their tracks. We'll find them. We'll hunt them down and find them, and when we do, we'll follow the chain of command right to the top. What they tried last night translates to two counts of attempted murder. That'll put Kurt Robb behind bars for life. Then we squeeze Paulie Metzger again, cut off their source of funds, and Spider is history."

A doctor on rounds arrived just then. With mild amusement I watched Jonathan reverse the usual physician/patient interaction. The doctor started off with the "good news" that we "might be able to go home by the end of the week." By the time he left the room ten minutes later, he'd agreed that Jonathan was going home at the end of the day.

Kurt Robb had reason to be jittery.

I got to my office at noon. Between the phone calls from friends and the inquiries from the press, I was able to do about two hours of actual trial preparation before I left the office at six o'clock.

I'd originally planned to go back to the hospital to help Jonathan get home, but discovered by midafternoon that I'd just be in the way. The Missouri Attorney General, sensing a significant photo op, decided to personally escort Jonathan out of the hospital and transport him home in an official state of Missouri limo with a five-motorcycle police escort. Jonathan was big news, and the attorney general—a politician to his core, with designs on higher office—was eager to bask in the media spotlight. He staged an "impromptu" press conference on the hospital steps. As the videocams whirred, he reared up on his hind legs, denounced the incident as "an attempted assassination," and vowed "to bring down the sword of justice upon the cowardly necks of the fiends responsible for this abomination, as God is my witness."

So I skipped the circus and drove straight to Jonathan's house to help prepare his daughters for their father's home-coming. The housekeeper had wisely shielded the girls from all media reports of the incident. All they knew was that Daddy had been in an automobile accident and had broken an arm and a leg. It turned out that that's all they needed to know. When Jonathan came through the door, moving smoothly on crutches and smiling at his daughters, it seemed inconceivable that less than twenty-four hours ago he'd been hanging upside down in his car, battered and barely conscious. The gauze had been unwrapped from his head and replaced by a large bandage placed on his forehead at an angle that made it seem almost jaunty. The cuts and bruises seemed less raw, and the black eye didn't look quite as prominent now that he had his color back.

I felt a little like the fifth wheel at the joyous family re-union, so after we got him settled on the couch in the living room with a cup of hot chocolate and his daughters at his side, I kissed him good-bye and said I'd call him in the morn-ing. On the way to my car, I noted with approval the aug-mented security arrangements. There were now two state Highway Patrol cars parked in front of the house and two plainclothes officers with crackling walkie-talkies moving down the driveway. It was the first worthwhile thing the at-torney general had done all day.

Benny taught an evening seminar on trade regulation and dropped by afterward to cheer me up with massive quan-tities of Chinese takeout, including an entire container of Mongolian Beef for Ozzie. Suffice to say, Ozzie treats Benny with a degree of veneration that one normally associates with the disciples of a charismatic religious leader. In Ozzie's world, Benny was the Dalai Lama.

Benny hung around to catch the ten o'clock news. Jonathan was the lead story. Fortunately, I was just the nameless "other attorney accompanying Mr. Wolf" who "escaped with minor injuries." There was footage of the attorney general making his vows on the hospital steps.

"Give me a break," Benny groaned after the attorney general made his vow. "Sword of justice? That knucklehead couldn't find his own butt with both hands and a copy of *Gray's Anatomy*."

The piece ended with a live remote of Bishop Kurt Robb outside the Spider headquarters, wearing his green beret and tinted glasses.

"That's preposterous," Robb said with a chuckle when asked if he was aware that the attorney general had targeted his organization as a suspect in the accident, "but I'm hardly surprised. That so-called attorney general is nothing more than a rank hairball coughed up on the carpet of Missouri politics. You don't have to be paranoid to wonder if this whole accident was staged." He turned to face the camera, by now in complete control of the live interview. "And here's something else to ask yourself. A man driving along the highway crashes through the guardrail and goes over the edge. What's your first thought? Alcohol, right?" He smiled and shrugged. "I wouldn't be at all surprised if they discovered a little too much Mogen David in his bloodstream." He turned to the reporter. "Well?"

The question caught the reporter off balance. "Pardon?"

"Have you asked the attorney general, madam? He's hurling around some serious charges. Have you bothered to ask him the blood alcohol level of the Big Bad Wolf?"

She stammered. "Uh, that's a subject, well, uh, not that I know."

He turned back to the camera and shook his head sarcastically. "This is freedom of the press? What a sorry state of affairs."

CHAPTER 21

L egal fictions were part of the world of law long before publishers named a category after them. Those original fictions—the true fictions, if you will—have always been more powerful than the ones that jostle for space on the bestseller lists. That's because legal fictions are at the core of the law, and the core of the law is metamorphosis. Consider the corporation, a golem created out of inanimate objects as if from a witch's brew: take a set of cryptic phrases, add three whereas clauses, stir in a special corporate seal, and—presto—the thing lives! Or observe the alchemy of the libel action, where that ethereal abstraction known as a person's reputation is transmuted into a tangible piece of property.

Metamorphosis comprised the first order of business Monday morning when the thirty-six designated men and women filed into the courtroom. They were a motley collection—young and old, fat and skinny, black and white, urban, suburban, and rural; some with graduate degrees, some without high school diplomas. But inside the courtroom they were no longer ordinary folk. Now they were the "venire," ready for the voir dire. At the end of that process, six would undergo the final transformation by raising their right hands, repeating the enchanted words, and—presto—they'd become the engine of justice charged with determining Ruth Alpert's fate in the trial of *United States ex rel. Ruth B. Alpert* v. *Beckman Engineering Co.*

Although jury selection in a federal civil case is usually a streamlined process, there was nothing usual about this case. It would take all morning to cull through the venire panel for our six jurors plus one alternate because Judge Wagner would be asking each prospective juror a list of forty-six questions carefully designed by a team of psychologists and sociologists at Trial•Edge, the Chicago jury selection consultants retained by Beckman Engineering.

As the morning droned on, I studied the prospective jurors, hoping that they were picking up the contrast between the plaintiff's counsel table and the defendant's. Facing the jury at the defendant's table were Kimberly Howard; her unctuous aide de camp Laurence Browning; one of Roth & Bowles's interchangeable young male associates; a harried female paralegal; and Conrad Beckman, today attired in the standard first-day-of-trial outfit: an impeccable dark suit, starched white shirt, and power tie. Seated on the other side of the defendant's table were two consultants from Trial•Edge, another young male attorney, and another harried paralegal.

The two consultants were frenetically typing coded data into their laptop computers as each prospective juror answered the questions on the list. That data was being transmitted to a more powerful computer in the back of the courtroom manned by another pair of consultants, one of whom was wearing a headset that kept him in contact with a support team at another location. The mother computer was processing the data and updating lists of Top 6 and Bottom 6 prospective jurors, which it transmitted to the screen of the laptop computer on the table in front of Laurence Browning.

From my seat at the plaintiff's table, I could see the lists roll and change on Browning's computer like the flight departure boards at O'Hare. I'd heard that Trial•Edge had been conducting jury pool surveys and focus group studies on the case for more than a month. By the time this trial was over, Beckman Engineering would have paid them over $150,000, which was more than their opening settlement offer to Ruth. With all the technicians, lawyers, and paralegals involved, the defendant's jury selection operation seemed like a mini-version of the NASA launch team in Houston.

Over at our table, Mission Control consisted of Ruth and me.

Period.

We didn't have the money for consultants or laptops loaded with proprietary software. So we did our jury selection the way it had been done for centuries: by intuition. We listened as each prospective juror answered the judge's questions and then we jotted down not-so-coded data onto our low-tech notepads—sophisticated, calibrated observations, such as *Maybe?* and *He gives me bad vibes* and *Yes!* and *Don't trust a woman with that hairdo* and *No way!*

Occasionally, as the morning dragged along, I glanced back to the gallery and tried to pick out members of the press. Scattered throughout the ten rows of benches in the courtroom were a dozen or so reporters, some of whom I recognized, including the local stringers for the *Wall Street Journal* and *BusinessWeek*. Last Friday, as part of a flurry of final pretrial orders, Judge Wagner opened the proceeding to the public. The unsealing of a court file involving claims exceeding $100 million against a major St. Louis corporation snagged the attention of the local media and some of the nationals. The *Post-Dispatch* ran a big article on the case in the Sunday business section. I'd received a call late Friday afternoon from a reporter with *Forbes* magazine, which had ranked Beckman Engineering last year as one of the fifty best-run private corporations in America. She was somewhere out there in the crowd.

At twelve-thirty, Kimberly and I went up to the bench for our last voir dire sidebar with Judge Wagner. We each handed Her Honor a slip of paper with our final preemptory strikes. She looked at them, nodded, and gestured us back to our seats. She conferred a moment with her clerk and her bailiff, and then turned toward the group of prospective jurors, which had been whittled from thirty-six to twenty-two.

"Ladies and gentlemen," Judge Wagner said, "if I call your

name, please take the seat I indicate in the jury box. Mr. Fernandez, seat one. Miss Deutsch, seat two—"

As she called out their names, they stood self-consciously, one by one, and filed into the jury box to take their assigned seat, which was the seat they would occupy for each day of the trial.

"Mrs. Trotter, seat three. Miss Jahnke, seat four. Mr. Hagen, seat five—"

When they were all seated and facing the bench, Judge Wagner turned to the ones left behind, thanked them for their patience, and told them to report back to the clerk's office after lunch. As the unchosen filed out of the courtroom, I turned my gaze toward the jury box and studied them, this jury of our peers. I couldn't help but wonder if all those fancy consultants at Trial•Edge felt any less unsure of these seven men and women than I did.

Judge Wagner had the jury stand, raise their right hands, and be sworn in.

"Ladies and gentlemen of the jury," she said after they were seated again, "the Court will be in recess until two o'clock, at which time the trial will begin with opening statements. Let me remind you that you are not to discuss the case among yourselves or with anyone else from now until the case is over. The bailiff will now show you to the jury room." She paused and gave them a friendly smile. "We'll see you at two o'clock. Have a good lunch."

Benny was waiting for Ruth and me in the hallway outside the courtroom. Ruth was meeting one of her girlfriends for lunch, which was what I had suggested this morning, since I knew I would need some time alone to get ready for opening statements. I'd told her to meet me in the courtroom at a quarter to two.

I filled Benny in on the morning's proceedings as we walked over to Crackers for soup and a sandwich. We still weren't ready for trial, of course. I still had investigators out there looking for potential witnesses, and my opening statement consisted of one page of hastily scribbled notes.

We got a booth in the back of the restaurant and placed our orders. When the waitress left, Benny leaned forward and said, "I found some intriguing stuff on our little resort town."

"San Carlos?" I said, wavering between curiosity and dread. I was curious to learn whether Benny had discovered the town's mysterious connection to Ruth's case, but I dreaded the thought that his news might further complicate this far-too-complicated case.

"I started with Nexus," he said. Nexus is a computer data bank that contains full-text articles from hundreds of newspapers and periodicals.

"Any hits?" I asked.

He nodded as he pulled a folded set of papers out of his jacket pocket. "Four. Three were exactly what you'd expect: features in travel magazines on South American resorts. But check out the fourth."

He handed me a sheet of paper. It was a photocopy of an article that had appeared in the October 30, 1995, issue of the *New York Times*. The story described an awkward public relations problem confronting "this picturesque ski town." Erich Priebke, a prominent local citizen was under house arrest while the Argentine Supreme Court tried to decide whether he would be extradited to Italy to stand trial for his participation in the killing of 336 Italian civilians at the Ardeatine Caves outside Rome in 1944. Apparently, during World War II the charming Señor Priebke had been Captain Priebke of the German SS.

If it were only Priebke, the article explained, the residents could shrug it off as one bad apple. But what made the town's leaders so uneasy was the way the controversy focused attention on a dark chapter of the history of San Carlos de Bariloche. According to the *Times*, the town had once been a "haven for Nazis who fled Germany after World War II." In particular, it was rumored to have been a sanctuary for former

SS officers involved in the operations of the concentration camps.

I looked up at Benny in astonishment. "I can't believe this."

Benny nodded. "Neither could I. I ran another computer search through one of those oddball databases." He unfolded the other two pages. "This appeared back in 1972 in some Jewish publication called *Jacob's Review*. It's from an article on the novel *The Odessa File*. By the way, did you know that there really was an organization called Odessa?"

I shook my head. "No."

Benny looked at the first page. "The name is an acronym. I can't remember the German, but in English it stands for the Organization of Former Members of the SS. Do you remember that thing Harold Roth mentioned to you? Die Spinne?"

"Sure."

"I thought it was a curse. You know, like 'Die Motherfucker.' And maybe it is, but the only guy named Spinne I could find was some Danish composer from the seventeenth century."

"What would they have against him?"

Benny shrugged. "Beats me. The next closest word I found was spinney, which is a small forest. Die Forest?" He shook his head. "Doesn't make sense. But check this out."

I flattened the pages on the table and read the paragraphs that Benny had highlighted with a yellow marker:

The most formidable of the other secret confederations was Die Spinne comprised of officers in the SS-Totenkopfverbände (the SS-Death's Head Formation), the storm-trooper division in charge of the concentration camps. By 1944, many of the senior officers of the Death's Head Formation, aware that the war was lost and under no illusions as to how they would be treated afterward, made secret arrangements to escape and carry on

Hitler's plans. In late 1944, at a secret conference at the Maison Rouge hotel in Strausbourg, Die Spinne was established. According to papers found in a dark blue envelope taken off an SS colonel in the internment camp at Ebensee, the chairman of the conference made the following statement:

> "The battle of France is lost for Germany. Steps must be taken for a postwar underground campaign to achieve by clandestine means what we have failed to achieve by open war. We must seek and establish contact and links with sympathetic foreign firms and be prepared for taking up large-scale credits after the war if our goals are ever to be achieved."

I looked up at Benny in wonder. "This is incredible."
He nodded. "Read on."
I looked down at the text:

By the end of 1944, Die Spinne had established safe houses, forged papers, trained guides and go-betweens, plotted routes for border crossings, and arranged for sanctuaries in Spain and Italy, often in monasteries. The main escape route, known as the "B-B axis," ran from the town of Bremen to the Italian port of Bari, and from there to Spain and South America.

Members of Die Spinne all had proper papers and arrived at their new destinations with substantial financial resources at their disposal to enable them to become partners in major enterprises. This was due, in no small part, to the meticulous records of assets maintained by the Death's Head Formation of the wealth confiscated from the concentration camp prisoners. In May of 1945, according to records seized by the invading Russian army, a special department of the Reichsbank sent several crates of "dental gold," valued at $5 million, to the Aussee area of Germany, where it was shipped to a bank and then transferred to San Carlos de Bariloche, a mountain village in Argentina that was rumored to be the international headquarters for Die Spinne.

I put the pages down and looked at Benny, "Is it possible?" I said, my head reeling. I checked my watch. "Oy," I said, reaching for one of the halves of my tuna sandwich, "I've got my opening statement in thirty minutes." I shook my head and leaned back in the booth. "Oh, Benny, there's too many loose ends."

"What can I do?"

I tried to give him a plucky smile. "How about writing a note from my mother. 'Dear Judge Wagner: Please excuse Rachel from Court this afternoon. She's not feeling well.' "

Benny smiled and reached across to punch me gently in the arm. "You'll be awesome. The jury'll love you. Now what can I do to help?"

I gestured toward the article I'd just read. "Check with one of our students. Maybe Josh. See if he can run those two dates through the computer."

"Which dates?"

I finished the sandwich half and took a sip of iced tea. "The ones we found in the *Post-Dispatch*: April 21, 1942, and November 11, 1943. Have him check the newspapers in the other five cities."

"What other cities?"

"Chicago, Springfield, Memphis, Gary, and Indianapolis." I checked my watch again.

"Rachel, go. I'll hook up with you after court."

I reached into my wallet and handed him a twenty. "Here's for lunch."

"That's way too much."

"Lunch is my treat. Gotta run."

As I reached the door, I heard him call my name. I turned to see him standing at our booth. He gave me the thumbs-up. "Good luck, gorgeous!" he shouted. His booming voice turned heads throughout the restaurant. "Knock 'em dead!"

Grinning, I waved and turned toward the door, buttoning my coat as I headed into the cold, my thoughts churning anew as I tried to focus on the opening statement that I was supposed to deliver in less than thirty minutes.

CHAPTER 22

To her credit, Catherine Wagner kept her feelings hidden from the jury. I knew she didn't like me professionally or, apparently, personally. I also knew that she was secretly, and occasionally not so secretly, leaning toward my opponents. A person with her Republican ties would naturally favor Kimberly Howard and Kimberly's client. Especially Kimberly's client. Beckman Engineering and its founder had long been stalwarts of the GOP in Missouri. Nevertheless, in the jury's presence she was the very essence of the neutral judge.

And thus, when the jury was seated, she gave them a welcoming smile and announced, "We will now hear opening statements from counsel for the plaintiff and the defendant." She turned to me with a cordial expression. "Ms. Gold?"

"Thank you, Your Honor."

I stepped around the table and moved toward the jury box, stopping about six feet from the rail. I paused to study their solemn faces. I was wearing my first-day-of-trial outfit: a stylish worsted-wool sheath dress in a brown mini-check pattern under a matching jacket. The dress was fitted and hemmed above the knee. The jacket reached to mid-thigh. I had on sensible flats, gold earrings, no necklace, no bracelet. A serious outfit for a serious case.

"Cheating," I said to them, my voice subdued. "That's what this case is about. Cheating. When all the evidence is in, I will stand before you again and remind you of what I am telling you today. This is a case about cheating."

I paused, scanning their faces. They were paying attention.

"We're here," I told them, "to prove to you that Beckman

Engineering conspired to defraud the United States government out of tens of millions of dollars. Specifically, Beckman Engineering and five other companies got together in a secret scheme, and the goal of that secret scheme was to make millions of dollars by cheating on a series of government bids. Cheating. That's what this case is about."

I moved back to the plaintiff's table, relieved that I'd gotten that far without an interruption. I'd sensed that Kimberly was about to leap to her feet with an objection, and it might well have been sustained. This was opening statement, not closing argument, and I'd opened out near the border between the two. Time to return to more familiar themes.

"My name is Rachel Gold," I told the jury. I placed my hand on Ruth's shoulder. "This is my client, Ruth Alpert. As Judge Wagner explained to you earlier, Ruth has a special title in this lawsuit. She's not the plaintiff. The United States government is the plaintiff. Ruth is what's known as a relator. That's a fancy legal term for what many of us call a whistle-blower." I watched the jurors carefully, trying to sense whether they were following me. It was so hard to read their faces.

"Ruth is the whistle-blower here," I continued. "She's the one with the courage to call your attention to a special type of cheating called bid-rigging. But the claim we're here to present to you doesn't belong to Ruth. It belongs to the United States government. We intend to prove that the United States government has been swindled by a group of companies who decided that they could make a whole lot more money by cheating instead of by playing fair."

Now was the time to segue into the central function of the opening statement, which is to explain to the jury what you believe the evidence will prove. Unfortunately, that was a problem here. To begin with, our case still hadn't fully jelled, and our proof was going to be disjointed. Ruth was my only friendly witness, and she had very little firsthand knowledge to offer. Most of our evidence would be coming from the mouths of hostile witnesses, many of them employees of

Beckman Engineering. That meant I'd be fencing with witnesses over every point. Almost as bad, some of those hostile witnesses, such as Otto Koll, wouldn't even be in the courtroom; I'd have to present their testimony by reading aloud excerpts from their depositions. And finally, as with most conspiracy cases, the key evidence was circumstantial. Max Kruppa's American Express receipt was about as close to a smoking gun as I was likely to get, and it wasn't that close.

All of which meant that I had an especially important job to accomplish in my opening statement: I had to prepare the jury for the fact that this case was not going to unfold before them in a neat, orderly fashion. I needed to help them understand that I was going to be building a mosaic of evidence, tile by tile. If everything broke our way, a clear picture would emerge when the mosaic was complete. If not, it wouldn't matter to them because the judge would throw out the case long before they'd be called upon to render a verdict.

I moved back toward the jury box. "Evidence in a real trial," I explained, "isn't like evidence in those courtroom dramas on TV. In the real world, evidence arrives in bits and pieces. That's because witnesses can only testify to what *they* witnessed, and no one person ever witnesses the whole story." I shrugged. "In a real courtroom, you sometimes hear the end of the story first, and you don't hear the beginning until the last day of trial. It can be confusing unless you have a blueprint."

I paused. "When I was a little girl, I wanted to be a carpenter more than anything in the whole world. I even had my own tool belt. I wanted to build houses." I smiled. "Well, that's the analogy that comes to mind. Over the next two weeks or so, I'm going to be building a house in front of your eyes. I've ordered all the supplies, but they're going to arrive at different times. You'll see. A whole bunch of boards will arrive one morning, a truckload of pipe the next, electrical wiring that afternoon. Without a blueprint, you'd have no idea what this house is going to look like. But if I give you that blueprint, then when you see each piece of evidence arrive, you'll be able to recognize it and know where it fits. You'll be able to say, Oh, yeah, those are the bricks for the chimney. Ah, that looks like the paneling for the den. Hey, there's the cedar for the deck out back."

Several of them were smiling or nodding. They hadn't zoned out on me yet. I leaned back against the edge of our table. "So let me give you the blueprint. Let me tell you what this house of evidence is going to look like."

Thirty minutes later, I returned to my seat and watched as Kimberly Howard rose to address the jury.

"A blueprint for a house?" she said with mild disdain. "When you make the kinds of accusations that Ms. Gold just made, you better have a house that can withstand a tornado." She shook her head firmly. "But the blueprint you just heard is for a house of cards. We're going to show you that there's nothing there, ladies and gentlemen. Those walls are paper-thin, and that, of course, is the problem with a house of cards. At the slightest breeze, the whole thing collapses. And let me assure you, ladies and gentlemen, my client plans to do a whole lot more during this trial than blow hot air."

Two of the male jurors chuckled appreciatively, and Mrs. Trotter—the black cleaning woman—nodded her head.

Not a good sign.

Kimberly shifted gears and became entirely businesslike as she opened her loose-leaf notebook. For the next ninety minutes, she proceeded to escort the jury through what she believed the evidence in the case would show. It was an exhaustive—indeed, exhausting—presentation, and most of the jurors were looking exhausted by the time she rounded the final turn.

"As for damages," she said, pausing as if to contemplate the topic, "I shall not have anything to say on the subject now. We shall learn that damages need never be considered unless the plaintiff establishes a right to recover them. Without liability, there can be no damage." Another pause. "When we come to the conclusion of this case, I shall have an opportunity to address you again. I think you will agree with me at that time that there is no right to recovery here—that there is no liability."

She closed the book and gave the jurors a firm smile. "I thank you for your attention. I shall look forward to addressing you again at the close of the case."

She turned and moved toward her chair, glancing at me, her face set in grim determination.

I called Ruth as my first witness. Although she had no direct knowledge of the bid-rigging conspiracy, I knew that the jury's interest in hearing from her would be especially high. She was, after all, the reason we were all here. She was also, like all *qui tam* relators, vulnerable to the charge that she was nothing more than an avaricious bounty hunter, in it just for the money—a charge Kimberly had already floated during her opening statement.

For that reason, I wanted her in the witness stand today, even if it was already almost four o'clock when she raised her right hand and swore to tell the truth, the whole truth, and nothing but the truth. I probably had no more than an hour's worth of questioning and ought to be able to conclude her direct examination before we recessed for the day. It would be just enough time for Ruth to make a first impression on the jury, and Ruth made good first impressions.

It would also give Kimberly Howard and her troops all night to prepare for Ruth's cross-examination, which was just fine. I was convinced that the most devastating cross-examination of Ruth was a succinct one demonstrating that she had no direct knowledge of any key issue in the case. But I suspected that Kimberly wouldn't be able to resist the chance to grind Ruth into the ground right at the outset of the case. After all, she had deposed the poor woman for thirteen days. Within those 2,506 pages of deposition transcript—including almost 200 pages of questions and answers on various unsubstantiated charges that Ruth had taken paperclips, pencils, and other office supplies home over the years—were plenty of questions that Kimberly would be tempted to ask again in front of the jury.

I was hoping Kimberly would be tempted. I also hoping she'd underestimate the risk. Kimberly was an excellent cross-examiner, but she had a rigid authoritarian style. While that might play well when the witness was an arrogant corporate executive, Ruth was hardly that. Seated in the witness box in her floral-print dress with her big purse on her lap, she was a grandmother from *Mister Rogers' Neighborhood*. You could almost imagine her opening that big purse and removing a small tin of fresh-baked tollhouse cookies to offer to the jury and "to you, too, Miss Howard." If Kimberly tried to take her on a Bataan death march during cross-examination, it could generate a lot of sympathy for Ruth—and thus for Ruth's case. Or so I hoped.

The timing worked out perfectly. I spent an hour and fifteen minutes with Ruth on the stand. We went through her personal background and her years of employment at Beckman Engineering. Over Kimberly's repeated objections, the judge allowed Ruth to give a brief description of the vaguely sinister hints she had heard within the office about the bidding process on certain federal government contracts and her difficult decision to take on her former employer in this lawsuit. It was like waving a red flag in front of the defendant's table. Everyone on their trial team was glaring at Ruth when, at 5:17 P.M., I turned to Judge Wagner and said, "I have no further questions, Your Honor."

The judge announced that we would be in recess until the following morning at 9:30 A.M. After the judge, jury, and court personnel filed out of the courtroom, Ruth and I started packing up for the night. Benny joined us at plaintiff's table just as Kimberly and her entourage marched out of the courtroom, leaving in their wake three clerks and a paralegal to repack the trial boxes and transport the essential stuff back to whichever Roth & Bowles conference room was now serving as the *Alpert* v. *Beckman* war room.

"Way to go, Ruthie baby," Benny said with a big grin.

"You were kicking some major butt up there today, girl."

Ruth covered her mouth and giggled. "Oh, my goodness, Benny, the things you say."

He turned to me. "How'd the openings go?"

I shrugged. "Okay, I guess."

"Oh, Benny," Ruth said fervently, "you should have heard Rachel's speech. My goodness, it was beautiful."

"Hey," Benny said, "you think I'm surprised? I've said it before and I'll say it again. She's got the legs and she's got the looks, and if I ever decide to make an exception for smart women with balls, Rachel Gold is first in line for the title of Mrs. Benny Goldberg."

I glanced up from my trial notebook and placed my hand on my chest. "Oh, be still my heart."

"So *nu*?" he asked. "What's on the agenda for tomorrow?"

I looked around to make sure no one from the other side was in earshot. "They'll start with Ruth's cross-examination," I said softly. "That'll take all morning. Maybe even into the afternoon." I reached over and squeezed her elbow reassuringly. "But she's ready."

Ruth took a deep breath and sighed. "I hope so."

"Who's your second witness going to be?" Benny asked.

I frowned. "I'm not sure. A lot depends on how long Ruth is on the stand. I might read Otto Koll's deposition. I might put the Max Kruppa documents into evidence. Or, I might even call the big guy."

"Conrad?" Benny asked, surprised.

"Maybe." I was packing up my stuff as we talked. "It depends on how things go."

I didn't want to put on any of my expert witnesses tomorrow. It was too early in the case for that. And I certainly didn't want to spend half a day with one of the Beckman Engineering employees dueling over the meaning of various bid documents as the early momentum in our case slowly leaked out. If I was going to call Conrad Beckman to the stand, it was better to do it early on. That way he wouldn't be sure how many cards I was holding.

I closed my large trial briefcase, snapped the clasp, and looked up with a smile. "Well, guys, Day One is history. Let me call Jacki and see what's cooking."

I called from one of the pay phones down the hall. Benny and Ruth were standing nearby. When the call ended, I turned toward them with a pensive expression and glanced down at my notes.

"What?" Benny asked.

"Jonathan called. He found a name for me. Kurt Lindhoff."

"Who's that?" Benny asked.

"He was on the St. Louis police force back in the forties and fifties. He's dead, but his daughter lives here. She's in her sixties, some sort of therapist. Apparently, she's willing to talk to me tonight."

"How does she fit in?" Benny asked.

I turned toward Ruth and gave her a sympathetic smile. "Her father was the homicide detective assigned to your uncle Harry's murder."

CHAPTER 23

At precisely eight o'clock, Ingrid Lindhoff opened the door to her inner office. "Rachel Gold?"

I stood up. "That's me."

She gave a formal nod. "Please come in."

For some reason I'd pictured a marriage counselor as warm and bubbly and cheerful, but Ingrid Lindhoff was no Dr. Ruth. She had the lean, angular look of a long-distance runner, with slate gray eyes, high cheekbones, and thin lips in a square, compact face. Her outfit was no-nonsense: white blouse, beige skirt hemmed just below the knees, black flats. No perfume, no makeup, no jewelry. Her iron gray hair was cropped short, accentuating her widow's peak.

She took a seat behind her desk and motioned toward one of the chairs facing it. Her office matched her appearance. Solid, functional furniture on a gray carpet, three drab pen-and-ink rural landscapes framed on the walls.

"Thank you for seeing me," I told her.

"Your client was related to Harry Rosenthal?"

"Harry was her uncle."

"I see." Her entire demeanor was precise and reserved.

"I understand that your father investigated the case," I said.

"Both cases. Mr. Rosenthal's murder in 1943, and Mr. Bernstein's murder the prior year."

"I didn't realize he was assigned to both."

"He wasn't assigned. He *volunteered*."

"Oh, I see." But I didn't. She must have sensed it.

"You are Jewish, Ms. Gold?"

I stiffened slightly. "I am."

"As you know, both victims were Jewish." She leaned forward, steepling her hands beneath her chin. "My father was a German immigrant. His family moved to America when he was five. They settled in South St. Louis with the other German immigrants." She paused. "My father was a proud American, Ms. Gold. It was at the crux of his identity. His patriotism was a prime motivation for his decision to become a policeman. He believed that it was his duty to stand guard over the American Dream. Those are his words." Her eyes seemed to go distant for a moment, a wisp of a smile tracing her lips. "Kurt Lindhoff was the sort of man who could say something like that without sounding corny."

"Why did he volunteer for those two homicides?" I asked.

"Because of Hitler," she replied, almost matter-of-fact. "He despised Hitler, he despised Nazism, and he especially despised the German Americans who supported Hitler. He viewed the German-American Bund as a personal affront. He denounced them at meetings and handed out leaflets against them on street corners." She paused, smiling at a memory. "Once, the Bund held a rally at the Friedrich Jahn monument in Forest Park. My father helped organize the anti-rally. They hired a biplane and pilot for the afternoon. The pilot flew over the rally, and my father dumped several buckets of horse manure onto the demonstrators."

I laughed. "That's wonderful."

Her smile faded. "A few nights later a gang of masked thugs dragged my father into an alley and beat him severely. He spent more than a month in the hospital."

I winced. "Oh, no."

She nodded. "But he was a hero in South St. Louis. Most German immigrants were loyal Americans." She leaned back and crossed her arms over her chest. "My father viewed the Bund members as traitors to America and traitors to God. He loathed their anti-Semitism and their racism. That's why he volunteered to work on those homicides." She paused. "It started as a personal crusade. Unfortunately, it became an unhealthy obsession."

I could see how she might be an effective marriage counselor. Although she exuded no warmth, she was no doubt a meticulous diagnostician.

I removed my portable dictation machine from my briefcase. It was about the size of a deck of cards. "Would you mind if I record this?" I asked. "I don't always trust my notes."

She nodded. "That's fine."

Over the next forty minutes, Ingrid Lindhoff described her father's quest to solve the two murders—an obsession that consumed his waking hours, wrecked his marriage, and ultimately destroyed his life. Myron Bernstein had been the first homicide victim. When Harry Rosenthal was killed eighteen months later, Lindhoff volunteered for both cases. He knew enough about Nazi Germany and the Bund ideology to understand the significance of the two murder dates. Although other detectives were assigned to each case, Lindhoff pestered his superiors for months until they relented and put him in charge of both investigations. He was thirty-seven at the time. The assignment would become his life's work.

He spent full time on both cases for more than a year, but in the spring of 1945 his superiors informed him that all personnel assigned to the investigation were being reassigned to other, newer cases. Although he could remain nominally in charge of the investigation, they expected him to take on a full caseload of other homicides. After all, they explained, a fresh batch of unsolved murders had been added to their department's inventory since Harry Rosenthal's death, there were no solid leads in either of the so-called Nazi cases, and the word from City Hall was that Homicide better start arresting some murder suspects pronto. Ironically, he received the news on May 8, 1945, the day after Germany surrendered.

Kurt Lindhoff was a good cop. He accepted the decision and his new caseload without complaint. But he remained far more than nominally in charge of the Bernstein and Rosenthal investigations. He continued to work both cases hard, squeezing in time at night and on weekends. Ingrid Lindhoff was in high school at the time, and she could remember going to bed most nights before her father got home from work. Not surprisingly, her parents' marriage crumbled. Within weeks after Ingrid started her freshman year at the University of Missouri, her mother left her father and moved in with her spinster sister.

"He changed," she said, a touch of melancholy coloring her otherwise rigid features. "My father had been the classic Germanic type, obsessed with order and cleanliness. He used to spend an hour after church every Sunday morning scrubbing our porch and front steps."

But no longer. The house began to deteriorate physically. By the time she graduated college, one of the awnings was torn, the paint on the outside was peeling, the grass was uncut, and one of the shutters was hanging at an angle. She recalled her dismay over what she saw when she visited him. The whole house smelled of musty cigar smoke and stale beer. There were files on the two murders spread throughout the house. The kitchen was a disaster area, with piles of dirty dishes in the sink, dozens of empty cans of beans and chili on the counters and table, and swarms of fruit flies everywhere. Her father slept most nights on the couch in the living room. Dirty socks and underwear and shirts were strewn on the floor. Crackpot informers and other oddballs would drop in at all hours of the night with "hot tips" on the cases. And at the center of this swirling chaos was her father, once the spit-shine lawman, now a disheveled kook.

"It was quite distressing for me," she said.

But her father remained focused and confident. "Just a matter of time, Ingrid," he used to promise his daughter. "There's no statute of limitations for murder. We'll find the bastard."

And, surprisingly enough, he did.

In the fall of 1955—nearly twelve years after Harry Rosenthal's murder—the newspapers announced the arrest of a suspect in the murders of Harry Rosenthal and Myron Bernstein. Ingrid showed me a photocopy of the article from the

Globe-Democrat. It included a picture of her father posed with the suspect on the steps of the police headquarters.

I studied the photograph with fascination. Detective Kurt Lindhoff was a thick, bull-headed man with a flattened nose and squinting eyes. He was wearing a dark fedora and a wrinkled raincoat over what appeared to be a suit and tie. According to the picture caption, the skinny man in handcuffs standing next to him was Herman Warnholtz. I recognized the name from Harold Roth's reports. It was difficult to make out Warnholtz's features in the photograph because of the shadows. He had a narrow, almost gaunt face, with prominent cheekbones and deep-sunk eyes beneath projecting eyebrows. He was wearing a cap and a jacket over what appeared to be a laborer's shirt and pants. According to the article, Warnholtz was a "local contractor alleged to have once been active in the now defunct German-American Bund."

Within a few days the grand jury indicted Warnholtz for both murders. Kurt Lindhoff was ecstatic. Warnholtz pleaded not guilty at his arraignment, and trial was set for early spring of 1956. But Lindhoff's initial euphoria began changing to anxiety as the trial date approached and he realized that the culmination of his life's work was now in the hands of the prosecutors.

And then the playing field shifted ominously.

"A new lawyer for Warnholtz appeared," Ingrid explained.

He was a fancy dan from Nashville named Rufus von Reppert, who wore cream-colored double-breasted suits and spats, spoke with an elegant Tennessee drawl, and arrived with an entourage of assistants, secretaries, investigators, and law clerks. Rufus booked an entire floor of the Chase Park Plaza and turned it into his trial headquarters. Every night at nine sharp he stepped off the elevator at the Tenderloin Room, usually in the company of his lovely personal assistant Luanne, and the maître d' would escort the two of them to their corner booth for dinner.

But appearances were deceiving, for Rufus was no effete

dandy. He was a brilliant criminal defense attorney with an impressive number of acquittals and hung juries. On the day before Warnholtz's trial was to begin, Rufus pulled off a dramatic coup by convincing the trial judge to dismiss the Harry Rosenthal murder charge for insufficient evidence.

"My father was livid," Ingrid said.

But the jury convicted Herman Warnholtz of murder in the first degree for the death of Myron Bernstein. The trial judge sentenced him to die in the electric chair, and the court of appeals affirmed six months later.

"Was he executed?" I asked.

Ingrid shook her head. "The governor commuted his sentence to life in prison."

I frowned. "Why?"

"No one knows. Governor Roy Thompson was a lame duck at the time and entered the order during his last week in office. My father was convinced that someone bribed him or threatened to blackmail him. There were rumors that Thompson was a homosexual, which is apparently why he decided not run for reelection when his term ended." She paused and shook her head. "I think the governor's decision pushed my father over the edge."

"How so?"

"Warnholtz was in the penitentiary outside Jefferson City. My father drove there once a month to visit him."

"Why?"

She sighed. "My father vowed that he'd find the necessary evidence to convict him for the Rosenthal murder. He'd drive down to prison to taunt Warnholtz, to tell him that he'd watch him die in the electric chair." She shook her head sadly. "It became a pathological fixation. In 1961, my father resigned from the police force to devote himself full time to the case. The last time I saw him was on his birthday, June 22, 1963."

She came to the house to wish him Happy Birthday. Her father looked terrible—haggard and unshaven—but he was also almost delirious with excitement. He claimed to be on the verge of a major breakthrough in the Rosenthal case. He told her, "I'm going to finally see that Nazi bastard fry."

"What was the breakthrough?" I asked.

She shrugged and shook her head. "Probably nothing. My father died a week later, and I certainly couldn't find any breakthroughs in the records he left behind."

"How did he die?" I asked.

She seemed to contemplate the question before answering. "They found his car in the middle of the Chain-of-Rocks Bridge at three in the morning. It was empty. There were no witnesses. They recovered his body from the Mississippi River three weeks later. The medical examiner ruled it a suicide." She paused.

"You have doubts?"

She shrugged. "I've read the literature on suicides. Denial is a common reaction among the surviving family members. Even where the fact of suicide is manifest, the survivors try to rationalize it away." She crossed her arms and frowned. "I've tried to be professional about this. My father was mentally unstable near the end. But still, I do not believe that he was suicidal." She gave me a rueful smile. "Then again, it's difficult to be professional about personal matters."

Ingrid Lindhoff's nine o'clock arrived on schedule. I thanked her for being so generous with her time.

"It was my pleasure, Rachel." She walked me to the side door. "My father died with unfinished business. I suppose that's the way most of us will exit, but his death still troubles me." She put her hand on my shoulder. "An unsolved murder must be every bit as distressing for the relatives of the victim. Please tell your client that my father went to his grave convinced that he had solved it correctly the first time. Perhaps that will help her."

I sat in my car in front of her office for a long time mulling over what Ingrid Lindhoff had told me and how it might fit with what I already knew. I seemed to be stumbling through a maze of mirrors inside a haunted house. Familiar images kept emerging out of the shadows, each time in a different place. I couldn't tell whether I was moving toward a solution or just wandering in circles.

Finally, I started the engine and pulled onto the street. As I headed home, I called Jonathan on the car phone and filled him in on the meeting. After I finished, I said, "I need one more favor from you."

"Sure."

I told him I wanted to try to close the loop on Warnholtz. When did he die, and where? Were there any living relatives? If so, where were they today? That sort of thing.

"The prison authorities keep some records on former inmates," he said. "I'll make a call in the morning."

"That's great. Now tell me how you're feeling."

"I'm getting there. I may go to the office for a couple of hours tomorrow. Good luck in court, Rachel."

"Thanks. 'Bye."

As I pulled into my driveway I slowed to wave at the two officers in the police car idling in front of my house. At Jonathan's insistence, the security detail had been expanded to include me, too. I was not merely another victim of the highway assault, he argued, but a potential witness as well, and someone sure seemed determined to eliminate potential witnesses to that incident. On the prior Saturday night a pair of southern Illinois fire departments had responded to the report of a fire behind an abandoned warehouse. They arrived to find the smoldering remains of a late-model pickup truck. Inside were the blackened corpses of two adult males, both burned beyond recognition. The truck had dents along the passenger-side panel consistent with those on Jonathan's car. The prospects of tracing the truck to its owner had been impeded by removal of the license plates and the VIN number. The prospects of identifying the victims through dental records or fingerprints had been impeded by removal of their heads and hands.

Although the security patrol should have been reassuring,

it seemed to have the opposite effect on me. Every time I peered out my window and saw that police car parked under the streetlight, it triggered an image of those charred and headless corpses seated upright in that burnt-out truck.

CHAPTER 24

R uth Alpert, God bless her, drove them absolutely crazy. Kimberly Howard strode into the courtroom that morning with a gleam in her eye and a fifteen-page cross-examination outline in her hand. She was, as they say, loaded for bear and ready to rumble. Problem was, she had the wrong scouting report. The only bear Ruth resembled was a Teddy, and she wouldn't have known a rumble from a rhumba. Even their outfits were a mismatch. Kimberly had dressed for the part of steely legal assassin. She wore a severe gray pinstripe suit hemmed short, starched white blouse, dark hose, and spiked heels. Ruth, who'd been a little chilly on the witness stand yesterday afternoon, had added a pink cardigan sweater to the latest in her series of frumpy, floral-print calf-length dresses. As for me, I'd aimed for somewhere in the middle today: a navy pinstripe shirtdress with cream collar and cuffs, hemmed above the knee but not as short as Kimberly's.

Kimberly spent an increasingly frustrating five hours—three before the lunch recess, two after—stalking Ruth from one testimonial forest to another without ever getting close enough for a kill shot. Even when she seemingly had Ruth trapped in a contradiction between her deposition testimony and her trial testimony—the ultimate cross-examiner's bull's-eye—Ruth glided away. Ordinarily, cross-examination through use of prior inconsistent testimony is a powerful, low-risk way to undermine a witness's credibility, and frankly, Kimberly was one of the best at the technique. In a hearing in another case, I'd watched her adroitly draw and quarter a witness using prior testimony like honed surgical knives. Although the inconsistencies between Ruth's deposition testimony and trial testimony were not glaring, there were plenty of minor ones in all those transcript pages. Kimberly's goal was to highlight enough so that the cumulative impact would destroy Ruth's credibility. It was a technique that would work with a typical witness.

But Ruth was no typical witness.

"I see," Kimberly said, a pitiless smile forming at the corners of her mouth. "And when Ms. Gold asked you that yesterday afternoon, you said yes, correct?"

Ruth nodded courteously. "I certainly did."

"I take it that your answer today is also yes, correct?"

Ruth gave Kimberly a puzzled look. "Why, of course, dear. It was yes before, it is yes today, and it will be yes tomorrow."

"Why, of course," Kimberly said, the sarcasm dripping from her voice. "It was yes before, it is yes today, and it will be yes tomorrow. However"—dramatic pause—"it certainly wasn't yes last December fifth, was it?"

Ruth looked confused. "I am afraid I am not following you, dear."

Kimberly turned toward Laurence Browning, who smugly held out the transcript from that day of Ruth's deposition. There was a red tab attached to a page about two-thirds of the way toward the back. Kimberly flipped it open to that page as she approached the witness.

"Ms. Alpert, allow me to show you page 193 of the transcript of your deposition from last December fifth." She placed it on the front ledge of the witness box and spun on her heel to face the defendant's table, where Browning was waiting with another copy of the transcript open to the same page. She moved toward Browning and took the copy. "Line fourteen, Ms. Alpert," she announced, back to the witness. She turned to face Ruth. "You'll see that I asked you precisely the same question. Please, Ms. Alpert, be kind enough to read to this jury the answer that you gave back *then*."

Ruth frowned at the page. "Oh, my goodness," she said. She reached down and lifted up her large purse. She placed it on her lap and unsnapped it.

"Ms. Alpert?"

"I am terribly sorry," Ruth mumbled. She was rummaging through her purse.

Kimberly turned toward the jurors. She crossed her arms beneath her breasts as she tapped her foot, the former beauty queen seizing center stage to heighten the drama.

"There," Ruth said with an embarrassed smile as she held up her glasses case. "I am afraid that I am blind as a bat without these." She put on her reading glasses and peered over them at Kimberly. "What line was that, dear?"

Perfect, I said to myself.

Kimberly glared at her for a moment, the tension seeping out of the scene. "Fourteen," she said through clenched teeth.

Ruth studied the page and looked up, puzzled. "Now I am a confused."

Kimberly smiled. "I thought you might be, Ms. Alpert. Why don't you just read aloud what you said."

Ruth looked down at the page and then up at Kimberly. She shook her head. "I didn't say anything at line fourteen. I believe that you are the one speaking there, my dear."

Kimberly looked down at her copy with a frown and read it. "Uh, right. Line fourteen is my question. Read your answer."

"You mean the one at line sixteen?"

Kimberly gave her an irritated stare. "Yes," she hissed. "Read it."

Ruth looked down at the page again. "It says here, 'Probably not.' "

Kimberly nodded triumphantly. "Exactly. Today your answer is yes. But on December fifth it wasn't yes, was it? It was 'Probably not.' Correct?"

I had been watching the jury throughout. If I had to guess from their expressions, the impact of this so-called contradiction was far from what Kimberly had hoped.

"December fifth," Ruth mused.

"Excuse me?" Kimberly said, much louder than necessary.

Ruth frowned at her uncertainly. "December fifth?"

"Yes, Ms. Alpert. December fifth." There was an accusatory edge to her voice. "Remember that testimony?"

Ruth pressed her finger against her cheek in thought. "Miss Howard, was that the eleventh day of my deposition or the twelfth?"

I fought back a smile as I saw one of the jurors, Mr. Fernandez, turn to his neighbor in surprise. He raised his eyebrows in astonishment at the realization that Kimberly had subjected Ruth to twelve days of deposition.

"The eleventh, I believe." Kimberly acted nonchalant.

Ruth flipped back through the deposition. "That was such a long day," she said. "Do you remember the weather that day, Miss Howard?"

Kimberly was trapped. She had to answer. "Not particularly."

"Oh, my heavens, it started snowing at noon. Remember?"

"No." Kimberly's frustration was apparent as she realized that somehow she had lost control of this witness.

"I remember that day," Ruth continued. "It—"

"Please, Ms. Alpert, can we—"

"Objection, Your Honor," I said, standing up. "Can the witness be allowed to finish her answer?"

Judge Wagner looked from me to Kimberly and back to me. Expressionless, she said, "Sustained." She turned to Ruth. "You may continue."

Ruth smiled at the judge. "Why, thank you, Your Honor." She turned to Kimberly. "I remember that day so clearly, Miss Howard." She paused, her brow wrinkling in distress at the memory. "It started snowing at noon. The snow kept getting worse, and you had so many questions for me. So many. I remember it was dark by the time you asked me this one." She held up the deposition transcript. "You see, it's on page 193, and the whole thing is 226 pages. I remember I was so worried about driving home from downtown in all that snow." She shook her head. "I am terribly sorry, Miss Howard. I must have been confused when I gave you that answer. But I am not confused today." She paused to smile at the jury. "I promise." She turned back to Kimberly. "And that answer is most definitely yes. Yesterday, today, and tomorrow."

She closed the deposition transcript and gave Kimberly Howard a smile warm enough to melt butter. All six jurors and the alternate were beaming.

"There," Ruth said with a satisfied nod. "I hope that clears things up for you, dear."

And so it went. Kimberly scored a few points with Ruth's inconsistent answers, and she certainly was able to underscore what we had readily conceded at the outset, that Ruth lacked direct knowledge on several important factual issues in the case, but those were superficial wounds. By the time Kimberly Howard finally turned away from the witness and announced to the judge, with barely concealed exasperation, that she had no further questions, I was feeling good enough to charge the witness box like the triumphant catcher rushing the mound at the end of the World Series and lift my client in the air with a big hug.

But this was a courtroom, and this particular game of hardball was far from over. I stood up, nodded at my client, and turned toward Judge Wagner. "I have no further questions, either, Your Honor."

We took a fifteen-minute recess.

I spent the first five minutes assuring Ruth that she'd done just fine. I spent the rest of the time debating with myself over my next witness. The safe choice was Otto Koll. Indeed, his testimony was literally a no-brainer. He wasn't in court and he wasn't within the subpoena power of the court, which meant I would have to read his deposition to the jury. That was something I could almost do in my sleep. And that was the problem, of course. It was nearly four o'clock, and my fear was that reading a deposition transcript at this late hour would put the jury to sleep. That was the worst possible use of Otto Koll's deposition. I wanted those jurors fresh and alert when they heard Otto Koll answer, "I don't recall," to dozens and dozens of questions that could be answered truthfully that way only by someone in an advanced stage of Alzheimer's disease. Koll's testimony was strikingly implausible, and I didn't want to dilute any of that implausibility by reading it to a fatigued audience. Moreover, if I waited until tomorrow, I could put Benny in the witness box and have him recite Otto Koll's answers while I read the questions. That would make the deposition reading a far more interesting event for the jury, and hopefully give all those "I don't recalls" an even greater impact.

No, what I needed now was a way to perk up the jurors and underscore the contrast between my client and Beckman Engineering Company. The choice was obvious, although hardly enticing.

When the jurors had reassembled in the jury box and the court personnel were back in their places, Judge Wagner looked down at me from the bench and said, "Call your next witness, Counsel."

I stood and turned toward the defendant's table. "Plaintiff calls Conrad Beckman."

Beckman glanced inquisitively at Kimberly, who tried to keep a poker face.

Excellent, I said to myself.

He rose and moved toward the witness box with stately dignity, looking every inch the chairman and founding father of Beckman Engineering Company. Although the jury had missed it, the brief silent exchange between Beckman and his counsel confirmed what I'd suspected: they hadn't anticipated that I'd call him as a witness in my case. That meant they hadn't yet prepared him for his testimony, having assumed that they would have plenty of time to do so before he took the stand in their side of the case.

Nevertheless, an unrehearsed Conrad Beckman was still a dangerous witness, and putting him on the stand in the middle of my case was a risk akin to poking a stick at a rattlesnake. My goal was to give him a few careful jabs—just enough to make him rattle and show his fangs—and then back off before he struck.

Beckman raised his right hand and allowed the clerk to swear him in. He took a seat in the witness box and gazed at me as if he were here for nothing more demanding than an eye exam. I placed a blowup chart of the six companies on the easel, positioning it so that he and the jury could see it:

Company	Date of Formation	Founder/Current CEO
Beckman Engineering Co. St. Louis, MO	1944	Conrad Beckman/Conrad Beckman
Beek Contracting Co. Gary, IN	1934	Albert Beek/Louis Beek
Eagle Engineering Memphis, TN	1938	Max Kruppa/Arnold Cornfeld
Eicken Industrial Indianapolis, IN	1952	Henry Eicken/Charles McCambridge
Koll Ltd. Chicago, IL	1947	Otto Koll/Otto Koll
Muller Construction Co. Springfield, IL	1953	Edgar Muller/Edgar Muller

"Sir," I said, pointing toward the chart, "you are familiar with the companies on Plaintiff's Exhibit seven, correct?"

He gazed at the chart for a moment and nodded. "I am."

"Over the years you've attended meetings with the founders of each of these companies, correct?"

"I have."

"Would it be fair to say that your relationship with the founders goes way back, in some cases even to a time before they founded their companies?"

Kimberly was on her feet. "Objection, Your Honor. Irrelevant."

Judge Wagner looked at me. "Counsel?"

"It's directly relevant, Judge," I said. "Plaintiff contends that Beckman Engineering has participated in an illegal conspiracy with these five companies. A conspiracy requires a special relationship among the co-conspirators." I paused to point toward the chart. "These are private companies, each run for decades by its founder. The nature and length of Mr. Beckman's relationship with these other gentlemen is thus critical."

"Overruled," the judge announced, turning to Beckman. "You may answer the question."

Beckman pursed his lips as he considered his answer. "I have known these gentlemen for many years," he said calmly, "along with the principals of dozens of firms. Ours is a small industry, Miss Gold. Just as you may know dozens and dozens of your fellow attorneys, many of whom are your competitors, I know many of my company's fellow contractors."

My question had been capable of a yes or no answer. Thus, everything he said after the first eight words was technically nonresponsive. I could have moved the court to strike it from the record, but that would merely emphasize it for the jury. Moreover, Judge Wagner was not about to let me put Conrad Beckman on a short leash. Given that fact, my best strategy was to ignore his speeches and keep nudging him in the direction I wanted him to go.

"But let's focus on these five companies, sir," I said in a pleasant voice as I pointed again toward the chart. "Your relationship with each of these founders dates back before World War II?"

"Objection, Your Honor. Irrelevant."

"Overruled."

Beckman studied the chart. "Miss Gold, three of the five companies did not even exist before World War II."

"I realize that, sir. My question had to do with the *founders* of the companies. You had a relationship with each of those men that predated World War II, correct?"

"A relationship?" Beckman asked rhetorically. "Perhaps I knew them. I don't know whether I would call that a relationship."

"Fair enough," I said with an amiable smile. I moved over toward the jury box. "Let's try to figure out what to call it, Mr. Beckman." I stared at the chart and pointed toward the entry for Eagle Engineering. *Might as well hear his rationalization early on.* "Why don't we start with Max Kruppa. Tell us about the origins of your relationship with him."

Beckman crossed his arms over his chest and wrinkled his brow, as if trying to remember. "I can't recall where or when I met Mr. Kruppa, Miss Gold. Max was a German immigrant. During the years before World War II he still had strong feelings about the old country. He knew that my parents came from Germany. For some reason, he thought that made a special bond between us. I recall that he tried to interest me in certain German-American organizations."

"Which German-American organization, sir?"

Beckman rubbed his chin. "This was many years ago. I believe it was originally known as the Friends of the New Germany."

"The Friends of the New Germany changed its name, didn't it, Mr. Beckman? It became the German-American Bund, correct?"

He fixed me with dead eyes. "You may be right, Miss Gold." He paused and shrugged. "As I said, that was many years ago."

"So you and Mr. Kruppa were both members of the German-American Bund?"

He shook his head. "I don't know about Mr. Kruppa's affiliations. I certainly was not a member. I will concede that I attended one or two of their meetings, although curiosity was the primary motivation. They held their meetings in the neighborhood where I grew up." He paused. "I am not proud of that, Miss Gold. I was a teenager, and I did some stupid things back then." He turned to the jury and shook his head with chagrin. "Frankly, I regret it."

It was a masterful parry. His answer contained just enough truth and exactly the right tone of contrition to make any effort at follow-up too dangerous. I'd poked the stick, and the diamondback had made sure I heard his rattle. Although I could use the English translation of Kruppa's letter to argue to the jury that Kruppa must have been writing to someone with far more than a mere "curiosity" in the American Nazi movement, it wasn't a clear shot, and I'd risk antagonizing the jury in the process.

Beckman had already conceded the key point—namely, that he had attended at least two Bund meetings. He dismissed his actions as the foolishness of youth, and the more I harped on it, the more I risked giving Kimberly an opening to rebut it with character evidence. Judge Wagner wouldn't need much of an excuse to let Kimberly put on a conga line of testimonials from the heads of all the charitable organizations that had given him awards over the years. By the time they were done, he'd be St. Conrad.

So I moved on.

He conceded, in an almost offhand way, that he had known each of the founders of the other four companies for several decades.

I didn't come right out and ask whether his company had been a co-conspirator in the bid-rigging conspiracy. No sense lobbing that fat pitch over the plate. He'd get plenty of batting practice when it was Kimberly's turn. Instead, I tried to keep my pitches around the edges of the plate. It wasn't easy. I showed him a blowup poster of Max Kruppa's seemingly incriminating American Express receipt. Beckman readily—indeed, almost casually—conceded that he'd attended meetings over the years with different industry representatives. Then he turned toward the jury to assure them that his company had never participated in any discussion of bids or pricing at those meetings.

As for the words that Max had scribbled on the back of the receipt in the box entitled "business purpose"—*"Meet w/ Koll, Muller, Beckman, Beek & Eicken to divide up pending federal IFBs*"—he shrugged them off. "I was not at that meeting, Miss Gold, and I certainly would not want to speculate as to what Max meant by those words." He shook his head sadly. "It's a shame he isn't here to tell us himself."

I poked the stick a few more times before Judge Wagner announced that court would be in recess until nine-thirty the following morning. When the last of the jurors had filed out of the courtroom and the door had swung closed behind them, Kimberly jumped to her feet.

"Your Honor," she said, her face twisted in anger, "Miss Gold is using this lawsuit as a vehicle for running a smear campaign against one of the most respected and revered citizens of St. Louis." She gestured toward the gallery. "She's playing to the press out there while she shamelessly attempts to prejudice this jury with totally irrelevant gossip that is more than half a century out of date." She flung her arm toward me. "In the name of fairness and decency, defendant implores the Court to enter sanctions against this woman."

Judge Wagner turned a stern face toward me. "Well?"

And once again we rehashed the same evidentiary issue we'd argued several times before, and once again Judge Wagner cut it off with a stern warning.

"You are on very, very shaky ground, Ms. Gold." She spoke slowly and clearly, presumably to make sure that every member of the press heard her words. "It was your decision to open this can of worms. I'm warning you right now that you had better be able to reach in there and pull out a big fat night crawler before this trial is over or I'm going to give this jury a special instruction on attorney misconduct that'll make your curly hair stand on end." She stood up and turned to leave the bench. "That's all for today."

CHAPTER 25

The phone rang at quarter after six that night. I was slumped on the couch in the corner of my office with my shoes off, my feet up, and a half-empty bottle of Samuel Adams Boston Lager resting on my lap. Exhausted, I turned toward the phone and tried to will myself up.

"I'll get it." Benny walked over to the credenza and lifted the receiver. In a ridiculous Japanese accent, he announced, "Dese are Raw Office of Honorable Rachel Gold."

He listened a moment and grinned. "Hey, dude. Yeah, rough day in court, but she's holding up." He looked over at me and winked. "Jonathan, you wanna join us for a traditional Jewish meal? No, man, I'm talking about the food of our people: Chinese takeout."

He listened a moment and then laughed. "Come on, dude, remember that passage in the Haggadah? Let's see, how's it go? 'Rabbi Elazar, the son of Azariah, having come to Bene-Berak on the night of Passover, said, Verily, I am like a man of seventy years of age, yet I have never found a matzoh-meal version of potstickers that doesn't taste like fried ca-ca.' You sure? Hey, I understand. Yeah, she's right here."

He brought the phone over to me. "It's Mr. Wonderful. Listen, I'm going out to the car for a moment. I think I left the rest of the brewskis out there."

I took the receiver. "Hi," I said in a listless voice.

I had a road map of Missouri open on my desk when Benny came back with three more bottles of Samuel Adams.

"They were hiding under the dry cleaning," he said. "What are you looking for?"

"Potosi," I said.

"Potosi?" Benny said, as he set the bottles on the desk. "There's nothing down there but the prison."

"Exactly." I tilted the takeout container of Hunan chicken and used the chopsticks to scoop out the last of it. Chewing slowly, I studied the map.

The Potosi Correctional Center occupies the slot within the Missouri penal system that Marian does within the federal system. It houses the eight hundred or so inmates classified "maximum custody" or "risk to the public," all of whom are serving at least twenty-year sentences. It also houses Missouri's death row inmates, whose final seconds are spent strapped to a gurney in a special room in the prison infirmary known among the inmates as "the cage." The condemned man gets to watch as the white-coated attendant meticulously swabs his arm with rubbing alcohol to protect him from, heaven forbid, contracting an infection from a contaminated needle used for the lethal injection.

Benny had a baffled expression. "Who the hell is in Potosi?"

I looked up at him. "Herman Warnholtz."

Benny's eyes widened. "He's still alive?"

"Barely," I said. "He's in his eighties and has terminal cancer."

"How did Jonathan locate him?"

"Easier than you'd think. One phone call to someone in the corrections division. They ran the name through the computer and pulled it right up. Jonathan had someone in the A.G.'s office call down to Potosi to tell them that I needed to talk to Warnholtz as soon as possible. He told them it had to be at night because I was in trial all day." I checked my watch. "I have an appointment in two hours if I want it. All I need to do is call down there to confirm it."

"You've got an appointment tonight?" Benny repeated in disbelief. "Just like that?"

I shrugged. "Jonathan called in a favor. It's not as if Warnholtz has a prior engagement."

Benny came around the desk to look at the map with me. "Where the hell is Potosi?"

"There." I pointed to a spot about ninety miles south of St. Louis in the heart of the Lead Belt mining district.

He studied the map for a moment and turned to me. "Are you really going down there tonight?"

I shrugged. "Maybe it's just a wild-goose chase, but I have to do it."

Benny frowned. "Even if this creep knows something, what makes you think he'll tell you?"

"I don't, but I'll never find out if I don't try. What's the worst that could happen? I drive a four-hour round trip for nothing, right? I'm still home before midnight. How bad is that? It'll be quiet in the car, I'll be able to think about the case, maybe come up with some good ideas for cross-examination. Oh, and I bought myself a treat last weekend: Bob Marley's greatest hits. I can listen to that, too."

Benny stared at me for a moment and uttered a weary groan. Silently, he opened a bottle of beer, took a big sip, swallowed, and rolled his eyes heavenward. "I can't believe this."

"What?"

Grumbling under his breath, he turned toward the phone, lifted the receiver, and punched in a number. As he waited for it to ring, he shook his head in frustration.

"Hi," he said into the phone, his voice subdued. "It's me. Listen, something's come up in this case. They're going to need my help tonight. Yeah, I'm real sorry. Maybe we can get together later this week. Sure. I'll call you. Take care."

He hung up and stared at the phone.

"Oh, Benny, you didn't have to do that."

He snorted as he headed over to get his coat. "Right. Did you happen to notice where Potosi is located? Smack dab in the middle of *Deliverance* country, that's where. And you're planning to head down there alone? And at night?" He slipped on his coat. "Let's roll."

"Benny, you really don't—"

"Enough," he said, holding up his hand to silence me. "Move it, woman."

I was, of course, delighted and grateful. I called the prison to confirm the appointment, and then I stuffed a yellow legal pad, my portable dictation machine, and three dictation cassettes into my briefcase. On the way down the walk toward my car, I asked him who he had called.

"Who?" He looked over at me and shook his head sadly. "Here's a hint: what do you call a sexy twenty-one-year-old aerobics instructor who can suck a golf ball through a garden hose?"

I knew the punch line, but it took a few seconds to get the point. "Oh, Benny," I said sympathetically, hugging his arm. "You're an angel."

"An angel?" he said sarcastically. "No, I believe 'imbecile' is the correct term for someone who just passed up an evening of, shall we say, high-impact aerobics to spend some quality time inside a state penitentiary with a Nazi cretin doing life for murder."

"Well," I said, kissing him on the cheek as I slipped my arm through his, "you're my imbecile, and I think you're the greatest."

"Words suitable for an epitaph. Oh, well, as Bob Marley would say, 'No woman no cry.' "

Look at the bright side," Benny said impatiently. "If you marry him, at least you can start getting laid again."

We had exited the divided highway about ten miles back. We were now on Highway 47, an unlit state road that cut west through St. Francois County and into Washington County. We were definitely in the boonies now, many miles from the nearest *minyon*.

I glanced over at Benny in the darkness. "You know what my sister said? She told me that Jonathan is what you'd call a real Jew."

"Oh, really?" he said caustically. "Did you tell her that her husband is what you'd call a real putz?"

"She didn't mean it as an insult, Benny. It's just that he's so . . . well, you know."

"Religious?" Benny put his hand over his chest in mock horror. "What a disgrace."

"Benny," I said, exasperated.

"Listen," he said, holding up his hands, "if it was me marrying him, you could understand my reluctance."

I gave him a baffled look. "Huh?"

"I'm talking about a female version of me, okay? I'm making a cogent point here."

A female Benny Goldberg. The image made me giggle.

"What I'm saying," he continued, "is that we'd be like oil and water, Jonathan and me. I'm about as likely to spend a Saturday morning at a synagogue as I am to have an elective colostomy. But look at you. What more could any nice Jewish boy pray for? You light the candles on *Shabbat*, you fast on Yom Kippur, and you've got a tush that would make the Ayatollah recite the *Shema*. The perfect Jewish wife." He paused. "Right?"

I looked over at him with a smile. "I thank you, and my tush thanks you, but neither one of us has any idea what you just said."

"Look, Rachel, it's not like you're marrying some Lubavitcher zealot in a black coat and felt hat who gets his jollies throwing rocks at cars. The man's got cable TV, for chrissakes. I even watched *Beavis and Butt-head* with him one night."

"Now there's a testimonial."

We'd reached Highway O, which was about two miles east of the town of Potosi. My smile disappeared as I turned right at the intersection. It was up ahead, a few hundred yards down Highway O, looking more like a space-colony garrison than a high-security prison. We stared at it as I drove slowly along Highway O. The prison consisted of a group of low-slung, gray-block modules topped with huge rolls of coiled razor wire that shimmered beneath the powerful overhead spotlights. Facing Highway O was the large gray door where the hearse drives in and out on execution day. I'd read somewhere that the grassy expanse on either side of that road fills with black crows on execution days.

We passed through the first checkpoint and parked in a guest spot near the entrance to the administrative building. Once inside the building, we moved through another checkpoint, this one with a guard behind a glass enclosure, and then we entered the spartan waiting area. Five minutes later, deputy assistant warden Billy Dillard came out to greet us. He was a pudgy man in an off-white short-sleeve shirt and a wide iridescent tie held in place by a Southeast Missouri State tiepin. In his forties, Dillard looked remarkably like an updated version of Oliver Hardy, right down to the unkempt black hair and splayed little mustache. He'd obviously been briefed in advance and instructed to be courteous.

"I talked to one of the paramedics an hour ago," Dillard explained as he escorted us down the hallway and through the first of several checkpoints. "He said Herman seemed alert."

"That's not always the case?" I asked.

Dillard pursed his lips and shook his head. "Oh, no. I'm afraid Herman's in bad shape."

"What kind of cancer does he have?" I asked.

"Prostate. Inoperable. He's dying. He's lost a lot of weight in the last three months. They don't give him more than a few weeks, a month tops."

"What kind of inmate was he before the cancer?"

"Well, ma'am," he said thoughtfully, "he's been a resident here since this facility opened. He was transferred from Jeff City with a clean record, and he's never been a problem here. He pretty much keeps to himself. Likes to do woodwork. It's his hobby, you might say. He subscribes to one of those carpenter magazines and works down in the prison shop a couple days a week—or used to, back before the cancer got him. Tables, chairs, that sort of thing. We donated some of his stuff to the local library. He was a pretty decent carpenter in his day."

We stopped at the prison infirmary checkpoint. The guard acknowledged Dillard's arrival with a nod and a polite "Evening, sir."

"Where'd they put Herman, Ray?"

"Room C, sir."

We followed Dillard through the main section of the infirmary, past the execution room (with curtains drawn over the observation window), and down a short hallway lined with doors. Dillard stopped in front of the one marked "Room C" and peered through the narrow observation slot. Then he opened the door and stepped in.

"Herman," he said in a loud, artificially cheerful voice, "here are the folks I told you about."

Dillard turned and gestured for us to join him. I filed into the small windowless room, followed by Benny. A hospital bed dominated the room. I stood at the foot of the bed as Dillard introduced us to Herman Warnholtz.

I was surprised and I was disappointed. This was not the Herman Warnholtz I'd expected to see. Perhaps it was the ravages of age and disease, but there was no sign of the brute in the shrunken ghost that gazed up at me from the bed. He may once have been a Nazi thug who headed a vicious gang named after the SS guards that ran Treblinka and Buchenwald. He may once have celebrated Hitler's birthday by tying up a Jewish shopowner with baling wire and incinerating him in his store. But these were not the eyes of the Devil's henchman. These were weary eyes—faded blue but still clear—eyes that seemed almost benign. This was a dying old man, a faded stick figure with sunken cheeks and a bald head sprinkled with age spots. His arms were at his sides on top of the sheet, the skin as thin and fragile as tissue paper. A slight palsy caused his left hand to make a faint patting noise on the sheet.

"Good evening, sir," I said.

He nodded in acknowledgment, a tiny movement of his head.

As he stared at me, I thought of his old adversary, Harold

Roth. Both men so young and vibrant back in the 1939, decades later so withered and frail, Harold now dead, Warnholtz soon to follow.

"I'm here to ask you some questions," I continued. "I hope you'll be willing to answer them."

"About what?" His voice was soft and husky.

"Conrad Beckman, sir."

He frowned. "Why?"

"Because you knew him."

He gazed at me, his eyes closing. "What makes you say that?"

"Because I know things about you, sir."

His eyes remained closed. For a moment I thought he was asleep, but then he asked, almost in a whisper, "What things?"

"I know about the Deutsche-Horst family camp along the Meramec River." His eyes opened and then narrowed. I continued. "I know that you were one of the camp counselors, along with Rudolphe Schober and Conrad Beckman."

His expression was blank, but his eyes were now alert.

I met his stare. "I know about the Death's Head Formation. I even know about San Carlos de Bariloche."

He studied me. "How?"

"I just do." I shrugged. "But I don't know the whole story. I know that Conrad Beckman was active in the Bund before World War II. I know that he did a major construction job down in San Carlos back in the fifties, and I know that he did it with one of his competitors."

"Who?" Warnholtz asked in his hoarse voice.

"Who?" I repeated, unsure.

"Which competitor?"

"Eagle Engineering."

"Eagle?" he repeated in a whisper, searching his memory.

"Down in Memphis," I explained. "Max Kruppa owned the company."

"Max." He nodded, a faraway look in his eyes.

"You knew Max?"

He seemed to contemplate me for a moment, and then

closed his eyes. "Long time ago," he said. "Who cares anymore?"

"I care. I think it might hold the key to my lawsuit."

His eyes still closed, he asked, "Who are the others?"

I told him about the bid-rigging conspiracy and the names of each of the company founders.

He listened in silence. I waited. Eventually, he opened his eyes and turned toward Billy Dillard. "I'll talk to her. Alone."

Dillard shrugged. "You sure, Herman?"

He nodded and turned toward Benny with a frown.

I shook my head. "He's my colleague, Mr. Warnholtz. I need him to stay here."

He mulled it over. "Fine."

He waited until Dillard had closed the door behind him. Then he turned to me, his eyes narrowing. "I never was a snitch."

I nodded, not sure where this was going but not wanting to derail it by saying the wrong thing.

"I did my time," he said after a moment, his voice still hoarse but now more forceful. "I never said a thing. Not even to that madman Lindhoff." He paused. "But he let me down." There was bitterness in his voice. "He promised he'd take care of my wife and son. But when my wife died in 1964 . . ." His voice trailed off. His eyes seemed to lose their focus. "Pretended he never made that promise. Pretended he didn't even know who I was. He let them put my boy in the state mental hospital." He shook his head. "Not a damn thing."

He squeezed his eyes closed, as if the memory were too painful to bear in the light. I waited. When he finally opened them, they were moist. "That was wrong," he said in a whisper.

I nodded, feeling a tug of compassion in spite of myself.

He looked up at the ceiling, as if he were addressing God. "He broke his promise," he said, his voice stronger. There was more color in his face now. He leveled his gaze at me, his eyes burning. "So I'm breaking mine. I'm a dying man. I'll answer your questions."

"Who broke his promise?" a I asked.

He seemed to grit his teeth, as if gathering the resolve to clear this first hurdle. "Conrad Beckman," he said, his voice laced with anger.

"I see," I said, keeping my expression neutral. I gestured toward the chair along the side of his bed. "Would it be okay if I sat down?"

He nodded.

As I came around the bed and sat down, he turned his head to watch me. I was close enough to hear the raspy strain in his breathing. I set my briefcase on my lap and opened it.

"May I take notes?" I asked as I removed a legal pad and a pen.

He nodded.

I held up my portable dictation machine. "May I use this as backup, in case I can't read my notes?"

He nodded again.

I set the dictation machine on the nightstand and pressed the Record button. I glanced back at Benny, who had moved into the far corner of the room. He was leaning motionless against the wall with his arms crossed over his chest, his expression solemn. I turned to Warnholtz, who was gazing up at the ceiling again.

"Mr. Warnholtz, I'm going to ask you some questions about Conrad Beckman and his company. How long have you known Mr. Beckman?"

He turned to me. "We grew up in the same neighborhood. Back in the 1920s."

"Okay. That's one of the subjects we're going to talk about. I'm also going to ask you about Mr. Beckman's relationship with the men who ran the five other companies that we believe were co-conspirators with Beckman Engineering."

He shook his head. "That might be a waste of your time. I been inside for forty years."

"I understand that, sir. I'm interested in the period before your incarceration."

He gave me a curious look and raised his eyebrows. "How far back?"

"That depends, sir. How far back does your knowledge about those men go?"

He considered the question. "Well, pretty far. For some, even before Die Spinne."

That name again.

"Who was he, Mr. Warnholtz?"

"Who?" He frowned.

"Spinne, sir. Who was he?"

"Who?" he repeated, puzzled. "You mean what."

Now I was confused. "Wasn't Spinne a person?"

He stared at me for a moment, and then his face broke into a smile. As I stared at him, at that grinning bag of bones, the rib cage visible beneath the sheet, the neck a gristly stalk, the sudden awful irony made me shudder. In his final days Herman Warnholtz had become the mirror image of one of those haunted Auschwitz survivors.

"Why are you smiling?" I finally asked.

"You don't know German, do you?"

"No, sir. I don't."

He nodded, amused. It was an awful grin, the skin stretched paper-thin over his skull, the thin lips pulled back from brown, crooked teeth worn down to stumps. A death's head grin.

CHAPTER 26

I got home at twelve-thirty. At two o'clock I was still wide awake in bed, staring at the ceiling, my mind racing. I almost called Ruth to tell her about the interview. Instead, I played part of one of the tapes again to reassure myself that it hadn't all been a dream. I finally drifted off to sleep somewhere around three and awoke with a start at five-ten. I was so antsy I threw on my jogging clothes and took Ozzie for a brisk thirty-minute run.

I was at my desk at six-fifteen drafting my application for a writ of *habeas corpus ad testificandum*, a mouthful of legal mumbo-jumbo that, if granted, would compel the superintendent of the Potosi Correctional Center to transport Inmate #2574312 to the courtroom of the Honorable Catherine Wagner the following morning to give testimony in the matter of *United States ex rel. Ruth B. Alpert* v. *Beckman Engineering Co.* If, however, Herman Warnholtz was too ill to travel, the habeas application requested that I be allowed to take a videotaped deposition at the prison to show to the jury.

I had it in hand when Judge Wagner summoned us into her chambers at 9:00. A.M. to go over the morning's schedule. "Are you done with Mr. Beckman?" she asked, shuffling through some papers.

"I have a few more questions for him, Your Honor. Depending upon other testimony, I may call him again."

"I hardly think so," Kimberly said, turning to me with an glare. "Ask now or forever hold your peace."

I kept my eyes focused on the judge. "There's no need for Your Honor to resolve that issue before it's ripe."

Judge Wagner looked up from her papers and fixed me

with a chilly stare. After a moment, she asked, "And after Mr. Beckman?"

"I'll be reading the deposition of Otto Koll."

"Alone?"

"I'll have an assistant in the witness box to read the part of Mr. Koll."

"Who?" she asked.

"Professor Goldberg, Your Honor."

"Oh, come on," Kimberly scoffed.

Judge Wagner gave me a severe look. "I assume you will impress upon *Professor* Goldberg the fact that he will be appearing today in a United States District Court and not the Comedy Club."

"He understands that, Your Honor."

"And after the Koll deposition?"

I went through the rest of my plans for the day: testimony from a Beckman Engineering employee in the government contracts division, presentation of a series of summary exhibits prepared from Beckman Engineering's bid documents, and— if time permitted—the beginning of the testimony from one of my expert witnesses.

"There's one last item," I said. I handed a copy of the habeas application to Kimberly and the original to the judge. "Plaintiff has learned of an important witness. As you see from the application, he's an inmate at Potosi."

I waited until the judge finished reading the four-page application and my attached affidavit. When she looked up from the documents, I continued, "He has direct personal knowledge of the conspiracy, Your Honor. I'd like to put him on tomorrow morning. He is, however, quite ill. If he's too sick to be transported to St. Louis, I ask for leave to do a videotape deposition one night this week."

Judge Wagner looked over at Kimberly. "Counsel?"

I could tell from Kimberly's expression that she hadn't the foggiest idea who Herman Warnholtz was. It confirmed my hunch. I'd been purposefully vague in my habeas application and in what I said to Judge Wagner about the witness. That's because I assumed that there was only one person connected with Beckman Engineering who would have any idea of the significance of Herman Warnholtz's testimony, and that person was not in Judge Wagner's chambers. I almost felt sorry for Kimberly.

"Defendant objects," she said, regaining her mettle. "This is trial by ambush. Miss Gold doesn't have this man on her witness list. We have no idea who he is."

"Your Honor," I said, "up until two nights ago I had no idea who this man was, either. Mr. Beckman, however, most assuredly knows exactly who he is. I drove down to Potosi after court yesterday to interview the witness and learned that he has direct personal knowledge of critical facts going to the heart of this case." I took a deep breath and exhaled slowly. "I believe that Mr. Warnholtz's testimony will destroy the defendant."

"Please, Counsel," Judge Wagner said, "save the hyperbole for the jury." She turned to Kimberly. "I'm inclined to grant this application in part." She looked at me. "Given that Mr. Warnholtz is quite ill, I'm reluctant to order him brought to St. Louis. I'll have my clerk check with the prison officials this morning to get a clearer sense of his medical condition. If he's strong enough for a videotaped deposition, I'll order one to take place in Potosi on Saturday. If the witness has any admissible testimony, we'll play the videotape to the jury next week."

When we returned to the courtroom, I kept an eye on Kimberly. She gathered her troops into the corner to explain the Herman Warnholtz development. The huddle broke with one of the younger associates dashing out of the courtroom door, no doubt to return to Roth & Bowles to launch a frenzied search for information about Warnholtz.

Kimberly signaled for Conrad Beckman, who had been sitting in the front row of the gallery with two of his assistants going over certain business matters. Beckman joined her in the corner. I watched them closely. He listened to her carefully, rubbing his chin as she talked, his face set in a contemplative expression. When she had finished, she nodded toward me. His eyes followed her gesture. Beckman and I stared at one another. I expected some reaction, perhaps a flicker of anxiety or a flash of anger, but his eyes were dead, his face a blank. I turned away, troubled.

Conrad Beckman settled into the witness chair, a placid expression on his face.

"You understand that you are still under oath?" I reminded him—and the jury.

He nodded. "I do."

"Do you know a man named Herman Warnholtz?"

Another nod, completely unruffled. "It's been many years. We grew up in the same neighborhood."

"When was the last time you saw Mr. Warnholtz?"

He seemed to think it over. "A long time ago," he said, shaking his head. "Probably not since before World War II."

"Mr. Beckman, were you and Mr. Warnholtz ever anything more than childhood pals?"

He gazed at me, his expression almost serene. "Not that I recall, Miss Gold."

"When you were both adults, Mr. Beckman, were you and Mr. Warnholtz ever members of any organizations together?"

"Not that I recall, Miss Gold."

I walked over to the chart showing the other five companies and their founders. "When you were both adults, Mr. Beckman, were you and Mr. Warnholtz ever present at any meetings also attended by any of these men?"

"Not that I recall, Miss Gold."

His composure was impressive, and unsettling. He knew what was coming, possibly as soon as tomorrow, more likely by videotape early next week. Could his strategy be to simply tough it out, to deny Warnholtz's allegations, to characterize them as the ramblings of a bitter, dying killer? Or was he simply conceding what he knew he had to concede—that he grew up in the same neighborhood with Warnholtz—while refusing to budge on any important issue?

No matter. I'd established all I needed to establish through Beckman. The rest would come from Warnholtz's mouth.

"Mr. Beckman, is there anything else of significance that you recall about your relationship with Herman Warnholtz?"

Beckman leaned back in the witness chair and frowned in thought, or at least pretended to. After a long pause, he shook his head. "I don't think so."

"Is there anything that you and Mr. Warnholtz did together that you feel like sharing with this jury?"

"I don't think so."

I paused. "Are you sure?"

He observed me coolly. "Nothing comes to mind, Miss Gold."

I turned toward the judge. "No further questions."

Benny and I finished reading the deposition of Otto Koll to the jury shortly after noon. Judge Wagner announced that court would be in recess until two o'clock. After the jury filed out of the courtroom, I started gathering my papers.

"Counsel," Judge Wagner said, "please approach."

Kimberly and I stepped toward the podium. Judge Wagner was holding my writ application in her hand.

"My clerk spoke with the warden down at Potosi." She looked toward me with an expression that bordered on sympathy.

I caught my breath. Something was very wrong.

"There has been a change of circumstances down there," she continued. "I'm afraid your application has been rendered moot, Ms. Gold."

I gripped the podium for balance. "Moot?"

"The inmate passed away during the night."

"He's dead?" I was numb. "How?"

Judge Wagner shrugged. "Apparently in his sleep. His cancer was terminal." She took out her pen and scrawled *Denied, Moot* across the first page of my writ application. She looked up and nodded firmly. "Ladies, I'll see you back here at two."

CHAPTER 27

Herman Warnholtz was dead, but I had the tapes. Nearly two hours of my questions and his answers. Powerful answers. Astounding answers. Unfortunately, every answer carried the same warning label: inadmissible.

I'd reached the evidentiary barricade known as the Hearsay Rule, and I needed to find the right key to unlock that gate. I had only ninety minutes to find it. But before heading upstairs to the law library to start my search, I sent Benny down three flights to the U.S. Attorney's office with instructions to double-check on the security arrangements and make another copy of the audiotapes. The originals were stored in the evidence vault in the U.S. Attorney's office, thanks to some assistance from Jonathan this morning. My paranoia level—already high when I called him for help at eight in the morning—had jumped even higher with the news of Warnholtz's death. His disease may have been terminal, but I was certain that cancer was not the cause of death. That type of convenient coincidence only occurs in fiction.

The Hearsay Rule.

For fans of courtroom drama, no scene is more familiar than that of opposing counsel leaping to his feet to declare, "Objection! Hearsay." But for the trial lawyer in a real courtroom, as opposed to the one up on the silver screen, no doctrine is more tangled and frustrating.

The Hearsay Rule.

In the usual hearsay situation, there are two witnesses: the one on the witness stand and another one outside the courtroom. The one on the witness stand is essentially the repeater:

his role is to tell the jury what he heard the other one say. The repeater meets the basic requirements for admissible testimony: (1) he's under oath, (2) he's present in the courtroom so that the jury can eyeball him, and (3) he's subject to cross-examination. But the *real* witness—the one whose statement is being repeated—isn't under oath, isn't in the courtroom, and can't be cross-examined.

"What did you *hear* him *say*?" Thus, hear-say.

Objection, Your Honor.

Sustained.

Simple as that. But . . . it's rarely that simple. Sometimes an important witness, someone who ought to be in the courtroom to testify, isn't there. Maybe he's out of town. Maybe he's dead. Or maybe the key statement is a written one—perhaps in a letter or a police report or a hospital record. Each of those documents can contain highly relevant information for the trial, but each is a classic example of an out-of-court statement. How does one cross-examine, say, a purchase order?

And thus the hearsay dilemma for the judge: the choice between evidence that is less than ideal and no evidence at all. In grappling with that dilemma, the courts have carved out dozens of specific exceptions, each for a situation where other factors supply the trustworthiness that the Hearsay Rule was designed to ensure. The challenge for the trial lawyer is to find the exception that opens the gate to the hearsay evidence he wants to present. That was certainly my challenge. The audiotapes were classic hearsay: (1) Warnholtz wasn't under oath; (2) he wasn't in front of the jury; and (3) he couldn't be cross-examined, at least not in this lifetime.

I rooted around in the evidentiary grab bag for ninety minutes and returned to the judge's chambers with a few possible fits, including the Dying Declaration, the Co-conspirator Exception, and that battered skeleton key known as Rule 804, which will unlock the gate when no other key fits, but only if the court determines that "the interests of justice will best be served by admission of the statement into evidence."

"Audiotapes?" Kimberly said in outraged disbelief. "Your Honor, that is the rankest of hearsay. Moreover, it is thoroughly tainted by the surrounding circumstances. To begin with, Mr. Warnholtz was serving a life sentence for a crime so heinous that it undercuts any contention that he could be a credible witness. In addition, he was in the final stages of a terminal disease that in all likelihood had blurred the line between reality and illusion. The man could have been hallucinating for all we know."

"Judge," I said, holding up an audiocassette, "this is an excerpt from the interview. All I ask is that the Court withhold its decision until listening to this, perhaps during our afternoon recess. I can assure you that Mr. Warnholtz was completely lucid throughout the interview. The testimony on this tape is more compelling than you can possibly imagine."

"Testimony?" Kimberly repeated disdainfully. "Don't try to dress up that murderer's blather with fancy names."

"Your Honor?" I said.

Judge Wagner frowned, clearly troubled. "What?"

I leaned across the desk and placed the audiocassette on her blotter. "Please listen to it, Judge. I realize this is an unusual request. I wouldn't make it if I didn't believe it was important."

Judge Wagner lifted the cassette and studied it carefully. "I'll listen to it, Counselor," she finally said, shifting her gaze to me, "but I wouldn't get your hopes up."

I didn't. But when we took our afternoon recess at 3:15 P.M., I prayed that she'd listen to at least some of it. The tape I'd given her lasted twenty minutes and included two excerpts—one having to do with the bid-rigging conspiracy and one that was far more chilling.

The recess was supposed to last fifteen minutes. Judge Wagner didn't return to the bench until three-fifty, and when she did, her demeanor had changed. Gone was the buoyant authority figure. She seemed pale, almost subdued. Before the jury filed in, she asked me when I could supply her with a full copy of the interview tape.

"Right now, Your Honor." I reached into my briefcase. "I have an extra copy with me."

"Leave it with my clerk."

Kimberly jumped to her feet. "Your Honor, I assume Ms. Gold has a copy for us as well."

Judge Wagner looked at her dully. "What?"

"A copy of the interview tape, Your Honor. Defendant is entitled to review it as well."

Behind me, I could hear the buzz in the gallery. There were at least a dozen reporters back there. None of them had any idea what we were talking about, but all had now heard the word "tape" several times.

I stood up. "With the Court's permission, we'd prefer to wait until Your Honor has had an opportunity to listen to the entire tape before we start distributing copies."

"Miss Gold may *prefer* to keep us in the dark," Kimberly said angrily, "but her preference is irrelevant here. Defendant insists upon a copy of the tape."

Judge Wagner shook her head. "I'll review it tonight. We'll decide tomorrow whether copies are appropriate."

The first call came at six-fifty that night. We were sitting around my conference-room table eating pizza at the time—Benny, Ruth, my mother, Jacki, the five law student volunteers, and me.

"It's for you," Jacki said, handing me the phone.

I took it reluctantly. Putting my hand over the receiver, I whispered to Jacki, "Who is it?"

"Some woman." Jacki shrugged. "Probably another reporter."

I sighed. "Hello?"

"Rachel, this is Catherine Wagner."

It took a moment. "Oh, hello, Your Honor."

The others in the room immediately hushed.

"I just finished listening to the tape."

"Oh."

I waited, tense. The others in the room were staring at me.

"My God," she finally said. "It's, well, it's overwhelming."

"I know." My spirits jumped. I gave a halfway thumbs-up signal to the others in the room.

"But Kimberly has a point," she continued in a concerned voice. "What if the disease had affected his mind? Or even worse, what if it's all a lie? What if he was consumed with jealousy over Conrad Beckman's success and decided to try to ruin him? What if this is all just a revenge scheme?"

"But why wait all these years?" I said.

"Perhaps, but that same question applies even if everything he said is true. Why wait all those years?"

"Because no one asked." I was growing concerned. I could sense I was losing her. "He explains on the tape, Your Honor. Lindhoff was the only one who ever tried to get information out of him. After Lindhoff died, no one bothered to ask him. And even if someone had, even after Beckman broke his promise, Warnholtz knew that he'd be a dead man if he talked. But that was no longer a factor at the end. Death wasn't a threat. Whether he talked or not, he was still dying of cancer."

There was a long pause.

"I'll need corroboration," she said.

"Pardon?"

"That tape is hearsay, Rachel, and the most dangerous type. Good God, the stuff on there is toxic. It'll destroy Beckman's reputation. He'll never recover. I must have corroboration before I let anyone hear it. I need independent confirmation that what that man told you is true."

"What kind of corroboration?"

"That's your problem, Rachel. But without it, that tape isn't coming into evidence."

The second call came ten minutes later while we were trying to decide whether the newspaper articles that Zack and Jake had been able to locate from the other five cities would be sufficient corroboration for the judge.

"It's Stanley Roth," Jacki said, as she handed me the phone.

"Rachel," he said, "we need to talk."

I shook my head in exasperation. I didn't have time for this. "Why, Stanley?"

"We have a new settlement offer. I think you and your client will find it extraordinarily attractive."

I closed my eyes and exhaled slowly. "Just give me the dollar amount over the phone, Stanley."

"It's a little more complicated than that. We need to talk in person, Rachel. I'm calling from a meeting at the Hyatt down at Union Station. It ought to be breaking up around ten. I'd be happy to drop by your office if you're still there that late, or I can come by your house if your prefer. Which sounds better?"

That's when it clicked.

I opened my eyes.

The Hyatt.

Union Station.

I was dumbstruck.

"Rachel?" he said. "Are you still there?"

"Uh, fine, Stanley. I'll meet you there."

"You mean at the Hyatt?"

"Right."

"I'm more than happy to come to you."

"No. The Hyatt."

"Well," he said with a chuckle, "if you insist. Let's meet in the Grand Hall. I'll buy you a drink."

"I'll see you at ten."

"Excellent. You won't regret it, Rachel."

I hung up and stared across the table at Benny. It was as if we were the only two in the room.

"Nu?" he finally said.

"Union Station."

He frowned. "So?"

"Judge Wagner wants corroboration."

It took him a moment. "Ah," he said with a smile. But the smiled faded. "You think it's still there?"

I shrugged. "Why not?"

"Why not?" He shook his head. "Because they renovated the whole damn building."

"Not that part."

Benny leaned back with a frown and crossed his arms over his chest. "After all those years?"

I smiled wearily. "You have any better suggestions, Professor?"

The others were watching us closely.

Benny studied me as he pondered the question. Finally, he gave me a wink and grinned. "What the hell, eh?"

I nodded. "My point exactly."

CHAPTER 28

The Grand Hall at Union Station is surely the most dazzling room in St. Louis. Carefully restored to its 1890s splendor, it now serves as the lobby and lounge of the Hyatt Hotel. There are sweeping Romanesque arches and a glorious barrel-vaulted ceiling six stories overhead. The walls and ceiling are decorated with gold leafing, bas-relief, Numidian marble from Africa, Vert Campagne green marble from France. Above the main entryway is a stained-glass mural depicting three seated women as symbols of the three great U.S. train terminals of the 1890s—New York, St. Louis, and San Francisco. Framing the stained-glass mural is the Arch of Whispers, so named because a soft whisper at one end of the huge marble archway can be heard at the far end.

On other nights, normal nights, pleasant nights, I've sat in one of the easy chairs sipping a glass of wine, usually with a friend or a date, and imagined the wonder on the faces of railroad passengers of the 1920s as they stepped into the Grand Hall for the first time. But not tonight. Tonight, the Grand Hall could have been an abandoned airplane hangar, a rusted Quonset hut, a vacant warehouse. I had other things on my mind.

It was ten o'clock. Benny and I sat facing each other across a low cocktail table in the middle of the huge room. There was a lounge pianist playing old show tunes off to one side. Standing alongside the piano was a jowly businessman in his sixties all gussied up in a blue blazer, gray slacks, and fresh tan. He kept the beat with a lit cigarette as he beamed down at the blonde at his side. She was young enough to be his daughter and seemed to be having trouble working up much enthusiasm for Mr. Wonderful or for the *Oklahoma!* medley on the piano. Scattered on couches and love seats throughout the room were small groupings—business travelers, conventioneers, sleek young professionals on dates. Benny and I looked out of place in our jeans and sweatshirts. I had on hiking boots, Benny his green Converse high-tops. We'd dressed for the task facing us after the meeting with Stanley Roth. Instead of a briefcase, I'd brought a backpack weighted with equipment.

The waitress arrived with my cranberry juice and Benny's Anchor Steam.

"Does Ruth have a settlement number?" Benny asked.

I shook my head. "Not after the tapes."

"What if she could clear a million?"

"That's exactly what I asked her. She said no."

Benny took a sip of his beer. "No to a million bucks? Does she realize that if Catherine excludes those tapes, the settlement value is going to plummet big time?"

"I explained it all to her. She understands."

Benny glanced over and said, "Ah, here comes the bagman."

Stanley Roth was approaching from the lobby area of the hotel, moving with grim determination in his dark business suit and Burberry overcoat.

"Hello, Rachel," he said in his smooth, confident voice.

I nodded. "Stanley."

Turning to Benny, Roth said, "And you must be Benjamin Goldberg." He reached down to shake Benny's hand. "I've heard fine things about you at the law school."

The strained chitchat ended when the cocktail waitress arrived to take Roth's drink order, a sparkling water with a twist of lime. After she left, he turned to me and leaned forward, focusing those blue eyes like lasers.

"I'll get to the point, Rachel. Beckman Engineering has determined to put this case behind it and move forward. Rather than haggle and play games, I'll give you my settlement authority. Under the *qui tam* claim, your client is entitled to as much as thirty percent of any recovery. My client is willing to stipulate to that percent." He paused. "Beckman Engineering is prepared to pay three and a half million dollars to settle the case. Your client's thirty percent share is one million fifty thousand dollars. In exchange, your client would sign a confidentiality agreement and turn over all documents and tape recordings. That way we'll achieve genuine closure. Both sides will be able to walk away from this lawsuit and move forward without any baggage." Another pause, this one underscored with a firm smile. "Well, Counselor? Do we have a deal?"

I shook my head. "No."

"No?" He tried to remain affable. It was an effort. "Isn't that a decision for your client to make?"

"It is, and she has. We spoke earlier tonight."

He studied me, his eyes narrowing. "Are you saying that Ruth Alpert is prepared to walk away from a million dollars?"

I nodded.

After a moment, he leaned back in his chair with an annoyed frown. "Okay, let's hear the counteroffer."

"Don't have one."

His face reddened. "That's—that's absurd. How can you reject a million dollars without a counter?"

"Because we know your client won't agree to one of our terms."

His eyes narrowed. "Which is?"

I gazed at him calmly. "A signed confession."

He snorted. "For God's sake, Rachel, are we back to my crazy uncle's paranoia?"

"You mean your *murdered* uncle?"

He shook his head in irritation. "I am surprised at you—and disappointed. You're trying to turn this into a crusade—some lofty battle between good and evil. Well, that's not what it is. It's just a lawsuit, young lady—an ordinary commercial lawsuit, and one of dubious merits at that. I suggest you get down off your white charger and start considering your client's best interests." He leaned forward, his eyes flashing. "We are offering a million dollars. A million dollars! My God, how can you possibly—how can you *responsibly* advise her not to accept it?"

"I didn't. She made the decision on her own. Ruth Alpert has a lot more guts than you and your client ever imagined."

"Guts?" he said caustically. "More like greed. Foolish greed."

I shook my head. "You still don't understand, do you, Stanley?"

He stood up and glared down at me. "I understand plenty," he snapped. "I understand that your client is going to be bitterly disappointed. I understand that even if you somehow pull off a sleazy emotional victory before the jury, your client will never see a penny of it. Beckman Engineering will fight you at every level of the judicial system, and they'll fight that war with resources you couldn't even begin to imagine. We will grind her into the ground."

"You know what, Stanley? They had a name for the Jews who helped the Nazis run Auschwitz. They called them *capos*." I stood up and moved in close, dropping my voice. "You're nothing but a *capo* in a three-piece suit."

He stared at me, the vein in his temple throbbing. "I feel sorry for your client, but not for you. Never." He turned and strode off.

A moment later the waitress arrived with his sparkling water.

Y ou really think so?" Benny asked.

We were standing in the darkness behind the fountain sculptures across the street from Union Station. The frolicking mermaids and spraying river gods were frozen beneath a dusting of snow. We were facing the front of Union Station, known as the Headhouse. It covered two city blocks.

The Headhouse was modeled after the walled medieval city of Carcassonne in southern France. There were massive turrets and a heavy limestone facade and Romanesque arches and a maroon Spanish tile roof. No less an authority than Frank Lloyd Wright had described it as "a noble structure—full of vitality and dignity."

At the eastern end of the Headhouse a clock tower soared 230 feet into the night sky. The illuminated clock facing us showed the time as 11:05. Rising just above the slanted roof of the clock tower was a slender, peaked turret—a minaret that seemed to sprout out of the northwest corner of the tower.

As we stared up at the clock tower and the little minaret, Herman Warnholtz's words echoed in my head. *I told him if anything bad ever happens to me, I got a man with orders to turn 'em over to the cops. Those records were my life insurance policy, you see? Except I don't need no life insurance anymore.*

"But why there?" Benny asked.

"Because that's where his brother worked. He was a janitor at Union Station. You heard what he said. He said his brother knew all the nooks and crannies, the best places to hide things."

We studied the structure in silence.

"It's been, what," Benny said, "forty years? What are the chances?"

"Only one way to find out."

"Jesus, Rachel, how the hell are we supposed to get up there? It's like a goddamn fortress."

He was right. From where we stood, Union Station looked more like a medieval castle in France than a train station in Missouri. But if it looked like a castle, perhaps it was built like one, too, with lots of corridors and passageways and cubbies. I surveyed the upper levels of the Headhouse as I tried to picture the inside of the structure. It had originally contained—in addition to the Grand Hall, the hotel, and the restaurant—dozens and dozens of specialty rooms: ticket offices, waiting rooms, telegraph and telephone centers, offices for various railroad companies. I could see lots of darkened windows, which probably meant lots of rooms and corridors beyond the public areas.

A pair of massive turrets flanked the main section of the

Headhouse. They stood nearly as tall as the steeply slanted roof. Set in the curved outer walls of each turret was an ascending spiral of tall, narrow windows, which presumably tracked a spiral staircase inside. I thought of the barrel-vaulted ceiling of the Grand Hall. With any luck, the spiral stairs reached that high. I'd read somewhere that the ceiling of the Grand Hall, so solid and substantial in appearance from below, was actually a separate structure suspended from the roof. If so, that meant that there had to be access to the crawl space above the ceiling for maintenance of the suspension cables and stained-glass skylights.

The clock tower was at the far left end of the main structure. Although there was no public access to it, *someone* had to have access to it, if for no other reason than to perform routine maintenance on the clocks. If we could find our way into the passageways above the public areas we might be able to find an entrance to the clock tower.

Earlier tonight, after the call from Stanley Roth, I'd toyed with the idea of contacting Jonathan to have him try to get a search warrant, but I decided not to. I didn't know whether a tape recording of a dead convict constituted probable cause for a warrant; nor did I know whether Jonathan would be tainted if I sought his advice on the subject. If there was something important concealed in that clock tower, I didn't want to give any criminal defense attorney a basis to exclude it on a technicality. If it was really up there, Benny and I could bring it to the law enforcement officials in our capacity as private citizens.

I turned to Benny. "Let's check it out."

The best place to check it out was from the arcade, which was an arched passageway that overlooked the Grand Hall one floor above the main level. Although the time was nearly midnight, we weren't as conspicuous as I'd feared. The promise of dramatic views of the Grand Hall had lured others up to the arcade. There was a trio of businessmen ahead of us, an older couple in tourist attire across the way, and an elderly man with a cane behind us. We tried to blend into the sparse night-owl crowd, although a close observer would have noted that we were concentrating on scenery far different from the other strollers. Specifically, we were searching for doorways and passageways.

Eventually, we peeled off from the others to head west down one of the corridors above the hotel registration area. There were doors along the way. Many were marked NO ADMITTANCE, all were locked. I wasn't discouraged. This was a big structure, and the folks who'd normally be moving around the back corridors were maintenance workers and members of the building trades, not security specialists and Secret Service agents. We saw painting equipment—tarps, two stepladders, paint cans—along one hallway. Another had a large floor polisher leaning against the wall. I knew that it was just a matter of time before we found an open door.

I was right. As we moved along a dimly lit corridor at the western edge of the Headhouse, we found a stairwell door propped open. Benny took one of the flashlights out of my backpack and handed it to me. I led the way. The top of the stairs opened onto a narrow hallway with several doors. The first door on our left was unlocked. Inside was a tiny room filled with cleaning supplies and mops. The second door on our right was also unlocked. Inside were wall lockers and a deep sink. We took another flight of stairs up—this one much steeper—and opened the door at the top.

There was a noticeable drop in temperature as we stepped into what at first appeared to be an enormous, unfinished attic. The air was chilly and musty. I paused to get my bearings. A wooden walkway ran the entire length of the room along the wall to our left. To our right was an immense object that seemed to swell up out of the floor in the middle of the room like the sloped, ridged backside of a huge sea serpent—so massive that it blocked our view of the other side of the room. The nautical image was reinforced by the twenty or so steel cables tethered to it like hawser lines, and by the series of narrow catwalks, one every twenty feet or so, that ran up the side of the thing from the wooden walkway. I pointed the flashlight overhead and moved the beam along the steepled underside of the roof. There were cables anchored up there as well, which confirmed what I had assumed. We were standing above the Grand Hall, and the massive thing suspended to our right was the top side of the barrel-vaulted ceiling.

We moved down the walkway along the entire length of the ceiling, pausing to note that the stained-glass "skylights" had powerful fluorescent bulbs suspended above them that mimicked sunlight for those in the Grand Hall below. At the far end of the room we passed through a doorway, down a long flight of stairs, along another corridor, down another flight of stairs, and into what appeared to be the dilapidated remains of a old ballroom. The floorboards were dusty and warped, the walls were exposed brick, and there were rusted support beams standing at odd intervals throughout the area. I swept the flashlight beam around the room slowly, trying to get my bearings. We had started west of the Grand Hall, moved east over it, and were now even farther east. We had to be getting warm.

We walked to the far end of the room and went down another set of stairs.

"Over there," Benny said.

I aimed the flashlight to where he was pointing. The beam illuminated an archway cut into the side wall. I moved toward it cautiously. As we got closer, I could make out a metal stairway through the arched opening.

"I think we found it, Benny." I could hear the excitement in my voice.

We stopped in the doorway, and I pointed the flashlight upward. The metal stairway zigzagged along the interior walls like the stairs on a park ranger lookout tower.

I swept the beam across the ground. "Yech."

There were dead pigeons on the floor—dozens of them. Some obviously dead for years—just feathers and bones. Others more recent. I picked a careful path through the corpses over to the ladder. Benny followed.

I pointed the beam upward again.

"What is *that*?" I asked, squinting.

About two-thirds of the way up the tower there was a large roundish metal object that filled up most of the interior space. It was difficult to make out details this far away with just a flashlight. "Some sort of water reservoir?"

"Maybe," Benny said. "Could be this thing used to double as a water tower for the building."

I lowered the beam and stared at him for a moment. "Well?" I was grinning.

He tilted his head back and studied the stairs for a while. Then he looked at me and winked. "You have a fascinating law practice, Counselor."

CHAPTER 29

It was indeed a water reservoir—rusted and neglected, long since abandoned. The stairs snaked around it, and the air above it was much colder than below. We climbed past narrow windows, more like slots cut in the thick walls. The wind whistled through them. I paused to peer out of one. It looked north over Market Street and the immobile fountains across the street. Another quarter turn up the stairs, another open window, this one looking west over the maroon tiled roof of the Headhouse.

Behind me, Benny was gasping. "Time-out," he wheezed, slumping onto a stair. "Christ, my heart sounds like a tympani drum."

I came back down several stairs and sat next to him. I shined the flashlight overhead.

There was a platform less than thirty feet above. I put my hand on his shoulder and gave him an encouraging squeeze. "We're almost there," I said.

Benny leaned back, saw what the beam was illuminating, and nodded, his breath still wheezing. I sat quietly, listening to his breathing return to normal.

"By the way," I said, "I'm impressed with your tool collection."

"Most women are."

"I'm referring to your tool tools, you goofball." I lifted the backpack and shook it, rattling the equipment inside. "You always put yourself down as a Jewish mechanic, but when we needed a chisel and a special hammer, you came through like a champ."

He shook his head. "I got those from my neighbor. He's some sort of genetic freak."

"How so?"

"He's a urologist but he isn't Jewish. Probably the only Gentile urologist in the Midwest. And a goy through and through. Took me down to his basement. Place looked like a TrueValue Hardware wet dream. I ask him for a hammer, he shows me a wall that looks like the goddamn Hammer Hall of Fame. I took two for tonight—a normal one and a big mother that looks like it once belonged to Thor."

I was smiling as I stood up. "Come on. Let's find the judge her corroborating evidence."

The platform overhead turned out to be the clock landing, and it had clearly been refurbished since Warnholtz began his prison term. All four clocks were new, with whirring electronic motors and special illumination bulbs. There were wires and cords and electric panels. Even more important, there were additional stairs. I had mistakenly assumed that this platform was the highest point in the tower, but in fact the clocks were set in the walls about fifteen or twenty feet from the top of the tower.

We left the clock platform and headed up the stairs into complete darkness. There were no windows up here. I clicked on the flashlight as we reached the final landing. The wind howled outside.

"The northwest corner," Benny said as he turned, trying to get a fix on our location. His breath vapored in the frigid air.

I moved the flashlight beam slowly around. The area was a square, and three of the four corners were standard right angles. But the fourth one was beveled—essentially a narrow extra wall set at a diagonal into the corner from floor to ceiling. I tried to visualize the outside of the clocktower. The little minaret was attached to the northwest edge of the tower. The beveled corner must have been the common wall with the minaret.

"This is it," I said, pointing the flashlight beam.

I kneeled in front of the wall and set the backpack on the floor. Unlike the other walls, which were made of brick, this beveled corner was composed of limestone blocks. The blocks were a little longer than regular bricks and about twice as high—about twelve inches long, five inches high. I shined the light along the masonry as I moved my other hand slowly over the blocks and mortar.

Benny was kneeling beside me and unzipping the backpack. "Where's it supposed to be?"

I replayed Warnholtz's words in my mind. "Five from the left, three up from the floor."

We counted. I held the flashlight close to the wall. The masonry looked the same as what surrounded it.

"He was either a helluva bricklayer," Benny said as he positioned the chisel against the mortar, "or full of shit."

Fifteen minutes later, Benny had cleaned out the mortar on all four sides of the block. It took the two of us several more minutes to loosen the block and slide it out of the wall. It was an ample piece of limestone, far heavier than an ordinary brick. Benny reached his hand inside the opening and scooped out loose pieces of mortar.

"There's something hard back there," he said as he brushed out more debris.

"Let me see." I leaned down with the flashlight to train the beam on the opening.

"Well?" he asked.

"Look."

He put his head close to mine as we peered inside. The flashlight illuminated the lower-left quadrant of what had to be the front of a safe.

"Whoa," he said quietly.

To expose the entire door of the safe, we needed to extract three more blocks. Fortunately, the opening created by the first brick sped up our task. We had the other three blocks out of there in under fifteen minutes. Once we'd cleared away all of the loose pieces of mortar, I shined the flashlight in the large, square opening. The sturdy little safe was in good condition. The numbers on the combination lock were clearly visible.

"What was the combination?" Benny asked.

"Hitler's birthday: April 20, 1889." I peered into the opening and trained the flashlight beam on the combination knob. "I'm guessing it's four right, twenty left, eighteen right, eighty-nine left."

I guessed right. On the second try, I pulled down on the little handle. There was an audible *click* and the door swung free.

"We're in," I said.

I opened the door and shined the light inside. The safe contained one thick manila envelope bound with twine. I reached in and lifted the envelope out of the safe and through the opening in the wall.

"Let's get the hell out of here," Benny said. "I'm freezing."

"Wait." I sat down with my back against the wall. I placed the manila envelope on my lap. "Let's just take a peek."

I fumbled with the knot until Benny, exasperated, opened his pocket knife and cut through it. I pulled off the twine and opened the big envelope. It was filled with papers. I carefully removed them, making sure not to get any out of order, and I placed them on the ground between us.

I lifted the top page. It was an old, yellowed bill of lading. I wasn't used to reading them, but from what I could decipher, it pertained to a consignment that left the Port of Buenos Aires in South America on a vessel named *La Guardia* on June 7, 1948, and arrived in the Port of New Orleans thirty-three days later. The bill of lading was difficult to understand: parts were in Spanish, parts were in English, and many of the entries, including the weight of the goods shipped, were in abbreviations that I didn't understand. But the goods themselves were identified quite succinctly: DENTAL GOLD.

The next several documents made up the paper trail that followed the shipment from the Port of New Orleans to St. Louis via two different railroad trains. When the gold reached

St. Louis, it was unloaded and transported to the Gravois State Bank & Trust, where it was placed in the vault. Sixteen days later, according to the documents, the gold was sold to a dealer in Chicago named Hubert Schwinn for the sum of $300,000, which was placed into Account #2438712, a new account opened that day at the Gravois State Bank & Trust in the name of "Die Spinne." The next document was a carbon copy of the signature card for that account. I held the card up and shined the light on it so both of us could see. It was dated August 12, 1948. There were two signatures, each one neat and legible: Herman Warnholtz and Conrad Beckman.

I turned to Benny. "Time to go. We've got a long night ahead of us."

I helped him close the safe and shove the four limestone blocks back into place in the wall. He slipped on the backpack and adjusted the straps. It was his turn to carry it.

We'd passed the clock landing and were almost at the water reservoir when Benny stopped.

"What's wrong?"

He shook his head in disgust as he slipped off the backpack and set it on the stairs.

"Please, please," he grumbled as he unzipped the bag and shined his flashlight inside. "Aw, shit."

"What?"

"I left the damn chisel up there."

I shined my light overhead. "You want me to?"

"Naw, it's my fault. I'll go get it."

"You sure?"

"Yeah, yeah. I need the exercise. I'll meet you below."

"I can wait."

"No, go ahead." He turned and started up the stairs. "See if you can get your bearings there, figure out how we get out of this dump."

I waited a few minutes. I could hear him trudging up the stairs and cursing under his breath. But by the time I'd squeezed past the rusted water reservoir, his footsteps and grumbling were no longer audible. With the manila envelope under my arm, I mulled over possible exit routes as I continued down the stairs. We'd entered the upper section of the Headhouse on the far west side, had crossed over the center section, and were now at the eastern edge of the building. Instead of a fifteen-minute hike all the way back to the other side, we might be able to find a stairway and an exit nearby.

I reached the bottom of the stairs and paused to listen. From far overhead I could barely hear the muffled echoing of Benny's footsteps. Clicking on the flashlight, I carefully picked my way between the pigeon corpses and through the arched opening.

I hadn't taken more than a few steps when a powerful beam of light flashed in my face. "Well," said a deep, resonant voice, "look who finally came down from her tower."

Startled, I stumbled backward a step, squinting into the glare.

He chuckled. "I don't suppose you're Rapunzel, eh? Not with that hair."

I was unable to see him, unable to see anything. Although flustered, I remembered the archway. It was directly behind me. Benny was on his way down. Trying to shield my eyes from the light, I staggered off to the side, moving in a wide arc, trying to draw him with me, away from the archway. The whole time he kept the beam of light on my face, like a prison spotlight. Blinded, I heard the scrape of his shoes as he followed me.

"Whoa, sister," he said with a chuckle. "Hold still. Turn off your flashlight."

I did.

"Who are you?" I said, my voice shaking, still backing away from the archway. His voice was familiar. I struggled to place it. "Are you a guard?"

Another chuckle. "Not the kind you're hoping for. Where's the Pillsbury Jew Boy?"

I stood there dazed, squinting into the light. I recognized the voice. I couldn't believe it.

"I asked you a question. Where's the Pillsbury Jew Boy?"

"He went to get the car. He's out front waiting for me."

"Left you here all alone?" Another chuckle. "Pretty little girl like you. Fat boy sounds like a pussy to me." He shifted the beam to the manila envelope under my arm. "You find something interesting up there, Rachel Gold?"

The sound of my name made me flinch. "Who are you?" I asked, stalling for time, my heart racing.

"Answer my question first."

He had his back to the archway. Benny might be in earshot. I had to warn him.

"*Who are you?*" I shouted. "*Who are you?*"

"Ssh," he said. "No need to get all in a lather here. If I was going to hurt you, I'd have done that already."

"What do you want?" I asked, struggling to keep control of myself.

He shifted the beam toward the envelope again. "Just that."

I pulled it closer to my body.

That made him chuckle. "You don't have much leverage here. First of all, you're inside this place illegally. I believe you lawyers call it trespassing. Second of all, you're unarmed. Third, you're alone. I have an automatic in my jacket and three men waiting up those stairs back in that old ballroom. They're armed as well. But don't worry. All I want is that envelope."

"Why?"

"We lost track of you and the Pillsbury Jew Boy back there—in fact, we didn't figure out where you'd gone until one of my men spotted a flashlight moving up the clock tower." Another chuckle. "Doesn't take a rocket scientist to figure there must be something awfully important inside that envelope—important enough to make you break into this building in the middle of the night in the middle of your trial. That kind of behavior is just unusual enough to get me thinking that maybe, just maybe, whatever's in that envelope has something to do with our dearly departed Herman Warnholtz. Now, if that's the case, I can—"

There was a sudden *Whomp.*

He groaned in pain as something hard clunked to the floor. His flashlight beam gyrated. There were the sounds of heavy footsteps charging, then an *Oomph* of a collision. Two bodies crashed to the ground. I clicked on my flashlight just as Benny was raising his claw hammer. He was straddling the other man, who was facedown on the floor. Benny smashed the hammer down hard into the middle the man's back. I could hear a rib crack. He smashed it again. Another crack.

I grabbed Benny's arm. "Enough. There are others back there."

Benny looked up at me, his eyes wild. He nodded and got to his feet. We both stared down at the man on the ground, who was whimpering.

"This way," I whispered, pointing the flashlight toward the east.

"Wait."

Benny leaned over and grabbed the man by his shoulder. He pulled him to his side and shined the flashlight on his face. We were staring down at Bishop Kurt Robb. His glasses had been knocked off in the fight, his nose was scraped and bloody. He winced in pain.

Benny turned to me. "You got tape in that backpack?"

I nodded.

He raised the hammer over Robb's head and waggled it menacingly. "Keep your mouth shut, you Aryan asshole, or I'll crack your head open like a soft-boiled egg." He turned to me. "Get me the tape."

I dashed over to the archway and grabbed the backpack. On the way back, I dug around and pulled out the roll of duct tape. Benny tore off a long strip and handed it to me. Then he leaned over Robb, shoved him onto his stomach, and yanked his arms behind his back, holding his wrists together.

I squatted next to him and wrapped the tape several turns. Benny let go of Robb's hands. They fell limply against his back.

Benny reached for the duct tape and tore off another long

strip. He handed me the strip of tape, grabbed Robb by his hair, and pulled his head off the ground. "Say cheese."

Benny looked over at me and nodded. I positioned the duct tape over Robb's mouth and wrapped it around his head twice.

When I was done, Benny leaned in close, still holding Robb's head by his hair. Robb's eyes were darting around in fear and pain.

"Pillsbury Jew Boy, eh?" Benny said. "Well, guess what, motherfucker? Fourth quarter just ended. Final score: Jew Boy one, Spider zero."

Benny released his grip and Robb's head conked against the ground. He made a muffled groan.

We headed quickly toward the eastern end of the building, hoping that Robb and his men had entered, as we had, from the west side. I looked back as we reached a stairway. Off in the distance I saw two flashlights moving in our direction.

"Hurry," I whispered.

We scrambled down the stairway toward the door at the bottom, pushed through it, ran down a short corridor, came to another door, pushed through it, and found ourselves standing on the sidewalk on Eighteenth Street. I looked back with a wince, expecting the door to burst open.

"This way," Benny said, grabbing my arm and running toward Market Street. We jogged to the front of Union Station and the entrance to the Hyatt Hotel, where there were several cabs parked in a line. We hopped in the first one.

"Police station!" I shouted. "Hurry."

"Yes, ma'am." The cabbie shifted to Drive. The tires squealed as he pulled away from the curb.

We settled back, both of us breathing hard. After a moment, I turned to Benny. "How did you do that?"

"A hammer."

"No, I mean the first time."

"That was the other hammer. That big sucker. I snuck up behind him and threw it." He pantomimed a hammer throw.

"Right in the middle of his back. Whack!" He paused for a second and then smacked his forehead with the heel of his hand. "Ahhh."

"What?"

"His tools."

"Whose?"

"The urologist's. They're back there."

"Don't worry, Thor. We'll buy him some new ones."

CHAPTER 30

They were all in the courtroom that morning.

Ruth Alpert was seated at my side, and next to her was Benny. Conrad Beckman, looking especially dour, was over at the defendant's table seated next to Kimberly Howard. The two of them were surrounded by the usual entourage, with Laurence Browning officiously shooting his cuffs.

Out in the gallery every seat was taken. Stanley Roth had the aisle position in the first row behind the barrier on the defendant's side. He was going over some point with an intent young spin doctor from the St. Louis office of the public relations firm of Hill/Dowling. This was Hill/Dowling's first appearance in the courtroom. *Fasten your seat belts, fellas*, I thought. The rest of those two rows were packed with executives from Beckman Engineering and attorneys and paralegals from Roth & Bowles.

My mother was in the courtroom today, along with Ruth's grown daughter Barbara. They were seated in the first row on the plaintiff's side. Next to them were Jacki and my five law student volunteers.

The press was here in force this morning, both print and broadcast. Their numbers had been swelling each day. For those following their reports on the trial, our side was slightly behind on points. The *Post-Dispatch* reporter had decreed Conrad Beckman's testimony yesterday "impressive" and "forceful."

There were plenty of spectators in the gallery as well. The television accounts had been luring them into the courtroom in greater numbers each day.

And finally, there was a new group today: the law enforcement professionals. Jonathan Wolf was there, seated in the back row between two of his investigators, his crutches leaning against the bench next to him. I recognized a couple of FBI special agents, an agent from the Bureau of Alcohol, Tobacco and Firearms, an assistant U.S. attorney, and someone from the city prosecutor's office.

The only important people missing from the courtroom were my best witnesses: Gloria Muller, Harold Roth, and Herman Warnholtz—all dead. And Kurt Robb, of course. He was in lockup in the city jail on a variety of misdemeanor charges (trespass, assault) that would keep him on ice for another twenty-four hours. That ought to be enough time.

I glanced over at Benny. He looked wired this morning, and with good reason. Neither of us had slept a wink last night. I hadn't pulled an all-nighter since law school, but I was hanging in there so far. We'd left the police station at close to three in the morning. One of the cops drove us back to Union Station to retrieve our car. Sleep had been out of the question. There'd been just too much to do. Jacki, God bless her, had been a real trooper, as had my volunteers: they all came in at four-thirty in the morning to help assemble the exhibits, make the transparencies, and take care of the dozens of little tasks that needed to be ready before the trial resumed at ten o'clock this morning.

My first courthouse appearance this morning had actually occurred much earlier. I knew that Judge Wagner usually got to court by seven-thirty. Accordingly, I was waiting at the entrance to the judges' parking area when she pulled up at 7:25 A.M. I handed her copies of the financial records we'd taken from the clocktower, along with copies of the newspaper articles from the other five cities. I explained what they were, and then I drove back to my office praying that she'd concur. At ten to nine, her clerk called to inform me that Her Honor would allow the audiotapes into evidence with a cautionary instruction to the jury. I traded high-fives with my trial team and went back to gathering the materials for court.

At ten-fifteen, the courtroom buzzer sounded. We stood

as the side door opened and Judge Catherine Wagner swept into the room, her blond hair flowing behind her. She took her seat in the high-back leather chair behind the bench and turned toward the jury.

"Ladies and gentlemen," she began, "in a few minutes plaintiff's counsel is going to play an audiotape for you. It's an interview she conducted two nights ago with a man named Herman Warnholtz. At the time of the interview, Mr. Warnholtz was serving a life sentence for a vicious murder back in 1942. Mr. Warnholtz had terminal cancer at the time of the interview." She paused. "He died several hours after the interview."

I could hear a rush of whispers behind me. Her opening comments had ratcheted the courtroom tension several notches higher. I eyed the jurors. A few glanced at one another, but for the most part they sat with their arms crossed staring at the judge, their faces solemn.

"As a result," Judge Wagner continued, "all we have are Mr. Warnholtz's unsworn statements. Even worse, Ms. Howard never had an opportunity to ask Mr. Warnholtz any questions." She paused to smile. "We all know that Ms. Howard would have had some tough questions for him."

A few of the jurors smiled and nodded. The others just sat there, their faces grim.

Judge Wagner frowned and shook her head. "But sometimes we have to try to deal with evidence that's less than ideal." She gazed at the jurors. "What you're about to hear, ladies and gentlemen, is hearsay. You're going to hear a tape recording of a series of unsworn statements by a convicted murderer. I caution you to listen to this tape with a skeptical ear." She studied the jurors for a moment and then gave them a reassuring smile. "I am confident that you will do that." She turned to me. "Counsel?"

I stood. "Your Honor, we have a few exhibits that we'd like the jury to be able to see while they listen to the tape."

Judge Wagner nodded and turned to the jury. "In the audiotape, you will hear Mr. Warnholtz explain that at the time of his arrest in 1955, he asked his brother to hide certain documents in the clocktower at Union Station." She turned back to me. "Let's do that part now, Counsel."

I glanced over at Benny. "Plaintiff calls Benjamin Goldberg to the stand."

Benny stood and walked over to the witness box. As the clerk swore him in, I noted with relief that the shower, shave, and navy blue suit had him looking downright trustworthy.

I took him through the preliminaries—name, residence, occupation, etc.—and then had him describe our journey up and over the Grand Hall and into the clocktower. Benny was the perfect witness for this: he was, after all, an extremely articulate man with superb storytelling skills. The jury listened to him intently. Two jurors were actually leaning forward in their seats, enthralled by the tale.

"The safe was exactly where he said it would be," Benny explained to the jury. "Five limestone blocks in from the left, three blocks up from the floor."

"Tell the jury what happened next."

"Well, he said on the tape that the combination to the safe was Hitler's birthday, which happens to be April 20, 1898. So we gave it a try." He motioned with his hand, as if turning the combination knob. "Four ... twenty ... eighteen ... ninety-eight." He nodded. "Sure enough, it popped right open."

I paused. The jurors were hanging on Benny's every word. There wasn't a sound in the courtroom.

"What was inside?" I asked.

"A large envelope."

"Did you bring it with you today?"

Benny nodded. "Right over there," he said, pointing at the package in front of Ruth Alpert.

As I moved toward the table to retrieve the envelope, I glanced toward the gallery. The spectators were spellbound. Stanley Roth looked ashen. I carried the envelope over to Benny and handed it to him. "Take a moment to examine the contents, Professor."

He did.

"Can you identify them?"

He looked up with a confident nod. "These are the documents we found inside the safe."

I turned to the judge. "Your Honor, we offer this envelope and its contents as Plaintiff's Group Exhibit Forty-eight." I turned toward Kimberly. "I have an extra set here for defendant's counsel." I walked over and handed them to Kimberly, who looked too dazed to say a thing.

"Any objection?" Judge Wagner asked her.

From the expression on Kimberly's face, I could tell she was trying to get her brain to shift out of neutral into first. It took a moment for the gears to mesh. "Yes," she said uncertainly. "Hearsay. Lack of foundation."

"Overruled."

I looked at Benny and then the judge. "No further questions."

"Any cross-examination?" Judge Wagner asked.

As Kimberly rose and moved toward the podium, I saw Conrad Beckman grab the set of documents and pull them in front of him. He slowly leafed through them. For the first time in the trial, there was a look of concern on his face.

"*Professor* Goldberg," Kimberly said, having regained some of her spunk, "let's get this straight. You are a professor of law, correct?"

"Yes, ma'am." He was the essence of polite humility.

"And as a professor of law you *study* the law, correct?"

"Yes, ma'am."

"And you *write* about law, correct?"

"Yes, ma'am."

"And you *instruct* law students in the law, correct?"

"Yes, ma'am."

"Then perhaps you can instruct us, Professor. Last night, when you and Miss Gold were gallivanting around the clock tower, were the two of you—one a *professor* of law, the other a *lawyer*—were the two of you *violating* any laws?"

Benny gave her a sheepish grin. "Probably."

"*Probably?* Come now, Professor. Remember back to first-year property. I believe what you and Miss Gold committed last night is called 'trespass,' isn't it?"

Benny raised his eyebrows and nodded. "I believe you are correct."

"And while you and your cohort were in there *trespassing*, I believe you testified that you started chopping away at the mortar and tearing out bricks and otherwise *destroying* private property, Professor. That violated *another* law, correct?"

Benny nodded. "You're probably correct, Ms. Howard."

"As a matter of fact, indeed"—and here she paused to smirk—"as a matter of *law*, the only proper thing to have done if you really thought there might be something up there in that clock tower was to go to the police, correct? Go to the police, file a report, and ask them to search the clock tower. Correct?"

Benny shook his head. "Nope."

"No?"

He nodded. "Too risky."

I caught my breath.

Kimberly gave him an exaggerated look of puzzlement. "Too risky?"

I crossed my fingers. I knew exactly what Benny was doing: dangling the bait. Kimberly had been trained, as I'd been trained, to ignore that bait, to change the line of questioning, to move on, to never ask that next logical question, to never utter that most dangerous word in all of cross-examination. But even the most rigorous training can't overcome instinct, as I'd discovered on more than one unhappy occasion.

Kimberly stared at Benny as she moved back to the end of the jury box. Her position would force Benny to look at the jurors when he answered her next question.

"Too risky to go the police?" she repeated, her tone heavy with sarcasm.

"Yes, ma'am."

Here we go. Come on, Kimberly.

"Why?" she asked.

Yes!

Benny shrugged. "Because every time Rachel found a witness with incriminating evidence against your client, that witness died. Gloria Muller knew bad things about your client, and someone killed Gloria Muller with a shotgun. Harold Roth knew bad things about your client, and someone shot Harold Roth between the eyes. And Herman Warnholtz certainly knew bad things about your client, and now Herman Warnholtz is dead." He nodded his head thoughtfully, doing his Jimmy Stewart number. "You're right about that police report, Ms. Howard. We could have made one, but that wouldn't guarantee a search warrant, and even if the cops decided to get one, it might take a couple of days and the word might leak out before then. Frankly, Miss Howard, I was worried that anyone who was willing to kill people to keep out evidence against Mr. Beckman wouldn't hesitate to destroy these records"—he lifted up the manila envelope—"if we gave them half a chance. As a matter of fact, it turned out that we *were* being followed inside Union Station that night. When Rachel came down out of the clocktower—"

"*Stop!*" Conrad Beckman roared.

The courtroom was silent. Beckman was standing at counsel's table, one handing grasping the sheaf of financial records from the safe, his face scarlet, his eyes burning with rage.

"Counsel," he snapped at Kimberly.

She hurried over to the table. He grabbed her by the shoulder and started whispering to her furiously.

After a moment, Judge Wagner said, "Ms. Howard?"

Kimberly looked over apologetically. "Just a moment, Your Honor." She turned back to Beckman, who immediately started in again.

"Ms. Howard," Judge Wagner repeated, this time more forcefully. "*Now.*"

Kimberly nodded at Beckman and turned to the judge. "Your Honor, may we approach?"

Judge Wagner gave her a stern look. "Quickly."

I followed Kimberly up to the bench. The judge stared at

her with displeasure as we waited for the court reporter to join us with her shorthand machine.

When the court reporter had her machine set up, the judge shook her head at Kimberly and said, "Put a muzzle on your client, Ms. Howard, or I'll hold him in contempt."

"I apologize, Your Honor. Mr. Beckman is somewhat upset."

Judge Wagner gave her a withering look. "So am I."

"Judge," Kimberly said, "we'd like to settle the case right now. We're prepared to make a substantial offer."

Judge Wagner looked at me. I shrugged. "Your Honor, they made a substantial offer last night. My client turned it down."

"We're prepared to increase that offer significantly," Kimberly said quickly, keeping her voice low. "Assuming liability here—an assumption we would never make but for settlement—our damages expert has calculated the maximum exposure at forty million dollars." Kimberly paused. "We are prepared to offer that amount in settlement."

Judge Wagner was taken aback. "You're offering forty million dollars?"

"Right now, Your Honor. On the condition that this trial terminate immediately, and that all evidence, including the audiotape and the documents from the safe, be turned over to us for disposal in our sole discretion."

Judge Wagner turned to me uncertainly. "Counsel?"

Forty million dollars? Ruth's share would be twelve million dollars.

"I'll need to confer with my client."

She studied me for a moment, her lips pursed in thought. "Very well. Step back."

We returned to our seats.

Judge Wagner looked over at the jury. "Ladies and gentlemen, the court will be in recess for ten minutes."

She waited until the last of the jurors had filed out of the courtroom and then turned to all of us. "I'll expect to see counsel in my chambers in exactly five minutes."

"Your Honor," Kimberly said, "the defendant requests that the representative of the United States government be present in your chambers as well." She turned and gestured toward Philip Balding, who was seated in the third row. Balding was the skinny weasel from the Department of Justice who'd been assigned to monitor the case on behalf of the government—the same weasel who'd declined to take over the case last fall. I could still remember the gray November morning when Balding's letter had arrived.

Judge Wagner nodded. "That's fine with me. Okay, Mr. Balding?"

He stood up, anxiously buttoning the jacket of his wrinkled brown suit. He was wearing wire-rim glasses and a crooked gray bow tie. "Certainly, Your Honor," he announced in a nasal voice.

The jury was in the jury room, the defense team (numbering more than a dozen now) had staked out the conference room across the hall from Judge Wagner's chambers, the spectators and a gaggle of Beckman Engineering officials were milling in the aisles, and journalists were trolling the hallway outside the courtroom armed with notepads and tape recorders, ready to pounce on any warm body remotely connected to the trial who was foolish enough to venture out for the water fountain or the restroom. The only place with any semblance of privacy was the empty jury box, and that's where we huddled—Ruth, my mother, Benny, and I.

"But if I take the money, they won't play the tape," Ruth said to me.

I nodded. "That's the trade-off. Say yes to the money and the trial ends now. Turn it down, and we'll bring back the jury, play the tape, and get on with the trial. In two or three weeks, we'll hear the verdict. You could end up with more than their offer, and you could end up with nothing."

Ruth was struggling. "I just don't think I should settle. I

don't think I should." She looked at Benny and my mother.

Benny shook his head in wonder. "You sure, Ruthie? We're talking megabucks here."

"But I want them to know, Benny. It's for him, not for me." She turned to my mother. "Am I crazy, Sarah?"

My mother shrugged. "I'm not going to kid you, Ruth. You're acting a little *meshuggah*." She smiled and patted her hand. "But that's okay. In this life there are some things more important than money. And let's face it: you weren't rich before, so you're not giving away anything you already have."

I squeezed Ruth's hand. "Remember," I said gently, "this is *your* lawsuit, not ours. You had the courage to take it this far. Whatever you decide now is the right decision."

She looked at me, her eyes moist but fervent. "I want them to hear it, Rachel. For Harry's sake. I want them to know."

I put my arm around her shoulder and kissed her on the cheek. "Then they will."

Benny shook his head in wonder. "They'll know one thing for damn sure: don't mess with Ruth."

I smiled. Benny was right. Ruth and I had been battling this well-funded army of lawyers and paralegals and investigators and experts for months. We'd been dodging mortar shells and cannonfire for weeks on end, and we were still standing. Bloody but unbowed. I was enough of a realist to know that this war of attrition could still end in a smashing rout. Nevertheless, here we were, about to thumb our noses at a forty-million-dollar offer from one of the most powerful corporations in St. Louis. There was a certain demented glory to that. I was proud of her.

I gave her wink. "Let's do it."

I turned to the first row on our side of the gallery, where Jacki and my five volunteers were anxiously watching. I winked and gave them the thumbs-up. They answered with big grins. Zack pumped his fist in the air and hollered, "Yes!"

No?" Kimberly was practically shouting in outrage.

I shrugged. "She wants the tape played."

There were five of us in chambers: Judge Wagner, seated

behind the desk; Kimberly Howard and Stanley Roth for the defendant; Philip Balding for the government; and me.

Stanley put up his hand to quiet Kimberly and turned to the judge. "Your Honor, I'm afraid Miss Gold and her client have lost sight of the fact that this is a *qui tam* case. The real party in interest is the United States government. I've had an opportunity to talk to Mr. Balding earlier this morning and again during this recess. He's delighted with our offer and is prepared to recommend it to his superiors." He turned to Balding. "Tell them, Philip."

"Yes, indeed." Balding pulled at the loose skin over his Adam's apple as he nodded rapidly. "I am prepared to recommend the settlement."

"Forget it!" I turned on him, outraged. "You have no standing here, buster. None whatsoever." I stood over him, my face flushed with emotion, all the months of frustration suddenly bubbling over. "When we presented this case to you last year, when we asked *our* government to take it over and relieve us of the enormous burden of preparing the case for trial, you said no. You turned us down." I paused, catching my breath. "Well, guess what? We're turning you down." I jabbed my finger at him for emphasis. "My client is still the relator here, and that means she's still in charge."

He flinched. "Well, really," he said, shaking his head defensively. "I merely said that it appeared to be a reasonable offer. I didn't mean—"

"How would you know?" I demanded, glaring down at him. "My expert calculates the damages at over one hundred million dollars. Did you take that into consideration? Have you even read the reports of my experts?"

"Well, I—I—"

"Stop," Judge Wagner commanded. I turned toward her. She pointed at my chair sternly. "Sit down."

I sat down, still trembling with anger.

"Your client has rejected the offer, correct?" Judge Wagner asked me.

"She has."

"Fine." She stood up, resnapping the top buttons of her judicial robe. "Let's bring back the jury and get this case rolling again."

"But, Your Honor," Roth said, practically whining, "what about the government?"

Judge Wagner gave him a withering stare. "Forget the government, Stanley. They had their chance. Their dog's not in this fight." She turned to us and nodded decisively. "Let's go, folks. We have a jury waiting."

CHAPTER 31

*M*y *name is Herman Warnholtz."*

The sound system in the courtroom was excellent. His raspy voice boomed through the speakers.

"You know Conrad Beckman, don't you?"

"Yes."

"For how many years, sir?"

"We grew up in the same neighborhood. Back in the 1920s."

I could feel the drama in the courtroom, heightened by all of the delay and anticipation. Here he was, at last—a powerful, disembodied voice, speaking to us from a hospital bed in a maximum-security prison, ending forty years of silence to tell his story just hours before his death.

On the tape, I explained to him the nature of the bid-rigging conspiracy we'd alleged.

"Oh, yeah," he said.

"You knew about it?"

"Sure. I did the books."

"What do you mean, sir?"

"I was in charge of the records."

"Of the bid-rigging, you mean?"

"Oh, no. They kept track of that part. I kept track of the loans."

"What loans, sir?"

I watched the jury. They were mesmerized by this gravelly voice speaking from the grave.

"The loans from the Nazis. You know, Die Spinne. I knew about the bid-rigging scheme, sure. But that was Conrad's baby."

The jurors glanced at Beckman, who was frowning and shaking his head.

Warnholtz continued. *"It was a helluva good idea, too. Best way to make sure each of 'em could pay back their loan and start funding their end of the bargain. That's what Conrad told 'em."* Warnholtz paused to chuckle. *"Let me tell you something, young lady. You can earn good money on a government job when you know you can add an extra layer of fat to your bid."*

"Let me back up a moment, sir. You mentioned loans. Who got the loans?"

"All six of them, counting Conrad's company."

As the tape played, I propped the chart of the six companies up on the easel to help the jury follow his answer.

"Who were the six?"

"Well, you had Beckman Engineering, of course. Then you had Max's outfit down in Memphis. Eagle, right? You had Otto with his company up in Chicago. Henry was in Indianapolis."

"Henry Eicken, you mean? Eicken Industrial Company?"

"Yeah, I guess. Remember, we're talking 1948 when the money came in from Die Spinne. Some of them guys didn't set up corporations till the 1950s."

"You mentioned Beckman, Eagle, Eicken, and Koll, sir. Who were the other two in the conspiracy?"

"Well, you had Muller in Springfield, Illinois. That was Ed Muller. And then you had Al Beek up in Gary. That's six, right?"

"Yes, sir."

I watched the jury study the chart as Warnholtz explained the mechanics of the conspiracy in its early years—the group meetings three or four times a year, which he always attended along with Conrad Beckman.

"Mr. Warnholtz, you said that this conspiracy began back in 1948 with the loans from something call Die Spinne."

"That's right."

"I've read some about Die Spinne, sir. My understanding

is that it was a secret organization of former SS officers who ran the concentration camps."

"Yep. After the war they set up operations in South America."

"In San Carlos de Bariloche?"

"One group went there. There were others."

Several of the jurors were staring at Conrad Beckman. He was leaning back in his chair now with his arms crossed over his chest. He had his head tilted back and was gazing up, as if he were counting ceiling tiles.

"Tell me about the loans."

"Well, I never had the full picture. I don't think any of us did. Die Spinne spread money all around the world. They sent us a shipment of gold. Dental gold."

I had the transparency ready. I turned on the first overhead projector. The large screen showed the bill of lading from the vessel *La Guardia* on June 7, 1948. With the pointer I showed the jury the words "Dental Gold," which stood out clearly on the document.

"Dental gold?"

He chuckled. *"These were concentration camp guards. They had access, if you know what I mean. Jewelry, money, gold fillings. When the war started going bad for Germany, they smuggled out whatever they could. We sold the gold they shipped us—got three hundred grand for it. Cash. I set up the account, doled out the loans—fifty grand to each—and kept track of the records."*

"Why did they give you the gold?"

"Wasn't a gift. Seed money, you might say. Enough to get us rolling in our businesses. Fifty thousand was a lot of money back then, young lady. But we had to do more than just pay it back. Each of the six companies had to pay in a percent of its profits. That was Die Spinne's end of the bargain, you see? They wanted the money there for funding."

"For funding what?"

"Another Hitler, a Fourth Reich. That was the deal: they helped set us up in business and we had to finance Nazi op-

erations in this country. And let me tell you, that money built up fast. When I switched the account from Gravois Bank to Mercantile, we had a million dollars in there."

As he talked, I put transparencies up on the other five screens—all from the records we'd found in the clocktower. There was the account statement from the Gravois Bank showing an opening account of $300,000. Then the signature card with Conrad Beckman's signature. Then the six $50,000 disbursements back in September 1948, one to each of the co-conspirators. Then the spreadsheet showing the repayments over time. I ended the first series of transparencies with the account-closing transaction showing $953.421.45 transferred to Mercantile Bank.

I asked him about the bank records. He explained how he'd had his brother hide them in the clocktower shortly after his arrest.

"Why?" I asked.

There was a long pause. *"Because Conrad had changed."*

"In what way?"

"Maybe it was the money, or the good life, but I could tell his heart just wasn't in it anymore. Like he was trying to pretend all that stuff we done during the war hadn't really happened." You could hear the anger in his voice. *"And maybe I was starting to worry that if I didn't have some sort of leverage—something to hold him back, if you know what I mean—well, I might just end up in an early grave. So, when he sent that lawyer—guy named Metzger—to visit me in prison to ask about the records, I told him I had 'em stashed away safe. I told him if anything bad ever happens to me, I got a man with orders to turn 'em over to the cops. Those records were my life insurance policy, you see? Except I don't need no life insurance anymore."*

He rambled on about life in prison until I interrupted with a new question.

"Do you know what happened to all that money, Mr. Warnholtz?"

"Well," he said with a chuckle, *"I know some of it went*

for that fancy defense lawyer from Nashville, 'cause I sure didn't have that kind of money."

"Do you know whether any of it was used to fund Nazi operations in the United States?"

"I assume it was, but I don't know that for a fact, ma'am."

"You told me earlier that Die Spinne is German."

"It sure is."

"What does it mean?"

" 'The Spider.' "

Behind me I could hear the gasps. Over at the defendant's table, Kimberly Howard looked stunned. Conrad Beckman had his head down, his fists clenched. Back on the aisle seat in the first row of the gallery, Stanley Roth was dazed. The public relations guru seated next to him had a shocked expression.

There were six overhead projectors. I got the next set of transparencies ready as I heard myself on the tape pick up on one of Warnholtz's earlier, almost offhand comments.

"You mentioned that by the time you were arrested in 1955, Mr. Beckman was trying to pretend that all that stuff during the war hadn't really happened."

"That's what my gut was telling me."

"Exactly what stuff did you and he do during the war?"

There was a long pause. The hissing of the tape was audible throughout the courtroom. I gazed around. It seemed that every person in the courtroom was leaning forward, waiting for Warnholtz to continue.

"Well, it wasn't just us in St. Louis, you know."

"Who else, sir?"

"Those same ones."

"You mean the owners of those other five companies?"

"Well, yeah, although we weren't none of us companies back then. We met in the Bund."

"The German-American Bund?"

"Right, right. When that fell apart, we formed ourselves the Death's Head Formation. There were six chapters in the Midwest, and each of those men headed up one."

"*You mean Max Kruppa, Otto Koll—*"

"*Yeah, yeah. Same six.*"

"*How many were in the St. Louis chapter?*"

"*Oh, it varied up to eight or nine, but always the same three leaders.*"

"*Who were the three?*"

"*Well, me, of course, and Conrad. And then there was Rudy Schober. We went way back, the three of us.*"

"*Were you the head of the St. Louis chapter?*"

"*Me?*" He laughed—a raspy chuckle. "*Hell, no. Conrad Beckman was the chapter führer.*"

There was silence on the tape—just the background hissing noise. As the courtroom waited for him to continue, I remembered that moment in the prison infirmary, my surprise at what he'd told me. Harold Roth's informant had incorrectly identified Warnholtz as the leader. It was Beckman all along.

When I began speaking again on the tape, my voice was more subdued, as if I sensed but still couldn't believe where we were headed.

"*Tell me about the Death's Head Formation, sir. What did you do?*"

"*Well, we met, talked about the war, had some communications with SS commandants over in Germany. And then, well, the orders came down from Berlin.*"

"*What orders, sir?*"

"*That it was time to put Hitler's principles to work in this country.*"

"*How?*"

Another long pause. I asked another question: "*Mr. Warnholtz, was the order from Germany to kill a Jew on Hitler's birthday?*"

Another pause. "*Yep.*"

More gasps from behind me. Someone cried, "Oh, no."

I turned on the first overhead projector, which displayed the article from the April 21, 1942, issue of the *St. Louis Post-Dispatch* on the murder of Myron Bernstein. The headline dominated the top of the screen:

MAN DIES IN PAWNSHOP FIRE
OFFICIALS SUSPECT ARSON

"That's why you killed Myron Bernstein?"

"Yes."

"On Hitler's birthday?"

"Yes, ma'am."

Rage had started to creep into my voice. *"You thought that killing one defenseless Jew in St. Louis was going to bring Nazism to America?"*

"It wasn't just him. There were six."

Now it was my turn to pause.

"What do you mean?"

You could hear the dread in my voice.

"One in each city. We had it all coordinated."

During the pause on the tape, I moved down the line of overhead projectors, flicking them on one after the other. The headlines flashed, one by one, each from the April 21, 1942, issue of a different newspaper—from the *Chicago Tribune*, the *Indianapolis Star*, the *Commercial Appeal*, the *Gary Post*, the *Springfield Register*.

JEWISH MAN DIES IN SUSPICIOUS BLAZE

MYSTERIOUS EXPLOSION KILLS
OWNER OF COHEN'S DELICATESSEN

MAN DIES IN SOUTH SIDE INFERNO
POLICE SUSPECT NAZI TIE

Each article was a variation on the same fact pattern: a sadistic arson murder of a Jewish man.

There was a pause on the tape, and then my bewildered question, *"You mean six Jewish men were killed that night?"*

"Yep."

I gasped on the tape. And then, in a quieter voice, *"Oh, my God."*

I turned from the projectors to look at the jurors. Each one of them seemed to be experiencing the dismay I'd felt that night.

Warnholtz's voice continued, almost offhand. "*I suppose it was sort of a test, like one of them initiations. To prove we were really committed, if you get my drift.*"

"*Why are you telling me this, Mr. Warnholtz?*" I asked, "*after all these years?*"

"*Well, my time's about up. Cancer has me bad. Doctors don't give me more than three months. Guess this is one death sentence they don't hand out pardons for. Might as well answer your questions. Don't think I would have before, but no one's bothered to ask since that crazy Lindhoff.*"

"*That was the detective who arrested you for the arson murder?*"

"*The man was obsessed. More like possessed. Kept coming to see me, telling me he was going to nail me for the other one, telling me he'd watch me fry in the chair for that one.*"

"*What one was that, sir?*"

"*The jeweler. Rosen-, uh, Rosenberg or something.*"

"*Harry Rosenthal?*"

"*Yeah, that's the name. Died in, what, 1943?*"

"*November 10, 1943. Kristallnacht.*"

"*That's right. Kristallnacht. Anyway, that crazy Lindhoff was still on that case twenty years later, even after he quit the force. Almost cracked it, too. Changed his tune then. Wanted me to testify.*" He laughed—a wheezy snigger. "*Imagine that? Well, he was getting too close for comfort. I put out the word. Two weeks later, guess who gets himself thrown off the Chain-of-Rocks Bridge at three in the morning.*" Another snigger. "*I hear they ruled it a suicide.*"

There was pause on the tape. I walked over and turned off all of the projectors except for the one with the *Post-Dispatch* article on Myron Bernstein's arson murder. I removed that transparency and put up the one on Harry Rosenthal from the November 11, 1943, issue. The jury was watching me. Now they looked up to squint at the headline:

JEWELER MURDERED ON SOUTH SIDE
POLICE SUSPECT NAZI SYMPATHIZERS

In a crime that had veteran police officers shaking their heads in shock, the unclothed corpse of a south side jeweler was dumped from a moving car outside the third district police headquarters at midnight last night. The corpse was riddled with bullet holes and painted with swastikas, the symbol of the German Nazis.

I sat down next to Ruth Alpert and clasped her hand as we faced the jury, waiting for the tape to continue. I glanced at her. Her eyes were red, her lips quivering. I squeezed her hand.

"Tell me about that one, Mr. Warnholtz. Tell me about Harry Rosenthal's death."

"This time it was our idea," Warnholtz said. *"Things were going bad in Germany. We realized that it was up to us over here. So we picked Kristallnacht. Seemed a perfect night to kill a Jew."*

"Was it just the St. Louis chapter?"

"Oh, no. It was all six. But it was our idea this time. Well, I got to give credit where credit's due. It was Conrad's idea."

Another pause.

In the silence, Ruth let go of my hand and stood up. I looked at her curiously, but when I saw her face, I understood. There were tears on her cheeks, but her expression was firm. This was her moment. Hers alone. This was the reason she'd turned down a forty-million-dollar settlement.

"Did you kill Harry Rosenthal?"

"No, ma'am. I admit I was there. Rudy, too. But we didn't pull that trigger. No, ma'am."

I turned my head and looked slowly around the court-room. All eyes in the gallery and all eyes in the jury box were focused on Ruth. She was the sole person standing in the hushed courtroom—a lone figure bearing witness for her dear uncle Harry.

"*Describe it*," I said on the tape.

"*It weren't pretty, I'll warn you right now. We grabbed that Jew right out of his store. Hauled him off to a deserted boatyard near the river. Conrad had a can of red paint. I remember that part clear as day. Had me and Rudy strip the man naked. Tied him to a pole, we did. Conrad started painting swastikas on his body. Done it real slow and careful. Never said a word, and all the while that poor son of a bitch is crying and begging us to leave him alone.*"

Ruth turned toward Conrad Beckman. By then his were the only eyes not following her. He was staring down at the table, his brows furrowed, his jaws clenched.

"*Well,*" Warnholtz continued, "*when Conrad finished painting him, he stepped back and took out his pistol. Me and Rudy, we moved out of the way.*" He paused.

"*Tell me what happened, sir.*"

"*Well, he aimed that pistol and started shooting. Fired five bullets as I recall—couple in the arms, one in the thigh, two in the belly. The Jew was still conscious, but just barely. Had his eyes open, kind of silently begging, if you know what I mean. Conrad walked right up to him and shoved that gun in his mouth. Still hadn't said a word. Not a thing. He leaned in close, cleared his throat, and spit right into that Jew's face. Then he leaned away and pulled the trigger. Damn. Blew off the back of his goddamn head, brains everywhere.*"

Two of the female jurors were crying. I heard someone blow her nose and looked up to see that it was Judge Wagner herself. She was daubing her eyes with a tissue.

Through it all, Ruth remained standing. Alone. Her eyes clear now, implacable. She stared at Conrad Beckman's lowered head.

A long pause, and then my voice on the tape. "*That was my client's uncle.*"

"*Rosenthal?*"

"*Yes.*"

"*Well, like I say, I didn't pull the trigger.*"

A pause.

"*Mr. Warnholtz, I'd like to call you as a witness in this case.*"

"*You sure?*"

"*Is what you told me tonight the truth?*"

"*Yes, ma'am.*"

"*Would you be willing to repeat it in court under oath?*"

He chuckled. "*You mean, assuming you can find a way to haul this rotting carcass up there before I die?*"

"*Yes, sir.*"

A pause as he contemplated the question. "*Would Conrad be there?*"

"*Yes, sir.*"

Another chuckle. "*I just might like that. I spent forty years in this hellhole while Conrad's been living high on the hog, pretending he's some goddamn saint, trying to forget I ever existed. I wouldn't mind sitting in that witness chair and looking over at him in his fancy suit and saying, 'Hey, Conrad, guess what? I'm ba-a-a-ck.'*"

His laughter turned into a phlegmy coughing fit, then wheezing, and then the tape ended.

In the ensuing silence, I, too, had become a spectator. We all were. We followed Ruth's stare. We stared at Conrad Beckman, willing him to look up, willing him to face this brave woman.

And finally, he did. He lifted his head, his face empty, his eyes dead. He lifted his head and met Ruth's gaze. They stared at one another for what seemed an eternity.

And then he closed his eyes. He squeezed them shut.

And then he lowered his head, lowered it until his forehead rested on his fists on the table.

An eternity of silence. Judge Wagner cleared her throat. "Court will be in recess."

EPILOGUE

B lame it on the movies. I've always dreamed of a Hollywood ending to one of my trials. In my fantasy case, I
deliver a dazzling closing argument. There's not a dry eye
among the jurors as they file out of the courtroom to begin
their deliberations. Twenty minutes later, they send in a note
asking whether they can award my client more money than I
asked for.

But that's Hollywood. This was reality. The trial ended
abruptly during the recess.

"You blew the film rights," Benny later joked. Perhaps
too soon. Only last week Ruth was approached by a producer
with Touchstone.

But I'm getting ahead of the story.

The beginning of the end came with the arrest of Conrad
Beckman. When the last juror filed out of the courtroom, two
FBI agents stepped forward to cuff him and read him his
rights. The front row of Beckman Engineering officials, already numb, sat there slack-jawed as the feds hauled off their
leader with his hands cuffed behind his back.

The docket clerk summoned the rest of us into chambers,
where a stern Judge Wagner, still in her black robe, stood at
the window, her arms crossed, looking as much like a hanging
judge as a striking blonde possibly could. We took our seats
quietly.

She turned to the court reporter, who had just entered
carrying her shorthand machine. "Wait outside," she ordered.

The court reporter nodded meekly, backing out of the
room. I glanced around. Kimberly Howard looked absolutely
crushed. Stanley Roth, defiant during our last meeting in

chambers, seemed to have aged twenty years since then.

"Folks," Judge Wagner said, "the bailiff has the jury in the jury room, and that's where they'll stay through the lunch recess." She paced behind her desk for a moment. "They'll be sequestered for the rest of this trial. It's the only way to avoid a mistrial. Conrad Beckman is already in custody. The U.S. Attorney has advised me that other arrests will follow."

She stopped and turned toward Stanley Roth. "You have exactly one hour to settle this case, Stanley. When that jury gets done with Beckman Engineering, there'll be nothing left of that company but a spot of grease on the pavement. Make sure your client understands the severity of its peril."

He did. The case settled fifty-six minutes later for $70 million. Ruth's share was a cool $21 million, and my fee was ridiculously high. During the three weeks since then, we'd been having fun giving lots of it away. So far, Ruth and I had established (1) an endowment in her uncle Harry's name at the Simon Wiesenthal Center in Los Angeles, (2) the Harry Rosenthal Scholarship Fund at the National Holocaust Museum; and (3) the Harry Rosenthal Memorial Fellowship at the St. Louis Holocaust Museum and Learning Center.

Meanwhile, criminal proceedings had gone into hyperdrive on all fronts. The autopsy results on Herman Warnholtz revealed what I'd suspected: he'd been murdered. Last week an informer at Potosi implicated two other inmates, both members of a skinhead group with ties to Spider. Apparently, part of Bishop Kurt Robb's quid pro quo for the Die Spinne funds was the duty to silence anyone who might reveal the source of those funds. Although it was still optimistic to expect him to go down for all of those homicides, he was in a whole world of hurt anyway. Jonathan's grand jury had returned a multicount indictment of him and the upper echelon of Spider on various conspiracy and hate crime charges; moreover, the financial documents we'd found in the clocktower had roused the attention of that most dreaded of all legal juggernauts: the Internal Revenue Service. IRS agents literally put Robb and his organization out of business overnight by seiz-

ing every asset they could find, from bank accounts to office
furniture to the computer system in Spider's headquarters to
the color television, VCR, and kiddie-porno videos in Robb's
bedroom.

As for Conrad Beckman, I still wondered what must have
gone through his mind at his deposition when I handed him
Max Kruppa's German letter. Did he feel as if he'd been
yanked into another man's biography or his own nightmare?
Whatever his initial reaction, he'd have plenty of time to contemplate it. Murder has no statute of limitations, and that was
only part of his criminal troubles. A federal grand jury was
investigating criminal antitrust charges against Beckman and
the other bid-rigging co-conspirators, and Jonathan's sources
within the Department of Justice said that Otto Koll was already singing like the proverbial canary while staff attorneys
were passing out immunity to terrified Beckman Engineering
employees like Christmas candy. Conrad Beckman would live
out his days in prison.

Although a seventy-million-dollar settlement is a victory
to savor, I never got the chance. When I walked into my
office on the morning after the trial ended, it seemed as if
every client matter that had simmered patiently for weeks on
the back burner started bubbling over. I was swamped, working twelve to fourteen hours a day for sixteen days straight,
including weekends.

And then, to my delight, Jonathan announced that he had
an oral argument scheduled for a week from Monday in the
U.S. Court of Appeals in New Orleans. Did I want to join
him down there for a couple of days?

Yes!

New Orleans.

The perfect romantic getaway. An opportunity for two
busy lawyers to step out of their crazy professional lives and
give themselves a chance to decide whether to spend the rest
of their lives together.

New Orleans.

It might even lure Jonathan Wolf out of his stuffed shirt. Although I'm hardly the Holly Golightly type, the last time I was in New Orleans, attending a section meeting of the ABA, I snuck out of the evening cocktail party with a girl-friend from my Harvard days who's now the assistant general counsel of a major Philadelphia bank. We danced to zydeco music at the Cajun Cabin until two in the morning, shared a plate of beignets and several cups of café au lait with two drop-dead gorgeous musicians, and then, at three-thirty in the morning, headed off on the backs of their motorcycles for a party in the Warehouse District. We staggered into the morn-ing committee meeting wearing the same clothes we'd worn the day before.

Ah, New Orleans.

So I booked us the honeymoon suite at Le Richelieu on Chartres in the heart of the French Quarter. The plan was for Jonathan to go down alone on Sunday to prepare for his ar-gument, which was scheduled for 10:30 A.M. on Monday. I'd fly down in time to meet him for lunch in the French Quarter. And then, as I told Jonathan while I drove him to the airport early Sunday morning, we'd head back to the honeymoon suite for a serious discussion about sleeping arrangements.

Oh, well.

At least the plane arrived on time.

When I stepped out of the cab at Bayona on Dauphine Street at noon on Monday in the chic new outfit I'd bought especially for the occasion, I was not alone.

"Reservations for Wolf," I told the maître d'.

"Ah, yes, mademoiselle," he purred, studying the reser-vations book with his reading glasses. "Monsieur is already here. Party of two?"

"Party of four."

He peered down over the podium. "Ah, yes."

The maître d' led the way back to a romantic corner booth, where the bottle of champagne was already on ice and two crystal glasses were reflecting the candlelight. The change of expression on Jonathan's face was amusing to watch—

from surprise to bewilderment to concern to delight.

For there'd been a slight modification in plans. Jonathan's housekeeper, who'd had the beginnings of what appeared to be a common cold on Saturday, was in the grips of a bad flu by late Sunday afternoon—fever, chills, bad cough, congestion, the works. She could no more take care of Jonathan's two daughters than herself. Both of the backup sitters were out of town.

"Daddy," little Sarah shouted as she ran toward her father, "Rachel says we get to go on a real streetcar after lunch and then we can take a boat ride to the zoo."

He gave her a kiss on the top of her head and looked up at me with a twinkle in his eye. "Oh, really?"

I nodded and held up the book I'd bought in the airport bookstore: *A Child's Guide to New Orleans*.

Leah came over and gave her father a hug. "Rachel says that Leah and I get to sleep with her in a fairy-tale bed with a canopy overhead."

"Is that so?" he said, looking over her head at me.

"Where will you sleep, Daddy?"

Momentarily unsure, he looked at her and then at me.

I shrugged.

He rubbed his beard.

I raised my eyebrows.

He winked.

We both smiled.

AUTHOR'S NOTE

This is a novel. A work of fiction. It opens with the usual disclaimer about resemblances to actual persons, and well it should. There is no Conrad Beckman. There is no Herman Warnholtz. Nor, for that matter, was there ever a Death's Head Formation in the United States, at least to my knowledge. But there was one in Germany, a Nazi division known as the SS-Totenkopfverbände, and they were indeed in charge of the concentration camps. So, too, there was a Die Spinne, consisting of former SS officers, and by all accounts it did survive Hitler's fall.

There was no Harold Roth, but there were undercover agents just like him, and the reports they filed on the American Nazi movement in St. Louis during the years before World War II still exist. In researching this novel, I spent several spooky afternoons paging through those yellowed archives. I read about the St. Louis chapter of the German-American Bund, with its headquarters in a two-story building at 2960 Oregon Avenue called the Clubhouse. I read an undercover report describing the celebration of Hitler's birthday there on April 20, 1937, where Anton Kessler, führer of the local storm troopers, introduced the guest speaker, Walter Kappe, propaganda chief of the Cincinnati chapter of the Bund. Herr Kappe posed the following question to the cheering audience: "Why shouldn't the Gentile majority of St. Louis, defending itself against the Jewish Anti-American subversives, disfranchise Jewish voters, put them in the class of wards of the nation, and segregate them on reservations just like we did to our Indians?"

There was a Hitler Youth Camp, which opened on July

4, 1938, near Stanton, Missouri, and there was a Deutsche-Horst family summer camp near Meramec River off Lemay Ferry Road. The July 23, 1939, issue of the *St. Louis Post-Dispatch* did indeed have a headline that read:

10 ST. LOUIS BUND LEADERS
HAVE GONE TO GERMANY

And the article that ran beneath that headline is exactly as quoted in this novel. In the fall of 1939, Fritz Kuhn, national leader of Bund, did indeed travel to St. Louis to address a group of local storm troopers at the Liederkranz Club. The words he said there appear in this novel.

And so on and so on.

Although I know of no Conrad Beckman and I know of no Herman Warnholtz, I wouldn't be surprised if their doppelgängers are among us. As Rachel said, sometimes we seem Time's captives, running nowhere forever on ancient treadmills.

I hope she's wrong.

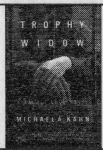

CHAPTER 1

You'd have thought this was my first time.

    Not even close.

I don't specialize in celebrities, but I've had my share. The list includes a member of the Chicago Bulls, two major-league baseball players, and the entire morning drive-time crew for one of the highest-rated FM stations in St. Louis. And that only covers contract negotiations and endorsement deals. I've sued Riverport on behalf of an Atlanta rap group in a gate-receipts dispute. When the case ended, the group's manager offered me a walk-on in their next music video. I told him I'd prefer to have my fees paid in full. I've represented a Hollywood star accused of trashing his hotel suite while on location here for a shoot—and we're not talking just any star. He made *Entertainment Weekly*'s "20 Sexiest Men" two years running. Alas, he's also two inches shorter than me and—as I learned while defending him in a four-hour deposition in a small conference room—afflicted with rhino breath.

But the odd thing is that I never felt the tiniest tingle before meeting any of them—not even a hint of that magical frisson that's supposed to radiate from real celebrities like, well, steam from a baked potato. And lest you get the wrong idea, I'm not one of those snooty types who professes to be above all that fawning. Far from it. I once was rendered dumbstruck on an elevator in the Met Square building when I realized that the tall man standing next to me was none other than number 45 himself—Hall of Famer Bob Gibson. For a diehard Cardinals fan, that's the equivalent of coming around the bend on Mount Sinai and finding yourself face to face with a Charlton Heston look-alike in flowing robes and sandals carrying two stone tablets. I rode several floors in flustered silence until I worked up the nerve to ask Mr. Gibson for his autograph, which he graciously signed on a sheet from my legal pad that I have since had laminated.

And that gaga response isn't limited to baseball gods. I would kill to spend an afternoon with Jane Austen. I would swoon like a schoolgirl before Clark Gable—especially the Clark Gable of *It Happened One Night*. And if Marvin Gaye were alive and well, I might just follow him from concert to concert like a Motown version of a Deadhead. With those folks we're talking frisson.

Cosmic frisson.

But not for my celebrity clients. For whatever reason, with them it always seems to be business as usual. Attorney-client. Strictly professional.

Until today.

Today I was driving halfway across the state of Missouri to meet my newest client.

A housewife.

More precisely, a former housewife. Probably the most famous former housewife in America, and surely the only one serving thirty-to-forty in Chillicothe Correctional Center.

Today I was definitely in the grip of that old black magic.

That's because today I was going to see Angela Green.

Yes, *the* Angela Green.

The same one whose murder trial came in at number 3 on *People* magazine's "Top Ten Murder Trials of the 1990s," just behind O. J. Simpson (no. 1) and the Menendez brothers (no. 2), but ahead of Timothy McVeigh (no. 4) and Jeffrey Dahmer (no. 5). The same one whose prime-time jailhouse interview with Oprah Winfrey drew a 41 share and ended with that shot reprinted in newspapers and magazines around the country—the one of Oprah, tears streaming down her cheeks, her head resting on Angela's shoulder as Angela gently patted her on the back. The same Angela Green who had Anita Hill deliver her acceptance speech in absentia at the *Ms.* magazine "Women of the Year" banquet, who caused a rift within the

NAACP when she was named one of its "Women of Valor," and who was the subject of Connie Chung's Emmy-nominated profile, which included those extraordinary testimonials from the prisoners who'd earned their high school equivalencies through the special tutoring program Angela helped establish at Chillicothe Correctional Center.

Yes, that Angela Green.

And this coming year—her seventh since entering prison—promised to be her biggest yet. The publication date for her long-awaited autobiography was just six months off. A major Hollywood studio had already snagged the film rights. According to a blurb in *Vanity Fair,* Whoopi Goldberg and Angela Bassett were vying for the lead role while Warren Beatty, Tommy Lee Jones, and Michael Douglas were in the running for the role of Michael Green. *Vanity Fair* picked Bassett and Douglas as the favorites, since "it would be almost too delicious for an Angela and a Michael to play the Angela and the Michael." Meanwhile, Angela's criminal defense attorney, Maria Fallaci, had her own book coming out late in October.

All of which translated into megabucks.

And where there are megabucks, there is usually a lawsuit. That's where I fit in. My name is Rachel Gold—Cardinals fan, daughter of Sarah, big sister of Ann, and, possibly, blushing bride and mother, assuming that a thirty-three-year-old bride isn't too old to blush or too young to become the instant stepmother of two adorable girls. But for the here and now, the only relevant role was lawyer, which is why I was driving through rural Missouri on this lovely Sunday morning in late June. I was somewhere in the northwest quadrant of the state, heading north on Highway 65 through a portion of Missouri I'd never been in before. According to a highway marker on the right, I'd just passed over the Grand River, although it didn't look too grand to me. Of course, when you grow up in St. Louis, it takes a whole lot of grand before any river can claim that label.

Chillicothe was the next exit.

Two hours ago I'd dropped Benny Goldberg off at the

University of Missouri in Columbia, where he was delivering a paper on antitrust law at a law school symposium. After my prison meeting with Angela Green, I was going to swing back down to Columbia to pick him up. On our way back to St. Louis we were planning to stop at a farm near Warrenton where Benny would introduce me to two new clients, Maggie Lane and Sara Freed, who were enmeshed in a dispute so outlandish that it had to be true. No one could make up such a story. Not even someone with a mind as warped as Benny's—and Benny's is as warped as it gets.

But Maggie and Sara could wait, I told myself as I pulled off the exit and drove into town. Chillicothe was a typical Midwestern village—chiefly frame houses, most built before World War II, a main street of redbrick buildings, including a bank and a pharmacy and a diner and a dry goods store. I turned down Third Street and slowed halfway down the block, peering out the window. Surprised, I rechecked the address.

I'd been to prisons before—in Missouri, Illinois, and Indiana—but never one for women. Men's prisons are geographically isolated—drab fortresses built on the outskirts of town, far from the women and children, grimly asserting to the world, *Here there be pariahs.* In this architecture of exile, Alcatraz is the quintessential model: a gray fortress on an island, cut off from civilization by frigid water, killer currents, and hungry sharks.

Chillicothe Correctional Center didn't fit that mold. Built in the 1880s as a home for wayward girls, the facility was located in the middle of a pleasant town in the gentle countryside. Its founders envisioned a pastoral haven where lost girls could find Christian salvation far from the wicked temptations of St. Louis and Kansas City. That vision produced a campus reminiscent of a New England women's college with several two-story redbrick buildings arranged like dormitories around a quadrangle.

Times change, though, and the home for wayward girls

was now Missouri's main prison for women, housing nearly six hundred inmates. The prisoners ranged from minimum security residents on work-release programs to death row convicts, of which there were presently three. Fortunately, Angela Green wasn't one of them. Nevertheless, when you enter prison at the age of forty-nine, a forty-year sentence might as well be life.

I pulled my car into the administration center parking lot and got out. Stretching, I turned toward the prison buildings across the street. There were several female inmates outside the buildings—some working on gardens, others strolling around the grounds. The only indication that this wasn't the Missouri branch of Mount Holyoke College were the gray work shirts and slacks worn by the women and the security fence topped with coiled razor-wire ringing the campus.

I checked my watch. It was almost eleven o'clock. I turned back to the administrative center, shading my eyes in the late morning sun. Time to check in. Time to meet my newest client. I paused a moment, grinning sheepishly. No question about it. I could feel the tingle.

We were in an attorney-client interview room, facing each other across the table. Unlike the interview rooms in men's prisons, which have all the charm of a concrete bunker at Normandy Beach, this one was softened by a few feminine touches, such as frilly curtains over the barred windows and a vase of irises on the rickety wooden table in the center of the room.

I was explaining the nature of the Son of Sam claim that had brought us together as attorney and client. Angela listened carefully, her chin resting on steepled fingers. Whatever celebrity excitement I'd felt in anticipation of our meeting had vanished the moment we met. Angela Green was someone you warmed to immediately, especially, I think, if you were a woman. It was a special connection, a sisterhood sort of thing that I could feel our first moments together. My reaction was typical, I suppose. This was, after all, the same woman who was adored within the prison not only by the inmates but by the guards as well.

The first thing I noticed about Angela Green was how human she looked. Although celebrities tend to seem diminished in person, here it was hardly Angela's fault. If clothes can make the woman, they can surely unmake her as well. Take the cover girl from a *Sports Illustrated* swimsuit issue, swap her thong bikini for a drab work shirt and an ill-fitting pair of Dickey slacks, deep-six the makeup, can the hairdresser, and we're talking, at best, the Before shot in a back-pages ad in *Cosmo*. While the media's two favorite adjectives for Angela Green were *saintly* and *regal,* try dressing Joan of Arc in the Missouri Department of Corrections' version of *haute couture* and she'd be lucky to pass for a janitor. As for regal, not even the queen of England could pull that off in prison grays.

Such was the case for Angela. Gone was the stunning African princess from her college days, the elegant suburban mother from her soccer mom days, and the coiffed matron from the final years of her marriage. In their place was a middle-aged woman who seemed older than her fifty-six years and heavier than I remembered from the *Oprah* special.

Nonetheless, Angela Green had presence. There was an aura of dignity about her—a quiet, determined dignity—that was palpable. Although her belle days were long over, she was still a handsome woman. Her skin was a deep mahogany that seemed to glow from within. Her hair—worn in a full Afro during her college days; tamed and straightened during her suburban days—was now braided in dozens of cornrows that reached to her shoulders. It was a striking look, especially for a woman of her age, and it gave her an air of authority. She had strong features—a wide nose; thick, bowed lips; full, high cheeks; broad forehead. But her most remarkable features were her eyes. They were dark and calm and wise. Although she was decades past her African princess days, it was no stretch to imagine Angela Green in the role of the village chief, seated upon her throne and resolving disputes among her subjects.

"I do not understand," Angela said, leaning back and shaking her head. Her voice was soft and husky, the words carefully articulated. "How can that child presume to make a claim against me? I am no relation to him."

"It's not his relation to *you*," I explained. "Under the Son of Sam law, the key is his relation to the victim. Members of the victim's family are the only ones entitled to sue."

"Family?" Angela frowned. "How is that child family to Michael?"

"He claims—well, actually Trent's lawyer claims—that he's the equivalent of Michael's son."

"Equivalent?" Angela repeated, puzzled. "What is that supposed to mean?"

"It's a doctrine called 'equitable adoption.' "

Angela shook her head, angry now. "Michael never adopted that tramp's child. He died before the marriage."

"I know." I gave her a sympathetic smile. "It's a stretch."

I explained the doctrine of equitable adoption, which the courts fashioned for that rare case where justice demands that a child be declared the rightful heir of people who never formally adopted her. In the classic "equitable adoption" situation, a married couple raises a foster child. Although they treat her as their own child, they never get around to making it official. If they die without a will or with one that refers generically to "any child of mine," their unfinished business lands in probate court. That's because the failure to adopt has significant legal consequences: a foster child is not an heir, while an *adopted* child has the same legal status as a biological child. Thus the equitable adoption doctrine typically comes into play in an inheritance battle between the unadopted child and the biological children, or—if no biological children—between the unadopted child and the deceased's blood relatives.

"The law is suspicious of these claims," I explained to Angela, "because the people who file them have a powerful incentive to lie about the dead person's intentions. The courts require the claimant to present direct evidence of a clear intent to adopt. Circumstantial evidence isn't enough. For example, one court ruled that claiming a child as a dependent on a tax return didn't constitute direct evidence."

Angela frowned. "What exactly does that mean here?"

"It means the court will carefully examine Michael's actions. The key issue is whether he expressed a clear intent to adopt Samantha's son. If so, did he do anything in furtherance of that intent?"

Angela narrowed her eyes. "And did he?"

"We don't know. We're at the beginning of the lawsuit. We haven't taken any depositions, especially Samantha's, and we haven't reviewed the documents. It's too early to say."

"How does it look so far?"

"We have some problems," I conceded, "but nothing fatal. We know that Michael signed a prenuptial agreement with the child's mother. In paragraph seven of the document he agreed to adopt her son. We know that he had an attorney prepare the necessary adoption papers. He also had an attorney prepare new wills for him and for Samantha. Although the wills were never signed, the plaintiff's lawyer claims that Michael reviewed and approved his draft two days before his death. The new will adds Trent to the list of beneficiaries and describes him as an adopted son." I paused. "Will the court find that to be enough evidence?" I shrugged. "It's too early to tell."

"He barely knew that child," Angela said quietly, her voice laced with frustration.

I reached across the table and laid my hand on top of hers. "We're going to fight it, Angela. We'll have plenty to say by the time of trial."

She took a deep breath and exhaled slowly. After a moment, she stood up and moved to the window. Pushing the curtain back, she peered out.

I waited.

She turned to me. "If that tramp wins, I will have Michael Junior and Sonya file their own Son of Sam claims. They are Michael's children, too. His only *real* children." She nodded decisively. "I'll bet that lawyer never considered that."

He didn't need to, I thought to myself. The Missouri legislature already had. The Son of Sam law barred any claim by a family member of the victim who also happened to be a family member of the killer. But I said nothing. No need to further demoralize my client this early in the case.

Instead, I explained our various defenses. She was interested to hear about the constitutional challenge to the statute, which would be led by the New York law firm representing her publisher. If we could convince the court to throw out the statute as an abridgment of the freedom of speech, the case would implode and we'd never have to worry about equitable adoption or our other defenses. She listened attentively, asking questions along the way.

When I finished explaining the legal issues, I went over a few more items regarding pretrial matters, including timing issues and the like. Then I had the deputy warden come in so that we could work out a confidential but efficient way for me to communicate with Angela by mail, phone, and fax—essential procedures given that St. Louis was a four-hour drive from Chillicothe.

I checked my watch after the deputy warden departed. We still had a few minutes before I had to drive back to Columbia for Benny. I had one more topic to broach. I wasn't quite sure how to begin, or where to go once we started.

Angela must have sensed it. "What is it, Rachel?"

I gazed at her for a moment. "I reviewed the file."

"Of what?"

"Your case. Everything. Court transcripts, pretrial motions, homicide investigation. Whatever I could get my hands on."

She frowned. "Why?"

"Good question." I leaned back in my chair and crossed my arms over my chest. "I'm not sure, Angela. I started with the trial transcript. Initially, I suppose I was looking for any stray evidence on the equitable adoption issue." I shrugged. "Maybe to see whether Samantha said anything back then about Michael's relationship with her son—back before her lawyer concocted this adoption theory."

"And did she?"

I shook my head. "Not really. Oh, she said he loved to play with Trent, took him fishing once, gave him a tricycle for Christmas—that sort of thing."

I paused.

"And," Angela said.

"And I saw other things."

"What things?"

"I'm not a criminal lawyer, Angela, but over the years I've had to look through a few homicide files. Yours was unusual."

She leaned forward, curious. "How so?"

I paused, searching for the right words. "There were loose ends."

"Such as?"

"Such as the murder weapon. It's not the sort of weapon you'd expect a housewife to use."

"Why not?"

"The serial number was filed off. The gun was untraceable. It's the kind you'd normally expect to find with a professional hit, the kind you'd buy from an illegal gun dealer."

She rubbed her chin, trying to remember. "I think they asked me where I bought it."

"They did. It's in the arrest report. You told them you'd never owned a gun."

She nodded. "That's true."

"So where'd you get it?" I asked.

She shook her head. "I have no idea."

I studied her for a moment. "Angela, if you wanted to buy that kind of gun, where would you go?"

"I have no idea."

"Neither did the police." I leaned forward. "That's my point. It was a loose end. The police were never asked to come up with an answer because it was never an issue at trial. Maybe there's a simple explanation for the gun, but it's certainly nowhere in the file."

Angela sighed and shook her head. "I supposed I blacked that part out, too."

"Possibly."

After a moment, she asked, "Was that the only loose end?"

I shook my head. "How did you get into his house?"

She frowned, trying to remember. "Did I ring the doorbell?"

"Not likely. He was shot coming out of the shower. He wouldn't have let you in with a gun in your hand and then gone back in the bedroom, gotten undressed, and taken a shower."

"Maybe the gun was in my purse? Maybe the door was open?"

"Maybe. The housekeeper said the door was locked when she arrived. It was the kind that automatically locks when you close it."

"Maybe I had a key."

"Did you?"

She shook her head in frustration. "I don't remember."

"Why would you have a key? The two of you had just finished a bitter divorce. There'd be no reason for him to give you a key."

"Maybe he gave the children a key."

"Did he?"

She shrugged. "I don't know."

"I assume you don't know how to pick a lock."

She smiled. "No."

"So how did you get in?"

"What did the police say?"

"Nothing. It's another loose end."

She stared at the table, frowning. After a moment, she looked up at me. "Are there other loose ends?"

I nodded.

"Such as?"

"Such as John."

John had been her alibi—her embarrassingly weak alibi. She claimed that on the night of the murder she had gone out for a drink with a nice young man named John, last name unknown, and woke up the next morning in Michael Green's bedroom with no idea of how she got there. The police found no trace of the mysterious John.

"In your police interview," I continued, "you said that you'd known John for a couple of weeks, that he used to come visit his mother in the hospital, right?"

She nodded.

"You said that you felt sorry for him. That the two of you became friends. That you used to have lunch together in the hospital cafeteria on the days you volunteered at the gift shop, right?"

"I did."

"So where is he?" I asked. "And *who* is he?"

Angela looked down at the table. "They think I made him up." Her voice was soft, muffled.

"Did you?"

She stared down at the table. When she finally looked up, her eyes were moist. "I wish I knew the answer to that, Rachel. Lord, I do. When I look back on those days, everything seems unreal, like I was living inside a dream." She gave me a sad smile. "More like a nightmare. I can't tell for sure what part was real and what part was imaginary. I believe John was real. I have a memory of the things we used to talk about at the hospital. I can close my eyes and see that young man."

She paused, closing her eyes. I waited. She opened them. In a discouraged voice she said, "I believe John was real."

"The police didn't."

She said nothing.

"But they didn't bother tying up the loose end," I said.

She gave me a puzzled look. "How would they do that?"

"By checking the hospital records. It couldn't have been that difficult to identify every female patient between the ages of, say, forty and seventy who'd been in the hospital for at least the two weeks preceding the killing. Once they had that list, they could quickly check whether any of those women had an adult son named John." I shook my head. "But they didn't bother to."

"Why not?"

Because of your lawyer's theory of the case, I wanted to say. Instead, I said, "Because they thought that they already had enough evidence."

She sighed. "They were right."